The Summer I Met Jack

ALSO BY MICHELLE GABLE

A Paris Apartment
I'll See You in Paris
The Book of Summer

The Summer I Met Jack

MICHELLE GABLE

ST. MARTIN'S GRIFFIN ☙ NEW YORK

THE SUMMER I MET JACK. Copyright © 2018 by Michelle Gable. All rights reserved. Printed in the United States of America. For information, address St. Martin's Press, 175 Fifth Avenue, New York, N.Y. 10010.

www.stmartins.com

Designed by Anna Gorovoy

The Library of Congress has cataloged the hardcover edition as follows:

Names: Gable, Michelle, author.
Title: The summer I met Jack / Michelle Gable.
Description: First edition. | New York : St. Martin's Press, 2018.
Identifiers: LCCN 2017055074 | ISBN 9781250103246 (hardcover) |
    ISBN 9781250103260 (ebook) | 9781250199607 (international edition,
    sold outside the U.S., subject to rights availability)
Subjects: LCSH: Young women—Fiction. | Socialites—Fiction. |
    Kennedy, John F. (John Fitzgerald), 1917–1963—Fiction.
Classification: LCC PS3607.A237 S86 2018 | DDC 813/.6—dc23
LC record available at https://lccn.loc.gov/2017055074

ISBN 978-1-250-10325-3 (trade paperback)

Our books may be purchased in bulk for promotional, educational, or business use. Please contact your local bookseller or the Macmillan Corporate and Premium Sales Department at 1-800-221-7945, extension 5442, or by email at MacmillanSpecialMarkets@macmillan.com.

First St. Martin's Griffin Edition: May 2019

10 9 8 7 6 5 4 3 2

For my father-in-law,
Tony Bilski,
my favorite "Polish DP"

PART I

A man sits on a patio, wrapped in a blanket and staring out to sea. It is cold in California this time of year, though much better than in New York, which is why he winters on this coast. He is old enough to do what he wants. Let someone else worry about logistics at the office, who's billing what hours, and the clients they should woo. He's sworn a hundred times he'll retire. Soon. Very soon.

His secretary comes outside. She wears a blue suit, and blue heels but in a different shade.

"Any luck?" he asks.

She frowns and extends the sealed envelope his way.

"It's the best I could do," she says.

The man turns the letter over in his hand, then tosses it onto a nearby table. He should probably ask her to type the address, as the woman's penmanship resembles that of a teenage girl. If teens wrote things by hand anymore. Oh, who cares. The destination is legible. Good enough.

"It's fine," he says, and leans into his chaise, eyes closed. "Thank you."

The secretary waits for further direction as the envelope flutters in the breeze. Before he meanders off into sleep, she has to ask.

"Do you think it's true?" she says.

At first, he doesn't answer. She assumes he's fallen asleep but, really, he's taking his time.

"We first met," he says, causing her to jump, "fifty years ago."

He opens one eye, and then the other.

"And over the decades she said many things."

He chuckles through his nose.

"*Many* things," he repeats. "Outrageous claims were made, some of which would make international news. But as to whether I believe it? I've never been able to decide. Not that my opinion matters. The only thing we can do is send the letter and wait for a response."

HYANNIS PORT, MASSACHUSETTS

The government wouldn't deport her, she didn't think.

Alicia was unclear on the particulars, but when a person emigrates to the United States under somewhat ill-begotten circumstances, she is not particularly inclined to raise her hand. She was probably safe, because where might they send her? Alicia was no longer a citizen of Poland, and they couldn't return her to the German camp. This was, she supposed, the upside to her statelessness. To be deported, you needed a home.

For a second, Alicia felt relief. Then she remembered a story she read, about a refugee who'd spent years on a ship, circling the globe, no port willing to let him through, like a crate of damaged goods.

Alicia sent up a quick prayer—or something like it—that Irenka would come through with the job.

"I do vat I can," she'd said in her choppy, harsh accent. "But no promisink."

A risky thing, to bet it all on a maid from Poland. But she had no other options on Cape Cod.

At least she had *this* job, her part-time work at the Center Theatre. She tried to wheedle Mr. Dillon into more hours, but he was rigid as a German.

"You can help George and Dewey during peak times," he'd said. "That's all I'm able to offer."

George was the Center's projectionist, a spindly man with a swoop of black hair and oversized black-rimmed glasses. Alicia thought the person running films should have better vision, but George seemed to do okay.

Dewey was the counter clerk, though he spent most of his time taking smoke breaks behind the stately brick building, or sometimes right in front, beneath the black and gold awning.

"No more than ten hours per week," Mr. Dillon said, "and only through the Indian summer."

"How about twenty?" Alicia countered, having noted Dewey's lack of industry.

"How about seven?" Mr. Dillon returned.

"But this is the perfect job for me. The first cinema in Poland was built in my hometown, in 1899. My mother was very proud of this. She'd tell any out-of-towner who'd listen!"

When Alicia first stepped inside the Center, her heart sang, for she'd finally, after nearly a year, found something in America that reminded her of home. Though the room was empty at the time, it remained grand with its red velveteen chairs and wide, noble balconies. She could almost hear the whoosh of the curtains and the sound of her mother's laughter tumbling over time and space.

"We probably saw twenty films a year," Alicia added. "In the good years, that is."

"Listen, I don't have to hire you at all," Mr. Dillon said, unimpressed with her cinematic background.

"Ten sounds fine," she'd mumbled, accepting brisk defeat, though this did not stop her from making one last request.

"Can I display my art in the lobby?" she asked. "You see, I'm a painter—"

"Do whatever the hell you want," Mr. Dillon said. "As long as it doesn't bother the customers. Or me."

As luck would have it, Mr. Dillon spent most of his time managing the Hyannis Theatre, over on the swankier side of town. Alicia was glad she'd picked the Center. Mr. Dillon wasn't apt to let a homeless Pole display her work on the glitzy west end.

Alicia stepped behind the counter. She could probably leave, as these were hardly "peak hours." Sunday matinees rarely were. In her brain, Alicia added up the time she'd worked that week. Should she push it to eleven hours, or twelve?

Alicia crouched down and slid one row of Boston Beans flush with another. The display looked sharp, artful almost. She let herself feel proud, and wished she could show Irenka.

"You vant to clean?" her friend had shirked when Alicia showed up on her doorstep last week, fresh off the bus from Oklahoma City.

"I don't *want* to clean per se," Alicia told her, "but being a maid would tide me over . . ."

"A maid! Bah! You cannot do maid! You terrible wit cleanink!"

Maybe so, but Alicia didn't plan to sweep floorboards for the rest of her life, and she could fake it well enough, for now.

"You still selling?" asked a voice.

Alicia jumped up. She shook her head, and the room blurred.

"Oh! Yes! Sorry!" she said, the man's Boston accent prickling the hairs on her neck. "I thought everyone was inside."

When Alicia caught eyes with the guest, everything inside her body seized. Before her stood a man, tall and tanned, with mussed reddish-brown hair and an untucked white shirt. He grinned, corner to corner, eyes crinkling at the edges.

"Wow, I must've really thrown ya," the man said.

"I apologize," Alicia said, panicked. "I wasn't expecting anyone to be out here. The second showing of the movie just began. If you hurry, you won't miss a minute. It's *In the Foreign Legion*."

As if he couldn't read the marquee. Mentally, Alicia rolled her eyes.

"Yeah. I know how it works," he said. "Stahrting from two fifteen, continuous. I prefer to sneak in late."

He pushed a chunk of hair from his forehead, and Alicia found herself mimicking the gesture. He caught this, and winked, causing Alicia to jolt once more.

It wasn't the man's handsomeness. He was attractive, no question, but he was also gangly, too thin. His hair was bushy and his head preposterously oversized compared to his reedy frame. Any objective poll would place his looks well below Ty Power's or William Holden's, yet there remained something special about him, something beautiful that had little to do with actual presentation.

But, yes, okay, he was handsome, and tan, and had one hell of a smile.

"So, you didn't answer my question," he said. "Are you still open?"

"You mean for refreshments?"

He laughed.

Holy snakes, the man had intensely straight and white teeth.

"Yes, what else?" he said. "Then again, maybe you can think of another reason I might want to hang out here?"

He said "here" as if it were two syllables instead of one. *He-ah.*

"Oh, er," Alicia stuttered. "There's not much else to do, aside from order refreshments."

"You must be new," he said. "I'd surely remembah your face."

Alicia blushed furiously and reached for a cup.

"Will that be a large?" she said.

"I didn't place an order."

"Asking 'What size?' is a much better sales tactic than 'May I help you?'"

"Well, I'm a suckah for a good saleswoman," he said. "So, I'll have a large Coke, as suggested."

"You've got it."

Alicia flipped around and began to fill his cup, wondering how it'd become so hot in that room. She fanned herself with a flattened popcorn box.

"By the way," the man said. "My name's Jack. Jack Kennedy."

"Kennedy?" Alicia blurted.

He was one of *them*—the family Irenka picked up after, the family Alicia hoped would employ her, too.

According to Irenka, there were some ten, twelve of them, maybe more. The father was a former ambassador; the kids all grown. The mother was penurious, and a tad odd, though Irenka held her in high esteem.

In her letters and in person, Irenka recounted stories about this crew, and their scrapes and shenanigans. They stole cars, broke limbs, and swiped food off one another's plates. The Cape was flooded with their unpaid bills, and the house was often flooded for real, as the family seemed unable to remember when they'd left a faucet running.

They were a family of slobs, Irenka claimed. They left their towels and bathing costumes strewn about the house.

"Worse dan pigs on farm," she insisted.

But Irenka must've been mistaken. Jack was in his shirtsleeves, and his trousers hung like old drapes, but Alicia couldn't imagine that anyone would consider him slovenly.

"Aw, hell," Jack moaned, "look at that expression. And you said 'Kennedy' like it was a swear word."

Sway-er. As he spoke, Alicia realized that while Jack had a Boston accent, his was different from those she'd already heard. It was the rhythm of his speech, and how it sped up, and then slowed. Sometimes his words pushed, and other times, they pulled.

"Kennedy," said like he was racing toward something.

"Swear," like he wanted the word to last all night.

"Judging by your reaction," he said, "I assume you've had the great misfortune of meeting my brother, Teddy."

Alicia thought for a minute, mind clicking through Irenka's tales. Teddy, he was the fat one, the youngest. He was prone to problems with boats.

"Teddy," the Ambassador once said, "if you leave with the boat, you come back with the boat."

"I've never met your brother," Alicia said. "But I've . . . heard some stories."

Jack snorted.

"I'll bet. Please don't judge our entire family by that one."

Alicia smiled weakly.

"I'm sure you're all lovely," she said.

Jack threw back his head and cackled.

"Said by someone who's obviously never met us. Listen, I hate to point out the obvious, but you haven't told me your name. Sort of makes me feel like I'm doin' all the work."

"Oh. Yes." She exhaled. "I'm Alicia. Alicia Darr."

Jack grinned, wide as the heavens, and extended a hand across the counter. Alicia brought hers to meet it.

"*Enchantée*," she said, inexplicably.

Alicia blushed yet again. French, of all things. She was at the Center Theatre in Hyannis, Massachusetts, not the damned Sorbonne. Maybe she should switch to German, to show him how many languages she knew.

"*Enchantée* indeed," Jack said. "Your accent is perfection. Where do you go to school?"

"I don't."

Jack scrunched his perfectly shaped nose.

"You don't attend school?" he said.

"I do not. The popcorn is delicious, have you tried some?"

"But you're not old enough to have graduated college."

"What's old enough?" she said. "In any case, I started out with lofty plans but didn't make it to university. The war, you know."

She looked away.

"Ah. I should've guessed. You're European."

"Am I?"

Alicia was not being coy. "European" was usually reserved for those from Paris, or Vienna, possibly Hamburg, worst case. She was from Poland, which most would regard as decidedly "Eastern Bloc."

Legally, though, Alicia wasn't from anywhere, "stateless" as her documents showed, her current home a mattress inside Irenka's closet. A person couldn't get much more displaced than that.

"So, you moved around?" Jack said with a wince. "Separated from family and friends?"

"Something like that."

He sighed, then blubbered his lips.

"Those Nazis. They were no fucking fun."

Alicia coughed out an astonished laugh, amused or deeply offended, either one.

Abruptly, Jack jerked his head toward something that'd caught his eye.

"You guys selling art now?" he asked.

"Oh. Um. Yes. It's something Mr. Dillon is trying out."

"Huh." He shrugged. "Well. Neat painting."

"Thank you?" Alicia said, craning past his (large, large) head.

He was inspecting a watercolor of Piotrkowska Street, Alicia's former home. Even though she'd created it, and studied it a hundred times, her heart sputtered as she took in the avenue's baroque buildings and its curled lampposts, restaurants, and shops.

"You painted that?"

Jack turned her way, one brow cocked.

"I did." Alicia nodded. "It's one of the prettiest streets in Europe. It *was* one of the prettiest streets. There's no telling what it looks like now. Well, enjoy your drink and the film. That'll be thirty cents."

"Anxious to move me on, are ya?"

He narrowed his green-gray gaze and leaned further over the counter.

"There's something familyah about you," he said. "We've met before. Have you been working here all summer?"

"No, I only started a few days ago. Do you need napkins? That will be thirty cents. As I mentioned."

"Really? A few days? Then surely you were here last summer."

He drummed his fingers on the countertop.

"You worked at the club? Teaching sailing? Tennis?"

"No, sir, not at all." Alicia wrested a napkin from its silver holder. "I've been in Hyannis less than a week. You should take one of these to your seat. Your drink will sweat thanks to the humidity. That'll be thirty cents."

"Only a week?" Jack said, appearing pinched. "That can't be right. I swear we've met before. You are so familiar and your face . . . well, it's unforgettable."

"You are mistaken," she said, staring at the floor.

Alicia could feel Jack's eyes on her as surely as she could feel the sun when she stepped outside.

"I'd like to get your number," he said.

Alicia glanced up.

"Excuse me?" she said.

"I'd like to take you out."

He reached into his pockets, but came up empty.

"You said you're new here, so I'd like to show you the Cape," Jack said, and picked up a receipt left by another customer. "Here, write down your number."

"My numbah?"

She had not meant to parrot his voice.

"I'm staying with a friend," she explained quickly.

"I'd be happy to meet her, too," he said, a glimmer in his eyes.

Alicia gave a hoarse chuckle.

"I don't know that you would be," she said. "Happy to meet her, that is."

"Wow," Jack said. "You're really making me work for it, aren't ya?"

Alicia snagged the slip of paper, and scribbled Irenka's information, hand quivering.

"It was fantastic to meet you, Miss Darr," Jack said.

He took the paper and rewarded Alicia with one last smile.

"Hope to see you again, very soon," he said.

Then Jack winked, and turned to go.

"That'll be thirty cents!" Alicia called out. "You still owe for the Coke!"

Jack spun around.

"Thirty cents?" he repeated. "That seems steep."

Alicia shrugged.

"It says right here on the sign, thirty cents for a jumbo."

"I thought it was a large?"

"I'm fairly convinced you said jumbo."

"I don't have any money on me," he said, without checking to be sure.

"Then you'll have to return the soda."

He closed his eyes and laughed.

"Don't worry, Alicia Darr. I'm good for it. You can put it on my account."

Before she could protest, or take possession of the drink, Jack vanished through the double doors. Alicia stood motionless, her body roiling with a great mixture of emotions. She was discombobulated, bewildered, and a little charmed. All that and poorer, given she was now thirty cents in the hole.

HYANNIS PORT

"I'll put it on the Ambassador's account," the cabdriver said as Alicia reached into her purse.

"I'm sorry, what?"

She stood on a circular driveway, peering into the taxi's window as a flag overhead thrashed in the wind. Behind her, a rambling white clapboard home leered through its green-shuttered windows.

"I don't need to pay?" Alicia said.

The ocean breeze was doing a number on the flag, and her skirt as well. Alicia leaned against the car to keep her decency intact.

"Mr. Kennedy has an account," the driver explained. "And I'm sure he'd want to pay *your* way."

"Oh, but I couldn't," Alicia said. "It'd feel like a—"

"It'd feel like nothing. He's so rich, money's practically coming out of his ears. Anyway, it's all paid out of New York. He probably doesn't even see the bills. Now, if you don't mind stepping away from the car, I need to get back for the cranberry express."

"Thanks for the lift," she said.

"Have a lovely day! And stay cool. It's gonna be a scorcher. Best you change out of that suit."

With that, he revved the engine, made one loop around the flagpole, and puttered off.

In her letters, Irenka said the Kennedys were one of the richest families in America. She'd described the house in exhaustive detail, but seeing it firsthand was another matter. It was somehow ostentatious and modest at the same time, like a beautiful girl who blushed when she attracted attention.

According to Irenka, the home had fourteen bedrooms, nine bathrooms, and a four-car garage. The basement contained a motion-picture theater, a wine cellar, and a hallway lined with a collection of dolls.

"Mrs. Kennedy keeps them down there," Irenka had written, "I think so the children do not scream."

The multiacre property also featured an enclosed swimming pool, a tennis court, a boathouse, two guesthouses, and a private dock. The lawns were well-tended, all the way to the sea.

Taking it all in, Alicia filled with the same flushing tingle as when she stepped off the bus at depot square. Hyannis Port exceeded any fantasy, with its quaint and tree-lined Main Street, charming storefronts, and sailboat masts bobbing in the harbor. And now, the Kennedy estate. Had she known Cape Cod might be like this, Alicia would've ditched Oklahoma long ago. Her luck was shifting. Alicia could sense it, as palpable as an ocean gale.

She approached the front door, feeling insignificant compared to the scope of the home, not to mention the ocean beyond. She'd seen the Atlantic before, of course, for weeks and from a battleship, but she'd never seen it like this. They should've plunked the Statue of Liberty right there in Nantucket Sound. This matched her American dreams better than anything in New York.

Alicia took the steps, one by one, the wood creaking beneath her shoes. Okay, so the home's exterior *did* need a new coat of paint and patches of dead grass broke up the lawn. But these imperfections were hardly worth mentioning, given everything else.

As she went to ring the bell, the front door swung open and a blur of person slingshotted out. It was a young woman, a petite, curvy thing who crashed to the floor upon contact with Alicia's right shoulder.

"Oh, excuse me!" the woman said, and popped to her feet.

She gathered the mess her stack of papers had made.

"I didn't hear the bell!" she said.

This woman was not much older than Alicia, midtwenties, most likely.

"Are you here to see . . ." She assessed Alicia for a minute. "Pat?"

"Um . . ."

"Jean? No matter, no matter." The girl waved her hand around. "They're basically all here. Last I saw, Mrs. Kennedy was in the kitchen with Eunice. Or is it Ethel you want?"

"I am actually here to see . . ."

"Mrs. Robert Kennedy is peacocking about somewhere," the girl said with a shake of her head. "Trying to lure people into games she's rigged to win. Anyhow, I'm off to post some letters for the Ambassador. Have we met? I don't think we've met. I'm Janet des Rosiers, Mr. Kennedy's personal secretary. Everyone calls me Miss Dee. Okay, then, help yourself inside. I'm off. Toodle-loo!"

Miss Dee said all of this without taking a breath, and then scampered down the stairs and toward a black car parked on the side of the house. Alicia remained frozen in place.

"Go on!" Miss Dee called out, unlocking the car door. "The house is open. Go right in!"

"Wouldn't it be impolite?"

"Oh, for Pete's sake."

With a huff, Miss Dee pounded upstairs and caught Alicia by her sleeve. She hauled her inside.

"Hello!" she shouted. "A friend of Pat's is here!"

Alicia began to second-guess the outfit she'd chosen that day: a gray flannel sheath and accompanying jacket with a deep-winged collar and sassy cuffs, purchased at a discount when she worked the Christmas season at Brown's. It was the best getup she owned, and probably too nifty for a maid, hence Miss Dee's confusion. But Alicia wasn't going to show up at the Kennedys' in immigrant wool, what with the possibility of running into Jack.

"Hello!" Miss Dee called out again.

She increased her pace and Alicia jogged to keep up, florals and checks whizzing through her vision. Soon they were standing in the kitchen beside two women: one older, one young. A mother and her daughter, from the looks of it. A large-brimmed straw hat was on the table between them.

"Miss Dee, I thought you'd left," said the older of the two, whom Alicia pegged as Mrs. Kennedy, based on Irenka's diligent description.

The family matriarch was petite, more so than Alicia or Miss Dee, a meter and a half at most. She sported large pearl earrings and perfectly curled and coiffed hair, these particulars not necessarily in accordance with the casualness of her linen blouse and pants. As for the daughter, she wore a striped one-piece playsuit, which served to spotlight her gangly legs and knobby knees.

"I was trying to leave," Miss Dee explained, "when I noticed a visitor no one bothered to let in!"

"Miss Dee, I'm glad you're still here," Mrs. Kennedy said, ignoring the problem of the improperly greeted guest. "It's imperative that we go over this summer's food bill as soon as possible."

"I showed you everything last week," Miss Dee said. "When we receive the next invoice, I'll bring it to you, right away."

"No, but you see, you haven't shown me *everything*. For example, I didn't see strawberries on any of the documentation, yet I've eaten strawberries in this very home!"

Alicia pondered the taxi driver's claims that no one bothered to mind the family's bills. If Mr. Kennedy didn't pay attention, Mrs. Kennedy surely did. Alicia was struck with a certain curiosity as to how she might appear on the invoice. *One woman, in transit.*

"Strawberries," Eunice said, and rolled her eyes. "Oh, Mother! Concern about fifty cents when you fly to Paris on the regular for new frocks."

Eunice's tone—or maybe it was the accent—surprised Alicia, coming out as if from a pellet gun. After she stopped speaking, the girl's harsh voice lingered on Alicia's skin, like a dozen small lacerations. Mrs. Kennedy's wasn't any smoother. Hers was high-pitched and crackly, like a phonograph scratch.

"Don't be sassy, Eunice," Mrs. Kennedy said. "The peak time is May and now that we're solidly into August, we can't be buying strawberries out of season."

"Like your dresses."

"That's enough."

She was interesting, this daughter who was about Alicia's age. Eunice wasn't as tall as she seemed, upon closer scrutiny. It was her extreme thinness that connoted a height not necessarily achieved. She had a broad smile and a broad face, and unlike her mother's perfect ringlets, Eunice's hair was a frizzy, auburn wreck. Yet there was something beautiful about her. No, that wasn't right. Perhaps "handsome" was the ticket. "Striking."

"I'm happy to discuss the strawberry requisitioning process later," Miss Dee said, "but I really must get to the post office before they close. Might we push this conversation to a later time?"

"Of course. Please, go post the mail. But we *will* discuss it. I won't forget!"

"I'm sure that's true. See you all later!"

Miss Dee ran from the room as fast as her shapely legs might carry her.

"Hello there," Alicia said, her heart galloping as the two women stared. "I'm here to see . . ."

Mrs. Kennedy stopped her with a finger.

"Hold that thought."

She bent over the table to scribble out a note. *Strawberries,* she wrote, and then Mrs. Kennedy pinned the note to her dress, alongside a half dozen other slips of paper. Alicia squinted to read them.

Recover settee
Sort magazines
Roosevelt

When Alicia lifted her gaze, she accidentally caught eyes with Eunice, who was analyzing her like a professor.

"You're here for Pat?" she said, her words again hard and fast, a well-practiced rhythm. "She's not here."

"That's okay," Alicia said. "I'm not here for—"

"Oh, how rude!" Mrs. Kennedy chirped. "We haven't introduced ourselves. I'm Mrs. Joseph P. Kennedy. . . ."

Mrs. Kennedy extended a hand, but as Alicia went to take it, Eunice jumped in.

"Since Pat's not here," she said, "maybe you can settle a dispute between Mother and me."

"A dispute?" Alicia stammered. "I'm probably not qualified—"

"No qualification necessary. You'd think a grown woman could pick out her own hat."

"You'd think . . ." Mrs. Kennedy muttered. "Honestly Eunice, you're the best of the Girls, yet your presentation is abysmal. If you'd *try* to be the least bit fashionable, it'd do wonders for your social life. It's a miracle you have any dates whatsoever in Washington."

Eunice leaned against a white wicker chair. She turned toward Alicia.

"See that hat on the table?" she said. "Whaddya think?"

"You really want my opinion?" Alicia asked, eyes drifting toward the hat she'd noticed when she first walked in.

If there was one thing Alicia could freely converse about, it was millinery. Oklahoma had been good for one thing, at least—her stint in the hat box at Brown's.

"Sure," Eunice said, shrugging her pointy shoulders. "Why not?"

"Stop pestering her," Mrs. Kennedy said. "I'm sorry. I tried to raise the Children with manners. But . . ."

"I do have some opinions on hats," Alicia said, voice thin. "As it happens."

"For example?" Eunice asked, lifting her brows as she crossed both arms over her chest.

"Well," Alicia started, "this coolie style is perfect for the summer, given its lightweight construction. And its wide brim balances bare arms while offering wonderful sun protection. But, when you're talking indoors . . ." She exhaled. "Small and neat can't be beat."

Alicia smiled and the two women stared, mouths open. Alicia blushed. There she went, spewing out corny advertising slogans again. As a girl, she'd developed her English fluency through tutors and teachers, but she learned *American* thanks to newspapers, radios, and TV.

"*Small and neat can't be beat?*" Eunice gawked.

"Something I learned working at Brown's," Alicia added, her blush deepening. "It was the largest department store in Oklahoma. What I meant was, smaller is better to show off one's profile."

"Yes," Mrs. Kennedy said. "That's exactly what I've been trying to say."

"You're here to see *Pat*?"

"Eunice has a date," Mrs. Kennedy said. "And she wants to wear a straw hat. For the love of all that's holy."

"We're at the Cape, Mother. He's seen me in a swimsuit."

"That's nothing to brag about."

Alicia's mind whirred as she struggled to keep pace with the back-and-forth, her ears ringing from their flinty accents. She longed for a piece of paper on which to jot *her* own notes, the things to follow up on later. Of course, she'd never pin them to her dress.

"How do you know Pat?" Eunice pressed.

"I apologize for the misunderstanding, but I'm not here for Pat." Alicia laughed. "I've never even met him!"

"Pat is my *daughter*," Mrs. Kennedy said, and pinched her lips together.

"Yes, sorry, let me explain," Alicia said. "I'm here about a job." Her voice squeaked.

"A job?" Mrs. Kennedy balked.

"Yes. My friend, Irenka Michalska, works here. She said you needed extra help through the rest of the summer and that I might be the one to fill this role? I believe she brought up my name?"

"*Michalska?*"

Mrs. Kennedy shook her head.

"That's the downstairs maid, Mother," Eunice said, one eye on Alicia. "You know, the husky one?"

"Ah, right. Irenka. That fleshy farm girl from Russia. Very religious! She's a dear."

"Poland," Alicia corrected.

"Religious" didn't sound like Irenka, though "fleshy" and "farm girl" certainly checked out.

"Yes, I'm starting to recall something about a 'friend,'" Mrs. Kennedy said, "but you don't look like a maid."

"Thank you. I hope to be an artist eventually but . . ."

"And how on earth do you know Irenka?"

"Really, Mother! Can't you see?" Eunice pointed, accusatorily, as if fingering someone for a crime. "She's from Russia, too."

"Not Russia . . ."

"You are?" Mrs. Kennedy's eyes bounced between her daughter and the immigrant who'd shown up in her kitchen out of the clear blue.

Alicia imagined that Mrs. Kennedy was right then questioning everything she'd ever believed about hats.

"I'm from Poland," Alicia said. "Though I left the country some time ago. I don't . . ." She gulped. "My family is gone."

"Your English is impeccable," Mrs. Kennedy said. "And you're quite lovely. You don't seem Polish at all."

"Oh, thank you?"

"I could tell," Eunice snapped.

She paused, chin lifted victoriously.

"Despite your . . . appearance, I could tell," she said. "So. You're . . . whaddya call it? Displaced?"

"I am a recent émigré, yes."

"Good grief. Why are there so many damned refugees on the Cape?" Eunice griped.

"You'll need to speak with Miss Dee," Mrs. Kennedy said. "She's in charge of the help, but just left."

"Can I wait until she returns?"

Alicia felt a headache coming on.

"You can't hang around," Eunice said. "Stay here. I'll find *Irenka*. Holy moly, I thought you people were supposed to come with your own jobs."

Eunice trotted off, muttering about the immigrant problem as she went. Alicia looked across the table to Mrs. Kennedy. She smiled meekly.

"You have a lovely home," she said.

"Yes," Mrs. Kennedy replied. "I'm thinking of buying new drapes."

Later that day, they were in the kitchen, Eunice's hat still on the table. Somewhere in the house, a bath had been started. Water whooshed through the pipes.

Alicia stood nervously, pulling on her new uniform, as sunlight streamed through the kitchen window.

"I'll need to get this taken in," she said. "Or taken up."

Anything so that the dress might fit a woman better than it would a crop of potatoes. Meanwhile, Irenka stood a few steps away, clucking.

"I cannot accept you be maid," she said.

"I don't have a choice, do I?"

Alicia yanked the apron strings tighter, and tighter still. There was a waist in there somewhere.

"I taut you find different job, wit your pretty face," Irenka said.

"They don't hire for pretty," Alicia replied.

"Don't they?"

"Well, if you hear about something like that, please let me know."

Alicia placed both hands on her hips and blew a string of blond hair from her eyes. The uniform was a far better fit for Irenka than it was for her, in a way that had little to do with measurements or length. With her ruddy complexion and stout build, Irenka was made for the back-breaking work tending to that house surely required. Alicia hated to think it, but facts were facts. Irenka was her one friend in America, and the only other Pole she knew, yet sometimes it was like they'd been born oceans apart.

A year ago, they were placed together at the YWCA in Oklahoma City, owing to their shared circumstances: Polish, unattached, and "young," although Irenka had several years on Alicia, exactly how many she'd not confess. Though they were similar in these obvious ways, at heart they were nothing alike.

Alicia spent her childhood in Łódź, a burgeoning, prosperous city in central Poland known for its culture and industry. As a young girl, she attended the opera, studied music, and showed an affinity for art. She dreamed of seeing her pieces in the world's most prestigious galleries. Connoisseurs would buy her artwork in Paris and in New York.

While Alicia blossomed in the country's second-largest city, her future roommate lived on the opposite side of Poland, in the hinterlands near Russia. Like most in that region, Irenka's people were farmers ("*I slaughter de pigs*") who maintained an existence of work and production. She had a meager education and never learned to read.

By the time they moved in together, the world had changed and thus their "differences" were preposterous, if such differences still existed. Irenka was no longer a farmer, Alicia no longer upper class, and neither girl was really "Polish" anymore. They were displaced persons—in the same boat, as they said, though their shared boat was also true in fact.

They'd both come to America on the USNS *General S. D. Sturgis* and found themselves in Oklahoma City, one of the cities willing to take their sort. Then Irenka learned of the job with the Kennedys, and off to Massachusetts she went. Alicia followed when she realized her brand of American dream could not be found in the dust bowl, in the one state not benefiting from a postwar boom.

"You vant dis job or no?" Irenka asked, and moved Eunice's hat from the table to the counter.

"I do," Alicia said. "I didn't mean to sound ungrateful. I'm pleased to have the work."

"Is only part-time. Until Labor Day."

"I know, I know . . ." Alicia said, nodding, for Irenka had reminded her of this a dozen times. "Part-time is better than no time. So, shall we get to it? Do you want to show me around?"

"Ya. Tour is good. Follow Irenka."

They started in the sunroom, which, aside from its Atlantic view, was a modest space dominated by a nubby orange couch and a pair of ratty, floral wingback chairs. Really, *all* of the Kennedys' furniture was on the shabby side of worn. Not to mention, the floors needed a good polish, the walls fresh paint, and Alicia didn't spy a single piece of art. She wondered how they'd outfitted their Boston home, or the New York apartment, or the spread in Palm Beach. She couldn't ask, for she'd never hear the end of it.

"Bah!" Irenka might say. "Not even Kennedy house is nice enough for you!"

Adjacent to the sunroom was a television room. After that, Irenka showed her the living room, and then the various pantries and utility closets scattered throughout.

"How do you keep it all straight?" Alicia asked.

"Everytink organized all de time," Irenka said. "You vill catch on! Probably."

"What's this?" Alicia asked, and stopped beside a bulletin board crammed with magazine and newspaper clippings, a dozen at least.

DULLES BARS RACE FOR SENATE IN FALL.

KOREAN REDS SLAY 26 G.I. PRISONERS.

"Dat is for learnink." Irenka tapped her head. "For de Children. Always de kids-who-are-adults must know de vents."

"The vents?" Alicia said with a squint. "I don't follow."

"De vents. Curranty."

Alicia noodled on this for a second.

"Oh," she said, and stifled a laugh. "Current events?"

"Dis is vat I said. I can always tell who not study. Usually it is Teddy. Eunice is best. If you cannot contribute, it's almost like . . ."

She thought about this, trying to drum up the words.

"If you don't have contribution," Irenka said, "it is like, you are nuttink. Come, I show you where dey eat."

Alicia nodded, skimming the board one last time.

VERBATIM RECORD OF YESTERDAY'S SESSION OF THE UN SECURITY COUNCIL ON KOREA.

That one sounded like a real humdinger, though Alicia appreciated Mrs. Kennedy's efforts. Father never made her read the "verbatim record" of any governmental proceeding—unless as a punishment—but Alicia was similarly expected to be up on the latest news.

On their way to the dining room, the women passed a door they'd breezed by the first time. Because it was open, Alicia took the opportunity to peek inside.

"Guest room?" Alicia asked, peering at the twin beds, which were outfitted in green and white coverlets.

"No, no," Irenka said, and clicked the door closed. "Is bedroom of oldest Kennedy boy. He is congress representation named Jack."

"Congressman?" Alicia said, heart racing. "Jack is a congressman?"

She didn't know what that entailed, but Alicia understood it as a political office demanding some degree of respect. Jack hadn't seemed notably stern or serious when she met him, but of course he'd been on holiday.

"Jack oldest son," Irenka grunted. "*Nie*. Oldest *now*. De Kennedys have loss in war too."

"It happened to most of us, I suppose," Alicia said.

After a cursory inspection of the cupboards, they proceeded through an arched doorway and into the dining room. Meanwhile, Alicia continued to picture the white and green room near the stairs, a bachelor's bedroom heavy with a mother's touch.

"Dis is where dey eat," Irenka said.

Alicia scanned the room. Whereas checks and flowers prevailed in the rest of the home, this was decorated in ivory and gold, replete with a polished rosewood table and exquisite china cabinets built into the walls. It was an elegant space, and reminded Alicia of Europe, before the war.

"Dey eat supper at seven fifteen. Butler serves de meals, but sometimes we help. De Ambassador, he sits at head of table. Mizz Kennedy at foot."

Irenka lowered both hands onto a chair.

"On right of Ambassador is Jack," she said. "Bobby on de left. Everyone else . . ." She wiggled her fingers. "Dey fill in."

"Everyone else is, who, exactly? Eunice?"

"Ya. Eunice. Pat and Jean. And de youngest, Teddy. De baby. But he is eighteen and going to university. Yet, still baby!" She rolled her eyes. "Sometimes I expect dey start carrying him! But he is very chubby."

"So I've heard."

"Ya. Once family sit, a woman says grace. Eunice, ush-ly. After grace, dey eat."

"And get quizzed on current events?" Alicia guessed.

"Also, sports. Winnink trophies. Losink trophies. Den Mizz Kennedy powders face and meal is done. Dis job very easy to predict."

"Easy to predict sounds perfect to me," Alicia said as they exited the dining room.

They walked along and Irenka explained the schedule for the rest of the day, and then reviewed the Kennedys' morning routines for tomorrow. Though it was not their duty to deliver Mrs. Kennedy's breakfast to her room, or prepare the Ambassador's customary poached eggs on toast, Alicia should familiarize herself with such particulars. In that house, ignorance was an excuse for nothing, not even if you came to this country on a ship. After all, the family's ancestors did, too, and they managed all of this.

"I tink dat is all," Irenka said. "You get hang of it sometime."

Alicia turned to her friend and smiled.

"With your help, I'm sure I will. You really have this place figured out. And, I must compliment you, your English has improved dramatically. I scarcely recognize your voice."

It was true; Irenka sounded nothing like the girl who left Oklahoma those five, six months ago. The "ink" on her "dinink" was less overt; her "thought" not as easily mistaken for "taut." When they met, Irenka had a very klutzy grasp of the language, and so Alicia insisted they speak English. Irenka worked on comprehension, while Alicia wrestled with her own accent, the "ink"s and "taut"s, not to mention "dis" and "dat."

"Th," she'd practice. "Thhhhh."

So peculiar, to put one's tongue against the teeth to talk.

They also worked on inflection. Americans had a spry and animated way of communicating, and if the girls spoke too deeply, they'd brand themselves as Poles straight off. Or, worse, people might think they were Russian.

"I try to improve de English," Irenka said. "Goink to church, it help."

"Church?" Alicia said, and wrinkled her nose.

It was the second mention of Irenka's newfound religion, which didn't square with what Alicia remembered. In Oklahoma City, she could barely drag Irenka to the basement mixers put on by the good ladies of the Catholic Church.

"Have you started attending—"

Alicia stopped as she felt the presence of something, *someone* else.

"What do we have here?" said a voice. "Some chitchat to pass the afternoon?"

A figure drifted into the full light of the hallway: a man. He was tall and thin, but with a midsection that told of his age. It was the Ambassador. Alicia found herself scooting behind Irenka.

"New employee, Mizzer Kennedy," Irenka said. "I show her vat's vat."

"My, my, a new employee," he said. "What's your name, sweetheart?"

"Dis is Barb . . . I mean, Alic*ja*. Alic*ja* Darr."

"Hello, Mr. Kennedy," Alicia said, her voice soft, especially against the backdrop of Irenka's brutishness. "I'm very pleased to be here."

"Dear, there's no need to hide," the Ambassador said, his small, round glasses glinting in the light. "Come say hello."

He extended a hand. When Alicia went to shake it, he pulled her toward him.

"Why you're a pretty thing, aren't you?" he said.

Alicia gave a bow of the head, which was not the correct response, but she was bewildered that anyone might notice her in such drab attire.

"Thank you," she mumbled, the sting of Irenka's eyes on her.

The Ambassador released her hand and gave Alicia another quick appraisal. Irenka moved between them, and crossed both arms over her heavy bosom.

"Ve fold linens," she said. "Before supper to be served."

"Of course," the Ambassador said with a grin. "I wouldn't want to get in the way of your work. Please, proceed."

He stepped aside. Irenka snatched Alicia's hand and dragged her forward.

"Nice to meet you," Alicia called out.

As they scuffled past the Ambassador, *something* brushed against

Alicia's rear. She glanced behind her, expecting to see a hallway table, or a stand packed with umbrellas tilting her way. But all she found was the Ambassador. Alicia shook her head. She must've imagined it.

"He's interesting," Alicia whispered, once they were safely out of earshot. "I'm surprised someone of his stature would bother with the help at all!"

Irenka answered with a deepening scowl. She didn't say a word, but at once Alicia understood that the Ambassador had never bothered with her.

Alicia wondered, had her currency gone up? A lowly refugee had caught the attention of an ambassador, and a congressman, too. With this knowledge came a flash of hope. No, it was more than hope. It was a plan.

The truth was, before she came to America, Alicia Darr had accumulated an enormous debt, one she'd never be able to repay using only cash. But maybe through the Kennedys, and the people who knew them, Alicia might elevate herself beyond her background, and her status of displaced Pole. Alicia needed to *matter*, and this family could show her the way.

HYANNIS PORT

Her new gig was part-time, but Alicia examined the Kennedys from dawn to dusk, diligently recording their physical characteristics, speech patterns, and myriad quirks. She'd already bought a second notebook.

The Kennedy personality was large in its variant forms, and after a few days, Alicia was well-schooled in each, which said less about her intuition (and mild spying) and more about the family's relentless need to show the world who they were.

Mr. Kennedy was the leader of the tribe, his wife a supporting player. The Children heeded the Ambassador more than they did their mom, and they were forever yapping at his heels like untrained pups. Just as she'd been warned, Mr. Kennedy was the only one with manners and savoir faire.

Unlike his offspring, he never swiped food from another's plate, or left clothes or trash for someone else to pick up. He didn't use blue language or brag about his wealth, as his daughters often did. Mr. Kennedy was polite to everyone, even Miss Dee, whom he treated not like a secretary, but like a beloved guest.

Then there was Mrs. Kennedy, the odd duck with her pinned notes, endless critiques, and religious adherence to rules and routine, including the routine of religion. She attended mass every day. Her closest friends were nuns.

The woman was shrill and slight, her diminutive stature not a fact but an earned prize. Weekly Kennedy weigh-ins had tapered now that the Children were grown, but Mrs. Kennedy continued to monitor everyone's physique with her unsparing gaze. She found countless areas ripe for comment and kept a notebook not only of the Children's weights, but their illnesses and dispositions, too.

The thing was, Mrs. Kennedy worked pretty hard at being Mrs. Kennedy, but the family didn't always notice. The Kennedys had formed a tight cocoon around their bawdy crew, yet she was somehow outside of it. "Don't tell Mother" was a frequent refrain, and despite her counsel, cushions didn't always get reupholstered, Eunice never bought a new wardrobe, and Teddy kept crashing boats.

Rose Kennedy was supervisor more than mother, and considered the whole deal an "enterprise" rather than a family. In that house, Mr. Kennedy nurtured. He doled out hugs. Mrs. Kennedy kept track.

It was no secret that Eunice was her mother's favorite, slovenliness and poor fashion notwithstanding. A "disheveled gypsy woman," as Mrs. Kennedy said. Eunice had an eccentric personality, and was energetic to the point of being high-strung. But she was the smartest and most pious of the bunch, the one Kennedy who'd ever saved an allowance, which was likely how she earned her mother's favor in the first place.

"Eunice would be the best politician in this family," Mr. Kennedy said, "if she were born with balls."

Then there was Bobby, who was quiet and a bit of a twerp. There was not enough of him—in any sense—to prevent him being overshadowed by his bigger and better siblings. Alicia never worried if she missed some Kennedy tidbit or bon mot, because Bobby was sure to repeat it soon after. Also, his choice of wife baffled. Ethel was loud, cutting, forever chomping gum and calling everyone "kid."

The only one who might still be counted as a "kid" was Teddy, bound for Harvard in the fall. Everyone loved Teddy. The women coddled him, the men treated him like a mascot, and Mr. Kennedy's face brightened the moment Teddy came into view.

Alicia saw quite plainly that Teddy could rob a bank or get kicked off an athletic team and be forgiven. He even managed to skirt the edges of his mother's eagle eye. Whereas Mrs. Kennedy demanded a family of thoroughbreds, sleek and lean and fast, she looked the other way when it came to Ted.

Teddy's closest sister, Jean, was pudgy, too, at least by Kennedy standards, a problem discussed at length both at the table and behind her back. Jean wasn't around often, and the family deemed her somewhat undignified. Maybe it was the way she appeared bored all the time, with her sleepy blue eyes.

Like Jean, Pat didn't visit much, living on the West Coast as she did. As the Kennedys so favored awards, Alicia would've given her top prize. Not only was Pat the prettiest, with her auburn hair and violet eyes, she was also the most sophisticated. She possessed a regal comportment, while remaining long on wit and charm.

Family, family, family was what they espoused, yet Pat lived in Hollywood and there was another sister, the oldest, missing like the oldest brother though presumably not due to war. Her whereabouts remained hush-hush, and the most Alicia could deduce was that this Rose Marie was either a nun or a schoolteacher in Wisconsin. Admirable professions both, but neither explained why she never came to Hyannis Port. Jeannette, the head maid, said she'd not been there in years.

And then there was Jack. Oh, yes, Alicia had compiled a thorough dossier on him, though her observations were made mostly from afar.

Jack had spent minimal time in Hyannis Port since she'd started the job. When he did saunter onto the premises, Alicia made immediate work of restocking the pantry, or cleaning the oven, anything to keep out of sight. Jack had taken her number that day, and Alicia didn't want "housemaid" to be the reason he'd not called. Nonetheless, Alicia managed to cull a few details about the man.

First, there was his reputation: a charismatic, going-places politician, the family's crown jewel. And there was what she had seen for herself: goofiness, a wry wit, the inability to arrive on time. Jack Kennedy was engaging, and even among his own family he commanded a room. But there remained something wooden about him, all the way to his walk.

"Boat accident," Irenka explained when Alicia found the guts to ask. "From de var. He saved de crew."

"He's a war hero?"

"Ya. Dat's vat dey say."

This, Alicia decided, was why Jack Kennedy fascinated her when no other American male had so far. In Oklahoma, she'd gone on a dozen dates. Fifteen? Twenty? There was no use counting. The boys were handsome and gracious, their jobs solid and their jawbones strong, but Alicia never experienced more than a vague appreciation for any of them. She'd begun to think that dating in America was a fluency she'd never master.

Then she met Jack. Alicia didn't feel romantically toward him, not exactly, as they'd met just once. But he evoked something that she couldn't entirely reason out, though she was starting to put it together. Jack Kennedy was older than the previous boys, thirty-three according to what she'd gleaned, and now there was the bit about the sunken boat. This had to be the answer. Alicia needed someone experienced, someone who'd seen the war.

Alicia sought many things when crossing the Atlantic, not the least of which was love. America was enormous, its reach almost incalculable. There must be a million Jack Kennedys out there, she guessed. Two million, perhaps. All she needed was someone like him, a man who was attractive and ambitious and wise to the world. In this ample, prosperous country, how hard could it be?

Alicia stood in the dining room, a pile of unfolded napkins on her right, articles from the Kennedy bulletin board on the left. Because of these clippings, she knew that Jack was currently in Washington, immersed in his congressional pursuits. Something about air mail subsidies and printing costs. She didn't entirely follow.

From what she'd read—not one, not two, but three articles on the subject—Jack was trying to compel the government to print instruction manuals for a possible atomic attack. The problem was the price tag, a steep $53,052.69. Alas, they'd spent three times that to print a Department of Agriculture cookbook last year.

"It's at least as important to know what to do in case of an atomic attack as to know how to cook," Representative Kennedy (D-Mass.) reasons.

It was a fair point, despite the unsettling hint of another possible war.

"Hello there," said a voice.

Startled, Alicia nearly popped out of her clompy white shoes.

"Hello, Mr. Kennedy . . . Ambassador Kennedy," Alicia said, breath in short supply. "I apologize."

Alicia shook her head. What was she apologizing for, exactly?

"It's okay. Call me Joe." The Ambassador walked a few steps closer. "Did I startle you?"

"Yes," she admitted. "I thought everyone was out for the afternoon."

"Then I should be the one apologizing," Mr. Kennedy said. "I would never want to put anyone off."

"Oh, it's fine! Really, my own fault for getting lost in my imagination."

The Ambassador was now directly beside her, his hand a hairsbreadth from hers. Alicia could smell his musty, summertime scent.

"It's lovely outside, don't you think?" she said, her heart faltering. "Did you get your horseback ride in earlier?"

"I did. Listen. My youngest, Teddy, told me the strangest thing."

Though he did not move, the Ambassador seemed nearer still. Alicia's hairline bubbled with sweat. When she dreamed of getting closer to the Kennedys, this was not what she had in mind.

"Really?" she said. "And what was that?"

Alicia reached for a napkin to fold and fold and fold.

"Teddy was at the Center the other day, picking up a copy of *Pretty Baby,*" Mr. Kennedy said.

Alicia nodded. They weren't due to premiere the movie for a couple of weeks, but all films at the Center were shown in the Kennedy basement first, before anyone else got a peek.

"Teddy was collecting the reel," Mr. Kennedy continued, "and saw you wiping a counter and organizing candy. I thought, how can that be? Surely, we pay her enough. I would hate for one of our employees to need a second job. I know Mother can be quite severe."

"It's nothing like that," Alicia said. "You pay the household staff generously. At the Center, I only work a handful of hours, and they let me show my art?"

She grimaced, hating how her voice came out as a question.

"You're selling art on the street?" Mr. Kennedy scowled. "Oh, no, you poor dear."

"Not in the street, in the lobby. And a perspiring . . . *aspiring* artist has to start somewhere."

"This sounds awful."

"It's not bad at all. I'm grateful for the opportunity, and happy to help with concessions on the side. I'm only in your employ temporarily—flex help, to carry you through the summer."

"Don't fret, my dear. I can talk to Mother about giving you more hours."

"No!" Alicia shrieked.

She reddened, and lowered her voice.

"Really, Mr. Kennedy, that's not necessary."

Panic washed over her. This was a great job, and the Kennedys were terrific theater, but if she stayed too long, she might never leave. Alicia understood how easily weeks spread into years. And she didn't come to America to be a maid.

"I enjoy the Center," she insisted. "The customers are kind and the projectionist is a funny little man named George. I spend half the time trying to figure him out, like a puzzle."

She laughed to herself.

"Plus, it leaves me time to paint," she added. "I can't be a housekeeper forever."

"Indeed. You are far too pretty to be a maid."

"Oh, thank you," she murmured.

As she began to fold her napkins with ever more diligence, the room's air seemed to stop. It was as though someone sealed them off when previously they'd relished a nice breeze.

"What happened to the articles on the board?" said a voice: cool and steely. "Has anyone seen my stories?"

"Good afternoon, Mother," the Ambassador said jovially. "How was golf?"

"Three birdies," Mrs. Kennedy answered, one eye fixed on Alicia.

"Holy gum! You should be teaching lessons at the club," he said. "Somehow you constantly improve while I only get worse."

"You should practice more." Mrs. Kennedy looked at Alicia. "Have you seen—"

"Oh!" Alicia yelped, suddenly remembering why the woman had come. "I'm so sorry. I have the articles right here."

"*You* took my articles?"

"Borrowed them, really," Alicia said. "I like to read while I fold laundry. It helps pass the time. I should've asked first. I'll put them right back!"

"My, my," Mrs. Kennedy said, her voice a bewildering combination of shaky and firm. "Aren't you an enterprising girl? Where did you say you were from?"

"Vienna," the Ambassador said. "She also works at the Center Theatre and is an accomplished artist."

"How nice," Mrs. Kennedy said, barely moving her mouth to get the words out. "I'm pleased that you're trying to acclimate to the country's culture. I find so many displaced persons are resistant to the arts."

"Oh, I wouldn't say that."

"They should have some sort of . . . program." Mrs. Kennedy fished a scrap of paper from her pocket. "A program that could take refugees on cultural outings."

"Winning idea, Mother."

Mrs. Kennedy scratched out a note, then slapped her pencil on the table. She pinned the paper to her dress.

"Perhaps you could start it with the church!" the Ambassador said.

"Yes, I think I will. I'm so glad to have thought of it."

Mrs. Kennedy straightened the note as Alicia strained to see the words. *Culture for the derelict,* it read. Alicia pressed her lips together to keep from speaking her mind.

Alicia was quite familiar with "culture," no Catholic ladies needed. In the 1930s, her family consorted with Europe's most renowned artists and writers and filmmakers. Father helped *found* the Polish Academy of Literature, and Alicia always read the works nominated for top prize.

If Poland wasn't good enough for Rose Kennedy, and surely it was not, Alicia had been to Paris, and many other cities besides. Even the ghetto in Łódź put on shows. It wasn't the *opéra national de Paris* (seven times), but despite actual starving, they weren't starving for art.

"Culture sounds wonderful," Alicia said, tightly. "I've missed it since I left Europe."

"Excuse me?" Mrs. Kennedy blinked.

"My parents were great patrons of the arts. When I was five years old, I saw Bruno Walter conduct *Das Lied von der Erde* with the Vienna Philharmonic. I still remember every note."

The Ambassador chortled, as if Alicia had told a great joke. Meanwhile, Mrs. Kennedy looked stricken, her church program shot to hell.

"Bruno Walter," Mr. Kennedy said, still chuckling. "Brilliant. I've met him, you know. He lives near our daughter Pat in Hollywood. Well, if you ladies will excuse me, it's two o'clock. I have a meeting with Janet."

He offered an amiable nod to Alicia, and then to his wife, and proceeded upstairs to his bedroom, where his two o'clock with Janet was customarily held. This meeting was always very . . . loud. Miss Dee must've been a vigorous typist.

Alicia caught Mrs. Kennedy's eyes as the sound of the secretary's bare feet pit-a-patted up the stairs. If Alicia were to look, she'd see that Miss Dee carried nothing—no notebook, no pen.

"You seem to be acclimating to America quite well," Mrs. Kennedy said, slicing through Alicia with her gaze.

Upstairs, the furniture began to creak.

"America is wonderful," Alicia said. "And this job is one reason why."

"What is dis in here?"

Irenka appeared in the doorway, filling the space with her bulwark style. Though their friendship had grown tense and thin, Alicia was grateful for another body in this room. Mrs. Kennedy's presence was suffocating, though she was small, about one-third Irenka's size.

"Mizz Kennedy. Did Alicja botter you?" Irenka wanted to know. "I tell her leave family alone."

"Everything's fine, Irenka," Alicia said, though this didn't feel entirely true.

"Yes, everything's fine," Mrs. Kennedy confirmed. "We were chatting about Miss Darr's upbringing. It's truly . . . unexpected. The Vienna Philharmonic. Can you imagine?"

Irenka glowered.

"Yes," she said, almost a grunt. "Alicia very world-y. She has much experience."

Alicia side-eyed her friend. Since Alicia had taken the job with the Kennedys, Irenka had soured toward her, for reasons unexplained. But Alicia knew better than to sweet-talk a Polish woman, especially one who'd lived so close to Russia.

"Please excuse me," she said to Mrs. Kennedy. "There's much to take care of and I don't want to fall behind. Irenka, I'll be in the kitchen if you need anything."

As Alicia slipped by, Irenka hissed, "*Tępa cipa.*"

Alicia pretended not to hear and instead reveled in the cadence of her native tongue. Polish was not a lyrical language, but she missed it sometimes.

"*To mi śmierdzi,*" Irenka added, a parting shot, and louder this time, for Alicia was already mostly down the hall.

"*Do widzenia!*" Alicia called gaily.

She probably should've been more upset to be called a bitch, and then a rat. But it was cute almost, decidedly old-world, compared to all the things hurled at her during and after the war.

Never mind Europe, though. There was a territorial dispute in that very home, over what, Alicia didn't care to guess. She had one aim and it was to get by, to endure the hostility and this job for a few more days, and a few more after that, until the next season came. It was how she'd survived weeks, months, entire years before.

Alicia couldn't predict the future but she was determined to build a life that would leave people no choice but to view her with dignity, respect, and maybe a smidge of jealousy, too.

ROMANCE BECOMES AFFAIR OF STATE
Long Beach Independent, August 26, 1950

HYANNIS PORT

Alicia had spent eight days with the Kennedys, but was unprepared for the full brunt of their energy when they were all in the house at the same time.

The shouting, the bickering, the constant one-upmanship. A door slammed here, something crashed over there, all those feet clobbering the stairs like a train that never stopped. Alicia wanted to ask, what was the prize? What was the sport in which they were all vying for first place? They exhausted her, and she wasn't even competing.

Alicia showed up early on a Saturday, after a raucous Friday night during which multiple persons were launched into the swimming pool. Jeannette was under strict orders to lock up the liquor, but the little squirrels found their way into it nonetheless.

On that day, approximately a dozen activities were scheduled, and Alicia was to assist with the preparations. While the Children and their friends rabble-roused outside, wearing ever more patches into the lawn, Alicia filled picnic baskets with hard-boiled eggs, hamburgers, hot dogs, Cokes, and beer. Once they finished pummeling each other, they were to sail to a nearby island for more sparring. Alicia packed the boats with the lunches and also footballs, baseballs, bats, and a smattering of other sporting equipment she found in the shed.

While the Children were gone, Mrs. Kennedy played French records and practiced the language, badly. Soon, way too soon, the troupe pounded into the kitchen, sweaty and sunburned and crawling all over the pantry like ants.

"I want another hot dog."

"Gimme some Cokes."

"Why does Jeannette always lock up the booze?"

"Who the hell put croquet balls in the boat?"

Alicia glanced up in time to see Jeannette thwacking Teddy on the chest with a rolled-up newspaper.

"Stop beating me, Jeannette!" he said, then sprayed a can of Reddi-wip into the air.

Teddy scampered out of the room, and his mob followed, punching and kicking each other as they went.

"This family," Jeannette said. "They are always hungry. For food, for sports, for everything."

"Yes," Alicia said with a snort. "I've noticed."

Jeannette had it the worst. The kitchen was *her* domain, but it was also the home's thoroughfare, the primary entry and exit point between the Kennedy universe and the outside world. This meant lots of smacking doors, scrabbly feet, and grabby hands, all day long.

"They're a pack of wild animals is what they are," Jeannette said, "every last one of them. They're either going to change the world or end up dead. Immortality or a tragic end."

"But who will achieve it first?" Alicia asked with a smirk.

"Definitely Jack," Jeannette said, shaking her head once again.

It was a wonder that she never got dizzy.

"Would you please make up some lemonade and tea?" she asked. "For the tea, use the recipe from the Royal Hawaiian Hotel. The large pitchers would be best. The Children are set to play softball and they'll be parched in no time."

"*Softball?*" Alicia said. "After all they've already done? Doesn't anyone need naps?"

"The mind boggles," Jeannette said. "Thank goodness for the Ambassador. They make fun of his rules, but he's the only one keeping them the slightest bit in line."

Alicia was inventorying the wine cellar when dinner began.

She didn't hear the bell but felt the thunderous rattle as family and guests descended upon the dining room. "Barbarians," "heathens," "untrained gorillas," all these words muttered by the help. Alicia didn't think they were quite as monstrous as described, although she'd never known so many people to be impaled by forks. Maybe Mr. Kennedy was on to something with his "only one drink before dinner" rule.

"Here's the list," Alicia said, walking into Miss Dee's office, which sat off the living room.

From where they were seated, they could hear the silverware ding, dishes clash, and voices hum. Every few seconds, someone made a joke, which was followed by a blast of laughter.

"Hmmmm," Miss Dee said, scanning the paper with her clear green gaze. "We're better stocked than I thought. We should have enough, but I'll confirm with the Ambassador to make sure."

She looked up, eyes sparkling.

"Thank you ever so much, Miss Darr. I realize this isn't in your job description but you're a tremendous help."

"Don't thank me," Alicia said. "I don't have a job description, really. I'm merely here to pitch in."

"And thank goodness for that."

Both women paused, and listened for a second as the Ambassador relayed the story of a problem brewing on Crete. A civil war was set to break out, thanks to a star-crossed love. A "modern Trojan War."

"Visualize a nineteen-year-old, raven-haired beauty named Tassoula," Mr. Kennedy said. "She is wealthy and politically connected. Her father is the Liberal Party deputy."

"Sounds like a hot numbah," one of the Children responded in his twangy Boston tone.

It was Bobby, no doubt. Teddy was more playful than uncouth, and Jack was never that idiotic.

"Her boyfriend is a thirty-five-year-old man named Costas," the Ambassador continued. "Costas is likewise quite wealthy, and he is reported to have the finest mustache in all of Crete."

"If that's his number one quality, then Tassoula should probably find another option," Ethel said, and Alicia cringed, bracing against her rough voice.

Ethel never earned hurrahs like the others did, though not for lack of trying.

"Are you bastahds gonna listen to Dad's story, or keep spouting off?"

"Language," Mrs. Kennedy sniped.

"Thank you, Teddy, but I can defend myself," the Ambassador said. "As I was saying, whereas Tassoula's family are noted members of the Liberal Party, Costas's family is wholeheartedly Populist, and his brother is *their* deputy."

"Jesus, that'd be like marrying a Republican. Someone should tell Costas that you don't have to propose to every broad you screw."

"Bobby!" Mrs. Kennedy squawked. "Enough!"

"If you'll allow me to continue," Mr. Kennedy said. "Now, despite their conflicting politics, the two fell in love and announced their intention to marry. Unfortunately, on Crete, any woman under twenty-one must get permission from her parents to wed. Naturally, Tassoula's father wouldn't stand for it. He decreed that he'd rather see his daughter dead than married to a Populist."

"Must be a swell guy," someone grumbled. "Politics over family."

Jack, it had to be Jack. He shared his family's Bostonian lilt but his voice was different somehow, apart. Alicia's heart began to trip over itself and she prayed Miss Dee wouldn't send her into that room. She couldn't ignore Jack, but she wouldn't be able to look at him either.

"Because Tassoula's father refused to allow the union," Mr. Kennedy said, "Costas kidnapped his young love."

"Alicia?" Miss Dee said. "Did you hear me?"

"Oh, I'm sorry." Alicia shook her head. "I didn't catch that."

"Sometimes it's challenging to focus in this house. I was wondering if you could assist with another task? Before you leave?"

"I'd be pleased to."

She needed the extra hours, but more than that Alicia wanted to hear the rest of Mr. Kennedy's story, the part about the kidnapping, and how it might cause a war.

"Here are notes from today's calls and meetings," Miss Dee said.

She placed a few sheets of paper on a nearby table as Mr. Kennedy explained that Tassoula's father armed three thousand men to defeat Costas, who'd decamped to Mount Ida, the birthplace of Zeus.

"I took these for the Ambassador this morning," Miss Dee said.

Alicia nodded, for she'd seen them together during the calls and conversations. As always, Miss Dee made notes with one hand, and held Mr. Kennedy's hand with the other.

"Can you read them aloud so that I may type them out?" Miss Dee asked.

She faced her Smith-Corona.

"Sure thing," Alicia said.

She took a seat as Miss Dee cranked the paper into place.

"When the archbishop visited Tassoula," Mr. Kennedy said from the other room, "the girl confirmed that she loved this man, and wanted to be married, and had left of her own free will. Now, the country waits. It's expected that a war will break out because no one is willing to budge."

"Wow!" said a person not of the Kennedy camp.

"That's wild!" said another.

"Begin on the first page," Miss Dee said, "and work your way through. This shouldn't take any time at all. Then you can go home and get on with your life."

"Will do," Alicia said, stacking the papers on her lap. "Ready when you are."

"Okay. Oh, wait. Damn it! I'm out of ink. Just one moment."

Miss Dee spun toward the wooden file cabinet behind her and began poking around.

"Hard to believe the entire country is wrapped up in this romance," said one of the guests. "Can you imagine if your fling became an affair of the state?"

"It's bound to happen to someone," Bobby said. "Men are always getting in trouble for taking off their trousahs."

"But a war? Usually sex scandals involve nothing more than a man screwing his secretary and his wife making a big demonstration about it. Throwing his clothes into the front yard, that sort of thing."

"I would like to know how we've degenerated into a discussion of sexual congress at the dinner table," Mrs. Kennedy huffed. "And I wouldn't call your example a scandal. No man is above falling in love with his secretary. That's at least half the point of them."

The conversation died, at least in Alicia's mind. What a thing to say, with Mr. Kennedy's own secretary seated footsteps away. Alicia looked toward Miss Dee, horrified. Here she'd been such a kind and gracious assistant, doing every last thing the Ambassador required.

"Miss Dee . . ."

The woman glanced over her shoulder and the two locked eyes.

"I'm sorry," Alicia started to say, but Miss Dee was not embarrassed, or even mildly perturbed.

Instead, she offered Alicia a conspiratorial wink.

"I guess the jig is up," she said with a laugh.

Miss Dee spun back around, fresh typewriter ribbon in hand.

"Shall we get to it then?" she asked. "I don't know about you, but I'm tired of listening to these Kennedys yammer on."

Alicia and Irenka worked twelve hours that day. It was after ten o'clock, and their shifts were over, yet they remained at the house.

"I need find sometink," Irenka said as she rummaged through Miss Dee's office, in the semidarkness, for a reason she refused to explain.

"We're going to miss our bus," Alicia said. "And Mrs. Kennedy is not going to be pleased with the prospect of paying us overtime."

"Mizz Kennedy is asleep."

Irenka opened a cabinet.

"What are you looking for?"

"We must lock house," Irenka said.

"I've never once seen anyone lock a door in this house."

"Shhh!" Irenka barked. "Dey tell me lock and bring key tomorrow. But Miss Dee never say where is dis key."

"The Children aren't here," Alicia said. "You know they never have their keys on them, or anything else for that matter."

The Kennedys traveled light, nothing but shirts on their backs, and sometimes not even that if the Kennedy in question was Teddy.

"Let's go, Irenka. You must've misunderstood."

"You still very bad maid. We lock de house."

"But *why*?"

"*Bo tak.*"

Alicia sighed. *Bo tak.* She'd forgotten the Polish phrase, an expression whose closest English equivalent was "because: yes." It had its uses, she supposed.

"Hello, ladies," someone said. "Is everything okay?"

"Mr. Kennedy!" Alicia said.

One hand flew to her chest and Irenka froze, hovered above Miss Dee's desk.

"What are you doing up at this hour?" Alicia asked.

Mr. Kennedy loomed in the doorway, tall and lank in his silk lounging suit. The light from the green desk lamp echoed off his precise, round spectacles.

"It is rather late," he agreed, "but when you get to be my age, beauty sleep seems a bit futile."

Alicia laughed dully as the Ambassador made several creeping steps toward them.

"Does Janet know you're snooping in her office?" he asked.

Mr. Kennedy detected her alarm, and chased the accusation with a playful wink.

"Don't worry. I won't tell Janet—Miss des Rosiers—a thing," he said, looking directly at Alicia. "It will be our little secret."

"There's no secret!" she said.

She glared at Irenka, who was suddenly struck dumb. Not that she was ever particularly . . .

Oh, never mind.

"Miss Dee told us to lock up the house and we're trying to find a key," Alicia explained. She glanced at Irenka. "Or was it Mrs. Kennedy who asked?"

"Mother hasn't locked up a day in her life," Mr. Kennedy said. "Much to Jeannette's consternation. She's convinced some criminal element will abscond with Mother in the dead of night. Demand a ransom. That sort of thing. She has the whole plot worked out."

It wasn't so outlandish, on account of their wealth. Not to mention, all those rumors of the "bedroom prowler." Alicia should probably bring this to the Ambassador's attention but she suspected Mr. Kennedy was already apprised of the man who snuck around at night and crawled into bed with the Girls' friends.

"Well, Irenka," Alicia said, "it's settled. We don't need to waste any more time hunting for errant keys. I appreciate you clearing that up, Mr. Kennedy. Thank you and good-bye."

Alicia scooted past the man, careful not to make contact, or sully his nice silk with her handmaid paws. Once through the door, she planted herself in the hallway.

"We don't want to miss the last bus," she said.

Irenka persisted in her suspended state.

"*Chodźmy!*" Alicia snapped.

Good grief. Irenka Michalska: the only person on God's green earth who could make a situation more awkward by doing absolutely nothing at all.

"*Teraz!*"

Mr. Kennedy padded farther into the office, his slippered feet plonking softly against the floor.

"Miss Darr is quite right," the Ambassador said, and lifted a letter from the desk. "No need to lock up."

And still Irenka did not move.

"I'm leaving now," Alicia said. "Are you coming?"

"Hold on a minute," Mr. Kennedy said as he inspected the envelope now in hand. "Janet forgot to mail this letter. It needs to go out by Monday. Would you take it to the post office for me?"

This question was posed to Alicia, though Irenka was closest to the desk.

"I'd be happy to," Alicia said, shuffling into the room.

She reached for the envelope, but Mr. Kennedy whisked it away.

"Gosh darn, she wrote the address incorrectly!" he said. "Allow me to fix it."

"Oh." Alicia blinked. "Okay. I can get it from Miss Dee tomorrow. It's Sunday, so it won't go out for another day anyhow."

"I'd prefer to take care of this right now and save Janet from one of her innumerable tasks. Poor thing."

The Ambassador pivoted sharply.

"You can leave," he told Irenka, who in turn scowled at Alicia.

Alicia had wanted to set herself apart from the other help, to say nothing of displaced persons nationwide, but this was not how she hoped to do it. "Top servant" was never her aim, and in fact it was Irenka's. Her friend's goal was upstairs maid and then marriage to a humble man, with eight to ten kids to follow. She was welcome to all of it, because none of these things were part of Alicia's dreams.

"Irenka can't leave without me," Alicia said, and reached for her hand. "We ride the bus home together and we'll miss it if we don't hurry. I'll get the letter tomorrow. It will be my top priority."

"I'll drive you home," Mr. Kennedy said as he ripped open the envelope. "Your friend can take the bus."

Irenka made a noise, like someone squeezing air from a balloon. Finally, she moved.

"But . . ." Alicia tried, though she likewise felt deflated.

This was getting uncomfortable, and fast. Alicia reminded herself that of all the people in the house, Mr. Kennedy was the most well-mannered. Even the Children preferred him to their mother. This letter was probably very important, as he was an important man.

"Mr. Kennedy, your offer is very kind," Alicia said as the front door clicked. "But I'd hate to put you out."

"Don't speak another word," he snarled.

Alicia gulped as he slid open a desk drawer. After locating a new envelope, he began to write.

MG Woodward
230 Park Avenue
New York 17, New York

It was the same address as on the original letter. Alicia was sure of it. Then again, why would he go to such trouble? She was probably missing a directional nuance, some American thing.

Before long, the envelope was sealed, keys were fetched, and they were in Mr. Kennedy's Rolls-Royce, motoring toward the east end. As they passed the empty bus stop, Alicia's stomach sloshed. Was it his driving? The family employed a driver, so Mr. Kennedy was not usually behind the wheel.

"Where did say you were from?" Mr. Kennedy asked as they veered onto Main Street.

They passed the New Yorker, the Panama Club, the Hyannis

Theatre, all of these places scheduled to close in the next couple of weeks. It seemed impossible that that side of town would be dark for the better part of a year.

"Vienna, right?" Mr. Kennedy said.

Alicia nodded. If she opened her mouth, she would surely vomit in his car. Her employment with this family had one week left, so there was no need to set facts straight. Austria or Poland, did it matter? At least he didn't mistake her for a Russian.

"You should be a model," he said. "An actress, perhaps. You know, I used to own a movie studio. My daughter Pat works in Hollywood and she's very well-connected. If you need anything, I'm sure she'd help you out. Your friend . . . now *she's* made for physical labor. But not you."

"An artist," Alicia managed to croak. "I wish to be an artist. I studied painting in Pol—back home."

"Ah, that's right. The Viennese artist." He waggled his brows. "It has a certain ring to it."

Now that he mentioned it, it rather did. Alicia smiled tightly.

"Turn here," she said, her voice at a high pitch. "It's the two-story house on the left. With the red truck in front, the lights on in the window upstairs."

Their window. Hers and Irenka's. Oh Lord, Alicia would give anything to walk in and find the Irenka from Oklahoma City, her onetime closest friend. So many letters, over so many months: Irenka's endless bragging about her job, and the Kennedys, and the gleam of their special type of rich. But what Alicia had mistaken for an invitation, she now saw as bravado, a way for Irenka to convey how far she'd climbed. Now Alicia threatened to overshadow her. This must be the explanation for their sudden discord. Alicia hadn't committed any other foul.

"Thank you ever so much," she said to Mr. Kennedy when they rolled to a stop.

She fumbled with the lock.

As the Ambassador leaned over, Alicia socked herself against the seat. How she prayed the neighbors were asleep. A Rolls was the swankiest ride in town and there was something unsavory about the combination of the car, the hour, and the girl.

"You are extraordinarily beautiful," Mr. Kennedy said, and, in one swift move, clamped down on Alicia's thigh.

She gave a jump, which did not put him off. Her uniform had hiked up on the drive and Alicia cursed herself for not taking care to keep it below the knees.

"Mr. Kennedy, I really should go," Alicia said, wondering if she'd have to change her name yet again. "I can see Irenka in the window. She is waiting for me."

Alicia summoned the strength to wrench herself from Mr. Kennedy's grasp. She kicked open the door and hustled toward the house, biting away the tears as the Rolls-Royce idled at the curb.

Alicia tiptoed into their room and tossed her handbag onto the desk.

"I thought you'd wait for me," she said to Irenka's back.

The woman was feigning sleep, and poorly at that. For Pete's sake, Alicia had witnessed Irenka's slumber at least a hundred times and this didn't come close to the real thing. She'd neglected the buzz saw snore, for one.

"I know you're awake," Alicia said, and unbuttoned the top of her uniform. "I made it home safely, in case you were worried. I don't appreciate being left to fend for myself. If the situation were reversed, I would've waited for you."

"De situation vould never be reversed."

Irenka flipped over. She looked Alicia square in the face.

"You vant to be alone vid Mizzer Kennedy."

"That is quite untrue," Alicia said, and wiggled out of her dress, stripping down to her pink slip. "I tried to refuse. You were there. You saw what happened."

"Refuse?" Irenka snorted. "I am sure you refuse nuttink."

"You are creating a rather elaborate story for someone merely trying to do her job."

Irenka sat up.

"I hate it," she said, trembling with rage. "I hate how you act like innocent. A good girl. Like you don't know anytink. You vant husband. Rich husband. But he vill never marry you. *Never!*"

"Mr. Kennedy?" Alicia laughed and lumbered toward her mattress. "Well that's a relief. He is already wed and rather old. Who'd want that many children?"

"Poor Mizz Kennedy!" Irenka wailed. "All dees vultures circlink, circlink. She is kindest, most virtuous voman in America."

"I'm sure she is." Alicia sighed. "But I don't know what that has to do with me."

She pulled on a black silk sleeping mask, a relic from her days (and employee discount) at Brown's.

"I know tinks about you," Irenka said. "Very bad tinks. You have made sin."

"Oh, Irenka," Alicia said with a chuckle, for she was too tired to be upset. "I'm not sure what you're referring to, but we've all sinned. The war had a way of blurring right and wrong. You know this."

"I see you. I see who you are. You disgustink."

"Well, lucky for you, I'll only be at the house another week. Then you can be rid of me for good. Not to worry, dear friend. Soon you'll have the Kennedys all to yourself."

The envelope lands on her desk. It's her first day. She's there for the summer, filling in for the assistant of an assistant, who's out on maternity leave. It's quiet this time of year, which she's been told is a blessing and a curse. At least she can wear her Metro shoes all day long.

She studies the envelope, which is addressed in loopy purple hand-writing and includes a peculiar lack of specifics. Because she doesn't want to be demanding, or seem like a doofus, she waits until her third day to ask for help from the guy in Payables. He's given her the eye at the espresso machine, several times so far.

"Do you know what to make of this?" she asks, deciding he's sort of cute.

The man from Payables is anxious to help and is shocked she's approached him of her own volition. This could lead to lunch, he thinks. Eventually drinks.

"Is that supposed to be an *address*?" he asks.

"I think so. It's very general. It reminded me of a letter to Santa Claus."

As she blushes at her lame joke, he spins around to his computer, and begins to clack.

"This person is real," he says. "Alas, no longer at this address."

He hands it back.

"Return to sender."

"Don't you have forwarding information?" she asks.

"Are you crazy?! We can't give student information to some rando! Think about it!"

"Sorry," she grumbles.

He realizes with great regret that there probably won't be any lunches. Meanwhile, she's determined, *Eh, maybe not that cute.* Later she'll eat a lonely turkey sandwich at her desk, in front of her computer. He'll berate himself for blowing it once again.

"Plus, I don't think you can forward mail to Rome," he adds, gently, he hopes. "A different mail system and all that."

"You're probably right."

The girl slumps toward her desk, envelope in hand. Once seated, she writes *No longer at this address* and circles the words. Just below she adds, *Try Rome.*

It's the best she can do.

HUMBLE REFUGEE MAKES GOOD

The Portsmouth Herald, September 1, 1950

HYANNIS PORT

Irenka was at work when Mrs. McGovern, the landlady, nervously tapped on their bedroom door. She came with unfortunate news.

"The fire marshal paid me a visit," she said. "There are too many people in this house. You will have to leave."

It surprised Alicia that a fire marshal might care about the occupancy of a private home, especially when the occupancy was four. Had they no immigrant families on Cape Cod? A dozen bodies packed into an apartment made for two? But Alicia was not one to question rules or laws, at least not out loud.

"Okay," she answered. "If that's what he said."

"He did." Mrs. McGovern nodded vigorously as she flushed a deep pink. "He said it. And if we don't comply, he'll report us for running a nonpermitted hotel, even operating a brothel."

"Excuse me?!" Alicia said with a laugh. "This must be the sorriest brothel in America! Rather, he could cite us for running an illegal convent."

"I really hate to do this to you," Mrs. McGovern said. "You *seem* like a nice girl, but I can't make waves at city hall. They're notorious for their retribution, and we couldn't survive if they revoked my husband's fishing license."

"Understood," Alicia said. "Think nothing of it."

The woman appeared genuine, and so Alicia took Mrs. McGovern at her word, even though the story did not add up, mostly because four was a small number by any account. But it was easier to blame a faceless bureaucrat than someone closer to home.

No matter. Alicia would press on. She had money now and it might be fun to get her own place. On her way to the Center that day, Alicia checked with a few people in town.

"A vacant room?" the baker Marty Martin said when Alicia stopped by the store. "A foreigner wants to let a room? This time of year? Good luck!"

"You'll probably have to relocate," said the Woolworth's manager.

As it turned out, Alicia's housing options were all too large, too dear, or too risky. She'd not soon let a bed in a boardinghouse otherwise filled with day laborers and unestablished fishermen. Dejected, Alicia straggled toward the Center. Maybe they'd let her stay there. She'd happily sleep beside the popcorn machine.

"I finally understand the expression," Alicia said when she walked inside.

George was at the counter, combing through the latest film-industry magazine. No doubt he'd soon regale her with details about movie financings gone awry, or stars that were difficult to insure.

"Which expression is that?" he asked, barely glancing up.

Alicia whomped her purse on the counter.

"On the Cape, never count on two sunny days in a row," she said.

"I think it was sunny yesterday and today," he said, brow wrinkled.

"That's not what I meant."

"Shouldn't you be at work?" he asked. "I mean, your other work. The real job."

"Not until later. I have some . . . personal business to tend to this morning."

She shoved a piece of hair from her eyes.

"Oh! Hey!" George slapped his magazine closed. "I sold one of your paintings."

"You did?!" Alicia perked up. "Really?"

"Yep. Last night. The big one. You know . . ." He twirled a finger. "The church."

"That's not a church." She shook her head. "You know what? Who cares! It can be whatever a person wants it to be! How much did you get?"

George reached into his pocket, then pulled a twenty from his wallet.

"Here you go."

He smacked it on the glass.

"Twenty dollars!" Alicia squealed.

She jumped over the counter to embrace the wonderful man.

"Oh, George! Thank you! Thank you so much!" she cried as he stiffened.

"Don't thank me," he said, worming out of her hold. "It's impressive, really. Twenty bucks is no petty thing."

"No. It's not." She exhaled. "Well, the sun shines on the Cape again. This money is needed—desperately." Alicia waved the bill. "I was kicked out of my room this very morning, by the fire marshal. So, I'm on the hunt for a new home."

"We have a fire marshal?"

"So they say. Alas, while twenty dollars is swell, apparently there's not a spare room to be found in this whole damned town."

Alicia looked around the lobby. Five paintings remained. She should start thinking about creating others, especially if this sale was the start of something more.

"Oh, George." She sighed. "I don't know what I'm going to do."

"You can move in with me," he said.

Alicia gaped. She felt mildly concussed, as if she'd just run into a tree.

"I can't live with you!" she sputtered. "Do you understand what you just said?"

George was so unskilled with general conversation, Alicia guessed that he was flustered, or trying out a joke. Also, he lived with his mother, who was unlikely to approve the bringing home of stray girls.

"Of course I know what I said. And you shouldn't be so quick to refuse, when your options are nil and something worse than that. We don't have a YWCA here. You could always go back to Oklahoma, I guess."

"You're a real pick-me-up, you know that? George. We've only known each other for a couple of weeks."

"Long enough that I've determined you're on the up-and-up."

"Have you now?" Alicia said, face twisting into an amused smirk.

"Yes. I've been tracking your movements. You haven't stolen candy or money once. And they said to be on the lookout for that sort of thing with DPs."

"I'm pleased to have exceeded your bargain-basement expectations of me."

"Our place is huge," he babbled on. "Your room would be on an entirely different floor from mine, and from Mother's. You'd have your own bathroom, and a hot plate. My sister got married five years ago and no one's touched her room since. Gosh, aren't you going to say anything? I've listed all these amenities. It'd be foolish of you to decline."

What choice did she have? George was right. It'd be unwise to refuse.

In the end, Mrs. Neill seemed glad of the arrangement, happy for the company of someone other than her undeniably odd son. That George Neill still lived with his mother was not the world's biggest riddle.

"I can't remember the last time I was this excited!" she'd cried, upon hearing the news.

That evening, with Irenka darning socks on the bed, Alicia crammed the entirety of her existence into a single suitcase, now a well-practiced art. As she latched it closed, Alicia felt heavy, exhausted by the weight of her own nostalgia. Irenka was her first friend in America and Alicia would never forget their days in Oklahoma: trying on clothes at Brown's, enjoying beers at Bishop's, talking about the men they wanted to meet. Alicia arrived in America one year ago. She didn't yet know if she was better or worse off than before.

Alas, Alicia's entire life had been one of moving on, and she'd not get hung up on this latest loss. She'd welcome Irenka back if asked, but people changed. Opinions changed. Circumstances changed. The two girls never had much in common, other than being female, Polish, and so similarly, pathetically displaced.

She wasn't needed at the Kennedys that day, so Alicia spent the afternoon with George, watching the rereleased, unedited version of *All Quiet on the Western Front*, followed by *My Blue Heaven*. Halfway through the second flick, she'd had enough velveteen and darkness for one day. Alicia collected her things, gave George a kiss on the cheek, and stepped out into the rosy dusk.

Alicia loved these hours on the Cape, after the temperature cooled and the sun began its descent. Up and down Main Street, restaurants hummed and people dashed, everyone brighter and more attractive in the generous light of eventide. Who needed Hollywood magic, with places like Hyannis in the world?

A block down, Alicia spotted a cluster of folks stopped to watch a street act. Ernie was the performer's name and today he made a show of spinning hula hoops from his neck, arms, and legs. The observers were boisterous, whooping and clapping. Good thing Ernie hadn't brought his monkey-on-a-string. Javier was easily spooked and prone to clawing at eyeballs when scared.

Alicia approached the group and offered Ernie a brisk smile. They were coworkers of sorts, at least in Alicia's mind. She tended to guests in the theater, while he entertained them outside. Ernie had any number of tricks: acrobatics, hoops, the occasionally performed and always injurious fire breathing. It astonished Alicia that, in America, one might fashion a career out of an assortment of bad ideas.

Ernie winked when he noticed her, but did not break his pace. After deftly removing five hula hoops from his person, he bent over and took to hooping on his rear.

A great holler went up from the crowd, which was mostly male save one little girl and her mother, who sensed the performance's imminent decline and promptly took leave. Just in time, too, as one of the onlookers soon shouted:

"Now do it on your prick!"

Alicia gasped. The comment came from a gang of man-boys cloistered off to the side. Based on the guffawing and backslapping, the offender was a squat man with saucer ears. Beside him stood a much taller fellow, oafish almost. Alicia took in a quick breath. She'd seen these two before, at the Kennedys'.

Don't be naive, Lem.

Shut up, Dave.

Behind them stood Jack Kennedy, live and in the flesh.

Alicia bit her lip. She scuttled backward a few steps as Jack looked up and caught her eye. He grinned, wide as forever, and gave a small wave. He recognized her! Jack Kennedy recognized her! She found herself both excited and relieved.

Alicia responded with a bob of her head. Then Jack waved her *over.* Alicia froze, at once sweaty and quite lubberly beneath her clothes. She followed fashion best she could, and boasted a kicky wardrobe for a Polish refugee, but Jack was probably used to the endless closets of his sisters, and whichever debutantes he wooed. At least she dressed better than Eunice.

"Hey there!" Jack called out, his voice booming as Ernie contorted himself into a backbend.

Around them, the crowd applauded.

"Hello," Alicia said, or mouthed, for she did not want to interrupt Ernie's show.

"Come here!" Jack said, and motioned her over again.

Despite the commotion, Jack Kennedy was impossible to ignore, and so everyone turned, even Ernie, who'd have a weeklong crick in his neck as a result. What could she do? With all eyes locked on her, Alicia plodded toward Jack.

"Hiya, candy girl," Jack said with his signature smile. "Getting off work?"

"Sort of," Alicia said. "I was at the Center, but not working. A colleague and I wanted to see *All Quiet* before it went back."

"Ah. A classic film. Personally, I think you should be *on* the screen, not watching it."

Alicia blushed. Either she really had that certain look, or the Kennedy men knew one way to flatter. Meanwhile, Ernie finished his performance and the audience broke up. Or maybe he'd stopped of his own volition, unable to compete with Jack Kennedy's inherent pizzazz.

"These are my pals Dave and Lem," Jack said, gesturing toward the men beside him.

Dave was the short, round one. Lem was tall, squinty, and suffered from a mean overbite.

"Remember these ugly mugs," Jack said, "for when they show up on wanted posters."

"Har, har," Dave said.

"Hello." Alicia extended a hand to each. "Alicia Darr."

"Dar?" Lem said. "Like D . . . A . . . R? Daughters of the American Revolution? My mother is a member. Her side of the family came over on the *Mayflower*. Did yours?"

"I did indeed come on a ship," Alicia said. "But it wasn't the *Mayflower*."

"Alicia!" shouted Ernie. "I'm off! Have a good one!"

"You too," Alicia said. "Well done. Another inventive performance. Next time bring Javier."

"We'll see. He's had a touch of the nerves. Right now, he's taking a resting cure."

"Give him my best."

"Friend of yours?" Dave asked with a barely detectable but undeniably present sneer.

"Yes," Alicia said, and lifted her chin. "He is."

"How does one become friends with a street performer, exactly?"

"The usual way. Ernie is a great fella and you never know when it might be useful to know a person with a monkey."

Jack chuckled as Ernie called out his final good-bye.

"Hold on, buddy!" Jack said, and raced over to the hat on the ground. "You deserve a few beans for your efforts. But bring the monkey next time."

Jack reached into his pockets but came up clean. He looked toward Dave and Lem.

"Flat broke, per usual," Lem muttered.

"Can one of you fellas help me out?"

"Sorry pal, I've got nothing," Dave said.

Jack looked pleadingly at Lem, who shook his head.

"No sir. No can do. You already owe me fifty-two bucks."

Jack swiveled toward Ernie.

"Can you wait here two minutes?" he asked. And to Alicia: "Promise you won't go anywhere? You'll stay in this very spot?"

Like Ernie, Alicia could only agree. With that, Jack hightailed it into Woolworth's, leaving Alicia alone with Dave and Lem.

"The bastard never has any cash," Lem said, saving her from having to start the conversation.

"The Kennedys are the richest SOBs in America," Dave said, "yet they never foot the bill. I've seen them borrow money from the collection plates at church."

"I don't understand," Alicia said, forehead wrinkled. "He's getting money from Woolworth's?"

Were they handing out loans now?

"He'll put it *on account*," Dave said. "Only Jack."

"All that damned money and somehow the Kennedy accounts never come due," Lem added.

Alicia smiled, unsure what to make of the ribbing among these men. So she stood there—dimly, she reckoned—waiting for Jack to return. When he did, he dropped three dollars into Ernie's pot.

"Thank you kindly," Ernie said, and collected his hat, the money, the last of his things.

He trotted off, whistling as he went.

"I'm famished," Dave said, and hiked up his pants.

Alicia blinked, wondering if she was supposed to stay, or leave, or what.

"I'm gonna grab a bacon and tomato," Dave said. "My stomach's growling and I can't hold out until dinner. The last time I tried to help myself to the food cabinet, Mrs. Kennedy shoved me onto a scale and made me fill out some sort of card."

"Aw, she's just trying to help," Lem said. "You've gotten a bit tubby."

"Better than being the Scarecrow's ugly cousin."

"You're an ass. But I'll join you. How about it, Ken? Can the delicate Kennedy stomach handle a bite between meals?"

"This hardy constitution? Are you kidding? I'm in. But you guys go ahead," Jack said. "I need a minute with this beauty."

The men snickered . . . in acknowledgment, or wonder, or some other reaction a refugee could never discern about an American boy.

"So," Jack said when his friends left.

He moved to face her, and Alicia was struck by the warmth of his attention, his Jack Kennedy sunshine. Somehow, he was tanner, impossibly more handsome in the low light. His cheeks were ruddy, his dense hair windswept and curled. Representative Kennedy looked like he'd just stepped off a boat, which was probably the very case.

"Is the Center opened on Labor Day?" he said.

"It is, although I'm not working then."

"Excellent." He grinned wider. "Listen. My parents host a big party every year. Lots of people. Great food. Unlimited booze. It's a gas."

Alicia gave a stingy smile. Yes, she was well aware of such a party and he'd be astounded to know in what detail. If asked, she could write out a full menu on the spot.

"You should come," he said.

Alicia barked out a laugh.

"Something amusing, Miss Darr?"

"Not at all," she said, giving her own toothy grin.

"You sure about that?" Jack said, and cocked a brow.

"You bet. I'm simply feeling merry on this glorious day."

"Uplifted by war movies, are ya?"

"Oh, it's not about the movie."

Alicia glanced at the ground.

"Wonderful to see you again, Jack," she said, trying to muster the courage to leave this magnet of a man.

"Hey! Where ya going?"

Alicia walked away, each step made as if in wet cement. Before rounding the corner, she stopped.

"By the by," she called out. "I read an article about you. A-bombs and cookbooks and whatnot."

"You did? Well, I'll be!"

"I quite agree with your position. If there's one thing I've learned, it's that it's best to be prepared. Well, have a delightful holiday. I'm sure your parents' party will be executed flawlessly and with every attention to detail."

Alicia turned to go, for good.

"Hey!" Jack shouted. "Hey! Alicia!"

She stopped, wanting to go back, but worried what might happen if she did. The next time Alicia saw Jack, she'd be in a maid's uniform, tending to the bounteous needs of his family, his friends, and all those pretty girls with gemstones clipped to their sweaters. This would prob-ably be the last she'd ever receive of his admiration, and so Alicia looked at him one more time. She wanted to remember the expression of someone like him, a man who saw something in her.

"Yes, Jack?" she said over her shoulder.

"Aren't you going to accept my invitation?" he asked. "To the Labor Day party?"

Alicia laughed, then shook her head.

"Oh, Jack," she said, head still moving. "I'd already planned to go."

"You knew about it?"

"As a matter of fact, the party at your parents' is the reason I'm in Hyannis at all."

THIS WEEK AT THE CENTER HYANNIS:
SO YOUNG SO BAD

HYANNIS PORT

Labor Day broke gray and dreary, a typical morning on the Cape.

But the gloom didn't dampen party preparations, or the commotion. A pinging, buzzy energy reverberated in the house. Jokes were told. Laughter rang. Mrs. Kennedy broke up countless squabbles in her rickety warble.

Late in the day, Alicia found herself in the kitchen pantry, hands clapped over both ears, her version of a break. When she stepped out, Alicia saw that the Kennedy sisters were hiding in the kitchen, too, thanks to their mother stalking about on high alert.

Alicia gave a curt greeting, and continued to work, invisible yet available at the same time; the perfect housemaid dance. It was Alicia's last day at the Kennedys'. She was almost sad to leave.

"I'm exhausted," Pat complained, coiling a piece of auburn hair around her finger. "And the party hasn't even started. Anyone want to play golf instead?"

"And miss the biggest shindig of the year?" Jean said as she nibbled on a slice of cake. "Mother would have a fit!"

She would likewise have a fit, Alicia thought, at the sight of Jean's careless snacking. Rose Kennedy viewed her average-sized daughter as well past plump.

"What would we miss?" Pat asked with a shrug. "The guest list is twenty-seven pages long. Whatever happened to good old-fashioned exclusivity? This place is giving me a headache."

"Aww, poor girl," Eunice clucked. "You'd better jet back to Hollywood before you collapse from fatigue. Shall I get the fainting couch?"

Jean tittered and brushed the crumbs from her mouth. Pat rolled her eyes with a harrumph. It was this kind of talk—gripes about regular Kennedy things like melees and mayhem—that earned Pat her reputation as moody and particular. To Alicia, it seemed like proper decorum and good taste.

"I'm flabbergasted you don't get invited to big, wild parties every night," Jean said, licking her fingers.

"Why?" Pat said. "Because I live in Hollywood? In case you haven't noticed, I'm not a starlet, I'm no Elizabeth Taylor or Marilyn Monroe."

"You're pretty," Jean said, "and a Kennedy. Not to mention rich as hell."

"No one cares about that," Pat said, then rolled her eyes again. "And thank God."

She pushed herself to standing. In the distance came a laugh from Bobby, followed by a signature Ethel bray. As to where Jack might be, Alicia couldn't guess. He wasn't in the house, but was due at any time. No one had said this, but the air had a certain brace to it, an expectation, like the lead-up to a sneeze.

"I'm going to change," Pat said.

"Yes, it's about that time," Eunice agreed, and followed her sister's lead.

Jean ogled an untouched sweet cake before sliding her gaze toward her sisters.

"Are you coming?" Pat asked.

"Sure," Jean answered with a defeated sigh.

As the three tramped away, Jean asked Eunice when Jack might arrive. A charge ran along Alicia's spine.

"Soon," Eunice said, her voice growing fainter. "He had some appearances this morning. Parades and such."

"Don't worry," Pat added, "we'll know the second Jack and his band of merry idiots drive up. They're impossible to miss."

Sure enough, Jack arrived with the men from the hula-hooping show and a gaggle of others besides. The family ushered him in like a distinguished guest, the king of their ruffian tribe.

Alicia resolved that while she would not seek out Jack—obviously—neither would she cower in shame. This was her last day as a maid, and life was on the rise. She'd sold a painting. Twenty dollars! There was no reason to hide.

From the moment he walked in, Jack took command of the party, always a pack of cronies at his side, a trickle of girls listing in his wake. Despite his personal retinue, Jack was easy to find. Whether at the bar, on the back lawn, or walking up from the cove, he shone brighter than the sun.

At dusk, Alicia was in the kitchen, plucking shards of glass from her stockings. She'd swept up three dozen mishandled drinks so far and her arms and legs were nicked and cut. Where was Mrs. Kennedy with one of her penny-pinching rebukes? Jeannette was right, they were all heathens.

Alicia paused, hands on the cool, sticky counter. It was nice to be alone in this room, the noise muffled and far away. She let her gaze drift out to where Jack held court, dazzling a flock of what she assumed were debutantes, based on what she'd read in *Mademoiselle*. The girls were pretty in their upscale, American way, albeit more attractive as a group than any one of them would've been on her own.

"Excuse me," said a voice, high-pitched but male.

"Oh! Hello!" She tore her eyes from the window. "Can I help you?"

When Alicia turned, she saw it was Jack's friend Lem, the tall one with the overbite.

"Heyyyyy . . ." he said. "Whaddya know? It's the gal from the theater, am I right? The dame with the street performer pal?"

"Yes, that's me," Alicia said, and tugged at her lumpy gray uniform. "I only work——"

She stopped herself, for Lem deserved no explanation.

"Did you need something?" she asked.

"Yes, actually. The bartenders are out of daiquiri mix."

"I think the caterers are aware," Alicia said. "But I'll check, just in case. It's possible they're walking out with it right now."

Her eyes darted to the window but she saw no daiquiris and instead Jack, encircled by an increasing throng of girls.

"Ah," Lem said, his gaze following hers. "Watching the master at work, are you? Per usual, he's charming the pants off them. Literally."

Alicia pretended not to register the joke.

"They are all very pretty," she said simply.

"Eh. Pretty but dull."

Alicia tossed her head back in his direction.

"Dull?" she said. "How can that be? They must have the best educations."

"School doesn't make someone interesting. Trust me, Jack is my closest friend. Those social register girls." He made a face. "It's not that he *likes* them. He likes to *mock* them."

"I hardly think that's——"

"They're wasting their breath," Lem said. "And their lip gloss and perfume. Jack needs someone who's interesting, unique, not the same as everybody else."

Alicia nodded, thinking, yes, they were all made from the same palette, weren't they? She herself could never pick out one from the others.

"He needs someone who can challenge him intellectually," Lem went on, "as well as in . . . other areas. Someone experienced, if you catch my drift."

Alicia's cheeks burned.

"I'm sure there are many who would fit the bill. . . ." she mumbled.

"Did you know he dated a Nazi spy? Jack never officially confirmed or denied the rumor, so it was probably true." Lem stepped up beside Alicia. "There's not a dame alive who isn't attracted to the bastard. Kind of sad to contemplate all the girls who pine after him, when he doesn't remember their names. If only they understood that he'll never settle down."

"Really?" Alicia looked at him. "You don't think he'll get married, eventually?"

"One day, I suppose. It's what's expected. He is a politician." Lem sighed, eyes lingering on his old pal. "Watch him standing there, jiggling his arm, tapping his foot. The man can't stand still. Nothing is ever enough for that guy. He's insatiable, in a thousand ways. There's not a woman alive who could ever be enough."

Alicia and Irenka were in the kitchen, alone for the first time that day. They'd worked dutifully beside each other for the past week, but their relationship was gone. What would happen when they left the Kennedys' that night? Would they ever have a proper good-bye?

"I go home now," Irenka said, and shimmied into her coat. "You stay and clean."

Alicia looked at the dishes lined up on the counter, the untold piles the caterers left behind. It would've been a tall task for the two of them, but Alicia was not up for the fight.

"*Do widzenia,*" Irenka said, and opened the door.

She set one foot outside.

"Wait," Alicia said.

Irenka hesitated, and in that split second, Alicia took her last chance.

"After tonight, I won't be working here," she said. "And—lucky you—you won't be forced to interact with me multiple times per week."

Irenka grunted in response.

"So, is this it?" Alicia asked. "Do you plan to speak to me again, or is the friendship over?"

"We are not friends."

"Ren." Alicia took a few cautious steps forward. "What'd I do? We had such fun in Oklahoma. You were the single decent thing about that place. Then you've invited me here, to the Cape, only to shut me out."

"I never invite you. My letters were to Alfreda and Zula. You stole dem."

"I didn't *steal* them."

Irenka's letters *were* mostly addressed to Alicia's roommates, but Alfreda and Zula passed them around. That was the point of bragging, wasn't it? To make it clear to *all* the girls how far from the YWCA she'd flown? Plus, Irenka swore the Kennedys needed more help, and there'd be room for any of them, if they came. She had to expect that the former Barbara Kopczynska would be the one with enough mettle to move to Cape Cod.

"You *tief*," Irenka insisted.

"I'm not a thief. Maybe you didn't invite me explicitly, but you were so enthusiastic about life in Hyannis. You said how much we'd love it here!"

"I do not like *you* here."

"What did I do? If you're worried that I'm going to take your job, then erase that thought right now. You have your life and I have mine—"

"I am much better maid."

"Of course that's true," Alicia said, thrilled to concede the title. "So, what's the problem? You liked me plenty in Oklahoma. What changed?"

Irenka sighed heavily. Then, ever so slowly, she rotated to face her former friend.

"I like Barbara Kopczynska. But it is *Alic-ja* here now."

"You're upset that I changed my name?" Alicia rolled her eyes. "That's silly. I had to, don't you understand?"

"You change de name, but you change much more. You are not same girl."

"I certainly hope not," Alicia said with a snort.

"You see? I am right."

"We've both changed," Alicia said. "And for the better. Isn't that why we came to America? To become . . . American?"

"But you change everytink. Your hair blond. Was brown before. You wear lipstick."

"Yes, okay, that's true," Alicia said with a small laugh. "My lips are redder and my hair is lighter. But that's all window dressing. Can't we agree that I'm the same person at heart? Take my housekeeping skills, for one. Terrible as always!"

Alicia gestured toward the cluttered counter, although the mess wasn't hers.

"Good thing it's my last day!" she added.

Irenka considered Alicia's argument.

"Maybe you right," she conceded.

Alicia exhaled. Perhaps they'd be okay.

"Yes, you de same," Irenka said. "Because you ugly person already."

Her face darkened, becoming shadowed beneath her fleshy brow.

"Ugly? Is this about the—" Alicia lowered her voice. "The Ambassador? Nothing happened."

"Hmph. So you say. You lucky I do not tell Mizz Kennedy he drivink you!"

"He drove me home once, in spite of my protests, and because you abandoned me."

"Poor Mizz Kennedy," Irenka said with a whimper. "All de tinks she doesn't know."

"Honestly, Irenka, you don't give the woman enough credit. She knows a whole lot more than she lets on."

To wit: One hour before, a handful of guests lingered in the sunroom, trading gossip on the Reds. Mr. and Mrs. Kennedy sat side by side on the pilled orange couch until Mr. Kennedy abruptly stood, summoned Miss Dee, and scampered upstairs.

"Look at that terribly faded pillow," Mrs. Kennedy said, staring at the space her husband left behind. "How embarrassing! I must replace it right away!"

Upstairs, furniture—and people—creaked and whined. The friends departed with as much grace as they could rally while Mrs. Kennedy rambled about the cushions, and then retired to her own bedroom.

Alicia's first impression was that Mrs. Kennedy was a tad slow, blind to the situation in her own home. But then Alicia soon learned that Rose Kennedy merely *played* dumb, which was a wholly different matter. It wasn't ignorance, but a choice, a subtle form of art.

"I give her lots of credit," Irenka said, as she fingered the cross she now wore at all times. "She is pious and godly. Unlike yourself. You forget, *Alic-ja*, I know vat happen before you come to America. I know about Germany and before."

"I could say the same of you."

"Not de same."

Irenka's eyes narrowed. They went a little red. On the counter, a dish clinked after slipping of its own accord.

"You sinful girl," Irenka said. "You pretty, but you wrong, on de inside."

Alicia flinched and Irenka released a fast, smug smile. Then she whirled around on her sturdy white shoes and plodded off, a farewell without so much as a good-bye.

A sinful girl? Alicia didn't think that of herself in that way, but neither was she free of sin. None of them were, really. When it came to survival in those wretched times, there was no black and white but instead a long continuum of gray. They'd all made trade-offs. The luxury of choosing between right and wrong was for other people, in other places, in other times.

Alicia would miss her friend, for Irenka taught her a great deal, like how to operate a dishwasher, and make a sandwich, and that one must first wet a sponge before putting it to use. Irenka even taught her something tonight, in their very last conversation, in a kitchen stacked with dirty plates. Hopefully, Alicia would never again have use for rags or mops, but she was grateful for the lesson that it was best to keep one's secrets locked in the past.

The most persistent guests had departed, the lingering scent of cigar smoke had at last dissolved into the misty sky. Even Teddy had slogged off to bed thirty minutes before, and he usually raised hell until dawn.

After ringing George to come pick her up (this wouldn't show on the Kennedys' phone bill, she didn't think), Alicia shut off the lights and made her way toward the front door. She'd miss this home and its rambling grandiosity, the shabby and well-loved furniture, the creak of the hardwood floors as the Kennedys clobbered about. But it was time to go.

Near the staircase, a figure materialized. Alicia lurched to a stop, her heart clonking around inside. Her first thought was of the rumored night prowler, but his glasses were said to be like the Ambassador's, and this person wore no specs.

"There you are," Jack Kennedy said.

Alicia checked behind her but no one else was there.

"I've been trying to hunt you down for hours."

"You have?" She wrinkled her nose.

"Yep. Saw you as soon as I arrived, but whenever I approached, you disappeared."

Alicia blinked in befuddlement. She'd tracked him that day, albeit peripherally and at a distance as she had a job to do, but never had they gotten closer than a car's length apart.

"I think you're confused," Alicia said.

"You're Alicia Darr, from the theater. The clothes are different, but I'd recognize you anywhere."

Alicia nodded, all speech having left. How was it that Jack Kennedy remembered her name? Maybe Lem wasn't right about every last thing.

"Long day, huh?" he said, and Alicia again nodded. "That's why I'm having one of these."

He showed her the daiquiri in his left hand.

"Want to share?" he asked.

"Beg pardon?"

"I'm asking, would you like to have a drink?"

"Yes," Alicia croaked. "Okay, sure."

"Come on," he said. "Follow me."

Alicia pattered after Jack, heart thrumming. She did not ask why they were going to his bedroom. It wasn't something to question, really, as she did not take this as a choice. She was a character in Jack's story, her plot written and directed by somebody else.

Once in his room, they sat on a bed, atop the green coverlet Alicia had laundered the day before. She remembered noticing that it'd pilled, and several threads had shaken loose. It did not seem like something for your favorite son's room. Because of this, the entire scene felt suddenly old-fashioned and domestic, the specter of Rose Kennedy all around. Alicia looked toward Jack as he set down his daiquiri, well out of her reach.

Without speaking, Jack leaned toward her, and she met him halfway. His lips, his tongue, they stunned her, for they felt like how she imagined they might. Alicia anticipated magic, she realized, something more than a kiss. Then again, that she expected anything was the biggest surprise of all.

In one move, Jack wrapped his arms around her and lifted her body on top of his. He did this with such deftness, Alicia barely had a moment to take stock of what happened. How was it that he was already on his back, with his pants off, Alicia's uniform hiked up to her waist?

He snatched the dress over her head, then tugged down her stockings. As he massaged Alicia through her underwear, Jack's eyes met hers for a quarter second, a full second perhaps. It was a pause, a question whether to go further, although no words were exchanged. Alicia nodded, bewildered, but wanting this still. So, Irenka had been right. She was a sinful girl.

Soon her pink silk drawers were stripped off. Jack eased himself inside and pulled down on her, anchoring her hips against his. He began to rock and pump. A drop of sweat rolled off her forehead and dropped onto his nose. He bucked more furiously and soon Alicia pulsed and tightened around him, to an unthinkable degree. Jack called out and lifted his hips, and she pressed harder to take in more of him.

A cascade of fits sent Alicia moaning and cursing, louder than him. She tried to temper these strange convulsions, but in the end could not and so she let herself go.

When it ended, they collapsed into a pile, lying there for a minute, maybe two. His heart beat against hers.

Then, as if startled, Jack pushed Alicia off of him and leapt to his feet. He began to dress, leaving her addled, not to mention naked and chilled. It was all so quick, a blur.

"You are something else," he said, latching his belt buckle.

How was he completely dressed? With an almost undetectable twinge of regret, Alicia rotated onto her side and pulled the green coverlet atop her body. Before putting on his shoes, Jack walked over and kissed Alicia gently on the head.

"Let me ask you something," he said. "How old are you?"

"Twenty," she answered, and pawed at the floor for her clothes.

When Alicia looked up, she saw the daiquiri sitting full and untouched on the bedside table, drops of water sliding along the outside of the glass.

"That was some show for someone so young," he said. "I loved it." Jack handed Alicia her uniform.

"Thank you" didn't seem like the appropriate response, for the compliment or the clothes, and so Alicia smiled weakly and tossed on the uniform. As she scooted upright, Alicia realized that her hands were shaking and her heart was beating fast. A minute ago, she felt pure ecstasy, and now she was overcome with the creeping sense of sick.

"Every girl should have an orgasm like that," Jack said with a chortle.

"Yes, I . . . uh . . . don't know what came over me. I'm sorry."

"Sorry?" he said. "Are you kidding me? That was terrific, kid. Too many broads are frigid, unable to enjoy themselves. Not that I'd know firsthand."

"Of course not," Alicia said, and stood.

Her legs were wobbly. She slipped on her shoes and crammed her stockings into her pocket.

"Hey," Jack said, his voice softening. "Was that . . . okay?"

"Yes, yes, perfectly fine," Alicia said, because of course if *that* happened, the overwhelming physical reaction from that unspeakable place, then of course everything was fine, much more than okay.

"Do you need a ride home?" Jack asked. "You don't live here, right? At the house?"

"No," Alicia said, and laughed.

Her body loosened.

"A friend is picking me up," she said. "I live on the east end, by the Center. Today is my last day, actually. I came to help a . . . friend. With the party."

"Ah, that's what you meant with your cryptic comment from the other day."

It took Alicia a second to remember the comment herself.

"Yes," she said, and glanced away.

"So, you won't be returning? To our employ?"

"No, I'll be moving on."

"Well, then." Jack flashed a grin and zipped his pants. "Sounds like I'll have to spend a bit more time at the theater. Here, I'll walk you out."

"Thank you," Alicia said in a whisper.

Jack showed her not out, but halfway to the door. After a hasty kiss and a somewhat rigid hug, he turned back. Alicia scuttled out onto the porch, panicked about what George must think. May God forgive her for corrupting that sweet boy.

When she reached the flagpole, George was idling in his mother's green Studebaker with the windows down. The only sound came from the crickets, and the gentle rumble of the Atlantic.

"I'm so sorry George," she said, sliding into his car. "I got held up. I feel terribly that you've had to wait so long."

"Long?" He kicked the car into drive. "It's been about a minute, two minutes tops."

Two minutes?

Alicia frowned. She looked at the clock on the dash. It'd been ten minutes since she'd called him. Ten measly minutes. Hadn't she rung an hour, a lifetime before? Sex with Jack Kennedy surely lasted longer than a drive from the east end.

Sex with Jack Kennedy. She'd had sex with Representative Kennedy. The realization began to hit her, in parts, like small, lapping waves.

"You okay?" George asked. "Your breathing sounds . . . funny."

"Yes," she said, taking in shallow gulps. "I'm fine, thank you."

Alicia squirmed and stretched her uniform taut over both knees. Thank God this was George; he'd never stop to question the whereabouts of her stockings. It was possible he didn't know women wore them in the first place.

"You seem a touch peaked," he noted.

"Yes. It was a long, strange day. That family . . ."

She didn't know how to finish the thought.

"Mmm-hmm." George bobbed his head. "They're a lot. Well, no more Kennedys for you. That's the good news."

"Yes, what a relief," she said. "No more Kennedys. Thank the heavens above."

POPE CONDEMNS "ART FOR ART'S SAKE"
St. Louis Post-Dispatch, September 5, 1950

HYANNIS PORT

The morning after Labor Day, Alicia went to mass.

It wasn't because of what happened with Jack. Alicia didn't feel all that guilty about their night together, and neither did she view it as a confession-worthy offense. Maybe her attendance was about nostalgia, or the solace of ritual. Or perhaps it was because she had nothing else to do that day, now that she was down to the one (part-time) job.

Donning a tartan dress in a color described as "burnt glass," Alicia packed her handbag and took off along South Street. St. Francis Xavier sat a few blocks up from the Neill home, right on High School Road, the dividing line between the west and east ends, the moneyed and the not. It was appropriate that a church might be in the middle, though technically St. Francis favored the rich side of the street.

Once inside the white clapboard building, Alicia snuck into a pew. Hopeful ladies beamed, fast to notice the fresh blood. With the strike of the organ came an unexpected sense of foreboding. Here she sat, in another country, five years from the war's end, and it still felt tenuous, like the Gestapo might crash through the doors at any moment and demand proof of who she was.

Alicia closed her eyes and reminded herself of how far she'd traveled from that life, figuratively and in fact. She breathed deeply, calmed by the Hail Marys and Glory Bes. Though she hadn't been to mass in a year, the rhythm returned easily, another language mastered. Alicia was happy almost, comforted as though she'd enjoyed a nice visit with an old friend.

As Alicia exited the church after the service, she whispered to herself, "I am Alicia Darr." Alicia Darr, the artist, the American, the burgeoning beauty, if she could be so bold. Alicia Darr, raised Catholic, now not necessarily belonging to any particular faith.

"Miss Darr?"

Alicia flipped around to find a curly-haired, power-packed force standing feet away.

"Mrs. Kennedy!" she said, alarmed or rattled, she wasn't sure.

"I thought that was you. . . ."

"It is! It's me!"

"Tuesday-morning mass?"

Mrs. Kennedy nodded approvingly and Alicia blushed. If there was any truth to the rumor that Rose Kennedy could read one's thoughts, it was right then dispelled. Alicia's head was full of Jack. His smile. His face. His skinny legs and very flat ass.

"Did you and your friends enjoy yesterday's party?" Alicia asked, speaking briskly. "It was a terrific event. You planned it well."

"So, you're Catholic," Mrs. Kennedy said, by way of answer.

"Yes. I am. I am Catholic."

"Color me shocked," Mrs. Kennedy said, her voice rough and rippled. "I knew the Catholic Charities brought many of you girls over to the States. I didn't realize you were one of them."

"I was indeed," Alicia said.

Mrs. Kennedy gave a side-eye of sorts, and Alicia weighed the possibility that she might know about her and Jack. He never would've told his mother, Alicia didn't think, but Rose noticed details and she was accustomed to the look of stolen sex, and the sound of it in her home.

"I attended school at a convent," Alicia blurted.

"What's that?"

"I went to convent school. In Europe."

Alicia hoped she hadn't used up all her prayers inside the church.

"Isn't that funny?" Mrs. Kennedy said, a half smile playing at her lips. "My daughters attended convent schools, too. The only place to raise a proper woman, if you ask me."

Around them, people bustled. A few shook Mrs. Kennedy's hand as they passed. Meanwhile, Alicia's skin glistened in the September sun. It suddenly seemed very hot and crowded on these Hyannis streets.

"I've heard that you're no longer working for us," Mrs. Kennedy said, after introducing Alicia to two older ladies, who were delighted to find such a youthful visage at Tuesday-morning mass.

"Um, yes, that's correct. But it wasn't that I quit!" she added. "I was hired as temporary help for the holiday. You probably knew that. . . ."

"What are you doing now? For work? You're the . . . ?"

Mrs. Kennedy took a second to analyze Alicia, head to toe. "The Viennese actress?" she said.

"Artist," Alicia corrected, though she did not bother with "Viennese." "I'm working at the Center, while I concentrate on my work. I'm a painter. I hope to attend art school one day."

"Art school?" Mrs. Kennedy formed her mouth into a straight line. "How . . . exotic."

"It was, er, something I trained for."

"At the *convent* school?" she scoffed.

"No. Before school."

Before the war.

Rose Kennedy gave another tight smile. Alicia decided to take her exit before she said the wrong thing.

"It was lovely to run into you," she said, and extended a hand. "*C'est bon de te revoir!*"

Mrs. Kennedy stared wide-eyed as she processed the words and, Alicia liked to think, the flawless accent. Perfect French coming from a refugee? *Quelle surprise!* Indeed, the pocket-sized woman was literally taken aback. She staggered backward, and almost tumbled down the stairs. Alicia caught her arm and pulled her to safety.

"Careful there," she said.

"I'm sorry, I don't know what came over me."

"I hope you don't mind me using French," Alicia said, and released the woman's arm. "I've heard you practicing with your records."

"Yes!" Mrs. Kennedy said, blinking several times. "The records! Thank you! Okay, it's time for me to go."

The two women shook hands, and Rose turned on her stubby heels. She was partway down the stairs when she paused to look back again.

"It was lovely to run into you," she said. "I mean that."

Alicia smiled. She could see, plain as the Cape sky, that in Rose Kennedy's exacting eyes, her stock had risen. It felt like some kind of coup, though Alicia didn't know how Catholic she really planned to be. Nonetheless, it was nice to impress someone so impervious and, more important, realize she'd maintained such a strong command of Catholicism and of French.

HYANNIS PORT

"I was just reading an article," George said one night, after the seven o'clock had let out.

Alicia was examining a collapsed convent wall she'd painted last week, a dramatic piece heavy with grays and blues.

"Who was it about?" she said, now eyeing the boot prints depicted in the soil. "Barbara Stanwyck? She seems to be your favorite these days."

Alicia took a step back, and put a hand to her chin.

"Barbara Stanwyck is a delight," George said. "But this article was about displaced persons."

"DPs?" she said with a small snort. "That sounds like a waste of time. After all, you have your very own DP, live and in the flesh. I'm pleased to entertain any of the curiosities you have about our sort."

"It's nothing specific. I only want to understand what life's been like for you."

"Aw, Georgie."

Alicia looked away from her painting with a little pout. She walked over and swung an arm around George's shoulders.

"You're the sweetest," she said. "An absolute gem. I'm glad to know you."

He shook her off, right on time.

George was fussy and particular and this was too much touching, and for far too long. If Alicia didn't live with Mrs. Neill, she would've thought George was raised inside a bubble by scientists evaluating the effects of social deprivation and poorly lit rooms.

"Tell me about these DPs," Alicia said, and moved to give him space. "What did the newspaper say?"

"It was an editorial," he explained, "about how the government is trying to train and educate them."

"*Them?*" she said with a smirk.

"It's not . . . I didn't mean . . ."

She waved him off.

"I'm teasing," she said. "Please, go on."

"Okay. . . ." He eyed her warily, as if she might bite. "Apparently, refugees are struggling to acclimate, particularly on the job front. I guess they're—the refugees—can't find jobs, or hold them down when they do."

Alicia's eyebrows spiked.

"I assume that you're about to offer a referendum on *my* ability to hold a job?" she said. "Feel free to keep that to yourself. The Kennedy gig was part-time, and if you think I want to pick up dirty bathing costumes for the rest of my life . . ."

"No, no, no!" All of George's features lifted. "That's not what I meant. Actually, it's the opposite. The writer was going on and on about how DPs can't find jobs, can't hold jobs, yet the one displaced person I know created two of them out of thin air, in a very short period of time."

Alicia chuckled.

"I wouldn't exactly call it 'thin air,'" she said. "Have you seen their house?"

"But somehow you managed to coax Mr. Dillon into paying you to hang around and look pretty."

"Aw, Georgie, I had no idea you thought I was pretty."

"And Paul agreed to no more than ten hours per week," George went on, face reddening, "but I saw your last paycheck, and it was for over twenty!"

"I'll take the hours where I can get them," Alicia said. "By the by, you don't seem to mind me 'hanging around' whenever someone spills a jumbo Coke, or when Dewey's swigging whisky in the alley."

"You have your uses."

"You're swell, George," Alicia said with a playful eye roll. "Now, the real coup will be convincing Paul to keep me on until next summer. Or until I hit it big in the art world."

"Don't worry about Paul keeping you on for now," George said. "This Indian summer is predicted to be the busiest yet. You're good for another month. Maybe thirty-five days."

"Thank you, that's very comforting."

Alicia wandered toward the candy counter.

"I'm glad you're here," he called out.

His voice echoed through the emptied lobby.

"Oh, you darling boy."

Alicia sighed as a tear slipped out. Dagnabbit, that kid was sweet to the core, even though he could bungle something as basic as "hello."

"I'm glad to be here, too," she added. "It gets better every day."

After wiping her eyes, Alicia began inspecting the candy stash. If there was one skill she learned at the Kennedys', it was how to take a good inventory. She noted they were low on Junior Mints.

"You know, today is my one-year anniversary," she said, picking a glob of ketchup off the glass with her fingernail.

"Your anniversary?" George screwed up his face. "Of what?"

"My arrival in the States."

"Really? Why didn't you say anything? That's a huge accomplishment!"

"Is it? Mostly I was thinking about how quickly time passes."

"But . . . one year! Don't they grant you citizenship now, or something?"

Alicia chuckled.

"Unfortunately, the process is a pinch more involved," she said.

Alicia thought of her paperwork in Oklahoma: a Declaration of Intent for Barbara Kopczynska—whoever that was—forever abandoned in someone's desk, in an office, in the middle of the country. Could she obtain citizenship as "Alicia Darr"? Her DP card said "Barbara," as did her resident-alien paperwork, but to use that name now seemed almost fraudulent.

"It's funny," Alicia said. "This past year has flown, but at the same time I only faintly recall how I felt when we drifted into port. Remembering that day is like watching a news program about someone else: stirring, yet distant."

"I can't fathom leaving home and traveling to the other side of the world," George said, shaking his head. "I've never left the Cape."

"Try it one day." Alicia squatted to rearrange a stash of Jujubes. "There's a great big world out there and you should see it. On the other hand . . ."

She leapt up.

"Hyannis is pretty top-notch."

How funny, Alicia thought, that they lived at the same address yet George's universe was alarmingly small. Then again, it was lovely that there were people like him, folks who knew the war only from a distance.

"Do you have family?" George asked. "In Poland? You've never said."

Alicia took in a sharp breath, surprised by the directness of his question. He was not customarily prone to such probing discourse.

"No," Alicia said, and walked to the other side of the counter. "Like so many millions, there is no one and nothing left for me in Poland, which is why you find me here."

George nodded and tightened his lips.

"People drink champagne in times of celebration, right?" he said.

"I believe that's the general custom. Why, is there something to celebrate?"

"Yes, of course there is! You!" He gestured toward her. "One full year!"

"George." Alicia put a hand to her heart. "That is so kind. But, really, it's merely the passage of time. Nothing to get excited about. I haven't done anything."

"I disagree. I think Mother has a Heineken in the fridge? Is that similar to champagne?"

"I don't think so," Alicia said. "But I do enjoy a cold Heineken."

She'd developed a taste for beer in the DP camp, the city of concrete barracks in which she'd lived while she awaited her visa. They didn't have enough water for the thousands of refugees, and what they did have was often contaminated. It was cheaper to give them all beer than to treat umpteen cases of dysentery per week.

"As far as I'm concerned," Alicia said, "a celebratory beer has champagne licked any day."

"Celebratory?" said a voice.

Alicia and George both jumped.

"What are we celebrating?" the person asked. "And where's my invitation?"

Alicia couldn't respond, for she was left dumbstruck when she realized the person speaking was Jack Kennedy. She had not expected to see him until next summer, if at all.

"Jack!" she said, lit up from the inside. "What are you doing here?"

How a million butterflies rushed into her stomach. That's what they meant by the expression, then. She hadn't previously known.

Alicia wasn't thick. She had no misapprehension that Jack's presence was any kind of affidavit on their night together. She was a (former) maid, and he was a wealthy congressman, and her ability to speak French and encounter his mother at mass did nothing to change that. No, the thrill in Alicia's belly was not due to any romantic notions but because of the very nearness of him.

"What are you doing here?" Alicia asked again, grinning.

She had not known her face capable of expanding that much.

"Shouldn't you be in Washington? Doing Washington things?"

"Ha. Well there's a lot more to being a congressman than doing 'Washington things,' and we're on recess. Fact is, I had a speaking engagement at the Kiwanis Club, and I figured why not pay a visit to my favorite Viennese artist?"

"Viennese?!" George squawked.

Jack turned to the man.

"Hello there, the name's Jack Kennedy."

He extended an arm, and George reciprocated the handshake like a regular human adult. Alicia's smile grew.

"This is my friend, George Neill," she said.

Jack nodded, then leaned against the candy counter.

"How was your Kiwanis speech?" Alicia asked.

"Eh. All right. If you want to know the truth, I only agreed to it so I'd have an excuse to see you."

Alicia's heart gave a leap, though she recognized the flattery for what it was: thin. But a girl couldn't argue with the way Jack said it, cute and sheepish both.

"Buttering me up, are you?" Alicia said with a blush. "No need to work so hard. I've already proven that I have no defense against your charms."

"Just how low is this defense, I'd like to know," he said, stretching closer. "When do you get off?"

"Soon. We're wrapping up."

"I have to go," George said, startling them both. "Alicia, you should lock up."

She gaped at him. George Neill was rather precious about the Center. He hid his keys when they were both at home. Once he dropped a set on the sidewalk and wouldn't let Alicia pick them up.

"I need to leave," he said. "Right now. I have a previous engagement."

"Oh." Alicia's eyes fluttered. "Are you going somewhere with your mom?"

"I know other people, you know."

With that, George grabbed his hat and vanished through the front door.

"One perceptive kid," Jack said as he walked to Alicia's side of the counter. "He can take a hint."

Alicia laughed nervously. Goose bumps ran across her skin.

"That could very well be the first time anyone's accused George of being perceptive," she said.

Jack smirked and took Alicia's hands in his. Her entire body slackened.

"So, Alicia."

He squeezed her hands. She warmed from the energy coming off him.

"Yes?" she said, with a croak.

"Are ya gonna take me for a tour or what?"

George would lose his wits if he saw Alicia like this, naked while in proximity to his beloved projector and all those cans of film.

But there was no time to worry about George Neill right then, given Alicia's company, and the *congress* they'd just enjoyed. Now Jack was seated, propped up against the wall. Alicia had her body curled into his. He'd draped a jacket over them both.

"You're so petite," he said. "So deliciously tiny and impish. Except for the breasts, of course. I could hold you like this all day."

Alicia recognized the exaggeration, but at least Jack was not hurrying this time. She squeezed her eyes closed and told herself to savor every second in this wondrous, dreamlike fog. Irenka was right about the sort of girl she was, but Alicia didn't care. She'd never been happier than she was right now.

The truth was, Alicia *enjoyed* sex. It was a devilish realization, but after what she'd been through, moments like these reminded Alicia that she was alive, a human in this world.

"You okay, kid?" Jack said, and kissed Alicia on the head.

She nodded, unable to speak, wondering if forever was too long to ask him to stay. A silly notion. Alicia shook it off.

Before long, Jack's spine got the best of him and he was forced to stand. With a grimace, he hobbled up onto his feet. From the corner, Alicia watched him struggle to dress. He seemed so old right then, so frustrated and unpoised, no glimpse of the cocksure Kennedy boy. Alicia wondered how he could be so many people at once.

"Well, young lady," he said, "I hope no other gentlemen have received your special tour."

"Are you a gentleman, then?" Alicia teased, and stood.

She hurried into her clothes.

"It depends who you ask," Jack said with a snigger. "Jesus, kid. You're funny, beautiful, and smart. A deadly mix."

As Jack wrestled himself into his shirt, pain ripped across his face. He reached out to steady himself.

"Careful of the projector!" Alicia yelped.

"I'm fine, thanks for asking."

Jack let go of the projector and massaged his lower back.

"I'm so sorry." She darted to his side. "I didn't mean to be insensitive, it's just that George is very finicky about his equipment. Please, let me help you."

"I'm dandy," Jack said, batting her away. "Just slept on it funny. Come on, I'm famished. I need a snack."

Jack shot toward the stairs and Alicia trailed after him. Once in the lobby, he ransacked the counter, as if it were a pantry in his home.

"What do we have here?" he said, plunging both hands into the popcorn bin.

Two fistfuls of popcorn—that'd be a medium? A package of Junior Mints. Coke directly from the tap. A little bit of this, a crumb of that. The total climbed.

Hungry, but too poor to join in, Alicia hopped up onto the counter and adjusted herself to show a large swath of leg. She was not a debutante, or a social register type, but she had some assets to be sure. Jack played fast and loose with actual money, but he had vast appreciation for the sort of currency Alicia possessed.

"Jesus, look at you," he said, and ran a finger along the outside of her thigh.

She shivered. Oh, the rapture of his touch.

"You're a specimen, Alicia Darr," he said. "The embodiment of womanhood. But shouldn't you be wearing stockings? We can't let any of your patrons get the wrong idea."

"It's your fault my stockings keep getting lost."

Jack studied her for a second, and an admiring smile formed. In that moment, and for the first time since she could remember, Alicia felt like a regular girl; she was no longer a refugee, or a person on the run.

"You might be a painter," Jack said, "but *you're* the work of art."

"Oh, shush."

Alicia blushed furiously.

"It's funny," Jack said. "You remind me of a woman I once loved. She was Danish. You have the same air: Nordic."

"I'm hardly Nordic."

She scooted off the counter. Alicia was parched; she'd have to sneak a pop after all.

"Tell me about your family," Jack said, straight from nowhere.

"Uh, what's that?"

She turned around, empty cup in hand. Jack stared at her with such intensity, Alicia thought she might combust.

"Your family," he said. "I want to hear all about them."

"I'm afraid that's not possible. . . ." she stuttered, filling the cup. It was mostly fizz.

"Why not?" he asked.

"Because I have no family."

"You have to come from somewhere."

Jack sauntered toward her, and Alicia backed up to the soda machine. Soon she was pinned between him and the ice tray.

"Vienna, right?" he said.

"Not Vienna," Alicia admitted. "Poland. I'm originally from Poland."

"Really?" He squinted. "I could've sworn you said Vienna."

"Hmm. Well. I've been to Vienna many times."

"What was it like?" he asked. "Growing up in a place like that? With all the Reds?"

"I didn't grow up with the Reds," she said, a bite to her voice. "They're why I didn't go back. We should lock up. I'm sure George is wondering where I am."

As Alicia tried to wiggle free, Jack pressed against her. Alicia stiffened and, as a matter of fact, so did Jack. Ten minutes had passed and already he was at full attention. Alicia wasn't the most experienced, but it was her understanding that men usually needed greater time in between sets. Jack Kennedy defied explanation, and the few things she knew of men.

"Why are you avoiding the question?" he asked. "About your family? I've memorized every curve to your body, but I don't know the first thing about your past."

"I don't have a family. This must be hard for you to understand, since there are so many of you scrabbling about. But all of mine are gone."

Alicia's nose began to sting. She shook her head, annoyed at herself for not keeping this part of herself behind a heavier gate.

"Sweet Alicia," Jack said, his eyes welling in return. "Even if they didn't survive, you had a family once. Let's talk about them. It hurts when you don't, when the world beats on, but you're stuck in the same place. I've lost people too, you know. My older brother. My very favorite sister. I dream about her almost every night."

"You do?"

Alicia and Jack looked at each other.

"Yes. I do. I try to talk to her, too. Is that odd?"

She smiled.

"I talk to Father all the time," she said. "Your sister, what was her name?"

"Kathleen, but we called her Kick, the perfect nickname. I'll tell you all about her, but first I want to know where *you* came from. I want to know who *you* are."

Alicia inhaled, her breath shaky as she gathered the nerve to reveal to Jack who she was, or who she'd been at one time.

She started with her parents. Her father was a wealthy industrialist, her mother a poet. They both loved art, and music, and books. Her father held great influence with the Polish Academy of Literature.

Alicia told Jack of her childhood home, which was grand and baroque. It lacked the scope of the Kennedy house, but was decidedly more grandiose, and festooned with emperor eagles, bull heads, mascarons, and swans. But then the war came, and they had to go.

Eventually their family split up, thereby sealing their different fates. Alicia was lucky. She was dispatched to a convent school outside Warsaw, and then a second school, deeper in the countryside. It was not necessarily safe at these convents—they were subject to raids and Luftwaffe bombs, too—but it was safer than anywhere else in Poland.

"I knew you were something special," Jack said when Alicia reached the end of her tale, which was really only the start. "I knew you weren't an ordinary broad."

"Is that so?" Alicia said, and dabbed her eyes with a napkin. "And what accounts for that opinion?"

Jack stepped back. The space between them seemed unnavigable, the size of the sea.

"You're only twenty," he said, "but you've seen so much. You're astoundingly brave. And then there's your wicked sex appeal." He winked. "As well as your impeccable French."

"French is the least of it. I know five other languages."

She checked the clock on the wall. It was getting late.

"We really should lock up," she said, sliding away from him. "George left ninety minutes ago. He's going to have a fit."

"Who cares about old George?"

"I do. I also care about my job."

She opened a cabinet and pulled out her pocketbook.

"Alicia," Jack said. "What are you doing?"

"Getting my things."

She held up her handbag.

"Aren't you going to tell me what happened with the war?" he said.

"You want me to tell you how the war began?"

"No." Jack laughed. "Don't worry, I'm smahter than I look. I actually wrote a book about the thing. What I meant was, what happened to you, and your family?"

"You wrote a book about the war? Really? What's it called?"

Jack laughed again.

"You're awfully good at dodging questions," he said. "You should be a spy, or a politician. Congresswoman Alicia *Dahr*-ling." Jack gave another wink. "Let me ask again. When the war broke out, you went to a convent, but it couldn't have been that simple. What are the details?"

Alicia sighed, pondering how she might arrange the story to satisfy Jack's curiosity, without divulging too much.

"Most of us in Łódź had to leave for one reason or another," she said. "The Nazis took everything, and to stay meant certain death. By 1939, they'd usurped my father's textile business. They were burning schools and universities, any symbol of Polish culture or literacy, any proof that we had worth.

"They began a campaign to target the intelligentsia, of which my father was a prominent member. I was young, nine years old, but I remember wondering how they could be after *us*. Surely, we were different, set apart."

Jack nodded, eyes glistening.

"We were wealthy, and my parents were smart, and we knew

important people. I thought we were special, and that this would save us, but none of it mattered. To the Nazis, we were all the same. Insignificant. Useless."

Alicia grew hot beneath her clothes. She tugged at her collar and cleared her throat.

"A group of us fled Łódź for another town in Poland—Radom—where we lived for a few years, until that was no longer safe either. Shortly after my twelfth birthday, my parents sent me to the convent and they went into hiding. When the war ended, they were gone and I found myself alone, working as a typist at a displaced-persons camp in Germany. I applied for a visa, and that's how I ended up here."

"Geez. That's a mighty short summary of a great big deal."

Alicia whipped out a tube of lipstick and began to apply.

"There's no use getting flowery about it," she said. "We all have complicated, sad stories from that time."

Damn, this boy was tricky. She'd have to be careful. Jack Kennedy had a crafty manner about him, a way of slipping right under the skin like he'd been there all along. Alicia had the sense she could tell Jack most anything, but the full story was too dear, too important to be passed around to shiny, white-toothed American boys.

"Okeydoke, Alicia Darr," Jack said, eyeing her thoroughly. "I can see that's all I'll get out of you today. But, let it be known, Jack Kennedy never gives up. I've yet to encounter a code I didn't eventually crack."

HYANNIS PORT

Jack Kennedy became a regular visitor, not only to Hyannis Port, but also to Alicia. Whenever possible, usually at the last minute and unannounced, Jack jetted up to the Cape for a rendezvous.

"I'm sorry it can't be more," he'd say, "but I had to see your face."

It was better than nothing and Alicia relished these brief windows of time when they sunbathed on the beach, dined at the Panama Club, and visited Alicia's bedroom after Mrs. Neill and George had gone to sleep.

Jack had a way of stretching time. He was a congressman running for reelection, yet was never too busy to probe Alicia about her job, or her interests, or what Europe was like during the war. He was thoughtful and inquisitive and Alicia felt like a subject he desperately wanted to understand.

"Why do you use so much blue in your paintings?" he'd ask. "Why do you make these harsh, almost unsettling moves with the brush?"

Though he admired her depictions of Poland, Jack thought she should "lighten it up" every once in a while. Alicia was in America now.

Seascapes were cliché, no question, but most folks had straightforward tastes and she'd sell a boatload to the tourists on Main Street. People wanted to look at pleasant, sunny things.

Alicia smiled but saw no way to take his advice. She could paint a seascape no problem, but why bother when she had the real thing nearby? What Jack didn't understand was that she painted Łódź, and the convent, because memories were all she had. There were no photographs, no keepsakes. She painted Poland so that she wouldn't forget.

Alicia couldn't explain this to Jack, despite how much he prodded for more. One of the things he adored about her—or so he said—was that Alicia never complained. She never donned a sour puss.

"How is it that you're always in such a good mood?" he'd asked. "So happy and upbeat? I know girls who bitch when the sun's too bright. But you, never. Why are you so incredible?"

If Jack Kennedy found her "incredible," Alicia didn't care to prove him wrong. He'd probably learn the truth one day: about Poland, and her parents, and everything that led her here. Alicia was deft at skirting questions, but she was bound to slip eventually. She'd put this off, though, as long as she could. Their days together were still fresh, their relationship wondrous and magical and new. Nothing lasted in this world, and Alicia understood that she must relish what she had, while it was still within her grasp.

One morning, on the hunt for cottage cheese, Alicia pattered into the kitchen to find an unexpected caucus consisting of George, Mrs. Neill, and a certain representative from Massachusetts, live and in the sun-tanned flesh.

Alicia froze in the doorway.

"I made flapjacks," Mrs. Neill announced.

"An improvement over my usual poached eggs," Jack said with a wink, and then bit into a piece of bacon.

He was in his shirtsleeves, rolled up, with both elbows on the table and hair that screamed for a trim. Alicia hadn't seen him in days, but the Neills might very well think he stayed the night.

"You need to eat more," Mrs. Neill said to Jack, full of cheer and without suspicion. "You're thin as a rail."

"Hello," Alicia said, and moved wholly into the kitchen. "How is everyone this morning?"

"Fabulous," Jack said. "But you're not dressed for sailing."

Alicia looked down at her outfit, a yellow sheath and matching "glamour cardigan," purchased at Abercrombie & Fitch's season-end sale. She had a small package under her right arm and a pair of heels dangling from her fingertips.

"But I do like the getup." Jack scrutinized the dress thoroughly. "You're making this room a helluva lot brighter."

"Yellow?" George said with a squint. "Do you think that's wise?"

Alicia shot him a glare.

"So, Alicier," Jack said, "Willie, George, and I were having a rousing debate. Have you seen the news?"

Willie? Mrs. Neill's name was *Willie?*

"What news?" Alicia asked.

Jack tapped the *Boston Daily Globe* that sat on the table before him.

"Hyannis Port is causing quite the stir in Washington," he said. "Turns out they don't know how to spell the name of our fine town."

"The question is whether 'Hyannisport' is one word or two," Mrs. Neill said. "According to Jack, they're creating new maps of Barnstable County and can't reach a consensus. Congress is deadlocked on the issue. Now they're calling around the Cape for the answer."

"It's one word, right?" Alicia said.

"Good girl." Mrs. Neill nodded. "Only the fancy sort, the summer folk, would think it's two. No offense, Jack."

"No offense taken. Hyannisport. One word." Jack wiped his mouth. "I'll let Washington know."

He snapped to his feet.

"So, are we going sailing?" he asked.

"Uh . . ." Alicia glanced at her package, and her shoes. "That sounds fun. . . ."

"Then you should probably change. Personally, I suggest a bikini."

George snorted. Alicia could feel him rolling his eyes.

"Okay," she said. "But could we stop by the post office on the way?"

"Golly, kid, I don't know if we have time," Jack said. "We should get on the water before it's too choppy, and I'm back to Washington later today. It's now or never, sweetheart."

"Then you must scoot!" Mrs. Neill—*Willie*—said. "I can post the package for you, if it's urgent."

"No, no, that's okay," Alicia said quickly. "I can do it later."

What was one more day? Then again, she'd been told there wasn't much time left.

"What are you mailing, anyhow?" George asked, brows knitted together. "What people do you know?"

"George!" his mother yelped. "What a question!"

"Hurry up, Alicia," Jack said, and snapped his fingers. "Chop, chop."

Alicia nodded, then pivoted on her stocking feet and scampered upstairs. She threw her shoes onto the bed, and opened a drawer.

She'd never been sailing, unless an immigrant ship counted, but Alicia spent enough time at the Kennedys' to know what American girls wore on boats. Thank goodness for west end sales, for Alicia had the perfect answer: a white and black polka-dotted halter top and black piqué shorts, with a red ribbon tied around the waist.

After tossing on the outfit, Alicia slid her would-be mail beneath a wad of stockings, then slammed the drawer closed. She grabbed a pair of deck-appropriate shoes, then rushed downstairs to meet Jack.

They walked the wood-chipped pathway, through the tall grass covering the dunes. When they reached the cove, Alicia took in the sea air, the sunshine, the blue skies. She watched as orange-legged piping plovers scurried across the sand, little bird bandits with their telltale black masks.

Soon, Jack was leading her past the break wall, and to the family's private dock. The last time she'd stepped on the pier's weathered planks Alicia was carrying picnic baskets that were so heavy she had indentations on her arms for hours and sore muscles for days. Now, she felt weightless.

"There she is," Jack said. "The *Victura.*"

Alicia smiled knowingly, as she'd seen the vessel before. "*Victura*" was Latin for "about to conquer." A perfect boat for Jack.

As he helped her on board, Alicia wondered, was it strange that this was the first they'd touched all morning? Didn't couples usually hold hands while strolling the shore? Then again, this was Jack, and that was not his style.

"This is a Wianno Senior," Jack explained, as he unstrapped the sail. "It was my fifteenth-birthday present and I've been in love ever since. Here. Take this, and help me rig the mainsail."

"Rig the mainsail?" Alicia balked. "I'm from Poland!"

He laughed.

"Well, Alicia *Dahr*-ling, you'd better figure out it, because a man needs a crew."

"But the boat . . . I'll damage it for sure!"

"Nah. This old girl is invincible. She was struck by lightning in 1936. In 1944, I rescued her from a hurricane. Hell, in the storm last week, Bobby and Ethel took her out and almost crashed three times."

He clicked something onto the top of the sail, then guided Alicia to help loosen the slack. Soon, they were wrapping rope around a crank. Jack told her to duck as he swung the boom across the boat.

"And away we go," he said as they cast off into the sun-dappled sound, the water lapping against the hull.

They picked up speed and Alicia's belly filled with a nervous flush. Jack was sitting beside her, on the back of the boat, guiding it with a large, brown stick. Alicia had envisioned something more substantial, a steering wheel, perhaps.

The boat sped up. Alicia gripped the seat's edge and squeezed her eyes closed. Oh, this sailing business was nothing like a battleship. It was disorienting almost, as if the wind was lifting them right off the water.

"Alicia!" Jack called, his voice weaker out here. "Look up! You're missing all the good stuff!"

She opened her eyes, amazed to be looking not at the other side of the boat, but the sky. Alicia released a scream.

"We're practically touching the water!" she said into the wind. "It's right there!"

If she wanted to, Alicia could reach out and brush her fingers across the foamy sea.

"I know!" Jack said, eyes dancing. "That's what's so great about this boat. Don't fret, sweetheart, we can't tip over. Lean back, Alicia! Let go!"

She took in a gulp of air, and tilted one degree, and then a few degrees more. She fixed her eyes on the sail and finally gave in to the whooshing grace of the boat as it skimmed along the water. Within seconds, Alicia was grinning as her hair flapped and the ocean spattered her face.

This was why she came to the States, for days like these. What had she been so afraid of? She was with Jack and the sea was an old friend. After all, it was this very Atlantic that delivered her safely into America's arms.

They'd planned a picnic on Egg Island, so Alicia was surprised when Jack anchored the *Victura* far from visible land.

"Are we eating on the boat?" she asked, peering into the water.

Five long, silver fish winnowed past.

"Maybe," Jack said. "But I'm not hungry. First, a swim."

She glanced up.

"I didn't bring my suit," she said, thinking of her new bathing costume: orange, with a wide wale and pearl buttons.

Then again, it was probably the sort of getup best left to sunbathing, and not an actual swim.

"Who needs a suit?" Jack said.

In one motion, he stripped to his skivvies. Then the skivvies came off, and he was in nothing at all.

Alicia gasped.

"Oh, come on." He rolled his eyes playfully. "Nothing you haven't seen before."

"But I didn't expect to see it out here! What if you get a sunburn?"

"That," he said, laughing, "would be the pits."

Jack stepped onto the bow, lifted both arms overhead, and dove into the deep blue. Alicia craned to look, waiting for him to resurface. When he popped up, he beamed, drops of seawater clinging to his lashes, his eyes greener than they were gray.

"Stop ogling and join in," he said, and slapped the water.

"Oh, Jack, I don't know."

It'd been ten years since she last swam. Would her body remember how?

"What don't you know?" he said. "Come on! Jump!"

Well, if nothing else, it was comforting to know he'd made water rescues before, of entire platoons. He even had a medal for this skill.

"Okay," she said, stomach fluttering as she stood. "Here goes."

She peeled off her clothes with more care than Jack had demonstrated, because, while the outfit had been on sale, it was still quite dear.

After stacking her things into a tight, neat pile, Alicia moved to the tip of the boat. She paused, the wind spraying goose bumps across her naked skin.

"Damn," Jack said. "Mermaids do exist. Are you going to save me if I have a heart attack on account of your unparalleled beauty?"

"No, Jack, I was kind of expecting you to rescue me."

Before she could chicken out, Alicia pinched her nose, closed her eyes, and leapt feetfirst from the bow. The water was warmer than she'd expected, saltier, too. She was thrilled to find that her churning legs could keep her afloat.

"This is incredible," she said, breathless with it all.

"I'll show you incredible. Get over here!"

Jack motioned, his arm rippling the water. Alicia dog-paddled toward him. Once she was close enough, he reached out and grabbed her with unexpected strength. Wrapping both legs around him, Alicia shivered, though she wasn't cold.

"You okay, kid?" he asked.

Alicia sighed, and rested her chin on his right shoulder.

"Never better," she replied.

They remained like that, locked onto each other, for some time. As Alicia's eyes followed the Atlantic toward the horizon, she wondered how there was anything important in this world besides the ocean, Jack, and a shiny wooden sailboat bobbing nearby.

HYANNIS, Mass.——A woman patron at a summer theatre laughed so hard that her upper plate flew out, sailed past the head of a man in front of her, and landed somewhere under the seats. A search party of employees recovered the plate.

The News-Herald, September 18, 1950

HYANNIS PORT

At the postal counter, Alicia held money in one hand, an envelope in the other.

How much to send? Alicia could never settle on the answer, because there was no right number. Her debt was immeasurable, not something to be reduced to dollars and cents. Maybe it was good that her sailing adventure with Jack forced her to wait a few days. It gave her time to think. On the other hand, their day together made the debt loom larger still.

Alicia had the crisp twenty-dollar bill from the sale of her painting, plus a collection of dollars and coins from the Center and the Kennedys, too. The boundaries of her budget were beginning to form, though Alicia was known to splurge on a new dress or paint supplies, but did not view the latter as a luxury. All this to say Alicia had money left over each week, but how much actually belonged to her was a formula she'd yet to solve.

"Something I can help you with, Miss Darr?" called the postman, as he leaned out the window.

"Oh, no." She shook her head. "I'm dandy."

"All right, but we close soon."

Alicia eyeballed the clock. It was later than she thought. There'd been an incident at the Center. During a showing of *Three Little Words*, a woman lost the upper portion of her teeth. Alicia and George spent twenty minutes checking beneath seats before finally locating it in the second row.

"I'll be out of your hair in a jiff," she told the postman.

She slipped the twenty into the envelope, then added a few dollars more, but took them out on second thought. What if she couldn't provide as much next time?

"Another overseas parcel?" the postman asked.

"Only a letter," she replied, annoyed he remembered this detail.

Alicia settled on the twenty. After scratching out a note, she sealed the envelope, then marched up to the counter.

"All set," she said, and handed over the letter. "Sorry for the delay."

The postman scanned the address, as he always did.

"Have you been busy?" she asked. "Or have things quieted now that we're at the tail end—"

"This will probably take some time," he said. "Nearly as much mail is being sent overseas right now as within the United States. Everything's all jammed up."

"There's no rush," she said, though this was not strictly true.

"Just don't blame me for any delay."

"Of course not."

After paying for postage and wishing the man a good afternoon, Alicia walked away with a bounce to her step.

Her slate was far from clean, but whenever Alicia sent something off, she felt one nudge closer to leveling the scales. Never mind its purchasing power, the money represented progress. It represented success. It said that Alicia Darr's journey to America, and thus her very life, was worth something yet. Twenty dollars per painting, at least. And whatever the value of Jack Kennedy's smile was.

Oh sure, she had some guilt for not sending more, but a person needed money to survive. Mrs. Neill refused to take rent, but Alicia had to compensate in other ways (buying groceries, sneaking pennies into the change jar) lest she inadvertently acquire another debt. It was probably time to open a bank account, she thought. Would her DP and resident alien cards be enough?

Mind weighing the particulars of the American banking system, Alicia found herself on South Street and most of the way home without having to think. Hyannis was now so ingrained, it was like she'd been there for years.

A block from the Neills', a familiar figure zipped out from a building and directly into her path. Alicia froze, unsure how to address this person, or whether she should.

"Miss Dee?" Alicia blurted. "Miss Dee, is that you?"

"Oh! Hello!" the woman said brightly, looking lovely as ever in a green suit. "Miss Darr! What a surprise! I'm sorry I didn't see you there."

"Don't apologize. I crept up behind you."

Crept up? What a choice of words.

"I adore your suit, Miss Dee," she said, the one rational comment her brain could hatch.

"Thank you. And, please, none of this 'Miss Dee' nonsense. That's a Rose Kennedy construct. She thinks the help can't pronounce my name and I play along. Sometimes, that's the best course with Rose."

As Miss Dee rolled her eyes, Mrs. Kennedy's tight, prim mug and tight, prim body appeared in Alicia's head.

No man is above falling in love with his secretary. . . .

"Please, call me Janet," Miss Dee said.

I guess the jig is up.

"Well, Janet, it's wonderful to see you," Alicia said. "Do you live here? In Hyannis Port? I always thought . . ."

She let her voice wane as she snuck a glimpse of the apartment building beside them. For Alicia, Janet was inexorably linked with the

Ambassador, and thus the Kennedy home. To picture her in an ordinary apartment scattered the pieces of a puzzle Alicia thought she'd nearly completed.

"You don't live at the house?" she said.

"Gosh, no, I live here." Janet smiled prettily. "When we're on the Cape."

"How nice," Alicia said, blinking like a muddled child. "I didn't realize the family was still in town."

"Not everyone. Only the Ambassador."

"Oh," Alicia said dimly.

God, what if Mr. Kennedy had seen her on the family pier, wearing nothing but Jack's wrinkled, sandy shirt? Luckily, they never went inside the actual house. Then again, why hadn't they? Was it because of Jack's dad?

"Miss Darr?" Janet said. "Are you okay? You look pink. . . ."

"I read in the paper about Mr. Kennedy's gift!" Alicia blabbed, glad for the two million he'd given to a Catholic home for dependent children.

Never mind the children, it was about to save Alicia from collapsing beneath a torrent of doubt.

"Those neglected children are so fortunate," she went on. "I mean, not fortunate in general, just, er, in this instance."

"I understood what you meant," Janet said, and broke out another triumphant smile. "Joe is the most selfless person I've ever known. Everything he does is for his family, or for charity. We are so proud of him."

Alicia nodded, marveling. Janet was an employee, yet when she spoke of the Kennedys, it was in terms of "we." During the day, she had full command of the house, upstairs and downstairs both. But at night, she was holed up in an ordinary apartment, on the humble side of town.

"I'd better go," Janet said, slipping on her gloves. "Joe is expecting me in a few minutes."

"Yes, of course. Have a lovely day. Perhaps we'll run into each other again."

"Possibly! Though we'll be in Florida, soon."

With one last smile, Janet slipped into her Buick and started the engine. Alicia remained on the sidewalk until long after Janet puttered out of sight, her head muddy with thoughts and questions she could not put into words.

The letter comes back, like a gopher you can't shoo from your yard. Even in death, his client is a pain in the ass.

Try Rome, someone wrote on the envelope.

He calls his secretary, who's in New York. She'll need to rummage through his files. He recalls an address in Rome. It was a friend's art studio, if memory serves.

When he rings, he learns that his secretary is on vacation. Wasn't she just on vacation? Maybe they pay her too much. He leaves a message, which she returns three days later, from Mexico. She's there with her boyfriend. What fifty-five-year-old woman has a "boyfriend," I ask you? A ridiculous term. He thought she was a lesbian on account of her hair.

"You can't help me from Mexico," he says.

"Oh, okay."

She is a little drunk from two margaritas at lunch.

"Why did you call me if you're on 'vacation'?" he wants to know.

"Someone from the office texted me that you'd called," she says. "I thought it might be urgent."

"It is urgent, but how are you going to help me from there?"

"I'll be back in seven days."

"Seven days! Haven't you already been gone two?"

"Three."

"Three! Good grief!"

"I can have Shari look." she says.

"Shari! Shari can't look!"

"Does it matter?" she asks with a sigh.

She's never this insolent, but of course there's midday tequila and her boyfriend starting to undress.

" 'Does it matter'?" her boss growls. "Yes, it rather does. There are people nosing around, waiting for news."

"Well, if Shari can't help, you'll have to wait."

She looks up. Her boyfriend offers a double thumbs-up. They're all dying for the boss to retire.

"Fine," the man says. "I'll wait."

He may be gruff but he's not unreasonable. That's what she's been trying to explain to the boyfriend, who wants her to quit.

"I'll send you an email," he says. "About what I need. You're in no shape to take notes now."

That she had margaritas at lunch is no great shock. He can hear it in her words. Meanwhile, the boyfriend is making his moves.

"Okay then, I'll speak with you next week," she says.

The man hangs up the phone.

Alone, at his desk, which overlooks the street instead of the ocean (a bad layout, he realizes), the man boots up his computer. He glances at the letter. How does one send mail to Rome? Something catches his eye. What imbecile got mustard on the envelope? He imagines some fat slob, eating a roast beef sandwich over a stack of mail.

The computer shows a welcome screen. Once the man remembers his password, and then also types it correctly after three tries, he googles how to send a letter to Italy. The results are discouraging. Italian post offices aren't even used for mail, but for paying bills. One purchases stamps at a tobacconist.

He soon learns that the internet is riddled with Italian postal calamities, and Rome is notoriously bad. There are countless stories of packages and letters received after months, or not received at all. One woman mailed her daughter a letter in July, and sent another on Halloween. Both arrived on the same day in December. Parcels often show up empty, or clearly rifled through.

The man jots down the rules for giving a letter the best shot. Thankfully, he is not desirous of sending weapons, hair, or human remains. He is likewise not interested in mailing clocks, footwear, or playing cards.

All envelopes must be white and addressed plainly, he notes. Anything colorful hints at celebration, and the possibility of money, especially if originating from the United States. If you send an envelope in pink or green or blue, count on it being opened, one hundred percent. Luckily white envelopes are all he has.

Soon the man is tired. He closes his computer and dashes off a letter to the secretary, to be received next week, and includes a ten-dollar bill. He estimates it will cost $6.04 to mail. She can keep the change.

WHITE ENVELOPE, he writes. *TYPE THE ADDRESS*.

In the end, the secretary will heed the first instruction, but not the second. She finds the request unnecessarily complicated and she prefers handwriting, a personal and somewhat old-fashioned touch. Why does the man always have to be so strict?

> Congressman Jack Kennedy, son of the former Ambassador, and
> Adele O'Connor have iced.
>> Around Town, by Ed Sullivan, September 27, 1950

HYANNIS PORT

Alicia hadn't expected to find Jack's name in the gossip pages.

She was unfamiliar with the word "iced," though of course it could only mean they'd gone cold. American idioms aside, who was Adele O'Connor and why hadn't Jack mentioned her before? It was good timing, at least. Alicia could ask Jack that night, in person, if she drummed up the nerve.

```
IN HYANNIS FRIDAY NIGHT WILL STOP BY AFTER
2200 MISS YOU= LOVE JACK
```

Alicia worked until nine o'clock, and despite her Jack Kennedy jitters, handled the candy counter like a pro. She came close to selling a piece of art to an older gentleman, but he got distracted and ambled off.

"Drat! Almost!" Alicia said, with a ping of triumph. "I had him on the hook!"

He didn't recoil at the twenty-dollar price, which was something, to be sure.

"He was making conversation," George said, ever the optimist. "I wouldn't get too excited."

"You really know how to make a gal feel swell," Alicia said, but smiled anyway.

"I don't know why you're under the misguided notion that you can sell a static painting to someone who's just watched a film. These are modern times. Art is picture and sound. Art *moves*."

"Please." Alicia rolled her eyes. "Most people view movies as a diversion, like a baseball game. Very few would consider it high art."

"So, you create 'high art' then?" he asked.

Normally, Alicia would've reminded George that some thoughts were best left in one's head. But she was too excited, her body racked by an almost devouring anticipation. She was seeing Jack tonight! It'd been awhile and there was quite a lot to say.

"All right! Good-bye!" Alicia called, the minute the clock struck nine.

George muttered something about the balled-up, lipstick-blotted tissues she'd left on the counter, though Alicia chose not to hear. She raced home to freshen up but, in the end, George walked through the front door long before Jack came.

He arrived shortly before midnight, never "on time" but instead forever "in the nick of," always catching Alicia seconds before she gave up. All he had to do was fire off one of his smiles, and she couldn't stay exasperated for long.

"Aren't you a sight," he said, and pulled her into him, the second she opened the door. "They don't make them like you in Washington."

He nuzzled her neck.

"Or anywhere."

"Jack," Alicia said, and pushed him away. "Not so fast."

She grabbed his shirt, and pulled him toward the living room.

"Aw, hell," he said. "You're playing coy? *Now?*"

"Coy. I don't know what that is."

Alicia shoved him onto the couch and twirled, skirt fanning out as she moved. She had on a new outfit that night: a white tube top tucked into a flared black skirt, with a bib necklace to finish it off. It was a kickier style than she normally wore, and more expensive, too. She wanted Jack to appreciate it before it ended up on the floor.

"Let's chat," she said. "We haven't seen each other in ages!"

"You're killing me, kid!"

Jack clutched his heart, and then his balls.

"Jack Kennedy, you're an animal. Surely you can contain yourself for five minutes before getting to the lights-out business."

"If you want to keep the lights on, I'm A-OK with that," he said.

"I swear you think about sex ninety percent of the time."

Alicia sat on the couch beside him.

"I assure you, it's much higher than ninety," he said. "Sorry, kid, it's your fault. You can't walk around looking like *that* if you expect me to behave."

"I can't decide if you're the world's biggest charmer," Alicia said, and swatted his shoulder, "or the world's biggest wolf."

"Can you blame me? You leave me positively weak."

"I'll check the box marked 'wolf.'"

"As for you, I'll check the one marked 'flirt.'"

Alicia chuckled, and thought back to all those months ago, in Oklahoma, when she'd returned from yet another date. As Alicia sprawled across the YWCA couch, she complained to Irenka that she'd tried with the banter and the come-hither and all that, but she still came across like a Pole who'd had too much vodka.

"It's hopeless!" she'd wailed. "I'll never find a proper boyfriend if I can't even flirt."

With that dead-eyed stare, Irenka asked, "What is flirt?"

Alicia tried to explain, to translate, but couldn't find the words.

"It's like teasing, almost," she said. "But sexier. Lighthearted."

"Vy you tease?" Irenka said. "Teasink is bad."

"Oh, never mind," Alicia said, a frequent response when it came to Irenka.

As for flirting, Alicia had come to accept this deficiency in herself. She'd grown up in a convent. The only men she encountered in her formative years were priests or Gestapo agents, and she didn't dare speak to either type. But, what do you know? In Hyannis, the flirting had clicked, like a language newly learned.

"You're in no position to accuse someone of being a flirt," Alicia said to Jack, radiating with the discovery of her newfound talent.

"*Accusing?* It's a fact, and I think it's swell."

"Jack." She sighed. "We haven't seen each other in ten days."

She squeezed Jack's knee, despite knowing how very prone he was to *heating up* with the slightest provocation.

Ten days. No wonder Alicia's nerves were revved, the thrill in her belly tormenting. Jack had been gone for so long, Alicia worried she'd have to master him all over again.

"Bed first," Jack said, and lunged her way. "Talk later."

Alicia laughed and nudged him onto to his rear.

"Okay, kid," he said, "you want to talk, let's talk. But better make it quick. You're driving me positively mad and I'm liable to take you right here on the couch."

"We're not alone in this house, you know," she said with yet another laugh, and then scooted away. "What's going on in Washington?"

"Washington? Good Lord, Alicia, please don't start talking legislation, or my boner will soften for good."

"You kiss your mother with that mouth?"

"No," he said.

"Let's talk about your campaign. Are you confident about regaining your seat? You're spending loads of time on the road."

"Sure, sure," Jack said, and tilted forward again, eyeing her hungrily.

"How's your family? What are they up to? Is your father here, or has he decamped to Florida?"

"My father? Why the hell are we talking about my dad?"

"Actually, I thought of him the other day, when I ran into his secretary Miss Dee. Janet, I guess, is what you call her."

"Yes, that is what we call her," he said. "Seeing as how it's her name."

He began to tap his foot.

"I didn't realize she had an apartment in town," Alicia said. "I thought she lived at the house."

"Why would you think that?" Jack asked, brow furrowed.

"Because her relationship with your father is very . . . involved."

Abruptly, Jack stopped moving, as if someone had cut his power.

"What are you getting at?" he asked.

"I'm not sure." Alicia looked at her hands. "They seem unusually intimate."

"Oh, brother." Jack groaned, and dropped his head. "Are you worried about my dad's sex life? Is that it?"

He turned to her again.

"I can arrange something, if you're interested. Wouldn't be the first time."

"Don't be a jerk," Alicia said, and touched her stomach, which felt like it had something crawling around inside of it. "And, no, it's not like that. I'm only trying to understand."

"Listen," Jack said. "You've met Mother. Have you noticed that she isn't the warmest sort?"

Alicia nodded, mouth open. Of course she'd noticed; everyone who worked at the Kennedys' had. The woman was harder, shinier, and more formal than her cherished rosewood table.

"Have you likewise picked up on her nose for details?" he said.

"That's one way to put it."

"You're a sharp girl, Alicia. Hell, that's half the reason I like being with you. But do you fancy yourself more perceptive than Mother, or the scads of others who go into and out of the house all day?"

"No, of course not."

"Then don't get excited about having uncovered some dark family secret, because you haven't. Unless you think Mother is a fool, or blind."

"No, I don't," Alicia said into her lap. "I believe she knows exactly what's going on with everybody, every last person."

Tears pushed against her eyes.

"I was merely asking," she said. "You don't have to be so nasty about it."

"I'm sorry," Jack said, hastily almost. "But Mother's *fine* with the state of things. She has her religion, and Father has his business, and together they have us. Take a gander at her house, and her bedroom overlooking the sea. Check out her closet, at the clothes bought in Paris last week. If you're thinking, 'poor Rose Kennedy,' then you can forget it. She wouldn't trade places with a damned soul."

Rose Kennedy *did* seem happy, in fact rather pleased with her station, not to mention her relationship with the one who mattered most—God.

"I'm sorry," Alicia squeaked, though she wasn't sure for what.

"Aw, kid," Jack said, and bumped her knee with his. "I know what you're thinking."

"Well, clue me in, as I don't know myself."

"First of all, my secretary, she's not my type."

"How comforting."

"And I'm not my father. To start, I'd never marry someone that Catholic."

Alicia laughed, though it sounded worn and rusty.

"Come on, kid, look at me."

She obeyed, eyes shimmering with tears.

"I am not Joe Kennedy," Jack said. "Sometimes people *think* that I am, but they're wrong. We have vastly different opinions on any number of topics, including marriage."

"Understood. I won't bring it up again."

"I should hope not," Jack said.

He went to stand.

"Shall we go upstairs?" he asked, then paused, taking in Alicia's countenance, and the way she was biting her lip. "What's the problem now?"

"Who's Adele O'Connor?"

His face jumped.

"Adele O'Connor? Where'd you get that name?"

"From the paper." She blushed. "The gossip pages. I probably shouldn't admit I read that muck, but there you go."

"Hell, everybody reads it. Tell me, Alicia *Dahr*-ling, what did this paper say?"

"That you two have 'iced.'"

Jack snorted and shook his head.

"It was a fling," he said, "that lasted about a week, ages ago. I couldn't even tell you what color hair she has. Couldn't pick her out of a lineup."

Alicia closed her eyes. Okay. This all sounded reasonable enough.

Jack reached out a hand to pull her up.

"Can we go to bed *now*?"

"I suppose," Alicia said, and staggered to her feet.

"Damn, you're hot to trot, aren't you? Try not to make a scene. It's embarrassing."

"I'm just tired," she said as they pattered down the hall. "Also." She stopped. "I should probably get one last thing off my chest."

"Jesus, you got a list or something? Next time send it in advance, so I can prepare my remarks."

"It's nothing major." She swallowed. "I only wish we spent more time at your place, instead of here, or at the Center."

"My place? In Georgetown?"

"No! Gosh no!" Alicia said, then wondered why not. "I meant here, in Hyannis Port. Although now that you mention Washington . . ."

"Weren't we just at the house?" he said. "I seem to recall sailing. A bit of skinny-dipping."

He winked.

"Yes, but technically we didn't go *inside*. It makes me feel . . ." Alicia let her gaze slide away. "That maybe you're embarrassed to bring me around."

"Aw, kid."

Jack wrapped her in a hug. Forget kissing, forget sex, forget nestling together in a tub. When it came to Jack Kennedy, an embrace was the rarest, most intimate gesture of all.

"I could never be embarrassed," he said. "As far as I can tell, you up my status by at least two hundred percent. Sure, we can hang out at the house. I figured it'd be weird, given you worked there. Weird for you, of course. I don't give a damn. You should've said something."

"Thank you, Jack. Thank you so much."

Alicia exhaled, realizing that she hadn't expected this answer. She'd envisioned a blazing smile, a quick "sorry, kid," and some compelling excuse, which she'd readily accept.

But Jack agreed, and more than that, he made it seem like she wasn't something to hide. The thought made Alicia weak, which was not the best position to be in when Jack Kennedy was goggling her like that.

"Since that's settled," Alicia said, and grinned, "I'm going to need help getting out of this skirt."

Jack kept his word and soon they were at the house more than they were anywhere else.

Alicia slept at the white clapboard home, she woke up there, she lolled about the sunroom and read on the porch. On sunny days, Alicia and Jack rode bikes on Longwood Avenue. They took sailing trips, and picnicked by the sea.

Sometimes, Alicia experienced a flutter of guilt when she tracked sand through the house, or left a cardigan on the porch or a dirty glass in the sink. Other times, it felt delicious and carefree.

When they weren't on the beach or sailing, Alicia and Jack were indoors, usually in the basement watching movies. Alicia missed so many important films during those frightening years: *The Wizard of Oz, Gone with the Wind, The Philadelphia Story,* and, of course, *Casablanca.*

"I think this is the beginning of a beautiful friendship," Jack often said, giving Alicia the shivers, every time.

Jack loved Hollywood but could never sit through a full reel. Fifteen, twenty minutes in, he took to pacing, tapping, scratching doodles on a pad. Jack Kennedy was never at rest, except while in the bath. Sometimes he took as many as four per day, with Alicia perched on the edge of the tub, reading a book or the latest news.

But these days were not to last. Jack was set to return to the campaign trail. He'd shown Alicia his October datebook, which looked less like a schedule and more like a full compendium of all venues in the commonwealth. Copley Plaza and Columbus Day parades and YMCAs throughout the district. The Young Democrats Club and the National Council of Jewish Women and every Kiwanis Club there'd ever been.

Alicia was perusing this schedule one afternoon when Jack lurched out of the tub. As he wrapped a towel around his waist, Alicia glanced up, a frown crossing her lips. It was a shock to see him in such stark and unadorned light. He was all skin and ribs.

"What's with the look?" Jack asked. "Wait, don't answer. You're admiring the legendary Fitzgerald breasts. Nipples that stand at attention like good soldiers."

"I'm not concerned about your nipples. I'm worried about your back."

"My back is my back. It'll always be there."

He hobbled toward his pants.

"This timeline is aggressive," Alicia said, sifting through the pages. "Do you really need to travel this much, to lobby for a job you already have?"

"Obviously," Jack said, a little huffy.

"Okay, okay." She inspected the list again. "Are you sure you're up for it?"

"Why wouldn't I be? Campaigning is vigorous, but I'm young. Well, not compared to you." He brandished a big, white grin. "But I'm a damned schoolboy compared to the rest of the bastards running for office."

Jack put one leg into his pants and then, very slowly, the other.

"Do you like being a congressman?" Alicia said, and set the papers in her lap.

"Do I like *being a congressman?*" he repeated. "I don't think anyone's ever asked me that. I'm helping people. It feels good to stand up for the needs of the folks in my district."

"But, do you like it?"

"Sure. Why not?"

Jack buttoned his trousers, then leaned against the counter. He gritted his teeth and squinched his eyes.

"Are you okay—"

"Yes, I'm fine," he said. "Old war junk."

He opened his eyes again.

"The thing is, Alicia, it's not about being a congressman."

In this light, his skin seemed more yellow than tanned. Alicia blinked, several times, to set herself straight.

"That's not all there is to me," he said.

"I barely understand what a congressman does, so I already think you're much more."

"What I meant was, this isn't the destination. I have places left to go."

"Gosh, you'd think United States representative would be enough."

"Oh, Alicia," Jack said. "I love your sweet unaffectedness."

He cocked his head, eyes shifting toward the window. Alicia wondered if he had yet another cramp in his neck.

"You remember that I had an older brother?" he said. "Who died in the war?"

Alicia nodded, and pushed herself off the side of the tub. She moved beside Jack, but did not take his hand.

"Joe Junior was the family's destiny," Jack said, "the person to lead us to greatness."

Her eyes flicked outside, to the sprawling lawn, and the Nantucket Sound in the distance. She turned to regard Jack. Hadn't greatness been achieved?

"He was going to be the first Catholic president of the United States."

"President!?" she yawped.

And here Alicia worried that she'd been too greedy with *her* American dreams.

"Yep," Jack said. "Alas, Joe Junior died and now the runner-up must assume the mantle."

"*You're* the runner-up?" she said. "I find that hard to swallow."

"It's true. Joe was good at sports, and at school, and he had a natural charisma that drew people like bait."

"Sounds familiar . . ."

"When I first got to Harvard," Jack went on, "I let everyone know that I wasn't as smart as Joe. I had to temper expectations, you see, so that people wouldn't be blindsided by Joe's sickly, disheveled little brother. I thought I'd go into teaching, or writing. But then he died, and now it's up to me."

Alicia scrutinized him for a minute, though Jack didn't notice, as his gaze was now cast toward his feet. She knew something about fulfilling a family destiny, even if, compared to his, Alicia's was small in scope, and not so spelled out.

"This is America," Alicia said, "the land of the free. Can't you do what you want?"

"Do what I want?"

Jack gave her the once-over.

"Why do *you* have to make your father's dreams come true?" Alicia asked. "What about Bobby? Or Teddy?"

Jack laughed bitterly.

"Nope," he said. "It's up to me."

With another grunt, Jack pushed himself upright.

"I understand," Alicia said. "Not about politics, and I've never had a brother, but I understand about being the one left behind. You see, I—"

"Alicia, there are seven of us," Jack snapped.

"Yes, of course," Alicia said, and then set her teeth into a clenched smile.

Suddenly, Jack dropped his towel and Alicia saw that he was for the moment pain-free. Whatever the situation with his back, or in his brain, Jack was ready to go with his lower half. As it were.

"Oh, dear." Alicia shook her head. "Don't you ever get tired?"

"You see? Who said anything about a bad back?" He grinned. "Now the question is, what are you doing over there? Come help this ailing man to bed."

WOMAN'S SIDE OF SEX-AND-WAR

The Washington Post, October 1, 1950

HYANNIS PORT

Whenever Alicia thought she had George pegged, whenever she'd convinced herself that he was the single-minded, artless, antisocial person he seemed, the boy would do something to rattle her entire worldview.

He might, for example, raise a topic unrelated to the cinema. Or he'd tell Alicia to give a man a pop (on him) because the fella was hard up for cash. And, every once in a while, he'd turn his insight on her, like a burst of light.

"Nothing," Alicia said, when George repeatedly pestered her about her mood. "Why do you keep asking what's wrong?"

Her voice was high, a mite shrill, especially compared to George's monotone.

"Because something obviously is," he said, watching a rag on the counter, as if expecting it to move. "You're distracted. I can't make you talk, but you're not fooling anyone."

He snatched the rag and began to clean, having determined that Alicia would not.

"It's Jack," she admitted. "He's leaving tomorrow."

"Isn't he always coming or going? That's sort of his 'thing.'"

"This time it's different. The midterm elections are next month." Alicia smiled, pleased with her deft use of the term. "He'll be campaigning until November, nonstop, and then his family spends December in Palm Beach. I don't know when I'll see him again."

"Can't you just ask?" George said, and pushed up his black frames.

"That'd be swell, but between the campaigning and his work in Washington, I'm not sure he knows himself."

They'd made no promises about what they were to each other, or what might happen when Jack revisited his off-season life. Alicia wanted to believe they'd last through the winter, but what did she know of relationships, really? Especially those that started in the sun.

Alicia wandered toward her paintings. She noticed they were all lightly covered in dust.

"There are benefits," she said, studying her artwork with a frown. "I haven't painted in ages. Life with Jack is such a distraction."

"That's how love goes. It has a way of taking over a person's life."

Alicia smirked. That George had an opinion on love was as big a revelation as one might find. Then again, he did watch a lot of Humphrey Bogart films.

She pivoted away from the paintings, shuffled to the candy counter, and held out a hand.

"Here," she said. "Let me clean."

"Do you?" George asked.

"Do I what? Want to clean? Not really but . . ."

"Do you love him?"

"George Neill!" she barked. "You can't ask a girl that! It's too personal!"

"Seems like a normal question to me."

George sniffed, then pushed up his glasses once again. Alicia crossed her arms.

"I don't know, George," she said. "Maybe I do, maybe I don't. With

Jack, it's different. It's more or less than love, something beyond the words I currently know."

"That makes no sense whatsoever."

"You're right." Alicia sighed. "I guess it's like this. When I'm with Jack Kennedy, he seems like the whole world. He makes me feel valuable, and important, and like I have a purpose. He can make me forget, for minutes, hours at a time, that I've ever been for a moment displaced."

Jack made supper for their last night together.

Because Alicia was well-acquainted with the "Kennedy stomach," she borrowed salt and pepper from Mrs. Neill, and had a snack before she left. Food: the one area in which the Kennedys did not shine.

They sat in the dining room, in robes, which seemed heavenly and diabolical both. When Jack went to fetch the first course, Alicia scurried over and sat in Mrs. Kennedy's spot, to test it out. She jumped back to Eunice's chair when Jack returned, with a silver platter in hand.

"*Bon appetit*," he said, and set it down.

He lifted the lid with flourish to reveal one pork chop and a solitary baked potato, sans butter.

"Looks wonderful!" Alicia said, glad for the pre-dinner snack.

She picked up a knife and fork, and began sawing. It took her thirty, forty seconds to gnash through the first bite.

"Delicious!" she said.

"Horseshit," Jack said, and threw his fork onto the table. "This is terrible."

"I didn't come for gourmet. Good or bad, there's still no place I'd rather be."

Jack laughed, and shook his head.

"I've got to hand it to you, kid," he said. "You *never* complain. It's like you've taken a course in stiff upper lips."

"What's there to complain about?" Alicia said, and meant it.

"The fact I'm leaving for one." He winked. "You don't seem the least bit sad, which makes this fella mighty insecure."

"But it's all an act, Congressman," Alicia said, and pushed her plate aside. "I'm quite distraught, especially since I don't know when I'll see you again. In the new year? Next summer? Never again?"

She tried out a smile, but found her mouth trembling, her eyes getting hot.

"Come on, now," Jack said, and patted her hand. "Don't be dramatic. It doesn't suit you. If nothing else, I'll be here on the seventh."

He tossed her one of his cute and wicked grins.

"The seventh?" she said. "Of October?"

Alicia tried to remember his schedule. Kiwanis or Rotary something-or-other on that day, she was pretty sure. Or was it the YMCA? They all looked the same, after a while.

"For a speech?" she asked.

"No," he said. "An art show. The best exhibition the Cape's ever seen."

"How can that be? The galleries close on Sunday for the season."

"Or do they?" Jack wiggled his bushy, unkempt brows. "On the contrary, my dear. My pal Marla owns one of the galleries on the west end. She's agreed to stay open later, so that you can show your stuff."

Alicia's heart began to race.

"But, Jack . . ."

"You heard it here first," he said, beaming. "Featuring, in Hyannis, Mass., on October seventh, the artistic stylings of a most talented Alicia Darr."

"Jack, that's . . ." She halted, all the breath having left her body. "I can't have an art show in a week."

Professional artists took *months* to get ready, and Alicia wasn't professional to start. All she had were a few lousy paintings, all of them already seen by the entirety of the mid-Cape.

"I'm not ready," she said. "I'll ruin your friend's reputation!"

"That's some thank-you," Jack said. "Planning this wasn't easy you know."

"I appreciate it, but . . ."

"Think nothing of it." He put up a hand. "Marla was pleased to support an up-and-coming artist. I told her that your stuff was top-notch, and she took my word for it."

"I'm sure she did."

Alicia hadn't imagined starting her career on Jack's good looks and charm, but she should probably take her breaks where she could get them.

"I don't know what to say. . . ."

"Don't say anything, except for yes. And we'll line up more shows, and more after that. Before long, you'll be known worldwide. No more shilling popcorn and Jujubes for you. You're blushing. Is that a yes?"

"Do I have a choice?" she asked.

"Not really," he answered with yet another maddening grin.

Alicia sighed and let the weight of what he'd done settle onto her.

"I'd better get to work," she said.

"You'd better. But, kid." Jack reached out and squeezed her hand. "Maybe paint something a little more, whaddya call it, lighthearted."

"Lighthearted?"

"Ya know, seascapes or something." He shrugged. "It's funny how you're so happy all the time, yet your paintings are so dark."

"Yes. Fancy that."

"Even though I'll see you in a week," Jack motored on, with that shiny, clarion confidence, all mention of her artwork for now in the past, "I must leave you something to remember me by."

Alicia rolled her eyes, certain he was seconds from shucking his robe. But instead, Jack reached into his pocket and pulled out a red velvet box. Before Alicia could look twice, he flipped open the lid to reveal a necklace glittering with aquamarines and diamonds.

Alicia gasped.

"I can't take it," she said.

They'd been tromping around his house and hers, having sex in a number of places and in a number of positions to boot. Yet this gift was the most inappropriate exchange between them. You didn't give someone diamonds for no reason. For a second, Alicia wondered what he'd ask for in return.

"Come on, kid. This isn't the Hope Diamond. Don't get me wrong, I'd give you that if I could, but Dad's always complaining that we spend too much money. This was the biggest piece of ice I could score, without hitting Pop's auditing threshold."

Alicia frowned. Talk of accounting was one way to kill a romantic surprise.

"I thought the floral pattern was perfect," he said, and nudged the box toward her. "Special and lovely, exactly like you."

"It's too ornate!"

"I'm going to send you to Mother for help on your thank-yous."

Jack stood and moved behind Alicia. His sleeve brushed against her cheek as he draped the necklace across her breastbone. A strand of hair caught when he triggered the clasp.

"I can't accept this," Alicia said as Jack sat down. "I'd be afraid to lose it!"

She fingered the jewels, which were cool and heavy against her skin.

"I have no experience with precious gems," she said. "It'd all end in disaster."

"First off, you're more precious than the whole deal and several times over."

Alicia turned away. If only Jack understood that her value had been established as far less, about a dozen years ago, in an alley in Radom. Alicia pictured her father's kind face, and the watch he gave to secure her fate. Could Father have saved all of them, if he'd had something like this?

"Anyhow," Jack said, "you'll probably take better care of it than a person with so-called experience. Last week Eunice left an eighteen-thousand-dollar necklace in a hotel suite in Chicago. It was stolen, of course."

"But at least your sister had a place to wear it. Visualize this neck-lace in Mrs. Neill's kitchen, surrounded by all that green linoleum. What a sight."

"Don't wear it in the kitchen, then."

He took a sip of wine and tipped his head.

"Why don't you stay here?" he said.

"Here?"

Alicia looked up.

"You bet. Why not?"

He asked this often. *Why not?* How wonderful to see life in that way. "Why not" to necklaces, to mansions, to national office. "Why not" to it all.

"I can't stay here without you," Alicia said. "It'd be . . ."

Odd? Lonely? Unseemly? Embarrassing when someone called the police?

"It's be strange," she said. "Not right."

"I would've thought by now, my house might feel like home. You've been in every corner of it."

"That's not true. I've never even been upstairs!"

"So?" Jack shrugged. "I've hardly been up there myself. Really, there's not much to it. Just a bunch of bedrooms. The movie theater and wine cellar are much more entertaining. As is my bedroom."

Alicia groaned.

"So that's your big hang-up?" he said. "You've never been up-stairs?"

"It's not a hang-up, merely a fact."

"Come on, then." He snapped to his feet. "I'll give you a tour, because I want you to think of this as your home, too."

"My home? I'm only the . . ."

Alicia clamped together her lips. Only the *what?* The former help? The new girlfriend? The something else?

"Are you coming?" Jack asked, mostly out the door.

"Fine," she said, rising to her feet. "Show me the untold secrets of the Kennedy manse."

"The lone secret is that the furniture is even more outdated upstairs than it is down here."

Jack took her hand while they walked, but dropped it when they reached the stairs. She fought a pout as he gripped the banister and lurched up the first few steps.

Of course, she thought. That was why his bedroom was on the ground floor, because the stairs were sometimes too much to take. She felt like an utter clod.

"I don't need to see your family's private quarters," she said. "Let's finish the wine."

"You wanted to see it, and that's what's going to happen."

Jack trudged upstairs with increased conviction. She followed, watching the floor so she didn't have to witness his shirks and grimaces. When they reached the top, he twisted out his spine.

"All right," he said, "prepare to be underwhelmed."

Jack led her from one end to the other, ticking through the bedrooms, which were as unremarkable as promised. One needed quantity over quality with so many children, Alicia supposed, though Mrs. Kennedy's floral and white-lace ocean-view suite was an exception. Rose hadn't been to Hyannis Port in weeks, but her sweet, powdery scent lingered.

When they reached the Ambassador's room, Jack hesitated.

"This is where Pop sleeps," Jack said, and prodded open the door with his foot. "It's nothing special. You can poke around, but I feel odd going inside."

Jack rotated away from his father's room, and Alicia stole a glance. Something caught her eye. It was a painting—a curious circumstance, as one of the first things she noticed about the Kennedys was their lack of art.

"Wait a second," she said.

Alicia took a few steps and stopped. Her legs went weak.

"Everything okay?" Jack asked.

"Your father's room," she said. "There's a painting in it."

Alicia heard the clomp of Jack's feet as he approached.

"Oh, yeah." He snorted. "That wretched thing. He bought it off some slut for twenty bucks. Caused a big uproar with Mother. Naturally, she was infinitely more peeved about the twenty bucks than the bimbo or the crappy art. He doesn't even like it. I think he keeps it up to prove some kind of point."

He snickered and Alicia stiffened.

"Sorry, kid," he said, "you probably didn't want that sorta peek under the Kennedy skirt. I know you're sensitive to the particulars of their relationship."

Alicia shook her head, for it was not about their marriage but instead the "crappy" art.

She recognized the painting. She recognized the building and its majestic domes and spires, the bone inlay and mosaic facade. It had been one of Alicia's favorite places in Łódź, which was why she put it on canvas.

"What building is it?" she asked, her throat dry, her voice crackling. "Do you know?"

"Probably a church or cathedral or something. Beats me." Jack grabbed her hand. "Come on, enough about my father's ill-begotten art. There are a few hours left until daybreak, and I need a week of Alicia, at least."

HYANNIS PORT

Alicia probably had more paint in her hair and on her body than on the canvasses themselves, but at least there was paint, and this was progress.

Was her work good? Was it awful? Somewhere in her flurry of production, Alicia lost the ability to tell. Mostly she saw indiscriminate smears of color; mostly she heard Jack's words.

Wretched. Crappy.

That Joe Kennedy was the owner of her one sold piece was a referendum on Alicia's talents, but whether for better or for worse remained a mystery. Alicia couldn't think about that now. She had to get ready for her show.

Her goal was ten. Alicia had the five unsold pieces, and she'd recently completed Park Źródliska and the Fabryczna railway station, to bring the total to seven. Partway through her eighth piece, a spinning mill, Alicia fell into a fit of despair and took a razor right through it. There was something garish and unsettling about the red of the mill. Now Alicia was trying a seascape, as Jack advised.

"Alicia."

She jumped, and spun around, crashing and knocking and nearly sending her entire repertoire into a dominoes-style collapse.

"George," she said, panting. "You startled me. I almost ruined my whole show."

Her offered no apologies, but George would not view this as a situation necessitating amends. Was it his fault that Alicia was jumpy? No, it was not.

"Don't worry about it," she said, slipping between easels. "It's nice to have some company. I could use a break."

"A break?" he said. "At nine o'clock in the morning?"

"It's morning?" Alicia's eyes bugged. "I thought you were just home from work. Good grief, I must've been at this all night!"

Mrs. Neill had granted Alicia use of the attic for her studio, thus accounting for the tight space and her inability to determine the time of day. Unexpectedly light-headed, Alicia placed a hand on a wood beam. She *had* been up all night, hadn't she?

"Are you planning on coming to work today?" George said. "You've missed three shifts so far and Paul is starting to ask questions. *You're* the one who got him to fire Dewey so that you could have more hours."

Alicia winced. She'd been a delinquent these days, it was true, but who had time to dole out Junior Mints when a gallery show was in the offing? It was a risk, but Paul paid her forty dollars per week. Alicia only had to sell a few paintings to compensate for the lost wages. Once this show was over, she could return to her job, and do it better than before. She'd even wear the ghastly uniform every day, instead of when she was in the mood, which was almost never.

"George, I can't go to work," Alicia said. "It's only for a few more days."

"Paul isn't going to buy that you've been 'sick' this long."

"You can survive without me. I'm no projectionist," she said with a wink.

"It appears you're making a joke," George huffed, "but who is the person responsible for delivering a film to the public? Who receives the jeers when something goes awry? With you out, I'm expected to work the candy and the projector, and the situation is ripe for catastrophe."

"But the Hyannis is closed for the season. Why can't Paul feed the films and you work the counter? For now?"

"Because I'm the projectionist," George said.

Alicia patted him on the shoulder.

"We know."

Alicia sighed and skated past George. It was stuffy in that room, a bit crazy-making. George was getting blurry as they spoke.

"I'm going downstairs for breakfast," she said. "If you'd like to join me."

"I already ate."

"You can still join me."

"And do what?"

"Oh, George," Alicia said, chuckling, feeling a tad maniacal. "You're such a funny man."

In the kitchen, Alicia found Mrs. Neill at the table reading a paper in her nightgown. Her gray-blond hair was teased and wild, her face still wrinkled from sleep.

"Good morning," Alicia said, and retrieved her cottage cheese from the icebox. "Is there still coffee? Or shall I make another pot?"

"Goodness! Alicia!" Mrs. Neill looked up, eyes wide with alarm. "Have you heard the terrible news? Your beau's grandfather has passed! It's right here in the paper." She tapped the article with one stubby finger. " 'Former Boston mayor expired at eighty-seven.' "

"Oh, no," Alicia said with a frown. "Jack must be crushed."

He was close with the politically minded John Fitzgerald, so close that they shared a name. Jack spoke of his grandfather often and, contrary to rumors, it was Honey Fitz, not the Ambassador, who convinced Jack to go into politics.

"Should we send flowers?" Mrs. Neill asked. "To the family? This is so devastating!"

Alicia nodded. Although, eighty-seven: that was some life. Plus, he'd passed after a "long illness," as it said right there in print. Alicia had never known anyone to live that long. Of course, she couldn't express these sentiments to Jack.

She peered over Mrs. Neill's shoulder and skimmed the article.

Yet to the last he held high hopes for a brilliant career for "John F's" favorite grandson, Congressman John Fitzgerald Kennedy, elected in 1946.

His daughter, Mrs. Rose Elizabeth Kennedy, wife of Joseph P. Kennedy, former Ambassador to Great Britain, is in Paris. . . .

Suddenly, George materialized in the doorway, appearing troubled, as if he'd walked in on someone else's compromised position.

"Mother, why are you in a state of mild hysteria?"

"There's been a death in the family!" Mrs. Neill cried.

"The family?" George said. "Are there people I don't know about?"

"I'm referring to Jack's grandfather!"

"Jack who?" His eyes skirted toward Alicia. "Jack *Kennedy*? Has anyone in this room even met the grandfather?"

"George, have a little compassion."

As Mrs. Neill and her son bickered about what might constitute an actual tragedy, Alicia walked toward the counter, picking chunks of paint from her hair as she went. She pulled a compact from her handbag, and checked her reflection. She did not look all that bad.

"I'll send Jack a cable," Alicia said, powdering her nose.

She swiped her lips with her trademark red.

"That's sweet," Mrs. Neill said. "Then you can, I don't know, bake him some sweets for when he comes to town, for the show? Oh, did I mention? I found Mr. Neill's tripod and camera. I can't wait to document your big day. Don't worry, I'll practice first!"

Alicia clicked her compact shut.

"Thank you," she said. "You're always so generous."

"So, you're definitely *not* going to work today?"

"Oh, Georgie, leave her alone. Work at a time like this? Really! But, Alicia dear, don't you want to change? Those dungarees have seen better days. Also, they are dungarees."

"It's fine," Alicia said, dazed.

Maybe it was the lack of food, or the lack of sleep, or the dust in Mrs. Neill's crawlspace. Or perhaps it was sadness for Jack, and for Mrs. Kennedy, too. Yes, Honey Fitz had enjoyed a long life. Even more reason that he'd be missed by the people left behind.

"I probably won't see anyone I know," Alicia said. "And it'll only take a minute."

"Work, Alicia?" George said. "The job you so desperately needed?"

"I'll see you all no later than ten."

03OCT50
JOHN F KENNEDY=
    322 OLD HOUSE BLDG WASHDC=

DEAR JACK SO SAD TO HEAR OF YOUR GRAND-
FATHERS PASSING WILL GIVE FULL CONDOLENCES
THIS WKND MUCH LOVE=
    ALICIA=

HYANNIS PORT

Alicia walked briskly down Main Street, the wind stirring her hair and stinging her lips. Mrs. Neill had broken the news, but Alicia had to see for herself.

She approached the glass door, and cupped both hands beneath the gold foil letters to peek inside. The room was dark and empty, nothing but four walls and a floor. When she stepped back, Alicia saw a paper tacked to the doorframe. The notice was weathered and the nail holding it up had already started to rust.

> *Thank you for a great season! See you in May!*
> *—Hyannis Gallery & The Cape Cod Art Association*

Alicia slumped on the doorstep. She pulled both knees in to her chest and let a few tears fall. How silly to cry about art in a world like this, but no one was looking and she'd been holding it in too long. Here was a sign—an honest-to-goodness sign—that Alicia would not get her chance.

She thought of Mrs. Neill, decked out in her nicest skirt, dead husband's tripod at the ready. She thought of George, spiffed up in black slacks and a skinny black tie, to match his specs and hair. And she thought of Jack. Alicia felt like she was disappointing him, too, though one would rightly see it as the other way around. Perhaps if she'd been a bit more special, a dash more talented, Jack would've kept his promise.

"What now?" she asked the sky and blustering clouds.

Her lantern-sleeved jacket flapped in the breeze.

Was she an artist, then? Or was she just a candy-counter girl? Alicia inhaled with a shudder. Maybe the answer didn't matter. Or maybe it meant everything.

"You left your paintings at home," said a voice.

Alicia looked up, then smiled through her tears. George had a camera looped around his neck, and was leaning on the tripod.

"The gallery is closed," he noted.

"That seems to be the shape of things."

Alicia pushed herself to standing and brushed off the skirt she'd purchased last week. It was the newest style, a slim wraparound number in a cinnamon hue. She'd almost bought the red, but didn't want to risk competing with her work. Alas, no one would see the art, much less be distracted by her.

"Do you like my outfit, George?" she asked, and exerted some effort at a twirl, though this season's silhouettes were not made for such things.

"I don't know anything about fashion," he said. "So I can't offer a review."

Alicia laughed and shook her head.

"I don't want a review," she said. "Only for someone to notice."

"Well." George cleared his throat. "You look beautiful. Is that okay to say?"

Alicia touched George's chin with a gloved hand.

"It's perfect," she said. "Thank you for making my day. Well, it's time to go home."

Purse hanging from the crook of her arm, Alicia walked a few paces before realizing she was alone. She swiveled toward George, who hadn't moved a stitch.

"I'd like to buy your paintings," he said.

"George . . ."

"I have a budget of one hundred dollars. How many can I acquire? I want the best pieces, of course. Not the seascape. Kind of seems like you gave up on that one."

Alicia laughed. For a second she felt okay.

"You can't spend a hundred dollars to make a girl happy!"

"I thought artwork was supposed to make the *purchaser* happy," he said.

"Yes, if the person buying it really wants the piece. It must speak to him; otherwise, it's just something colorful to put on a wall."

"Who says your work doesn't speak to me? Also, I don't think you're in a position to be asking someone *not* to buy your art."

"It's not your style. Remember what you told me? Art moves. It talks."

"I dunno what to say. I find myself invested in your work. It's melancholy. I like things that are dark."

"Spoken like a true projectionist." Alicia walked toward him. "You can't waste your money on this."

"Is it a waste, though? Or a good investment? It should go up in value, because I'm getting you on the ascent."

"I appreciate your very generous view of my future. It will go up, but only if I make a name for myself."

"Obviously you'll do that," he said, with a roll of the eyes.

Alicia laughed again. She did not expect to feel such lightness, given the message on the door.

"I'll sell you one painting," she said. "And you must choose it, not me."

"Fine. If that's the deal you want to strike," George said, and pulled out his wallet. "You need to learn to negotiate."

"I know what I'm doing, Mr. Neill," she said, and cocked a brow.

"Do you?" George said, and matched his brow to hers. "That's funny, because it seems to me that nobody ever taught you when to say yes, or how to say no."

CONGRESSMAN WOULD HELP

The Boston Daily Globe, October 13, 1950

HYANNIS PORT

When she heard Jack's voice, that unmistakable clip with its dropped *r*'s and extra *r*'s at the stretching of one syllable into two, Alicia did the absurd. She hid, in a closet, beside a bucket and a mop.

"She was here a second ago," George said. "Now . . . gone. I really don't understand her sometimes."

Jack laughed and Alicia's insides felt at once filled with feathers. She clutched her belly to squash them down.

"That's the way of broads, pal," Jack said. "They don't make any goddamned sense yet we love 'em all the same. Tell her I stopped by, would ya? I'm only on the Cape until tomorrow."

Alicia held her breath. Soon the Center's front door opened and then swooshed closed again. Alicia waited a full ninety seconds before slinking into the light.

"What was *that* about?" George wanted to know.

Alicia shrugged, because she didn't understand either. Jack sought her out, which was something, but so was the forgotten gallery show and the unanswered telegram. Alicia wasn't up for any half-baked excuses or, worse, no excuses at all.

"Isn't he your beau?" George said.

At first, she took this for a snide remark, and so Alicia looked at him crookedly in return. Then she remembered this was George, and he never meant any malice.

"That depends," Alicia said. "Would a beau arrange an art show and then forget, and then never acknowledge the forgetting in the first place?"

Alicia shook her head, embarrassed that she'd risked her job for a politician's promise. She knew better. Even someone like her, a refugee with next to nothing, even *she* had something to lose. How had Alicia not learned that by now?

"Sometimes life circumstances get in the way," George said.

"Excuse me?" Alicia blinked. "I'm surprised you're on his side."

"I'm not on anyone's side. But didn't someone die?"

"Well, yes . . ."

"And isn't he campaigning?" George said. "That's what you told Mother. A different city every night."

Alicia nodded reluctantly. The schedule, it'd been one explanation she'd given for his absence, a way to "save face," as the saying went. But it was also true, as was the fact of Grandpa Fitzgerald's demise.

"How come you always have an explanation for the most convoluted of circumstances?" she asked.

"That's funny," George answered, "I was going to ask how you always find yourself in the most convoluted of circumstances in the first place."

"I'll let you know when I figure it out."

Alicia meandered toward the front door and peered outside. The streets were quiet, other than the occasional dead leaf tumbling on the sidewalk. In front of the Center was a rack; attached to it was a single blue bike.

"Hey, George," Alicia said, slinking up beside him. "Is that Paul's bike out there?"

"Is it blue? Then, yes." He sighed. "Who rides a bike in this weather?"

"Do you know where he is? And how long ago he left?"

"Dumont's for lunch," George said. "About ten minutes ago. I don't care for the direction of this conversation."

"Perfect!" Alicia scurried to the door. "I'm having my lunch break now. If anyone asks, I borrowed Paul's bike! Not to worry, I'll take the utmost care!"

"You don't get a lunch break when you start at eleven!" George called, but Alicia was already outside.

After yanking the bike from its rack, Alicia wheeled it along, thinking she was lucky she wore the uniform that day, given the trousers involved.

At the corner, Alicia lunged up onto the seat and sent a prayer to the heavens. If anyone was up there, would He please help her body remember how to ride?

Alicia wobbled and weaved for several blocks, almost crashing into three different cars. In her path, seagulls squawked and then scattered. Somewhere, the ferry blew its horn. Then, her memories clicked into place, and soon Alicia was sailing down the road in something akin to a straight line.

She coasted toward Greenwood Avenue, where the homes got bigger, the trees denser. After a series of quick rights and lefts, Alicia swung around the corner and to the end of a cul-de-sac. She stopped beside the flagpole and dropped her bike into the gravel.

Marching up the front stairs, Alicia gathered her wits, and swiped the sweat that'd bubbled beneath her nose. She punched the bell, and was startled by the answerer. Mrs. Kennedy was tinier than she remembered.

"Miss Darr?"

Alicia smiled. That Rose Kennedy remembered her name was an achievement of some kind.

"Mrs. Kennedy, how are you doing?"

The woman didn't answer and instead surveyed Alicia, head to toe.

"Goodness gracious, what is that you have on?" Rose asked, making no effort to hide her distaste.

"It's a uniform. I didn't pick it myself."

"I should hope not. Dear, you have a lovely figure and that outfit is doing you no favors. Have you seen the latest collections from Paris?"

"No, I haven't had the chance."

"What a shame," Mrs. Kennedy said. "Please. Come in."

She gestured, and Alicia followed.

"I read about the passing of your father," Alicia said. "And I'm so sorry. He seemed like a formidable man. He was obviously quite dedicated to his family, which, as far as I'm concerned, is the best thing you can say about a person."

"He was a wonderful father, and that's only the start."

They proceeded farther into the home. Alicia didn't know whether to ask for Jack, or simply follow Rose to whatever room they were going to.

"I lit a candle," Alicia said. "For your father. At St. Francis."

Alicia flinched, jarred by her own fib. She hadn't attended church since the morning after Labor Day, but it seemed like the right thing to say, something that'd comfort a woman like Rose. Mrs. Neill had a candle in the house somewhere, Alicia reasoned. She'd light it tonight, in arrears.

"How nice," Mrs. Kennedy said, and smiled in her taut and lipless way.

She stopped and turned around.

"Remind me, dear, are you here to see Pat or Eunice?" she asked. "It must be Eunice. Pat's not here."

"Actually . . . it's Jack?" Alicia said, her voice leaping to new heights.

Rose studied her for a good, long while. Alicia was nearly ready to settle for Eunice when Mrs. Kennedy called out in her raspy, shrill voice.

"Jack! A young woman is here to see you!"

The house remained silent and Alicia's perspiration returned for a second show. She thought about the bike, and Paul, and her job, and wondered what she was doing at this house. How come she never recognized a risk until after she'd taken it? It was a wonder she was still alive.

"Yes, Motha?" said a voice.

Alicia wiped her top lip and glanced up, and there stood Jack, in the hallway, looking far too bright and tanned for midfall.

"Alicia Darr," he said, face breaking into a grin. "It's swell to see ya. But I gotta ask, what the hell took you so long?"

They sat in the sunroom, which was a different place in the low October light. Mrs. Kennedy had just left for her daily three-mile walk, this time pushing her mother in a wheelchair, a horsehair blanket draped over the woman's lap.

"Thanks for the telegram," Jack said, as Rose drifted out of sight. "Sorry I never got the chance to reply. I figured an in-person thank-you would be better."

"So, you did receive it," Alicia said, finding her steam about it beginning to cool. "I wondered, since I'd heard nothing in return."

"Sorry, kid," Jack said, and shook his head. "I probably received a thousand notes, calls, and cables. So many I couldn't possibly keep them straight. And, really, it's not a manners deal, to respond to a condolence."

"I suppose that's true," Alicia said, sinking into her seat, feeling foolish.

Of course Jack received a tidal wave of sympathy. Of course it'd be unwieldy to respond to each one. Jack was grieving, and he was campaigning, and he had a regular job, too.

"I know you weren't obligated," Alicia said, "I just wanted to be there for you. My heart hurt, to think of your sorrow."

"Aw, kid, you're sweet."

Jack launched himself to standing and began to pace the room.

"It's easy to forget," he said, "that he's gone. The campaign keeps me so busy that sometimes I don't have a second to think. Then some-one introduces me using *his* name, and it knocks me on my ass."

Jack sat down again, reclining into his seat back, stiff as a plank. Alicia noticed that his tan was yellowing, and he looked tired, and a bit jowly. She fought the urge to ruffle his hair.

"I'll tell ya one thing," he said. "It was a damned show, his funeral. Thousands lined the streets. He was loved. And he made a difference in Boston."

"He must've been so proud of you," Alicia said, thinking of the people she'd loved, and lost, and the funerals they'd never get to have. "How is your mother taking it?"

"Mother? What does she have to do with it?"

"It was *her* father."

"Yeah, well. Rose Kennedy's not so hot, as far as daughters go," Jack said with a grunt. "She didn't make it to the damned funeral. Too busy shopping in gay Par-ee."

He swirled a hand.

"Yes, but she tried, didn't she?" Alicia said. "I read in the paper . . ."

"Depends on one's definition of 'try,'" he said, and rolled his eyes. "She could've, if she wanted to badly enough. The woman has money and planes at her disposal, and she knew the end was near. It's a trav-esty, is what it is. The man gave her the world."

Jack slapped his hands together and jumped up.

"No use moping. He created a legacy, and that will live on. There's more to life than the breaths we take."

"'As tho' to breathe were life! Life piled on life,'" Alicia said, the words forming without her having to think of them.

Jack shot a glance in her direction, his top lip slightly raised.

"'Were all too little, and of one to me,'" he said.

Alicia grinned.

"'Little remains: but every hour is saved . . .'"

"Damn, she knows Tennyson too," Jack said. "Did I tell you that was my favorite poem?"

"No," Alicia said, delighted to have their minds meet in this way. "I love 'Ulysses.' It's so sad, yet inspiring at the same time."

"It's the perfect poem for my grandfather. Just like Honey Fitz, Ulysses isn't satisfied by his own accomplishments. He's not one to rest on his laurels, because there's always a new obstacle, a new challenge to face."

"Or a new challenge to *chase*." Alicia smiled. "Actually, the poem reminds me of you. Ulysses isn't ambitious, he's downright impatient for new experiences. And there's his affection for the sea."

"How'd you find out?" Jack asked.

"About your grandfather? It was in the papers."

"No. I meant about your parents. How did you find out they were gone?"

Alicia's face went white. She said nothing.

"Tell me, Alicia *Dahr*-ling," Jack said, his full attention locked on her. "You went from Łódź to Radom to convent school. And then, to my great fortune, you ended up here. But what happened after you left school? What happened to your parents? What are the details you left out?"

"I'm not really comfortable . . ."

"Listen, you don't have to tell me," he said, sounding needled. "You can ignore the question, and keep hiding behind your red lipstick and good cheer. But I ask as someone who knows you. I ask as someone who cares."

"I'd just turned fourteen," Alicia let slip.

Jack gave a close-lipped smile. She couldn't go back now.

"A group of us," she said, "older girls, we had moved to a different convent, farther from Warsaw. As I unpacked my things, Father Skalski summoned me to the chapel. He told me that my parents were captured in a roundup in Radom. My father was deported, and died in Treblinka. My mother was likewise presumed dead."

"Aw, kid," Jack clucked, his eyes devoid of their devilish glint. "I can't fathom hearing that, and at that age."

"It was truly awful," Alicia said through the gathering tears. "Alas, I wasn't the only girl in the convent to receive such news. I was lucky, in a way. So many had family members who vanished, unable to be traced. There is something to be said for a conclusion, if nothing else."

"Why do you have to be so damned gracious?" Jack shook his head. "I'm sorry, kid. I don't know why I keep saying that, but I can't think of anything better. Pretty pathetic for a guy who talks for a living."

"Don't apologize. I came to comfort *you*, not the other way around. Yet, here we are. I don't know how we traveled from your grandfather in Boston, all the way to my parents in Poland."

Jack chuckled dryly.

"I can tell you're about to clam up on me," he said. "I get it. I'm done with death for today, too."

Without warning, Jack sniffed his underarms.

"Jesus, I'm gamy," he said. "I'm going to change my shirt."

Alicia stared. That Jack never dwelled on anything, figuratively or in fact, was sometimes quite jarring.

"That's fine," Alicia said, remembering Paul's bike discarded on the drive. "I should go. I'm on a bit of an unauthorized lunch break."

"Do you have plans tonight?" he asked.

"Not as far as I know, but I'd have to check with George, to make sure."

"George?" he scoffed. "Don't tell me you're sleeping with that geek!"

"Jack Kennedy!" Alicia said. "What a thing to say! Of course I'm not sleeping with George. But I need to butter up everyone at the Center, because I've missed so much work."

"Missed work?" Jack said. "What's wrong? Were you sick and didn't tell me?"

"No, nothing like that. It was a few weeks ago. You might remember . . ."

"How about this," Jack said, slapping down her attempt to broach the topic of her failed show.

He went to sit beside her.

"Meet me at the Panama Club at nine o'clock."

Jack was close enough to touch, yet remained a hairsbreadth away.

"The Panama Club?" Alicia said, glancing at his trousers, despite her good sense. "Isn't it closed for the season?"

"It's closed to the general public, but I have my ways. Nine o'clock, Miss Darr. Don't be late."

With that, Jack stood and exited the room. The air at once went cold.

Alicia tried the front door, which was locked, then jiggled the side door, too.

The experience was all too familiar, with an extra reminder from the shuttered gallery a few doors away. After several more tries, she stepped out onto the sidewalk and peered up at the sign, and its alternating arcs of white and yellow.

"Looking for someone?"

Alicia flipped around to see the impish grin she so adored. There Jack stood, simultaneously dapper and ruffian, a sophisticated man crossbred with a disheveled boy.

"Why, hello, Representative Kennedy," Alicia said coquettishly. "Why are you cruising the streets at this inappropriate hour?"

"Why are *you* cruising the streets, one might ask?"

"I was scheduled to meet a handsome gentleman in this very spot, but he's not shown up. You'll have to do."

He laughed, eyes sparking in the dark.

"Then it's my lucky day. Come on." He jerked his head. "Follow me."

As she trailed Jack, Alicia noticed he was carrying a picnic basket, like the one used on the *Victura*. The nip in the air told of fall, but last summer seemed more than one season ago.

At the Panama's rear entrance, Jack fiddled with the door, eventually freeing the lock in a manner that'd get any other man arrested. Alicia pictured the headline in *The Barnstable Patriot:*

SCOUNDRELS BUST INTO PANAMA CLUB!

"Should we be here?" she asked, as Jack stalked confidently inside.

He led her through the kitchen, and to the ballroom, where he'd laid out a blanket. A Victrola and a set of candles were nearby.

"Is this for me?" she said.

"Sure. Who else?"

Jack plunked the basket onto the floor.

"I had Jeannette make us sandwiches, given my previous attempt at a meal."

"Smart choice," Alicia said, then lowered herself onto the blanket. "I'm famished. And thirsty, too."

"Good. I also brought beer."

Alicia sat on her left hip, and swung her legs to the right. These new slim skirts were not made for picnicking. Alicia wondered how Pat and Jean and Eunice navigated the change in style. Probably, for picnics, they always wore shorts.

Meanwhile, Jack took his time to sit. Once on the floor, he unwrapped two sandwiches, and poured their drinks.

"Chee-ahs," he said, and held up a glass. "To the magnificent A-lees-ier *Dahr*-ling, the prettiest girl I know."

They clinked glasses. Alicia took a sip. The bubbles tickled her throat. She'd have to make sure not to drink too efficiently.

"I hope you don't mind the setting," Jack said, and licked a stripe of foam from his top lip. "Or roughing it on the ground."

"I've certainly dined in worse situations."

"Ha. Me too. The campaign trail is nothing but 'worse situations,' one right after the other. Dingy rooms. Shitty beds. The most terrible food you could ever consume."

"Funny, I picture the campaign trail full of glitz and glamour. Swanky hotels, flashbulbs popping. You are a Kennedy, after all."

"If there was any glamour whatsoever, I'd bring you along so I didn't miss you so damned much."

Alicia responded with a happy sigh.

"I do like gettin' out there though," he said. "Dreary accommodations notwithstanding. Keeps my mind off stuff, too. Missing you. Missing Honey Fitz. Fuck." He shook his head. "I still can't believe he's gone. On the other hand, he outlived Kick and Joe. How the hell did that happen?"

"If only death had some logic. My father, he—"

"How would you want to die?" Jack asked.

"Beg pardon?" she said, forehead raised to the heavens.

"What would you pick?" he asked. "Shooting, freezing, fire, drowning, or poison?"

He rattled off these options, a rehearsed list. Alicia had been forced to contemplate her own death many times, but it was usually an either/or situation, nothing to do with the quality of it, nothing that invoked any degree of choice.

"I'm not especially keen to discuss this," she said.

"We're all gonna die at some juncture, kid."

While they'd indeed all die at some *junk-sha,* why think about that now? If she hadn't known Jack's history, she would've assumed such speculation was reserved for the sun-kissed and the privileged, people unaccustomed to loss.

"I'd pick poison," he said, with the assuredness of a scholar who'd mastered the topic. "Swift and easy. You wouldn't even know what's going on."

"It'd depend on the poison, and how it was administered."

Alicia knew a few who died that way. Her own father was gassed, which was more or less the same thing. "Easy" didn't seem like the right word.

"Trust me," Jack said. "It'd be the way to go. What's your choice?"

"I don't have one and I don't like this conversation. Death will come whenever it damned well pleases, and in its own way, and there's no use worrying about it in advance."

"You see?" Jack tapped a beer bottle against his right temple. "This is why we get along so well. We think the same way."

"I said nothing about poison."

"No, I meant about living in the moment."

Alicia tore the crust off her sandwich and took a bite. She did agree with Jack on this.

"Gotta get to the living, while the living is good," he said. "Personally, I don't think I'll make it past age forty-five."

"Jack!" She began choking on the sandwich. "What a thing to say!"

"It's true." He shrugged. "My back, plus my recurring . . . malaria . . . the doctors pump me full of chemicals all year long. A body can only take so much."

She looked down to see that her fingers were speckled with crumbs. As Alicia wiped her hands, she wondered if Jack was more affected by his grandfather's death than he'd let on. George was probably right. It was understandable—forgivable—that he'd forgotten her show.

"Alas," Jack said, and groaned as he moved up onto his knees. "My body might be shot to hell, but it can still dance."

He strained to start the Victrola. Soon, the music crackled.

"Come." He staggered to his feet, and offered a hand. "Let's cut the rug."

Alicia rose with caution, a confused reluctance, but was quick to soften into his embrace.

"I love this tune," he said, guiding her back and forth. "'September Song.'"

And the days grow short when you reach September

"It reminds me of you," he said. "Because we met in September."

Alicia closed her eyes. They'd met in August, but there was no use correcting such a fine point.

" 'September, November . . .' " he whispered in her ear, sending shivers along her spine. " 'These precious days I'll spend with you.' "

HYANNIS PORT

It was Alicia's first American winter—Oklahoma stayed relatively warm, so it didn't count—and she wasn't prepared for the total desolation after the holiday lights came down. The temperature didn't change all that much, yet the world was colder by large degrees.

In December, Hyannis had been magical. Shopwindows were decked out, each more impressive than the last: Osborne Refrigeration's sleigh and reindeer, Hyannis High School's nativity scene, and Bass River Savings Bank's forty-foot decorated Christmas tree. On Main Street, lights twinkled and Bing Crosby played on a loop.

Now the cheer and good tidings were gone, replaced by a thick sheen of frost. Bing's dulcet voice was exchanged for Communist hysteria, and Jack's absence didn't help Alicia's mood. In those winter months, they'd stayed in contact, but every minute was stolen, fleeting. They'd discussed a trip to Palm Beach, but time slipped away before they made plans.

"I don't really like Florida anyhow," he'd said.

They spent exactly three nights together, the most recent in

Boston, after Alicia undertook a journey involving two trains, a bus, and ninety minutes spent in the Hotel Statler lobby because Jack was always late.

But he was a busy man, so who was Alicia to complain? Jack was a congressman (reelected in November), and the key cog in the Kennedy machine. Now he was abroad, scoping out Europe's rearmament program with his pal Torby in tow. They'd been to England, and to France. The itinerary also included Spain, Italy, Germany, Yugoslavia, Greece, and Turkey. So far, he'd sent one cable, saying he wished she was there.

"I don't know why the Russians are surprised," Alicia said, late one night, while sitting in the family room with George, a newspaper in her lap. "Is it really shocking that West Germany would want to join forces with the West? Given the tyrants leering over their shoulder?"

"People don't usually regard themselves as tyrannical," George said, and flicked on the television.

"The Russians do," Alicia said. "And with great pride. I can't wait to hear what Jack thinks about it all."

George turned the television to *Amateur Hour,* his favorite show. Never a greater emotional investment had he made than in the lives of strangers who could sing and dance.

"I think the West Germans should arm themselves," Alicia said. "I don't trust those Russians. I don't trust them one bit."

George hated politics, and so Alicia was mostly speaking to herself. It helped to say it out loud, either way. She wanted to sound knowledgeable the next time she spoke to Jack.

As some pipsqueak sang on the stage, Alicia flipped through the paper to find ever more Russians and Reds. She sighed as the wheel spun on the television.

Round and round she goes, and where she stops nobody knows . . .

"Are you afraid?" George asked as a prepubescent baton twirler marched onto the screen. "That the Russians will invade West Germany?"

"I'm afraid of anything they might do."

"Yes, but West Germany is where you're from."

"For Pete's sake, I didn't think you were one of those types. For the hundredth time, I'm *Polish*, not German."

"Yes. We are all aware of your nationality." He rolled his eyes. "Our poor, displaced Pole."

Alicia glared at George, who didn't move. The only motion was the flickering of the television against his glasses.

"I didn't know you were so perturbed about my being a refugee," Alicia said. "I'll try to keep my homeless orphan status to myself."

"Oh, geez. Here we go again. You are the hardest person to have sympathy for."

"Wow, George," Alicia said, lips trembling. "I'm not sure how to take that. . . ."

"Since we're on the subject, are you really an orphan? By the strictest definition of the word?"

"I'm pleased to show you my displaced person card. In case you haven't noticed, I'm very much alone. Me, a few pieces of clothing, and a suitcase in my room. That's my entire world."

"I'd say you have more than a 'few' pieces of clothing," he grumbled.

"I don't have to put up with this," Alicia said, and stood. "When you're ready to apologize, I'll be upstairs."

She tramped across the room, slowly, to give George the opportunity to take back his words.

"So, you're an orphan."

"*Yes*," Alicia said, between clenched teeth.

"All alone in this world?"

"Do you have a hearing problem?"

"Hmm. Then you're sending money to Germany for the hell of it?"

Alicia's body seized. Cold fingers of panic ran along her spine.

"Excuse me?" she managed to croak.

"The money you send overseas, every week," George said. "Who is that for?"

It took her a minute to assemble the pieces of what George had said. When it all snapped together, Alicia gasped. They were being watched, like in Germany, and Poland before. Her life was once again at stake.

"Oh, God," she cried, "we're in trouble. If they're tracking me, and you're letting me live here . . . Oh, God."

Alicia sat down, and dropped her head into her hands. So, it was over. This was it, the disintegration of her big, fat American hope. Alicia could smell the ashes.

"Stop crying," George said. "Girls are so dramatic."

"We're being watched!"

"Being watched? I merely asked why you send money to Germany, when you've always said that you're alone?"

"Who told you?" Alicia looked up, her face red and tearstained. "Who told you about my letters? The government?"

"The government?" George said, and scrunched his nose.

On the television, the host told people to cast their vote by postcard or by phone. *Call JUdson 6-7000!*

"Good gravy," George said. "I didn't hear it from any spies or G-men or anything so exciting. I heard from my mother."

All of Alicia's dread, the clanging and collapsing inside of her, these things suspended. The situation couldn't be too dangerous, if Mrs. Neill was involved.

"How does your mother know?" Alicia asked. She lowered her voice. "Is she a spy?"

"A spy?" George said, almost spitting the word. "Cripes. No. She was chatting with the postman, and he asked when you were planning to bring your family to the States. Something about how it had to be cheaper than sending packages home every week. That was news to her, of course. And to me."

"The postmaster."

Alicia gave a rusty laugh. She hated that her mind had been trained to think the worst, primed to transform garden-variety gossips into instruments of insidious plots.

"Who's in Germany, Alicia?" George asked, facing her straight-on for the very first time.

Usually he looked at everyone sideways, or from the periphery, or not at all.

"It's not something I can explain," Alicia said.

"Who's in Germany?"

"I don't have to answer that. You're not my keeper, or a checkpoint agent."

George bit his lower lip and halfway shook his head. He stood and moved into the doorway. He wasn't going to watch the final act. That was unheard of, especially when it involved a children's musical troupe.

"My mother!" Alicia blurted.

He spun around, forehead raised.

"It's my mother," she said again, tears rolling down her face. "Every week I send her money, as much as I can. Every week I pray I'm one step closer to getting her out of that camp."

George seemed bedeviled by the information, like he hadn't known there were still *camps*. The war left millions without a home. Where did he presume all those people had gone?

Alicia explained that these were not the camps he pictured, nothing quite that grim. Mother's was more of a military-barracks-style outfit, a cinder-block town that, albeit charmless, still had schools and theaters and a library or two.

"It's been six years," George said. "Haven't people gone home?"

That was the problem. The Allies hadn't meant to keep the camps open for that long, but where was home, exactly? Very few of them could repatriate. Many places remained unsafe for Jews, or for anyone not wishing to live under Communist rule. Just because a paper had been signed, and a white flag waved, didn't mean attitudes had changed.

"But your mother?" George said. "I thought some priest told you that both of your parents were dead?"

Yes, a priest had said something along those lines. He said that Father had been rounded up, and had died at Treblinka. The last record of her mother was from a factory in Radom that'd been bombed twice, and Mother was therefore presumed dead. But "presumed" was just a guess.

After the war, with so many displaced, the Allies established tracking bureaus to help families reunite. Alicia left school and secured a job with one of these organizations as a typist, based in Bünde. After clacking out responses and requests for countless inquiries, Alicia completed one for her parents, just in case.

SEARCH BUREAU
CONTROL COMMISSION FOR GERMANY
ENQUIRY CONCERNING MISSING PERSONS
Kopczynski, Mordechai
Kopczynska, Felitzya

Alicia filled out the requisite information: their names, birth dates, birth places, and last known address. She recorded the date of their most recent communication, which was a staggering five years before.

It wasn't that Alicia believed she'd find them; she simply needed definitive proof that they were gone. Life was so transient, in the camp as in Europe, that it was hard to accept anything as the unmitigated truth.

News of her father shot back like a boomerang. He'd died at Treblinka, as Alicia had been told. And her mother? Nothing arrived on Mamusia for days, weeks, months at a time.

Then, one bright June morning, Alicia was filing discharged inquiries when her boss walked in with information for *her*. Mother had been found. She was alive, though not well, and residing in a DP camp in Stuttgart. The nurse who wrote the letter gave the address, and Alicia scraped together every last reichsmark and set off.

"How come you never told me you lived in a camp?" George asked, jaw slack with disbelief. "How do I not know this about you?"

Alicia shrugged. She wasn't hiding it, exactly. It hadn't come up.

"How long did you live there?" he wanted to know.

"About three years," she said. "Until I got my visa."

"You fled to the States." George frowned. "And left your mother behind?"

"You don't understand," Alicia said. "The camps were temporary. People *had* to leave the moment they could. No country would take the ill, or the elderly, or the handicapped or otherwise unable to work. My mother's health is very poor. They told us that there wasn't hope. She'd die in that camp."

As it had so many others', the past decade had decimated Mother's body, and her mind. She'd spent most of the war toiling in munitions factories and salt mines. After that, she lived in a series of concentration camps, though Alicia did not reveal this part to George.

"Don't you see?" she said as George remained fixed in the doorway, his features tweaked into a look of revulsion. "One of us had to get out, in order to save us both. The people who didn't seize their opportunities before the war, most of them ended up dead. Countries were starting to shut their borders and I had to take my chance while it was still available. By the time I received my visa, I was the only person under twenty still left at the camp, aside from the children who'd been born there."

In the end, the hardest choice Alicia ever made was really quite obvious. That's how it was for someone without options. The camps were not designed to last forever. Hundreds of thousands were scattered to the countries that'd take them, but no one wanted the sick. When the camps closed, what would become of them? There were only two ways to leave that place: with a visa or in a hearse.

Two old bags committed suicide this week, her mother last wrote. *It's not so sad. We'll die in this place, one way or another.*

Alicia had to earn enough to move Mother out, if for no other reason than to get her better care in her final days. Sure, the camp had a hospital, but did George ever wonder what happened to the doctors and

nurses from Auschwitz, Treblinka, and the rest? The ones who performed ghastly experiments and brutally hastened the deaths of millions? They were repurposed, sent to DP camps to take care of those
who survived, those they'd already tortured but not quite killed.

"I stand by my decision," Alicia insisted, as Irenka's words ran
through her head: *I see you. I see who you are.*

"My mother *wanted* me to go," she said. "I'll make a better life for
both of us. She's still young. Who knows, maybe a miracle will happen, and she'll recover. I dream of buying her a home, a cottage, at the
foot of a mountain."

A quaint, half-timbered, thatch-roofed *kotten* surrounded by but-
tercups, violets, and alpine rose. Not until she spoke the words did Alicia realize how complete the picture was.

"So that's your plan," George said flatly. "To get your mother out
of the camp?"

"It is," she said.

"Okay then, what are you doing about it?"

"George!" Alicia tossed up her hands. "Do you not see me in front
of you? I moved to America, is what I did."

"Yes, okay." George sniffled, pushed up his glasses. "I usually don't
bother pointing out the obvious, but this cottage? For your mother?
You do realize that you don't have a home for yourself?"

Alicia's mouth fell open.

"Does your mother want me to leave?" she asked.

"Of course not. She loves you like a daughter, more than her actual
daughter, it must be said. I think some part of her wishes, and believes,
that you'll stay forever."

Tears rushed to Alicia's eyes. Sweet Mrs. Neill. How kind. How
generous. Alas, Alicia was not getting drippy-eyed about the woman's
hospitality but instead the unintended weight of George's words.

She believes that you'll stay forever.

What's your plan, George asked, and he was right. Fact of the
matter, Alicia was hardly going to start one life at forty dollars per

week, much less two, especially when these lives had to be made of something more than skirting by.

"Have I offended you?" George said, and glowered. "That's not my intent. I'm just mystified. You realize how little you make, right?"

"So, you *don't* think I'll hit it big hawking Goobers to the summer folk?" Alicia said with a partial smile.

"Definitely not. Especially since you're perennially in danger of getting fired."

Alicia laughed, but said nothing.

"I thought the plan was your art," George said.

"It was. As you can see, it's progressing brilliantly."

She immediately envisioned the Center lobby, the *empty* lobby. Alicia didn't display her pieces anymore, and she hadn't lifted a brush in months.

"You're right, George," she said, "my plan is crap."

"Whoa." He held up both hands. "I didn't say that."

"Regardless, message received."

"I see why you did it," George said.

Alicia blinked.

"Why you came to the States," he said. "Alone."

She blinked again.

"You want to get your mom away from those doctors, obviously," he said. "But you also want to repay her for the risks she took, for getting you out of Łódź, and making sure you were safely at school."

Alicia bobbed her head. That was part of it, yes, though these actions belonged mostly to her dad.

"I hope you get that house for her," he said. "And yours, too. If you want it."

"I want both of these things, and more. George?" she said, a little absently, her mind starting to wander. "What's that American notion? A New Year's dedication?"

"New Year's resolution?"

Alicia nodded and walked toward him.

"I'm going to make one," she said. "A resolution. What do you think?"

"I don't know," he said, and scratched his neck, "these things usually only last a few weeks. They're kind of a joke, if you ask me."

"A drop of encouragement might be nice." Alicia rolled her eyes. "And this is no joke. Let it be known that within one year, everything will be different. My home. My career. My life."

"I don't think you're doing this right. I've personally never made a resolution—who has time for that—but it should be more, I dunno, specific. You want to lose twenty pounds. Take Sunday drives. Swear less. That sort of thing."

"I'd say a new house is quite specific. Or are you implying that I'm fat and swear too much?"

"No! Lord, no!"

"Let it be known." Alicia stomped her foot. "That by the thirty-first of December, in the year of our Lord nineteen fifty-one, I will be an entirely new person."

"Entirely new?" he scoffed. "As in one hundred percent?"

"Maybe not one hundred percent. There are a few good things in my life." She winked. "But, George Neill, wait until December. We'll still be friends, but I'll be so transformed you'll have to ask my name."

BOSTON

The night was cold; the wind whipped and coiled. All around cars honked. People rushed past, often knocking Alicia in their haste. The women rarely stopped. If they did, it was a second's hesitation before tromping onward, as though she'd never been there at all. But the men always paused to take a gander, or offer up a smile.

Alicia shifted between her feet to dance the shivers away. Not even Mrs. Neill's mink coat kept her wholly warm.

"Oh, just the one bit of fancy I've bought in my lifetime," she'd said, when offering it to Alicia.

How she loved that woman, and the ways she surprised.

Thanks to Mrs. Neill, she'd felt quite glamorous stationed beside the Boston Garden, decked out in the coat as well as a tidy black pillbox with rhinestones caught in mesh. But every minute was an hour in the sharp wind, and Alicia suspected that she now looked red-faced, chapped, and maybe a tad cheap.

She didn't confirm the time, but Jack was an hour late, at least. He couldn't have forgotten the ball, she didn't think. He'd sent a car to Hyannis to pick her up. They planned to stay the night in Boston, but

Alicia hadn't contemplated how she might get home, especially if Jack didn't show. The car that delivered her was long gone.

Two men walked past. One told the other to "check out that stacked cookie," then wondered how much her fee was. Alicia turned toward the station. Hopefully there was one more train that night.

"Hey!" called a voice. "Where do ya think you're going?"

Alicia exhaled. Jack. Right on time.

"Oh, Jack," she said with a sigh. "I thought you'd decided not to come."

She moved to face him, irritated that his chronic lack of punctuality resulted in her being mistaken for a whore. But one glimpse of Jack, and he hooked right into Alicia's heart. That shrub of hair, his broad and brilliant grin, and the tuxedo and his unfastened jacket, the pair of which did nothing to hide his gauntness, or the pair of crutches he leaned on.

"Crutches? Again? Jack, what is happening to you?"

Alicia rushed forward, and went to touch his cheek. Jack shirked, the slightest bit.

"Damn, Alicia, your hands are fuckin' cold," he said, throwing on a tight smile. "Despite the gloves."

"Fuckin' cold," she mimicked. "That's some way to speak to a lady."

She'd forgotten Jack's salty mouth, the way he dropped curse words in polite company the same as in company that was rough. People never seemed to take offense, though, probably because it was so easy to get caught up in his flashing intellect, the rat-a-tat of his voice, that unnerving charisma gleaming like gold.

"It's especially uncouth," Alicia said, "when the lady's hands are cold thanks to your tardiness."

"Aw, kid, I'm sorry. My clock's all screwed up and a meeting went late. I should've had Helen call, to let you know I was delayed."

"Helen?" Alicia squinted. "Who's Helen?"

"My new secretary? In the Boston office?" He shook his head. "Sorry 'bout that. I hate thinking of you out here, all alone in the cold."

"That's okay," Alicia said, through her teeth, thinking a call from Helen wouldn't have helped, seeing as how she left the Cape so many hours ago.

"Before tonight's over, you'll forget that you've ever been cold in your life."

"You're lucky I've missed you so much," Alicia said, her breath making puffs of smoke in the air. "But, darling, I have to say, you're terribly thin."

"What? Me?" He made a face. "It's the coat. It has what ya call a 'slimming effect.'"

"I see it in your cheekbones, in your eyes."

"Traveling's a bitch," he said. "The food, the strange hotels, the constant to-and-fro. Haven't been able to eat much since I got back. And, well, you see the crutches here."

He splayed one out, lifting his coat like the world's most endearing (and modest) flasher.

"I'll be better in a few days." He nodded toward the doors. "Shall we?"

Alicia followed Jack, which took some concentration thanks to his crutches and lurching gait. She didn't want to overrun him; Alicia knew he'd want to lead the way.

"Kid, you look terrific," Jack said when they reached the coat check.

Alicia waited for him to comment on the mink as he slid it from her shoulders. But Jack said nothing and passed it to the coat-check girl, along with his crutches.

"What a dress," he said.

Jack whistled and Alicia spun around twice. This was the reaction she imagined when she draped the frock across the counter and asked the saleswoman to ring her up.

"It's a velvet and satin sheath," she told him, and fanned out the shimmery, paper-weight skirt, "with overlay. Fresh off the presses. Or whatever term is used for the latest style. Your mother would know."

"That's some ingenuity right there." Jack grinned. "You can show off your legs, yet still be able to claim you're in a floor-length gown."

"Isn't America great?" Alicia fingered her necklace. "Do you like the ice?"

"Sure do. Looks fab."

Alicia smiled. Truth was, the necklace didn't really go with the halter neck, but she wore it because it was from Jack and therefore the best accessory of all, aside from Jack himself, banged up and hobbled as he was.

They walked inside and Alicia skimmed the program, to see what the night was all about. She'd never been to an event so grand.

72nd Annual Concert and Ball of the Fire and Protective Departments

Thanks to Jack's problem keeping time, they'd missed the concert and floor show. Soon, the medals of valor would be awarded. Jack was to present the Patrick J. Kennedy Medal of Honor, named after his grandfather, a former Boston fire commissioner. It was the first of what was to be an annual prize.

"I presume you're out for dancing," Alicia said, reviewing the list.

Fox-trot, fox-trot, fox-trot, waltz, fox-trot, fox-trot, fox-trot, waltz, fox-trot, waltz, fox-trot, fox-trot, fox-trot, waltz, fox-trot, fox-trot.

"Which is good since the only dance I'm skilled at it is the polka," she joked.

"Yep, yep," Jack said, surveying the room, a wrinkle between his brows. "Only the fox-trot and waltz here."

Within minutes, men began to approach, in pairs and in packs, to shake hands with the congressman and thank him for presenting the award. Jack returned their greetings hardily and with no shortage of back wallops, the very emblem of vim and vigor. Only Alicia could see the whisper of a grimace, the subtle gnashing of his teeth. Only Alicia (and the coat-check girl) knew about the crutches squirreled away.

Alicia met the mayor, the fire commissioner, and the department chief, and fifty more people after that. She met the intended recipient of the Kennedy Medal—a Negro, to her surprise. Every man in the joint wanted to shake hands with Jack, and more than a few women to boot.

"Oh, Jesus," Jack said. "Here comes that fella again. The one with the red nose? I wish I could remember his name."

"Randy," Alicia said.

Jack tilted his head in her direction.

"His name is Randy," she repeated, and smoothed her skirt. "Met your grandfather a few times. Retired from Rescue Company Number Four. Grumbled about how he surely would've received the Kennedy Medal had it been available at the time."

"Well, look at you," he said. "More than a pretty face. But we knew that."

Jack threw on a grin.

"Randy!" he said, voice booming. "We were just talking about you, ya old bastard. My lady friend was mighty impressed with your Fourth Company exploits."

Jack winked over the man's head, which was not difficult, as he was very short.

"She's a charmer," Randy said. "You should probably lock this one down before you seek a higher office. We all know where this is going."

Jack grabbed the man's hand again. He patted his back, and gave a little push, to move him on.

"Fuck," Jack said with a moan.

He slumped against the wall. He was in pain, but Alicia knew better than to point it out. Instead she inched closer toward him, so that he'd not seem so far away.

"I wish you weren't the belle of the ball," Alicia said. "I'm anxious to hear about your trip. What you saw in Europe. How things are shaping up over there."

"Aw, well, you can catch it on the television tomorrow night."

"Yes, me and the rest of the country," Alicia said, and rolled her eyes. "But I'd like to hear it from you."

Jack stared up into the rafters for a minute or two.

"They're certainly ill-equipped, militarily," he said. "Across the board. England, France, Italy . . . they're all under-armed."

"Is that unexpected, really?" Alicia asked. "They've just come out of a war. It's been six years, but really that's not so long."

"That's true," Jack said with a nod. "There's a certain war weariness and the thought of re-arming is not appealing to most. The problem is that Europe is weak, but they can't see it. The leaders seem borderline delusional, which is a problem as the Russian threat is real. Honestly, the only countries that impressed me whatsoever were Spain and Yugoslavia."

Alicia smirked. Jack called himself a Democrat but picked two countries with dictators as ideals.

"What about West Germany?" Alicia asked, a knot in her throat. "What's the sentiment there?"

"It's a precarious position. They're poised to be the most powerful country in Europe, but they've hit a roadblock. They need to join the Atlantic Pact, but are rightly worried this means automatic war with the Reds. Meanwhile, I don't know why *we're* still party to it. Europe is useless, if you ask me."

He closed his eyes.

"What about holding their ground?" Alicia said. "Why can't the Germans just stay the course?"

"You need weapons even for that."

"What was it like in West Germany?" she asked. "How did the people seem?"

"Like Germans, I guess."

Jack put more of his spine to the wall, and grimaced once again.

"Did they seem happy?" Alicia asked. "Well-fed? Are groceries in ample supply?"

"Why are you so concerned with the Germans?"

Jack opened his eyes.

"I'm not concerned with the *Germans*. . . ." she said.

"Jesus, look at that motherfuckah over there," Jack said. "He's smashed. . . ."

Alicia turned, then stopped as she sensed something—or someone—drift into her periphery. Her heart gave a hop.

"Mr. Kennedy!" Alicia chirped. "Mrs. Kennedy!"

Jack pushed himself from the wall. The red, white, and blue bunting clung to his pants for several seconds before detaching.

"Great to see ya, Pops," he said, pumping his father's hand.

Jack hugged his father, then bent toward his mother for a perfunctory kiss, his lips scarcely making contact at all.

"Dad, Mother, this is Alicia Darr."

"Yes, we've met," Alicia said quickly.

She regarded Mister, and then the missus.

"Nice to see you again."

"Why Jaaack," Mrs. Kennedy said, the hairs on Alicia's arms standing up with one strike of that creaky voice. "I hadn't known you were bringing a date."

"Didn't really think it needed an announcement. Next time, you'll be the first to know."

Jack tossed a glance over his shoulder, and it was then that Alicia realized the Kennedys had formed a circle and she stood firmly on the outside.

"Your girl looks lovely," Mrs. Kennedy said.

"Yes, yes, quite ravishing," Mr. Kennedy agreed. "She's the Austrian painter, correct?"

Alicia could not decide if she was part of the conversation, or blatantly eavesdropping. She inched up, to give herself a better shot at figuring it out.

"That's right. Damn it!" Jack looked toward Alicia. "Who's this guy marching over right now? Didn't he say something about a divorce?"

"Yes," she confirmed. "That's Norman Woods, with Ladder Company Twelve. His wife has 'Reno-vated' and he's confounded, feeling as though he's 'permanently in smoke.' His words."

"Damn, Alicia," Jack said, shaking his head. "I'd have screwed this all up if not for you."

"Hello, Mr. Woods," Alicia said, stepping around Jack, at once emboldened. "I was thinking, Jack here doesn't like to waltz, so if you have room on your dance card, save one for me?"

"I'd love that," Mr. Woods replied. "It'd be an honor to dance with the most beautiful woman in the room."

Alicia skipped to Jack's side, praying that her childhood ballroom-dancing lessons were still stamped in her memories somewhere. When she arced backward to smile at Jack, Alicia caught the sharp eye of the Ambassador instead. She shifted her gaze away.

"Mr. Burke!" she called out to a passing man, because, why not, she was on a roll. "Congratulations on the Walter Scott Medal. Very impressive!"

The man showed a flare of surprise.

"Why, thank you," he said. "I'm mighty flattered that such a lovely girl would care about a boring fireman's award."

"Rescuing a child from a burning building is not boring, and a hero is never dull."

"Quite right, Alicia," Jack said. "Helluva job, pal."

He rapped the man on his back, which sent him into a fit of coughs.

The rest of the evening continued like this. Parades of people tried to get a piece of Jack, and Alicia helped where she could. Jack was grateful, and Alicia's dance card filled in a blink.

"That girl sure knows how to work a room," she overheard Mr. Kennedy say.

Whether this was a compliment didn't matter, because Alicia felt like an asset to Jack.

After the ball, they stayed at the Hotel Manger, which was connected to the Garden. A good thing, too, as by the end of the night, Jack staggered more than he stepped. Once in the suite, they made love, and Jack dropped into a fast, hard sleep. Alicia was miles from tired, and so she shimmied back into her panties and curled up on a chair beside the window.

Alicia watched as Boston thrummed. She was all of a sudden overcome by the power and brightness of the city, and the country beyond. For the first time since she'd landed on these gilded shores, Alicia realized that as much as she loved America, there was a chance it might actually love her back.

He's bored, but in a postal facility that's the state of things. Plus, he's on a cold streak, not having found anything in weeks.

But one fine afternoon, a letter drops into his hands. It's from America, and there's no better kind. The envelope is white, with a lawyer's return, but the address is written in a mom-like hand.

Miss Serena Palmisano

The man thinks, *Ahò! Che culo!* What luck. A wife has borrowed her husband's stationery to send their daughter (or granddaughter?) a letter, including, no doubt, some cash to get by. Maybe this Serena is studying abroad. For the summer. Longer. He's worked it all out in his head.

He rips open the first envelope to find a second one—grimy, sullied by all manner of stamps. *Dai.* Perhaps there's no check for vacationing children after all.

Nevertheless, he tears open the second envelope, and his eyes go wide. There's no money but instead a reference to an inheritance, a "considerable estate." They might send a check, eventually. It's unlikely, but a man can dream and in fact that's the only way to get through a job like this.

He studies the addressee: Serena Palmisano. She lives on Margutta, which means she must be well-off. The man pulls out his phone and searches her name. He finds her Instagram account, and she is *strabella*. Super hot, as they might say in the States.

The man pockets the envelope, without bothering to look around. If anyone notices, they'll just assume he found something good. And, heck, maybe he has. It's not free cash, but a pretty girl can make a man almost as rich. He decides he'll fight the Italian postal industry's long tradition of poor service and deliver the letter himself.

Candidacies we expect . . . Congressman John F. Kennedy for Governor or Senator.

Politics and Politicians, March 18, 1951

HYANNIS PORT

Alicia almost couldn't trust her sight when she woke up late in the morning and found Jack asleep, laid out like a piece of lumber on his bed.

Nine o'clock might as well have been the afternoon. For a second: a shiver of panic. Alicia glanced toward him and saw his lashes flutter against the light of the morning sun. He opened his eyes.

"Hello there, handsome," Alicia said, pulling the blanket taut against her chest as she rotated onto her side.

A blond lock fell across her face. She blinked, lashes tangling with the strands of hair.

"Morning already?" Jack said with a grunt, and moved to meet her. "Good grief. How are you even prettier in the morning, without a stitch of makeup on?"

"I've always heard that Jack Kennedy can charm a girl in his sleep," Alicia said. "And now I know it's true."

Jack chuckled, mouth closed, then shut his eyes. Alicia sat still for a minute, listening to the birds twitter outside. Spring was almost here.

"Come join me," Jack said, patting the spot beside him.

"Are you sure?"

He nodded, and so Alicia scooted to the edge of her bed, stood, and crept across the slice of carpet between them, the very floor she once cleaned. She delicately lowered herself beside Jack, careful not to jostle the mattress, though it felt like cement compared to hers.

"Are you feeling all right?" she asked, nestling in.

Jack dipped his chin.

"Fine, fine," he said. "Back's a little off again. I hardly remember what it's like not to be in pain."

"I'd tell you to slow down, but you'd never listen."

He'd been busy these past few months, giving speeches, passing bills, visiting constituents throughout the state. That week he'd introduced a three-million-dollar fishing subsidy to the House and was the featured guest at an Evacuation Day banquet.

The reporters were starting to pick up on him, to notice that he seemed to be everywhere these days. Jack enjoyed the spotlight, though he was still hot about the journalist who called him a "very gaunt young representative."

"I'd like to see the fat asses at the paper!" he'd groused. "I'm sure those motherfuckahs are the picture of health."

Alicia laughed while thinking that "gaunt" was a generous way to describe a body that could've belonged to someone liberated from a camp at the end of the war.

"Jesus," Jack said, shifting in the bed, the groans of the springs matching those from his body. "I need to get to New York to see my doc, but I don't have the time."

"Yet you're about to start another campaign," Alicia said. "Sounds like a brilliant idea."

Jack's hair crunched against his pillow as he turned toward her again.

"Who mentioned a campaign?" he asked.

"I read the papers, Jack. The governorship or the senate? No use taking it easy, I suppose. What's the fun in that?"

"No taste for a man with some ambition, is that the problem?"

"I'm merely flummoxed," she said. "You finished one campaign and now it's on to the next? On top of your health issues?"

"Who said anything about health issues?" He scowled.

"You did. Or was 'I need to see my doc' code for something else?"

Alicia exhaled in frustration. She understood that Jack wasn't lying, necessarily. He was soldiering on, living two steps ahead, in the place he *wanted* to be instead of where he was. Alicia couldn't judge the man, as this sort of thinking was how she got through the war. Alas, their shared trait did not make him any less aggravating when he was "soldiering on."

"Are you really going to do it?" she asked. "Run for a new office?"

"That's the plan."

"Which one will it be?"

"As soon as I find out, I'll let ya know."

He paused for a moment and shook his head.

"I still can't stomach that Smathers made it to the Senate before I did. Who does the bastard think he is?"

"I'm sorry to be the bearer of bad news, but no matter which office you pick, you won't be the first. Unless you become king of the United States."

"Now there's an idea. I like it."

"I'm sure you do." Alicia rolled her eyes. "This will sound very Polish of me, but there is such a thing as too much ambition. God love ya Jack, but any proper Pole would tell you to be satisfied with what you have."

"I'm *very* happy with what I have," Jack said. "Extraordinarily so."

He reached out and pinched her side. Alicia yelped and rubbed the skin, now red.

"But, my dear," he said, "a man can be happy with what he has while also wanting more of it."

"I wish you luck," Alicia said, moving onto her back. "I shudder to think what might happen if you ever *lost* at something."

"Eh. The funny thing is, on some level, losing doesn't sound that bad."

"Politicians really are lying snakes, aren't they?" she said.

"Seriously, I think about it all the time."

Jack inhaled, his rib cage looking ever more like a chicken carcass.

"I dream of hopping off the carousel and flying far away," he said. "We could go to California, you and me. Get a hut on the beach. I'd sun myself eight hours a day, with you at my side."

"You'd never be able to sit that long," Alicia said.

"Then I'd take up surfing."

"And what would I do? Sunbathe? My skin is very fair."

"Have sex with me five times a day."

"Oh, is that all? So, I'd be cutting back, too."

"Hilarious."

"And how would I occupy myself the rest of the time?" she asked, thinking that sex five times a day would take an hour, at most.

But she liked the idea of it. The sun. The sand. The two of them. It'd never happen, but she liked it a lot.

"When you weren't exhausted by my deft lovemaking," he said, "you'd paint on the veranda, of course."

"Paint?" Alicia said, and swallowed, as if stuffing the word down. "What would I paint?"

"How should I know? You're the artist."

Alicia swallowed again. They hadn't spoken of it. They hadn't mentioned, danced around, or at all touched on her artistic aspirations since September. Though she'd almost revisited the incident a dozen times, it'd come to feel like something they'd agreed not to discuss. Did he even remember there was supposed to be a show?

"Geez, kid, what's that face?" Jack asked. "If you don't want to paint, then do something else. We'll be in Hollywood. You could become a film star. You have that air about you. I'll be the pool boy. The landscaper. A kept man, thanks to you."

Alicia sighed and looked his way.

"You sound pretty enthusiastic about this beach bum reverie," she said. "Which seems at odds with your dreams of 'higher office.' It makes me wonder, who wants it more—you or your father?"

"Does it matter, him or me? We both do, and there's not really a difference, I shouldn't think."

"Not really a difference? How's that?"

Jack took a second to consider this.

"We're Kennedys," he said. "All for one, and one for all."

"So, it *is* your father's dream?"

"Yes, and mine. What's with all the questioning?"

"I just want you to be living the life *you* want. And if that's in Washington, or in California, or—"

"Forget it. You wouldn't understand."

"No." Alicia glowered. "I wouldn't."

Jack heaved himself to his feet. Alicia remained in bed, wrapped in the sheets as palm trees listed in her mind. Jack had been talking nonsense, but it was quite delicious to imagine George feeding a reel into his projector, and seeing Alicia on the screen.

"I'm going to grab a shower," Jack said.

Just like that, the sand was blown from her thoughts. If only Alicia believed he could lose in November, then California would stand a chance.

"Okay," Alicia said, still dazed. "I'll make some eggs."

She swung her legs over the bedside and placed both feet on the nubby rug.

"Sounds fab," Jack said, marching across the room in his labored but proud waddle. "Coffee, too."

The door opened, then closed.

When Alicia heard water rush through the pipes, she lurched from bed, slipped on a robe, and made her way to the kitchen, feet sticking against the wood floors. As she reached for the coffee mugs, Alicia peered out through the white ruffled curtains, toward the family swimming pool, and the Nantucket Sound in the distance. Her heart let out a few extra beats.

Silly girl. What had she been thinking? Here she was, in a sprawling mansion on Cape Cod, beside the handsomest, most charming man she'd ever known. Yet she was picturing California, and the acclaim she'd find on another coast. Maybe Alicia was more American than she'd given herself credit for. Any good Polish broad would tell her to bring those thoughts back to earth, and be happy with what she had.

Alicia walked along, a bundle of clothes tucked beneath her arm. If she missed the next bus, she'd be late for work, and there was no good end to that. Either she'd be fired, like George always warned, or she'd have to listen to this same warning a hundred times more.

Someone was in the kitchen, Torby or Lem most likely, as Jack was off to Boston for a meeting with the Massachusetts Taxpayers' Foundation. His pals had come for the weekend and overstayed their welcome, as far as Alicia was concerned, which was why she was exiting through the seldom-used front door.

After gently clicking the door behind her, Alicia whirled around to find Torb balanced on the porch railing, like he'd been waiting for her to show.

"Oh. Good morning," Alicia said, her disappointment palpable, embarrassing to them both.

"Good morning," Torb answered, and took a drag of his cigarette. He flicked it into a nearby bush. "How is the Viennese artist this morning?"

"Hmm," Alicia answered. "Well, it was nice to see you. I'm off to catch the ten o'clock bus."

She jogged down the wooden stairs, toward the driveway.

"What happened to the art?" he called out.

"Excuse me?" Alicia said, and looped back to face him.

"I was at the Center the other day," he said. "To see *Mr. Universe*. You weren't there. And neither were your paintings. You still work there, right?"

"Yes, I do," Alicia said. "For now."

"Didn't you used to show your artwork in the lobby?"

Alicia nodded, her eyes flitting toward the road.

"And weren't you going to have a gallery show?"

Alicia regarded him warily, unsure if Torby was taking genuine interest, or about to demean her with one of his schoolboy digs.

"Jack told you about that?" she said.

"Of course," Torb said. "He mentioned that you're quite good."

Alicia gave a cough of surprise as she took in his droopy, wry gaze. Inexplicably, she started to laugh.

"Something funny?" Torb lifted his forehead.

"Yes. Well. I never had the show. Jack arranged it, but then forgot."

"Shit, Alicia, are you kidding? That's low-class, even for Ken. . . ."

"Oh, it's fine." She threw on a hard-fought shrug. "He was busy with his campaign, and then his grandfather died. My artistic aspirations understandably took a backseat."

"I should punch the bastard in the jaw the next time I see him."

"It's fine," Alicia said again. "It was an innocent mistake. The date slipped by."

"And you never brought it up?"

"No, I didn't. We don't see each other often and usually I'm enjoying our time together, not worrying about the past."

Alicia laughed again, embarrassed that she'd revealed so much. It was a miracle that Torb hadn't yet made any off-color remarks.

"Good," he said with a bark. "Good girl."

"Uh, what now?"

In the distance, a bus's engine roared.

"It's good that you haven't mentioned anything," he said. "You really understand him, clever girl. The quickest way for a broad to rid herself of Jack Kennedy is to come across as needy. You're smart to have a job and your own stuff going on."

Alicia smiled tightly. She didn't know about "smart," as her job was rooted entirely in her desire to eat and buy new clothes. And she couldn't be all that savvy to have missed the bus that would've gotten her there on time.

"Jack likes you," Torb said. "He likes you a lot. And I would know."

She smirked. Of course he would consider himself an expert on

Jack. Torb was an avid astrologist, and because they were both Geminis, he believed their friendship was literally "written in the stars."

"Ken missed you while we were in Europe," he went on, "and that bastard isn't the missing type. He thinks you're swell."

"Oh. Well. That's nice. He's, er, swell too."

"I'm sorry he flubbed your big day," Torb said. "But keep on painting. Keep doing what you love. And hell, next time you have a show, I'll make sure he's there. But don't ever mention what happened—"

"Or didn't happen," Alicia said, and cleared her throat.

"Quite right. It's best to let it slide."

"Thank you, Torby," she said, smiling with great exertion. "It's always nice to receive advice."

"Anytime, anytime." He laughed toward the ground. "All I can say is, thank God there's only one John Fitzgerald Kennedy in this world. Mankind could not survive more."

The bell jangled as Alicia walked inside. She sauntered up to the counter and squinted at the menu, debating what to buy. She'd just spent more dollars than she should've on art supplies, thanks to her conversation with Torb.

"Can I help you, Miss Darr?" asked the counter boy.

"Yes, I'll have an egg salad sandwich and a water, please," she said, and lunged onto the seat.

"Coming right up."

Alicia shifted to adjust her skirt, the stool squeaking beneath her. That's when she noticed the familiar coiffure of Janet des Rosiers.

"Hello, Janet!" Alicia called out, with a quick wave.

The woman jolted in surprise, the heels of her shoes lifting a centimeter before clacking to the floor again.

"Oh, hello there," she said.

The counter boy handed Janet a Coke.

"How funny to run into you," Alicia said. "Are Mr. and Mrs. Kennedy in town?"

"Only Mr. Kennedy," she answered in her pleasant way.

"You must've just arrived," Alicia said. "I was at the house not too long ago and I would've noticed if the Ambassador were there!"

"Is that right?"

As she watched Janet, she found her a bit . . . off. There was a tremble about her, like a drink bumped and about to spill. Janet's hair was flat on the top, her left eyebrow more filled in than the right. And her underpinnings didn't fit so well. Maybe the woman's grace wasn't as effortless as it appeared.

"And how is Jack?" Janet asked, stirring her Coke with a straw, bracelets clanging on her wrist. "He's been a bit under the weather, I know."

"Yes," Alicia said with a grim nod. "I'm worried about him, to be honest. He's so thin. I know he has a new campaign planned, but I hope he gets a break."

"I'm sure he's fine," Janet said. "The Kennedys don't like breaks. The faster, the better, in all things."

"But it's difficult to go fast on crutches," Alicia said with a half smile. "The poor man is so run-down, he was talking about chucking it all for California. It was a joke, but as Jack always says, 'Why not?' It's a decent idea, if you ask me."

"California?"

Janet's eyes expanded.

"Wouldn't it be a kick?" Alicia said. "I've always wanted to see Hollywood and doesn't every girl long for the big screen?"

"That's a cute little daydream." Janet plonked her glass on the counter. "Well, I'd better get back to the house, before I'm missed."

"Yes, probably best to hurry along. Tell the Ambassador I said hello. And please send my love to Mrs. Kennedy, too."

HYANNIS PORT

Rain ticked on the windows. The streets were slick. Inside the Center, *Magnificent Yankee* played onscreen, and in the lobby Alicia leaned against the counter, sighing over an opened newspaper. Atomic attacks, civilian defense plans, and Red spies: doom and more gloom than the weather outside. Now they were training Boston children for civil defense and converting schools into relief centers. How would this end?

"Stop fretting," George said earlier that day, when she'd agonized that thirteen-year-olds were being taught to carry stretchers. "There's nothing else to talk about right now, especially on the Cape. When summer arrives, that stuff will disappear. Soon the *Patriot* will return to fishing competitions, playhouse appointments, and strawberry crops."

"I should move to California," Alicia said. "It's never winter there."

Alicia glanced at the clock. The 2:15 show would end in a few minutes, and they'd enjoy an hour break before the next. The day already felt like forever.

Then, the doors flew open. Alicia lifted her head to witness a flock of women totter inside. They were in some type of uniform, a tan-colored minidress paired with tall boots. Behind them was a man with a wispy mustache and a very red face.

Alicia greeted the group, then ran a tongue over her teeth to check for lipstick. Why did she feel so unsteady? Not to mention, greasy and somewhat small? Alicia was used to being the most attractive woman in the room, but with these girls on the premises, her status was up for question. Her ghastly uniform did nothing to recommend her.

"Hello," she said, addressing the mustachioed man.

"Hi there, pretty lady."

He flashed a smile, then his ticket stubs.

"Don Class is the name," he said. "And behind me are the finalists for Coast Guard Queen. We're touring the Cape as part of our campaign, and figured we'd take in a show."

"That's magnificent."

Alicia tried to catch eyes with one or all of the girls, but they were busy rooting through handbags and fiddling with their hair.

"The entrance to the theater is right there," Alicia said, and pointed. "The current show is about to let out, and it's a bit of a wait until the next. I can hold on to your tickets if you wish to browse Main Street in the meantime?"

"We don't mind waiting," Don Class said. "Right, girls?"

He swiveled toward the six women: two blondes, two brunettes, and one each of red and raven-haired. A few of them gave listless nods. The black-haired girl pulled out a gold cigarette case.

"Let me get you popcorn and some Cokes," Alicia said.

"Sure. I'll take a jumbo Coke."

Alicia went to fetch his cup. He didn't intend to feed the Coast Guard Queens, it seemed.

"What'd you say your name was?" Don Class asked.

"I didn't." Alicia glanced over her shoulder. "It's Alicia Darr."

"Pleased to meet you, Miss Darr. It is a 'Miss,' isn't it?"

"Yes," she said, pausing to let the Coke de-fizz before adding a glug more.

Soon, Alicia heard the familiar click-click-click of the projector, followed by the dull murmur from the crowd. The film had finished. Within seconds, people would flood the lobby, and a few minutes after that, George would decamp from his lair.

"So, are you a model?" Don Class asked. "An aspiring starlet?"

The theater doors opened, and the people poured out. Or, rather, they trickled. The crowd was small that day.

"No, I'm only me, Alicia Darr, the girl who sells candy at the theater."

"Ha! 'Only you.' That's rich. You know, if I'd met you before our tour kicked off, I would've asked you to join my troupe. You'd make a fine addition."

"What troupe?" George said, materializing behind her. "And who are the dames in the khaki dropping ashes on the carpet?"

"They're the Coast Guard Queens, here to tour the Cape!"

Alicia said this with gusto, an antidote to George's tendency to doubt.

How can there be multiple queens? he might ask. *Who anointed them as such? And what does the Coast Guard need with a queen?*

"I'm not joshing," Mr. Class said. "You would've made a great addition to our stable of girls. I could've used an extra blonde, especially one with your figure. Your look is very of-the-moment."

"Thank you," Alicia said, blushing, batting her eyes. "I appreciate the compliment."

"Oh, brother," George griped.

Alicia handed Don Class the soda. As he reached for it, Alicia noticed the chunky gold ring on his pinkie finger.

"Where are you all from?" she asked.

"The girls . . . I don't know. Different parts of the country. Pennsylvania or whatever. I'm from California."

"California?"

Alicia perked up, as if the sun had at last broken through the clouds. George mumbled something, but Alicia didn't hear him.

"Yep," Don Class said. "Los Angeles, to be specific. Hollywood-land. I'm a talent scout by trade, escorting these fine candidates as a favor. You know what?"

He reached into his pocket and groped around, his wristwatch jangling.

"Let me give you my card," he said. "If you ever want to try your luck in Hollywood, I'll hook you up."

"Mr. Class, that's very generous," Alicia said. "But I can't pick up and move to Hollywood! That'd be more foolish than fun."

"Obviously," George said.

"I'm not prone to flights of fancy," she added.

"Flights of fancy?" Mr. Class scoffed. "Nah. You only need to know the right people, and you're looking at one. I'd make it easy for you. I own a house where all my up-and-coming starlets live, rent-free, until they make it on their own."

"Really? You set them up?"

"Sure, and I'm certain I could get you gigs within minutes of you stepping onto the tarmac at LAX. And, ya know, it's sunny in California right now. None of this miserable weather."

He jerked his thumb toward the door.

"It rains in California too," George said.

"Does it?" Don Class smirked. "You may be right, but it's so infrequent we can all pretend that it never happens at all." He returned his attention to Alicia. "I'd pay your way. You'd certainly be worth the investment."

"This is ridiculous," George said, and yanked the card from Mr. Class's chubby fingers. "Since when did wolves start carrying business cards?"

"George!" Alicia squawked. "Why are you being so rude? Mr. Class, I'm sorry. Please excuse his abhorrent behavior. He's not good with people."

"It's fine. Your boyfriend is being protective. I don't blame him."

"He is most definitely not my boyfriend."

Alicia gestured dismissively with her hand.

"I get it," Mr. Class said. "Some stranger walks into your place of work and invites you to Hollywood. That sounds like the start of a true-crime story. But they can vouch for me."

He nodded toward the Coast Guard girls, who were still lolling about the lobby, smoking cigarettes and propping themselves up on potted plants and displays, as if they couldn't be bothered to stand on their own.

"Feel free to perform due diligence on my background," Mr. Class said. "You'll find my résumé unassailable. Have you ever heard of Lana Turner?"

"Who hasn't?"

"I got Lana her start. Ava Gardner, too. Hell, Gloria Swanson has a house right here in Hyannis Port. Call her up, and she'll give you the scoop."

"Gloria Swanson," Alicia said dreamily. "How I loved her in *Sunset Boulevard*."

"Something tells me you'd have the talent to beat them all."

"What a load of crap," George muttered.

Alicia shot him a cutting glare. Then Don Class took her hand, and kissed it gently.

"A pleasure to meet you," he said. "I'll leave you to your work. The girls and I should probably take our seats."

"You have some time before the next show. . . ."

He grabbed his Coke, offered Alicia one last wink, then ambled off, whistling as he went.

"George!" Alicia said, and flipped around.

She grabbed both of his shoulders, and gave him a shake.

"Can you believe it?" she said. "A bona fide talent scout wants to fly me to Hollywood!"

"I cannot believe it, as a matter of fact."

Alicia flicked him with the back of her hand.

"You need to dream a little," she said. "California! Can you stand it?"

"But you live here."

"For now! Relinquish the card, bucko," she said, and extended her palm.

"You can't go to Hollywood."

"Yes, I can. That doesn't mean I will. It's a long shot and would depend on so many things, but it's not out of the question. So, I'll keep Don Class's information, should I need it in a pinch."

"What about Jack?"

"What about him? You're the one who called him . . . what was it? Oh, right, a 'shifty, horse-toothed political puppet.' "

"He's not that bad," George said, mumbling again. "Sometimes I get too . . . colorful."

"What's that? Jack Kennedy's charmed even you?" Alicia bumped him with her hip. "He really can do anything."

"I don't understand," he said. "You've been in the United States eighteen months and you've relocated twice. Now you want to go to California? I realize you're not accustomed to stability. . . ."

"That's one way to put it."

"But has it ever occurred to you to stay longer, to see how things might work out?"

"You would have the luxury of saying that, wouldn't you?"

Alicia let her arms fall to her side. Was George really not going to return Don's card? For a second, she had the fleeting thought that he wanted to keep it for himself.

"Sometimes waiting is the worst decision a person can make," Alicia said. "A million Jews would agree."

"But Paul finally likes you. He hasn't mentioned firing you in the last month. And you appear to be in a romantic relationship with Jack. Things are good, and *now* you want to leave?"

"George." Alicia exhaled. "I didn't say I was leaving. But it can't hurt to talk to the man, can it? Give myself another option? And what's wrong with being flattered by a talent scout seeing something in me?"

"Of course he does, you're beautiful."

"Oh, George." Alicia gave him a pout. "That's the nicest beautiful anyone's ever called me."

"Here's your dumb card," he said, holding it up.

"I don't want it," Alicia said.

"Take it."

"No."

"Suit yourself."

George crumpled it and tossed it into a bin on the far side of the room.

"I'd better get ready for the next show," he said, and pivoted on his shiny black shoes. "Can't disappoint the Coast Guard Queens. Queens. Of all the ideas."

Alicia waited, listening to the pit-a-pat of George's feet as he retreated. As soon as she heard the projection room close, Alicia shot across the lobby and rescued Don Class's card from the trash. She flattened it against her chest, then slid it into the pocket of her uniform.

She'd probably never use the card, or look at it again, but if nothing else, it represented one option, another second chance. When things went south and you had to leave town, it was best to have an escape route in mind.

That evening, Alicia found a letter waiting for her on Mrs. Neill's table, the envelope stark and ominous in the dim kitchen light. She approached it cautiously, as her stomach filled with a snowballing dread.

After ripping it open, like ripping a bandage off a knee, Alicia scanned the words and saw that Mother's letter was short but not sweet, and riddled with complaints about her fellow DPs, and Alicia, too.

What do I need with your American money? she wanted to know. *And how did you get so much? What sorts of tricks are you up to?*

For several more lines, she further chided Alicia, then concluded with her customary death toll. Three people had met their ends in the last week, though more were "sure to die at any time."

We can't all go to America, you know.

Alicia read the letter a second and a third time. Mamusia's writing had deteriorated in the past year, the shaky penmanship proof that she was not the woman she'd known. This was not the avid reader, or the cinema fiend, or the person who'd steal into Alicia's room when Father's parties became too charged.

"Barbara," she'd whisper, for Alicia was Barbara then. "I'm bored with these government men. Let's sneak into the cinema. Let's visit a café."

How Alicia loved that beautiful, vibrant mom. Of course, they were *all* better before the war.

"Oh, Mamusia," Alicia said with a sniffle, then wiped her eyes. "*Przepraszam.* I'm so sorry. I love you."

Alicia refolded the letter and placed it in her purse, next to the wrinkled card from Don Class. Well, if her earnings didn't impress Mother, a career in film surely would. She imagined her mom at the camp, bragging about her movie star daughter, and also boasting about the daughter's beau, who was handsome and interesting, especially for a "government man."

DISILLUSIONMENT ON WAY TO STARDOM
New York Close-Up, May 1, 1951

NEW YORK

Alicia's glass was heavy all night, only a sip or two gone before someone filled it again. Every few minutes, another bottle cracked, and more champagne bubbled down wrists and onto the table.

They were at the Stork Club in New York City, a place Alicia had ogled in the gossip rags. It seemed like a fantasy to be there, and she'd never forget her debut.

When they arrived, a doorman unlatched a solid gold chain and waved them through. Someone handed Alicia a gardenia, and ushered them into a pink-lit, wood-paneled room. As they squeezed into the banquette, Alicia caught her reflection in one of the dozen or so mirrors. She did not recognize this woman with the makeup, the jewels, the wind-tousled hair.

Jack's friends piled in after them, demanding champagne and caviar before they sat down. Alicia didn't order, but she refused nothing and soon found herself enchanted by the saltiness of the caviar, and the dry prickle of the champagne.

"You okay?" Torby asked, an hour into the evening.

He'd noticed Alicia's halfhearted effort at conversation, the way her eyes were drifting about the room.

"Sure, all's nifty," Alicia said, using the word for the very first time. "Just letting Jack catch up with his chums."

She loved Jack's brain, and admired his head for politics, but could pro-and-con General MacArthur's retirement speech for only so long before letting her mind wander to other things. The latest dress. A new crocodile handbag. The beaches in L.A.

"You see?" Torby said, and pointed his cigarette in her direction. "This is exactly the sort of thing that makes you a winner in my book. You sit there, pretty as a picture, not demanding an ounce of recognition. Your subtlety gives you more allure."

"Mmmm," Alicia said with a smirk she hoped to pass off as a smile.

She never would've guessed Torb Macdonald favored modest types, given the large-busted blonde right then pawing at his forearm, unconcerned that her nipples were partially exposed.

"Hey, Billings," Torb called out to Lem, who sat directly across from them.

The woman cooed and preened.

"Don't you think Alicia is the top broad Jack's brought around?" He looked her way. "And that's quite the accomplishment, since he goes through women like water. Or like the shitty soup he eats, which is basically the same thing, but with salt."

Lem chuckled, though it seemed forced. Alicia had been with Lem enough to understand that he enjoyed Jack best when there were fewer people along.

"She's a gem," he agreed, in a monotone.

Alicia got the sense Lem didn't care for her, but as he possessed all the charm of a walrus, and with the teeth to match, she didn't let it bother her too much.

"No airs," Torb went on. "No pretentiousness. You're not the least bit of a pain in the ass."

"Thank you for your *very generous* comments," Alicia said. "I've always dreamt of not being a pain in the ass."

Even Lem had to break face for that.

"What are you fuckahs bullshitting about?" asked Dave Powers, who sat to Torb's right. "And did someone say 'ass'?"

"We were talking about how much we like Miss Darr," Torb said, not really answering Dave's question, either way.

Alicia was starting to grow uncomfortable. She was being sold, but to what end she didn't know.

"Oh, yeah, she's a peach," Dave said with a nod. "Smart. A hot numbah. Plus, she doesn't try to befriend our wives, which is swell."

As he cackled, Alicia's stomach turned over. Dave Powers gave her the willies. He was too slick in public, too crass in places like a VIP room, and, more importantly, this was the first Alicia had heard about any spouses. Until that moment, she'd assumed Jack's friends were bachelors. The girls with them that night Alicia had taken for girlfriends, not secrets kept from wives.

"Speaking of ass," Dave said, right on time. "Who's that piece? The brunette? She's pretty, but seems a tad uptight. I was thinking that Dr. Powers could give her one of his special *injections*."

"Jesus," Alicia muttered, as Torby let out a guffaw, and Lem reddened.

"Yeah, go offer her one of your legendary injections, Powers," Torb said. "Gives new meaning to the phrase 'Don't worry, you won't feel a thing.'"

"Fuck you."

"That's Helen," Alicia said. "Helen Doyle, Jack's new secretary."

"Niiiiiice," Dave said. "So, does Jack need her services tonight? Or might she be up for some dictation from me?"

He gesticulated toward his groin, and Alicia shuddered. She didn't like to imagine Dave thinking of Helen in that way, chiefly because she didn't want to picture Jack taking a similar view.

Alicia preferred secretaries of the thick-ankled, matronly variety but, sadly, Helen Doyle was pretty. And young. She worked out of the Boston office, which did not explain why she was right then in New York. Neither did it explain what Alicia walked into earlier that night.

When she arrived at Jack's suite at the Waldorf Astoria, exhausted and bedraggled following her train-and-bus odyssey from the Cape, a woman answered the door. Alicia peered around her to find Jack sitting on the bed.

There was nothing untoward about the situation. Both parties were fully clothed, though Jack looked rumpled, as he usually was these days. The woman, still nameless at that point, wore a long, black sheath. Her sable hair was drawn into a low chignon and her cheeks were flushed.

"Hiya, kid," Jack said, his expression brightening though he made no move.

"Hello," Alicia answered, sneaking a glance at the flawless porcelain figure now stationed at Jack's desk.

She was delicate, like a child, or an undernourished baby deer.

"Hello there!" Alicia called out. "I don't believe we've met!"

She took five brisk, confident strides to greet her.

"I'm Alicia Darr," she said, and stuck out a hand.

"Helen Doyle," the woman replied, with a soft, cold handshake.

"Helen's my new Boston gal," Jack said, reading through some memo or speech. "You two should get yourselves acquainted."

"I think we just did," Helen said, gathering her things. "Please ring if you need anything. Is the plan to meet in the lobby at nine o'clock?"

"You bet," Jack said.

"That's in ten minutes," Helen said. "Please be prompt. Not even you could lose track of time before then."

Jack laughed, and Alicia fumed, though everyone had acted perfectly appropriate and polite.

"She's coming tonight?" Alicia asked, as soon as Helen was out the door.

But Jack had no inclination to talk guest lists right then. He pounced on Alicia like a jackal, ripping off her clothes as if skinning prey. They were both finished and dressed in time to meet Helen downstairs at nine o'clock, on the nose. When they walked up, she inspected them disapprovingly.

"I don't like her," Alicia whispered.

"Helen? How come? She's nice. Though, to be honest, I'm not sure she's the sharpest tool."

It was all Alicia needed to hear. Pretty was great, but Jack needed smart, too. Also, he didn't like brunettes.

Now Dave Powers was leering at the poor girl like she was a twelve-ounce steak. Helen Doyle was out of her element, out of place, and could probably do with some consideration from a well-heeled man.

"I think you're right, Dave," Alicia said, and took a swig of champagne, eyes still on Miss Doyle.

"There's a first time for everything," Lem mumbled.

"Helen Doyle is a strange bird," Alicia said. "But I'm sure she'd relish a little medical attention, courtesy of Dr. David Powers."

"That was quite the night," Jack said when they returned to the Waldorf. "I hope Lem made it to his room, and a maintenance man doesn't trip over his passed-out body in some corridor."

"I have the same wish for us all," Alicia said, grabbing her head.

How much champagne did she drink, exactly?

Jack dropped onto the bed and went to remove his shoes, his face contorted in agony. Alicia would've helped, but she'd long since learned not to interfere.

"I saw you talking to Torb and Dave," Jack said as he tried to extricate himself from his socks. "Anything interesting to report?"

"Not really."

Alicia removed her elbow-length gloves, wondering if she should bring up Helen Doyle, and the fact she'd gone to Dave's room. But

Alicia had the odd sense that Jack would be irritated, if not outright chapped.

"The highlight was Gloria Swanson, of course," Alicia said instead. "I couldn't believe my eyes when she walked up to our table in that jewel-encrusted turban. It was rather comical to watch all of you trip over yourselves to find her a chair."

Ultimately, Gloria wedged herself between Jack and Alicia, and then asked where Joe was. Through it all, Alicia was dumbstruck and clammed up. It was her first celebrity sighting, and what a way to start.

"Gloria's a helluva dame," Jack said as Alicia slid out of her dress. "You barely spoke two words to the woman."

"I know! I couldn't find a thing to say. I felt like the biggest yokel around."

Alicia turned toward the mirror and took a second to analyze her reflection: the blush slip, the smeared makeup, the necklace from Jack that never matched what she wore. Alicia thought diamonds went with everything, but this was not a proven fact.

"I met someone a while ago," she said. "A talent scout from Hollywood who's worked with Gloria. He said I have the looks for film."

"I'll bet he did," Jack snorted. "Sounds like a great line. I've probably used it myself."

"I don't know. He seemed on the up-and-up. He even offered to pay my way to California. I'm kicking myself, now. *That's* what I should've talked to Gloria about. I could have asked her opinion on Don Class."

"Don Class?" Jack shot up to sitting. "Are you joking? Man's a two-bit hustler. He probably just wanted to fuck you."

"He made no overtures in that vein," Alicia sniffed, and stretched to release the clasp of her necklace. "And it's not necessary to be so crass."

Though she was annoyed, it was nice to know Jack could be unreasonable and jealous like a regular man.

"You're going to be an actress now?" Jack said. "Is that it?"

"It's something I've been entertaining. People say I have the face for it and the art isn't going so well."

"You've barely given it any time! What did you expect?"

"You sound like George," Alicia said, and flung the necklace onto the bureau. "And maybe I've given it gobs of time. How would you know?"

"I don't like this idea." Jack sulked. "I don't like it one bit."

Alicia was about to respond, to say something about how she didn't like him living permanently on the campaign trail, when she noticed Jack glaring at the dresser.

"Did Don *Ass* give you that necklace?" he asked.

"What necklace?"

Alicia craned to look behind her, but was stumped, for the only necklace around was from him.

"That hideous thing you wear when you're trying to be fancy," he said. "It's so fucking gaudy."

Alicia let out a gasp. She picked up the necklace, and then swung it around, like a short and expensive lasso.

"This?" she said. "This is the piece of jewelry you're talking about?"

"I don't see any other chintzy pieces of costume ice in this room."

Alicia cocked her arm and chucked the diamonds at Jack. She caught him square in the forehead, and for a second she was happy as he wiped away a speck of blood.

"*You* gave it to me, you prick," she said. "When I tried to refuse, you told me that your sisters lose jewelry all the time."

"Aw, sure!" he said, eyes brightening. "That's right! Now I remember!"

Alicia shook her head and leaned against the dresser.

"How many diamond necklaces are you doling out, that you can't recall this one?" she asked.

"Come on, now," he said, struggling to his feet. "You're the most beautiful and interesting woman I've ever met. How could there be diamonds for anyone else? If you want to know the truth, Sarge picked it out."

"*Who?* Is that a nickname for one of your puckish friends?"

"Sarge Shriver is a friend of mine. He works for Dad in Chicago. I called *him* because he knows all the best diamond merchants. I wanted to get you the perfect piece."

Sarge Shriver's involvement was supposed to make her feel better, then? Alicia continued to scowl.

Jack walked over.

"Come on, gorgeous, don't freeze me out," he said, and pushed into her.

Alicia's tailbone smarted against the dresser's edge as Jack kissed her neck. He ran his mouth down her collarbone, and to the décolletage revealed by her slip. She should probably leave, but where could a girl go at one o'clock in the morning? If Alicia walked through the lobby at that hour, she'd probably get picked up in a vice raid.

And so, she succumbed to Jack, which was the easier and more pleasurable course. They started on the dresser, and ended on the bed. When all was through, Jack fell into his heavy stone sleep.

The next morning, as dawn spread across the city, Alicia didn't wait for him to wake up. With the first light through the window, Alicia crept from bed, wiggled into her traveling clothes, and counted her money, to make sure that she had enough.

After coaxing her hair into a less scurrilous state, Alicia laid last night's dress, and the gloves, across her side of the bed. She almost added the necklace but reconsidered, and slipped it into her handbag. On the way out the door, she grazed Jack's arm as she hurried past. She made it to the train station just in time to catch the Boston 7:05.

STAY AWAY FROM HOLLYWOOD!!
IF YOU HAVE GENUINE TALENT, A NEW FACE
AND UNUSUAL FIGURE, A TALENT SCOUT MAY
FIND YOU RIGHT IN YOUR OWN HOMETOWN
The Danville Advocate-Messenger, May 23, 1951

HYANNIS PORT

The Center was overrun, over-the-top, looking like the would-be funeral for every circus clown who'd ever lived. A person couldn't transport popcorn from counter to seat without smacking into a wreath, bouquet, or cluster of balloons.

"It's like the winner's circle of a shitty horse race," George said.

He'd taken to calling it "the carnation abomination," and Alicia didn't object. Jack remained on her bad side and she would not soon be swayed by gifts likely purchased by Sarge Shriver, or whoever had access to a "flower guy."

"I don't get it," George said, shortly after a delivery of chocolate, which Alicia left on the sidewalk for the Hyannis kids. "Are you split, or are you just mad?"

"No on being split, yes I'm mad. George, please stop moving."

Alicia sat perched on the counter, legs crossed, a sketchbook in her lap. Her friend's profile was taking shape. It was the first time she'd rendered a person instead of a place, though she'd not yet confessed to George that he was her debut subject.

"Why do you keep ordering me around?" he said. "So, do you *plan* to forgive Jack? Asking some business associate to pick out jewelry isn't the worst offense."

Alicia nodded, then scratched out a few more eyebrows. George's were pretty thick, now that she'd taken the time to examine them.

"I'll never understand women," he said. "Not if I studied for a hundred years."

"If you ever need help, let me know. I'll counsel you, free of charge."

"Yours is not the help I'd seek."

Alicia looked up from her pad. She narrowed one eye. George's face was disconcertingly symmetrical. Humans weren't made to be so even.

"What're you staring at?" he groused.

"Only you."

Alicia returned her eyes to the sketchpad, amused by this open secret. If George paid the least bit of mind, he'd recognize himself from fifty yards away.

"The thing with Jack is . . ." Alicia started, brushing her pencil upward to create the flecks of hair between George's brows. "He needs to understand that he can't always have his way. I honestly don't think anyone's ever told him that."

Alicia erased a few hairs. George's eyebrows were not that unkempt.

"All that stuff you've told him over the phone," George said, for he'd overheard a conversation or twelve. "About Hollywood and Don Class and the rest of it. Is that a game? Or are you serious?"

"It's all true. I realize you think I'm acting capriciously, but what girl wouldn't want the chance at fame?"

Alicia plunked down her sketchpad and slid from the countertop. A headache was approaching, as bad as a champagne hangover thanks to the flowers that were dizzying in sight and smell.

"Come on," George said. "Hollywood is a whim, a lark. You're just flattered that an agent noticed you."

"In case you're wondering, he's called me twice."

"Jesus Christ," someone said. "What is this unholy show?"

Alicia jumped, for she had not heard the door open. She peered over the flowers to see the tall, boxy noggin of Lem Billings.

"Lem!" Alicia said, and threw on a well-practiced mask of delight. "What are you doing at the Center? Here to check out *You're in the Navy Now*? He may be aging, but Gary Cooper is still a dream."

"No," Lem said, plowing through Jack's gifts. "No designs on Gary Cooper. I'm here to see you. This has to end, now."

End? The word sent a quiver of panic through Alicia. She'd acclimated to the flow of gifts, and watching Jack work so hard.

"Alicia Darr," Lem said, "what the hell are you doing to my boy? You're killing the poor bastard."

"How am I killing him?" she asked, somewhat irritated by this particular brand of American hyperbole.

"You know Jack hates being ignored. Cannot stand it. Some broad wouldn't screw him in '38 and he still won't shut up about it. And while I could take or leave you—"

"Thank you, that is very kind."

"I don't like seeing Jack upset."

"I'm not ignoring him," Alicia said, almost able to feel George shaking his head behind her. "I've been . . . busy."

"Working in a movie theater?" he scoffed.

"Yes. And I'd offer a referendum on your occupation, though I still haven't figured out what it is you do. Jack's assistants customarily wear skirts."

"I work at General Shoe. In Nashville."

"Nashville?" Alicia said. "That's the first I've heard of it."

How could he have a gig in Tennessee when he spent so much time in Massachusetts and D.C.?

"Listen, lady," he said. "You're making Jack crazy. Clinically insane."

If Alicia was not mistaken, Lem's eyes were beginning to well. Sometimes he acted like Jack's older brother, or an overprotective spouse, instead of a pal.

"How am I responsible for Jack's mental state?" Alicia asked.

"Women are evil sorcerers," he said. "Listen. There's a party, Wednesday night at the house. The entire family will be there to celebrate Jack's thirty-fourth birthday and Bobby's graduation from law school."

"Did Bobby finish as high as he was hoping?" Alicia asked.

"Higher. Dead middle of the pack."

"An improvement over expectations," she said with a snicker. "Will they be celebrating anything related to Teddy, do you think?"

A few weeks earlier, the youngest Kennedy had been kicked out of Harvard for cheating on a Spanish test, and the family had been figuring out what to do with him ever since. A dash of war heroism might be in order, if the Kennedys weren't so against Korea. But, they'd never cast him out. Alicia guessed that they reckoned Teddy's problem was not in the cheating, but in being expelled.

"Why are you telling me this?" Alicia asked with a sigh. "About the party?"

"Because the whole family will be there, and Jack wants you there, too."

"Yet you're the one who extended the invitation," Alicia said warily, despite the thrill rising in her throat.

Could she go? Could she socialize with the Kennedys like a regular guest? While she'd spent some time with Rose, and with Joe, as for the rest of them, they knew her as the girl who swept floors, packed their lunches, and mistook pool cues for something they might use on a beach.

"The invitation is time-sensitive, and Jack wanted your answer right away," Lem said. "With so much going on in Washington, he couldn't make it to the Cape."

"Jack Kennedy can't stand to wait for anything, can he?" Alicia said with a snort. "Alas, he'll need to wait for my answer. I'll think it over, but I have some decisions to make. There's a possibility I won't even be on the Cape when his birthday comes around."

"Jesus H." Lem rolled his eyes. "Not this Hollywood, Don Class nonsense. It drives Jack nuts, though perhaps that's the point."

"Me too," George piped in. "It drives me nuts, too. It's like, either go or don't. Stop talking about it. Stop dragging everyone else on your slow, boring ride."

"Weighing my options," Alicia said, and glanced over her shoulder to glower at George, "has nothing to do with Jack."

She turned toward Lem.

"Tell Jack that I'll either see him on the thirtieth . . . or I won't," she said. "That's the only answer I can give."

KENNEDYS BACK FROM PARIS

The Newport Daily News, May 29, 1951

HYANNIS PORT

Alicia paused at the front door, chin lifted despite the quaking beneath her butterfly-print dress. As her hands perspired through her gloves, Alicia threw her shoulders back and let the ocean breeze sweep across her face.

She rang the bell. Soon came the patter of feet, and the whirring of voices throughout the home. The Kennedys were present and accounted for, sure enough.

"Oh, hello," said the maid who answered, a girl Alicia didn't recognize.

She was Latin, which lined up with Mrs. Kennedy's preference for Dominicans over Eastern Bloc girls.

"Hi there." Alicia smiled.

Was Irenka on the premises? she wondered. She still worked there, which Alicia knew thanks to the small but active east end grapevine. Irenka was also dating a widowed fisherman who had five children and wanted five more, which was Irenka's very dream. Alicia wished her the best. It was funny how two Poles could behold America and see such different dreams.

"I'm Alicia Darr," she told the woman at the door. "A guest of Jack's."

"Please," she said, and waved Alicia through.

Alicia followed, the Kennedy ruckus intensifying with each step. To steady her nerves, Alicia focused on the skirt of her dress, and how the blue iridescent butterflies shimmered through the silk gossamer pleats.

"They're in the living room," the maid said. "Can I get you a pre-dinner cocktail? The others are having daiquiris."

"That'd be lovely," Alicia said, her voice creaky.

The woman hurried off.

At the threshold, Alicia stopped and smiled into a corner, the weight of the Kennedy gaze heavy upon her. When she finally let her eyes roam, Alicia took an inventory of the clan. There was Rose Kennedy and the new law school grad. Beside him, the expelled scamp. A very pregnant Ethel sat on the floor, and the sisters lounged on various chairs throughout the room. Everyone was there, except for Jack.

"He had an event at the Elks Lodge in Boston," Pat said, and strode across the room. "We're expecting him at any moment. Please, have a seat."

Pat took Alicia's hand and led her to a chintz chair.

"Hello, all," Alicia said, eyes skipping around the room.

She glanced from Rose Kennedy's decorative plates, to the wall of color-coordinated books, and then to the black baby grand. Atop the piano was a smattering of photographs: Joe, Honey Fitz, Joe Junior, and Kick. All of them dead, except for Joe.

"Oh! A butterfly print!" Rose trilled, chopping the silence with her ear-pinching voice.

Alicia looked at Mrs. Kennedy.

"Thank you," she said. "It's a new favorite."

"A copy of Dior's!"

Alicia shrank in her seat and folded her withering hands in her lap. She wondered how long she'd have to wait for Jack.

"We were discussing Korea," Joe said, and focused in on her.

Alicia sank further. Of all the bad luck.

"What are your thoughts on the war?" he asked.

A concert of Kennedy blues flew in her direction. Bobby tittered, in anticipation of her guaranteed misstep. His family called him "the shrimp," yet somehow, he made *Alicia* feel small.

"Well . . . it's clear the current approach isn't working," she started. "And I have to wonder, who is America hurting more? The Communists or itself?"

"Why, Daddy, that's almost exactly what you were saying earlier," Pat said brightly.

"Yes, yes," he said. "I quite agree with your assessment, Miss Darr. It seems you've been studying up."

"I also worry about how it's hurting Europe," she added, and was about to continue when Rose jumped in.

"The girls and I returned from Paris yesterday," she said. "I hope it's not going to end up like the last war, when we couldn't go at all."

"Yes, Mother, that was such a shame," Mr. Kennedy said, shaking his head earnestly.

With that, Rose steered the conversation toward the latest collections. How they'd gone from the Reds to haute couture so quickly, Alicia couldn't fathom. It took a special talent, she supposed, one that you were born into, instead of acquired. Alicia listened thoughtfully. It was helpful to know what to wear in the summertime, in any case.

Suddenly the kitchen door opened and then closed again, the familiar smack-clap Alicia once heard a hundred times per day. She straightened her spine, like a sentinel, but Alicia wasn't the only one tense with expectation. There was a definite hum in the room as everyone stared at the entryway, awaiting the arrival of their golden boy.

At first, Jack seemed unimpressed to find Alicia in his house.

"Hiya, kid," he said, with zero fanfare.

But when the group proceeded to the dining room, he yanked

her into a storage closet and whispered, "You just made my fuckin' week." His voice was hot, yet it sent goose bumps across every part of her.

"You're not wearing the necklace," he said.

Jack reached under her skirt. Alicia tried to shimmy away, but there was little room to move.

"Must've forgotten it," she said.

"I'll send someone to fetch it."

"Don't bother." Alicia pushed his hand away with decisiveness and force. "I think it's time for dinner."

"But first, a little fun."

"You're not going to have your way with me in a pantry."

"Why not?" Jack smirked. "I have before."

"Not with your parents nearby, creep. We'd better get in there before people start to talk."

"Argh!" Jack cried. "You're giving me a headache, not to mention a wicked case of blue balls."

Alicia swatted him and skittered past, out into the safe daylight.

The family, plus guests, convened at the rosewood table, and within seconds the conversation sparked, opinions and barbs whizzing about. Alicia joined in, where she could, but mostly she just watched.

"So, Pat," Jack said, digging into a dish of peas. "How's life in Hollywoodland? You still producing that radio program?"

"For now."

"When she's not vacating to Europe," the Ambassador said. "No man's ever going to take you girls seriously if you're constantly jetting around with your mother. And I don't have enough money for you all to spend like her, too. You'll need to find someone else to take up the tack."

"Oh, Dad," Ethel said, though he was not her father. "You have plenty of dough."

"Not the way you women go through it," he said. "And that includes you, Ethel."

"Of course Dad doesn't have enough money." Jean rolled her eyes. "He has to save it for Jack's campaigns."

"Ha! Too true!" Pat barked. "John F. Kennedy, straight to the top!"

She raised a finger in the air.

"Think of it like this, Daddy," Eunice said. "The golden child must have decent-looking sisters. Plus, if you're keen to marry us off, don't men like their wives to have panache?"

"Which is why I take you to Paris," Rose said. "To imbue you Children with some taste. Especially Eunice. I've seen scarecrows who dress in more flattering ways."

Though Rose's comment was stone serious, and Mrs. Kennedy *never* joked, the table erupted in good old-fashioned Kennedy howls, hardy and genuine and straight from the gut. All of them, that is, except for Bobby, whose laughter was like a brief shuffle. He didn't even talk like the others, having not inherited their charming, easy patter. Mostly he spoke in commands.

"Give me the rolls."

"Think about Korea this way."

"Pat, answer my question about Lana Turner."

"We don't need to worry about prettying up Eunice," Jack said, and bit into a pork chop.

He was talking with his mouth mostly full.

"Sarge is smitten," he went on. "That man is so desperate to marry you, you could wear paper bags, for all he'd care."

"Thank God," Rose said. "Because that's the state of things."

A great wave of hilarity again crashed through the room. Rose didn't find any of it amusing. With a sour-lemon face, she set down her fork and crossed both arms. Alicia was the only one to notice, or so it seemed.

"Seriously, Eunice," Jack said, gnawing on his food. "When are you going to marry the poor sap?"

"Who says I will? I have things to do."

"Working with women criminals," Rose said. "I pray you don't pick up their bad habits."

"I guess the real question," Jack said. "Is who's going to take care of Teddy now that Harvard no longer wants the task? Think we can get Sarge to marry him instead?"

"Hilarious," Teddy said. "The whole thing was a misunderstanding. Never would've happened if I weren't Catholic. You know how the Harvard types discriminate against us."

The table nodded in time.

"Hey, did everyone fill up their cars today?" Jack asked. "With the gas price wars starting at midnight?"

"Suddenly you're penurious?" Pat scoffed.

"I hope the driver has been apprised," Rose said. "If not, I'll have to dock his pay for the difference in price."

Everyone muttered their agreement.

"I, for one, am looking forward to summer," Joe said. "Did everyone read? Olivia de Havilland will be here, in person, in *Candida*. She's set to open the twenty-fifth season of the Cape Playhouse."

"I love Olivia de Havilland!" Jean said, sparkly and bright.

"Hear, hear," said Jack. "And she would've loved me, too."

"Oh, geez," Pat said, and met eyes with Alicia. "We're not supposed to bring up Olivia de H in Jack's presence. He's a real ass about the whole thing."

Jack grinned, like a naughty boy. *They should check his pockets for frogs and slingshots,* Alicia couldn't help but think.

"Olivia and I go way back," he said.

"He claims he could've bagged her," Pat added. "Jack has a very vivid imagination."

"I could've!" he insisted. "And she would've loved it!"

Jack turned toward Alicia.

"It happened like this," he said. "I was at her house, hanging out, chatting, the regular thing. As the minutes passed, she became undone by my charms."

"Please!" Pat groaned.

"I'd like to hear more about gas prices," Alicia said.

"Then," Jack continued, "Liv—that's what she told me to call her—gave me a house tour, no doubt a pretext to lure me into the sack. Unfortunately, I opened the wrong door, and tennis balls and racquets tumbled out, clobbering us both. She made me leave."

"I'm sure it was all about the racquets." Pat rolled her eyes. "She couldn't have been that attracted to you, if she let a little tennis get in the way."

Everyone laughed again, even Alicia, because she thought she should.

The dinner lasted three hours. As a whole, the Kennedys were moderate drinkers, a bit of a shock given their big and lusty personalities, and bootlegger roots. But that night the reins were loosened. Everyone was too busy celebrating, making plans for Jack, plans for them all.

All the way to the White House!

Nothing's stopping us now!

By the time Joe Kennedy tinged his glass to make a final speech, Alicia concluded that she fit as well as any non-Kennedy might. Blending in: her greatest skill.

"This has been a terrific night," Joe said as he stood. "And I'm certain we could solve all of Washington's problems with the brain trust in this room."

Everyone whooped and cheered.

"In honor of Jack's birthday, I think a speech is in order."

The Kennedys hooted again, but when Alicia went to look at Jack, she noticed that everyone was instead staring at her.

"Miss Darr?" Joe said. "Why don't you do the honors?"

"Me?" Alicia said with a cough. "Oh, Mr. Kennedy, I'm not very good with speeches."

"Or speech in general," said Bobby.

"Come on, Miss Darr. Up and at 'em."

"That's enough, Dad," Jack said. "She doesn't want to."

Bobby thwacked his hands together.

"You can't deny the invitation, Alicia," he said. "And you can't leave your fans wanting."

"Speaking of fans," Joe said. "Did everyone know that Alicia has been scouted by none other than Don Class, one of the best talent agents in the biz? Be careful, son, or she's going to ditch you for Hollywood!"

Alicia glared at Jack. She couldn't believe he'd told his dad.

"You don't have to give a speech," he whispered, misinterpreting Alicia's glare.

"No, Jack, I'm happy to toast you on this splendid occasion," Alicia said, standing, her legs and stomach weak. "Of course, I'm not well-practiced in speechmaking."

"Ha! You're not kidding!" Ethel cackled.

"But hopefully my adoration of you all will mask my lack of experience," Alicia said, evenly she thought. "I'm very pleased to be here, with this wonderful family, to celebrate this wonderful man." She looked at Bobby. "And his little brother, who has accomplished something, too."

Bobby flung a pea directly at her head, and Alicia ducked, though not in time. Her eyes darted around the table. Had Bobby Kennedy just thrown food at her? No one reprimanded him, so she had to be wrong.

"When I first met Jack . . ." Alicia said, pressing on, as something tiny and hard formed in her stomach. "When I first met Jack, I thought my hearing was off. You see, every person was staring at him in awe, as if he'd made some life-changing statement. But in my ears, he'd only said hello."

"Are you sure it's Jack you're thinking of?" Eunice asked.

"What room was this?" Bobby said. "The maid's closet?"

Sweat gathered at Alicia's hairline but she muddled on, knowing that to the Kennedys nothing was worse than a quitter, not even an immigrant with a shoddy toast.

"I soon realized," Alicia said, "that my hearing was fine."

"Lemme guess," Jean piped in. "It was a translation deal?"

"No." Alicia chuckled to keep from tears. "The point I'm laboring to make is that I soon realized people regard Jack that way all the time. He commandeers a room simply by walking into it and his smile is a benediction of sorts."

"Aw, shucks," Jack said with a complete absence of humility.

She was beginning to regret describing him in such flattering terms.

"He dominates a room like no other," she continued, pushing past her building doubt. "He's bold and funny and charming. And he's quite fun to watch."

"What about the *bed*room?" said Bobby. "How does he command that?"

Ethel bellowed and clapped. Her enormous belly jiggled. More peas sailed past.

"Come on," Bobby pressed. "Admit it. That's the only room you see him in."

Several people sniggered, but Alicia didn't stop to analyze which ones. Chest tight and vision blurry with tears, she folded her napkin and placed it on the table.

"Excuse me," she said, voice clackety like a freight train. "Thank you for a lovely meal, but I should go."

With that, Alicia bolted from the room.

"Was that necessary?" she heard Pat say. "Poor girl. Jesus H, no wonder so many people think the Kennedys are such pricks."

Alicia stood on the porch, shivering in her silk despite being so hot with shame. The *Victura,* freshly arrived from its winter at the boat-yard, bobbed in the distance.

She stared out across the sound, wondering how the night took such a crooked turn. More importantly, how was she going to get home? She refused to set foot back inside, but that's where she'd left her hand-bag, and it was where she might find a phone to call George.

"They're a bunch of cretins," someone said. "Lowlifes."

Alicia whirled around to find Pat, who gave her a sad smile and then offered a cigarette. Alicia didn't smoke, but she took one all the same.

"I'm trying to figure out where I went wrong," Alicia admitted, when Pat finally got the flame to strike in the damp air.

"Oh, kid . . ."

Alicia startled to hear Jack's nickname coming from Pat's heart-shaped mouth. If she took to calling her *Dahr*-ling, Alicia would be convinced that all Kennedys were pulling from the same book.

"You did nothing wrong," Pat said.

She blew a stream of smoke over her shoulder. Pat really was the prettiest of the sisters, especially in that misty moonlight. Never mind her auburn waves and striking violet eyes, Pat lacked the others' gawk and ranginess.

"Here's the deal," Pat said. "They loooooove to coax unsuspecting guests into inappropriate toasts so they can humiliate the speaker. It's a game. You're not the first."

"That's positively horrible," Alicia said. "Sorry, I know it's your family, but it's really quite ghastly. . . ."

"Oh, I agree," Pat said. "Why do you think I live on the left coast? Listen, kid, you handled yourself far better than most. Bobby doesn't usually resort to monkey antics unless he's run out of options."

"Be sure to let Bobby and the others know I've suffered far greater humiliation in my life. Vegetables in my hair isn't even in the top five, sorry to report. I know how much the Kennedys like to be *winnahs*."

"Ha!" Pat said. "I like it! You're all right, Alicia Darr."

She took another drag of her cigarette.

"No one told me there would be stargazing after dessert."

Another person moved onto the porch. Though she'd expected, hoped for Jack, the man who'd joined them was Joe.

"Sorry if we got a stitch rowdy in there," he said with sincerity so manufactured, Alicia swore she saw a plastic sheen. "The Kennedys can get carried away."

Alicia nodded because she agreed, though she did not accept his excuse. Who did these people think they were? A failed ambassador and heaps of money, plus one congressman elected from a small state. It was not the world's most commendable dossier.

"Jack sure loves having you around," Joe said. "We all do. You're a thrill to look at."

Alicia managed to push a "thanks" through her teeth.

"I'd better get inside," Pat said, and tossed her cigarette into a nearby rosebush. "Before Mother gets lonely and starts thinking about budgets again."

"No!" Alicia yelped. "Please. Stay."

Pat shrugged and shook her head. Her expression seemed to say, *Sorry, sister, I was being nice, but I didn't sign up for more than the basics.*

"Pat's right," Joe said. "Someone's gotta entertain Mother."

"What's the hubbub?" said a new voice, a fourth member to this uncomfortable party that Alicia so fiercely wished to leave. "No one needs to entertain Mother. You know she prefers to be alone."

It was Jack. Finally, Jack in third place, after Pat and Joe. Alicia scoped out the porch railing, pondering whether she had the strength to leap over and scurry off into the night.

"Let it be known I'm the only one who's apologized to Miss Darr," Pat said. "The rest of you are idiots. Razzing the poor girl. Get some class."

"It's all in good fun," Jack said.

"Some fun." Pat snorted. "If someone wrote a book about this family, the world would never believe it."

"She enjoys it," Joe said, lifting his expansive, shiny forehead. "Don't you, Miss Darr? At the start of your speech you called us . . . what was it . . . ?"

He checked with Jack.

"A wonderful family?"

"You betcha," Jack said.

"For Pete's sake, the girl is an *orphan*." Pat flung a hand toward Alicia. "She lost her family when she was still a girl. I'm sure she's just relieved to be involved in a group."

"That's not how I'd put it. . . ." Alicia began, weary of the way they all spoke as if she wasn't there.

And then: another set of footsteps on the wooden-planked porch. Alicia threw back her head and stifled a cry. How many more of them planned to come outside? She cursed Rose Kennedy for having so many damned kids, all of them hyper and yappy and crawling all over each other like puppies. Someone should neuter every last one of them.

"Can I help you?" the Ambassador asked formally.

Alicia looked up to find the feet were not Kennedy, which she should've guessed from the clunking stride. The steps, and the shoes, belonged to Irenka. And she was trying to join their group.

"Irenka!" Alicia said.

Her heart thrummed, her throat went dry. They'd not spoken in months, close to a year, but her old friend's mug felt like a lifeline. Maybe *she'd* retrieve the purse. She'd help Alicia get home.

"We're having a private conversation," Pat snarled.

"Did you call Alicja orphan?" she said.

"Irenka, just leave," Alicia said, her hopes at once dashed.

"She is not orphan," Irenka said, to Jack, and to Joe.

She plodded farther along the porch, aggressively almost, like a fairy-tale giant stomping out villagers.

"Irenka . . ." Alicia pleaded.

Where was her kindness, her humanity?

"She is not orphan," Irenka said again, her pronunciation remarkably clear, though she smelled quite strongly of booze. "Her name not Alicja. She called Barbara at home. And she has mudder, mudder still alive."

"What's a mudder?" Pat said.

"Where is Janet?" Joe asked, patting himself, as if he might've left her in some other coat. "She'll take care of this."

"Let's go, sweetheart," Jack said to Irenka. "You're in a state. I'll take you inside. Probably best that you have a nap."

"She has family!" Irenka insisted.

"She's a *displaced person*," Pat said.

"She has mudder. In camp. In Germany."

"Is this woman making any sense?" Jack asked Alicia.

She opened her mouth but found no response.

"You ask her how she get to America," Irenka said, hissing. "She prostitute herself. Whore. Get visa and leave mudder behind."

"Oh, *mother*," Pat said. "*Mudder*. I get it."

"Her mudder sick. Very ill. But not so ill as her dotter."

For what seemed like a great while, no one spoke, the lone sound from the crickets calling into the night.

"Guess I won't be retiring indoors," Pat said. "Time for another smoke."

The flick of the match was almost deafening.

"See?" Irenka said. "She does not deny."

"Alicia?" Jack said, hopeful.

Alicia bit her lip and shook her head. She didn't want to explain it here, like this, with Joe and Pat and Irenka listening, taking in every word. It was something Jack should know about her, but not in this way.

"How she describes it," Alicia said, "is not the story. It's not *my* story."

"Alicia," Jack said. "Are your parents alive?"

"My father died in 1942, at Tr—"

"Your mom," Jack snapped. "What about your mom?"

Alicia inhaled, tasting the sea air, Pat's smoke, all of it.

"It's true," she said, insides cratering. "My mother is alive."

She knew that with the Kennedys, her transgression was unforgivable. A person could lie or cheat or bribe or steal, as long as he remained loyal to his tribe.

"I never stated she'd passed," Alicia said. "It's a complicated situation. . . ."

"You lied," Jack said, face crinkling in disgust. "About your family. About your own mother."

"I can explain."

"Don't bother."

With that, Jack pivoted and went inside.

Whether Pat, Joe, and the traitorous Irenka followed him seconds or minutes later, Alicia would never know. As soon as Jack disappeared, Alicia did what she should've twenty minutes before. She vaulted herself over the railing and ran off into the dewy night.

The postal worker has strolled by Margutta four times, but he's not yet encountered the pretty Serena Palmisano. She'd stand out, as most residents on this quaint street are middle-aged.

On the fifth day, the man determines that these daily sojourns are no longer worth the effort. He has no evidence she lives here, and there are other treasures to unearth. Standing in her courtyard amid the ivy-covered terra-cotta buildings, he regards the envelope one last time and goes to chuck it in the bin.

Then he hears a crunch. He cranes to see Serena Palmisano walking across the gravel. He shakes his head once, to make sure she's really there. Yes. It is Serena, and she is accompanied by a very tall and handsome man, an American to be sure.

Serena is as lovely as the internet promised. She is slight, but feminine, and blessed with a sheath of straight, black hair, and round, soulful eyes. Her smile is large and white. The man considers that she has a few too many teeth. Also, her ears are a little big. Perhaps she's not perfect after all.

The couple breezes past and the man follows them inside. They stop at a bank of mailboxes. That's when Serena notices they are being shadowed. She turns away from the American and gives the postal carrier a funny look.

The man offers a darting smile and drops the letter into her mail slot, as though he's actually there to do his job. He takes his exit, winking as he passes.

Well, that was a waste of time. He had big hopes for that letter but now it's literally out of his hands. Maybe the girl will have better luck, though he can't imagine a resident of this building needing an inheritance. She clearly leads a charmed life.

After leaving the quiet Margutta and stepping into the noisy clamor of central Rome, the man picks up his pace, thoughts of Serena Palmisano growing faint. He hurries toward the sorting center with unusual efficiency, dreaming of what he might find next.

HONOR DEAD BY HELPING THE LIVING

Press and Sun-Bulletin, May 31, 1951

HYANNIS PORT

George found Alicia a mile up from the Kennedys'.

Jeannette had called from the house. She told him that Miss Darr had run off without her handbag, and left her heels in the lawn.

"This is an inauspicious sight," George said when he pulled up beside her.

Alicia wanted to keep walking but knew he'd follow, and why make it painful for the both of them? She reluctantly got into his car.

"Jack found out about my mother," Alicia told him. "And that's all I have to say."

"Did you explain why you left her in Germany?" He shook his head. "I knew this would happen."

"Thanks for your keen insight. And, no, I didn't explain because I never had the chance. I'm done talking about this."

They rode the rest of the way in silence.

Now Alicia was upstairs, on her bed, the butterfly dress fanned out around her. Her feet were cold, and grass clippings covered her toes and ankles. For hours she'd been staring blankly through the ging-ham curtains. It was almost dawn.

At about six o'clock, Alicia heard a car clambering outside. She peered through the window in time to spot a telltale Buick. Alicia watched as Jack lurched out of the car, then slammed the door behind him. He had Alicia's handbag tucked beneath his right arm. A small relief glimmered inside.

The doorbell rang. It was early, but the smell of coffee told Alicia that Mrs. Neill was awake. A polite resident would've intercepted the visitor but he was probably only there to drop off the purse. Anyway, Mrs. Neill would be pleased to see the man. Jack Kennedy charmed the dickens out of her, and it might be the last time their paths crossed.

Alicia listened to the soft patter of their voices, and the intermittent light chuckles from Mrs. Neill. She crouched onto the floor for a bet-ter eavesdropping spot, then decided to hell with it, she might as well meet her fate.

After straightening and fluffing her butterflies, a good match for her stomach as it happened, Alicia rushed downstairs before better judg-ment could take over.

"Oh! Alicia!" Mrs. Neill said as Alicia stumbled through the living room door. "I was coming to get you. You have a visitor. Jack posi-tively had to see you before returning to Washington. Isn't that sweet? I may be an old bag, but I adore a good romance."

Mrs. Neill winked, brushed Alicia's arm, and then padded upstairs. In all this time, Alicia didn't once glance at Jack. She was afraid of how he might look at her, and what he might see.

"Aw, Alici*er*," he clucked. "You're so bedraggled and cute. Still in your same clothes."

Alicia let out a sob and rushed toward him. But as she got near, Jack stiffened. Alicia wrapped both arms around her own waist instead of his.

"Are you here to drop off my handbag?" she asked, staring at the floor.

"Nah. Well. Yes," he said. "But I was coming over regardless. Seems like a few things need to be cleared up. I hate surprises."

"Trust me, I feel the same."

"But no one let you tell your story, and explain what that maid meant."

Alicia quickly glanced at Jack. His eyes were watery, just like hers.

"It's easy for me to say, don't do this, don't do that," he went on. "When I have the benefit of being able to make decisions from a very fortunate spot. When I thought about it, when I asked myself why you'd lie about your mother, I realized that people lie about their families all the time, to protect loved ones, or themselves."

Alicia stared, stomach tumbling. How was it he always found the right words, even when she was in the wrong?

"So." Jack plopped onto the sofa and pushed up his sleeves like he was about to draft a speech. "Let's get to it. You have a mother? In . . . ?"

"West Germany. Stuttgart."

She took a few steps forward, and a few more after that.

"And she's in a camp of some sort?" Jack asked.

A few scuffles closer.

"Yes," Alicia said. "A displaced-persons camp, where we both used to live."

Jack patted the cushion beside his.

"Now explain the rest."

With an exhale, Alicia lowered herself onto the couch. The dress crunched and her underpinnings were at once too snug. Of course, she'd been wearing them for twelve hours straight and they were meant to hold up breasts and rein in waistlines for only about six.

"I didn't abandon her," Alicia said. "I left, so that I could get us *both* out. Every week I send her money, as much as I can. Every week I'm one step closer to getting her out of that camp."

This was the easy part of her story. As far as visas went, it was Alicia or nothing. The camps were temporary and would soon close. Their only chance was Alicia, and the United States.

Alicia repeated the tale already told to George, but could not stop where she had before because George never asked if her name was Barbara. He never asked why a maid named Irenka might call her a whore.

You know that we fled Łódź in 1939 because my father's status put him at risk of being deported.

You also know that we went to Radom, a city in which we lived cautiously and on guard for several years. I couldn't attend school and so Father educated me himself, my classroom the crooked table in our shabby little home. During this time, Mother taught herself to sew, at Father's insistence and despite her dislike of the craft.

Papa had many talents, the chief of these his ability to spot a threat before it hit, like a train heard in the distance. In the summer of 1941, he sensed a shift, the heightening of tension. That's when he shuttled me off to convent school, and Mother to a factory, where she worked as a seamstress for the Wehrmacht. She wouldn't have had that job, and probably not her life, if not for Father forcing her to learn a trade. She also lied about her age, shaving off seven years. It helped that she was at that time so beautiful that people often mistook us for sisters.

Weeks after I departed for Warsaw and Mother assumed her factory job, the Germans initiated *aktionen* in Radom. They rounded up tens of thousands of citizens and sent them to the concentration camp Treblinka, where they were gassed. Some years later, I'd learn that Papa was in this group. After the heart and cunning he used to save his family, he died in an inhumane, brutal, and anonymous way, no difference between the criminals and the heroes, the sinners and the saints.

He'd sent me to a convent for "good girls" from affluent homes. I didn't know if I was good, and we certainly didn't seem affluent anymore, but they took me in. As I was not raised Catholic, Mother Superior and the others had some work to do. They taught me Latin, and the Bible, and the rhythm of the matins and vespers. I went through full Catholic rites. Several convents sheltered children during the war, but there was nothing false about my knowledge of the faith. I earned this, same as those who'd been Catholic from birth.

After two years, a group of us moved to Szymanów, where the sisters ran a boarding school for older girls. Szymanów was a long way from Warsaw and was therefore less dangerous, for a time. But immediately we had to confront frequent, unannounced inspections. German storm troopers descended in their black uniforms with red swastikas, crashing through our wall, barging through our doors. They requisitioned part of the convent to billet soldiers. By then, none of us were safe, not even the nuns.

While I studied under the sisters and endeavored to survive, Mother toiled twelve hours a day, sewing uniforms in a crowded, intemperate factory that was frequently bombed. From where she worked, she could hear evidence of life outside. Also, evidence of death, like the screams of people being hauled off in cattle cars.

Eventually, Mother was transferred to a factory in Warsaw, and then a munitions plant in Ludwigslust, followed by a salt mine somewhere in Germany. Then they sent her to a labor camp. She would move fifteen times between Łódź and the displaced-persons camp where we reunited.

They say the war ended in September 1945, but Germany unraveled many months before. In April, the Allies began liberating camps. They captured the Reichstag, and Hitler took a gun to his head. Finally, with the bombing of Hiroshima, the Allies had their victory. But a war never really "ends," does it? It's not like a holiday or a party, where everyone packs up their possessions and goes home. The signing of a treaty is the end of combat fighting, but the start of some new state.

Our state was this: homelessness, loneliness, confusion. All in, the overarching sense of being displaced. There were ten to twenty million in this position, a number too enormous to calculate. At the time, I still had a home at the convent, but my status was not secure. Father paid for me to attend school, but how much had he given, and would they let me stay? I was able to finish my schooling and left in 1946, a few months after my sixteenth birthday.

Father Skalski tried to trace the girls' families, but his information wasn't always reliable or complete. He knew about Mother's job in Radom, but after that he couldn't find a trail. My father was listed among the dead at Treblinka, a fact he disclosed on the occasion of my fourteenth birthday, which meant I'd never celebrate a birthday again. Why did I get another year, and not Papa? And how was surviving three hundred sixty-five consecutive days something to celebrate? I didn't *do* anything. It was pure luck, nothing more.

Though I believed the priest's words, the news read like fiction all the same. In my mind, Father left war-torn Poland to live temporarily in a different story, a place where he could enjoy literature and music and debate political topics without punishment. He'd pop into my world when the time was right. I had to stay at the convent in case he came. Also, I was afraid to meet real life.

"There's nothing for me to do out there," I'd said to Father Skalski.

He responded that I was a bright and faithful young woman, and would be fine. I had to go, he said, and start my life in this new Europe.

"And you must find your mother."

"Find my mother?" I'd gasped. "How do you propose I do that? Wander through Europe, hoping to bump into her?"

He went to write something as I scrambled to find a reason that might compel him to let me stay.

"I want to become a nun," I said.

I didn't want to be a nun. I wanted a home, not a pointless quest for someone I'd never find.

"We'd love to have you," he said. "But you must *try* to locate your family first. You can always come back, if a life of the cloth is truly what you want."

He handed me a list of the DP camps with the most Poles. The majority were in Germany, he said, so I should begin there. He'd gotten me a job at a tracking bureau in Bünde. It was a good place to start.

"Tomorrow," he said, "a soldier will escort you to Bünde. There you will earn a nice wage, and, with any luck, find the answers you seek."

I could say nothing but "thank you."

The next morning, on my way out the door, Father Skalski handed me some money, so I could get by. I wept over his generosity but later wondered if he'd done nothing more than return what was rightly mine. Surely in his desperation, Papa overpaid for the privilege of a convent school, though he would've viewed no price as too steep.

In Bünde, I realized there were millions of us rambling around the blighted country, trying to find loved ones across five hundred camps. Thankfully, the rumor web was thick and by 1947, I'd learned that Radomers were congregating in Stuttgart. My family wasn't originally from Radom, but it was the last home we'd had together so it was worth a shot. Father used to say, "Don't believe every rumor you hear; but don't ignore them either." So, on the inquiry form at the tracking bureau, I wrote "Stuttgart?" under "Other information." This was where I found my mom.

Mother was hospitalized when I arrived and therefore quarantined. They warned she probably wouldn't last the month. We'd hear similar warnings many times over the following years.

We finally saw each other, face-to-face, in the lobby of that hospital. Mother was in a wheelchair, an image that clawed right into my heart. I performed a quick calculation, and then did the math a second time. There'd been an error, I was convinced. The person before me wasn't in her thirties. This was an old woman, with white hair, and no teeth. Her hands were cracked, her nails peeled.

"Barbara?" Mother wheezed.

"No, that's not my name."

By then denying my life had become rote. Barbara Kopczynska? I'd never heard of her.

Then I remembered who I was.

"Yes, Mamusia," I said, tears rolling down my cheeks, "it is me."

I squatted beside her, and took her frail hands in mine, instantly regretting all my complaints about the convent schedule, and the dank quarters, and the billeting soldiers trying to have their way. It wasn't always happy, and it was hardly ever comfortable, but it hadn't taken me to the bone. What had Mamusia endured in five years, to appear as though she'd aged fifty?

I understood that I'd developed into an attractive woman, but I didn't stop to consider that Mother must've been similarly alarmed. The last time she'd seen me, I was a wispy innocent, miles from womanhood, and still unknowing of the horrors to come. That girl obeyed her mother, and worshiped her father, and was quiet and soft and kind.

When I first saw Mother, I thought, *Who is this old crone?* But, Mother saw a little girl acting too mature. I should've been in a pinafore, not wearing such a mature dress. Was I pretending to have breasts? And what was with the lipstick and that face? The doctors passing by snuck hungry stares. Mother knew nothing about me, but at that moment she saw that I was very plainly a bad girl. In Radom, her greatest fear was that she'd never see her daughter again, and I was a reminder that this fear had come to pass.

Our relationship started cold and distant, and worsened from there. Thanks to years of starvation and abuse, sickness racked Mother's body, everywhere including her mind. She yelled at me for childhood infractions and accused me of hiding her medicine. Once she asked if I'd given up Father to the authorities. She'd seen the worst of humanity and her guard was up. Thankfully, I'd developed a tough and callous stoicism over the years.

We persevered. I took a job as a typist with the camp administration and met the other residents in our makeshift community. The place resembled a city, replete with schools, businesses, and civic organizations. We could almost pretend that we'd resettled, right there at the camp. It was a decent life, but it wasn't built to last.

Countries like the United States, Canada, and Australia were admitting people for resettlement, and I put myself on the list despite my misgivings and the fact Mother would never be approved due to her health.

"I won't go without her," I'd told the man processing my paperwork. "How could I leave her here?"

The man explained that the wait list was long, as these countries limited how many displaced persons were allowed in each year. Probably by the time my name came up, Mother's illness would cease to be a factor. In other words, she'd be dead. His words were more comforting than I'd like to admit.

That summer, we learned that the camps were closing, and the Allies were winding up their DP sponsorship efforts. Panic overtook us all. There were a million of us left. Where would we go? Would we be subject to German rule once again? The idea chilled me to the core.

They were not fast in shutting down—thank God—and for the next two years I worked and painted and fretted nonstop. Mother either ignored or yelled at me. I kept a respectful distance, from her and the other DPs. Although I'd grown quite lonely, I hesitated in forming friendships, in being part of any "group." I would not soon allow myself to be identified by the songs I sung, or the gods I worshiped, or anything someone might one day deem wicked.

During this time, I developed a closeness with my boss, an American soldier. This friendship turned into the physical. He thought I was beautiful and smart. That I spoke six languages impressed him to no end. He was handsome and kind, though not the brightest, but he was enough at the time.

It's possible he was using me. There weren't many single, young women at the camp, fewer still in decent health, and none with my looks. I stood out. Many made passes, but his was the first I entertained.

The man promised he could get me to America. He had an aunt in Wisconsin willing to sponsor me, and such arrangement would ensure the fastest track. We were staring down the barrel of 1950—a new decade! I had to go, and take this opportunity. As for him, he was leaving, too.

"I can't abandon my mother," I explained, for the hundredth time.

"She despises you," he said.

"But she is my mom."

His last night at the camp, my soldier came to say good-bye. Mother was asleep and we got to it right at the kitchen table. She walked in as I straddled the man. She screamed, she screeched, she pummeled me all over, with both of her fists.

In a blur, I managed to pull on my dress, and the soldier escaped partially clothed. Through it all, Mother wept for all that she and Father sacrificed to give me. And now I was a common slut.

"You were supposed to be amazing," she said. "Now you're worthless, less than nothing. Dressing like a strumpet. Making love to any American who glances your way. Your father would be appalled. If this is what you're going to do with your life, it wasn't one worth saving."

The next day the soldier was gone and my papers were approved. I had an immigration visa in hand. I had to go. This was my chance to prove that I wasn't a "common slut" and that my life was worth the risk. I would do something grand, something meaningful. There was one place to make big dreams come true: the United States.

"That's why I'm here," Alicia said, voice shaky, as she reached the end of her tale. "And why Mother is still in Germany. My goal is to earn enough to buy her a nice house, and hire a nurse to help. Mother is young, but unwell, and I don't know how much time we have left. She hates me, but I owe it to my father to make sure she's all right."

Alicia let her gaze fall on Jack. She saw that he was fidgety and glistening with sweat, as though he'd been the one to confess.

"Hell, Alici*er*," Jack said, and shook his head. "That is fucked up."

Alicia nodded, not knowing whether he meant what happened to her, or what she'd done.

"I'm sorry for keeping this from you," she said. "But I'm not ashamed of the decisions I've made."

Jack stood and Alicia's heart plunked into her gut. As she started to speak—to protest, something—Jack offered the unthinkable. He spread both arms for a hug.

"Come here, brave girl," he said.

Alicia stood, legs warm and weak, and then she collapsed into Jack's chest and began to weep. The man was scrawny, stiff and thin, but it seemed like he could hold her up for days. Jack had the oddest way of making himself seem bigger, even when he was skin and bones.

"I hope you realize," he said into her hair, "that no matter what your mother thinks, you've accomplished what you set out to do. You've made a name for yourself. You've proven that the universe knew what it was doing when it kept you alive. Personally, I'm quite grateful. Not to be selfish about it."

Alicia laughed sadly.

"I don't know that I've made a name for myself." She pulled away and looked up. "But I've sent her money for this and that, minor luxuries that might improve her life. I've also been able to pay for medicines that she wouldn't otherwise get."

"It's so impressive what you've done. A refugee, no less!"

She bristled.

"I haven't done all that much. She's still sick, still in the camp, and still being tended to by Nazi doctors." Alicia sighed. "And while I'm making confessions, I should tell you about the necklace you gave me. The truth is, I sold it."

"You *what*?"

"That's why I didn't wear it tonight. I sold it and sent her the proceeds."

"Alicia." Jack released her from his hold. "That was a gift. I won't ask what you got for it. I'm sure you were swindled."

"I view myself as having a decent handle on the value of clothes and jewels," she said. "And I didn't think you'd care. You weren't the one who bought it!"

"Oh, geez, not the Sarge Shriver junk again."

"It was a rash decision, but I'm not going to spend time on that particular regret, as I have plenty of others to keep me busy."

"You're right," Jack said with a frown. "It's a stupid necklace. I'm sorry for giving you shit."

"No apologies necessary."

"Fuck. You know what? I knew you were strong from the second I met you. But that was a guess, and now I know for sure. How did you survive all that?"

Alicia smirked, for she'd given him the most cursory of overviews. Yes, she survived the move to Radom, and the convent, and the camp, but she could've spoken for hours about everything else she'd endured.

"I don't know if I *survived*," she said, "or was simply a day luckier than so many others. Through it all I told myself, *I only have to reach tomorrow*. At least I was in a convent. We were still in danger, but better off than most."

"You're a hero to me," he said.

"I'm no *war* hero, though," she said with a wink. "No one gave me a medal."

"That was easy. All I had to do was have someone sink my boat."

With an exhausted sigh, Jack sat. He tugged on his shirt, as if letting in some air.

"The soldier?" He studied her with a squint. "Did you love him?"

Alicia pressed her lips together for a second or two.

"I'm not sure that I loved him," she said, "but I believed in our romance absolutely. It was an enchanting thing in that moment of time. We didn't have to think about the future at all."

She sat beside Jack and smoothed her skirt over her knees.

"He helped me get my visa," she said, "but that's not why I fell for him. It's difficult to explain. He was handsome and kind and after going so long without human contact, it felt so *good* to be touched like that. I'm sorry if it sounds scandalous."

"I'm jealous," Jack said with an almost playful growl, "but it doesn't sound scandalous at all."

"Being with him made me feel alive, *human,* after not feeling that way for so long. And I wasn't the only one." She smiled. "When I first arrived at the camp, I was one of the youngest. And then, boom! Babies were being born, left and right. At one point, Stuttgart had the highest birth rate in the world, thanks to the DPs."

"I want to take care of you," Jack said, clutching her hands. "From now until forever. I want to make sure that you never feel unloved, or worthless, or desperate again. Alicia, let's get married."

"Jack! What a ridiculous thing to say!"

Alicia's heart fluttered and her palms grew sweaty. She refused to accept the world he was offering to her. He didn't mean it. Jack Kennedy was impetuous, full of big ideas.

"Dad's always saying a Catholic politician needs a Catholic wife," he said, "and you fit the bill."

"Not the same way your mother does."

"No one's *that* Catholic," he said with a snort. "Except possibly the nuns at your convent school. Anyway, I don't care what my father thinks."

"That's not true."

"It is. Dad has his opinions, and I have mine, and they're not always the same. You know, I keep telling the pols that I'm not Joe Kennedy. Why are you making me do it with you?"

Alicia would never mistake the two men, but as for Jack's future, there was no clear point at which the Ambassador's ambition stopped, and Jack's took over.

"I can give you everything you want," he said. "I can buy your mother a house tomorrow, and get her the nurse! Even though she doesn't deserve it. But if that's what you want, you'll have it."

Suddenly, Jack pushed himself off the couch and dropped to one knee. Alicia panicked and rushed toward him, thinking he'd taken a spill, that his back had betrayed him once again.

"Shall I call an ambulance?" she said.

"Alicia Darr," he said, looking into her face, "will you marry me? I don't have a ring, but I'll buy you the best one there is."

"Jack, no," Alicia said. "I'm not going to accept any hasty proposals."

She wanted to, very badly, but Alicia knew Jack's ways. She didn't want to say yes, and then have him change direction—or forget—by noon.

"It's not hasty," Jack said. "I've been thinking about this for a long time. The night of the firemen's ball, I resolved to make you my wife. I saw all of this in you, your strength, your intelligence, your bravery, though I didn't understand it at the time. I love you, Alicia. Please marry me."

Everything inside Alicia screamed. That Jack applauded her mind instead of her breasts or rear was so unlike him that she wondered if he was serious after all. And if he could love her after what she'd said, deflowered "Catholic" girl and all, then he could love her in spite of anything.

"I don't know," she said, though she did know, very much.

It seemed too rushed, too harried. Then again, that was the very way of Jack.

"I want to take care of you," he said again. "I promise to make everything wonderful, for the rest of your days."

"Oh, Jack," Alicia said with a nervous chuckle. "No one can promise that, not even you."

"Marry me," he said again.

"Do you really mean it? And will you still mean it tomorrow, and next week?"

"Absolutely." He broke out into a grin. "If you want to know the truth, Sarge picked out a ring."

Alicia threw back her head.

"Jack!"

"I'm kidding," he said. "I did consult him, but in light of a recent jewelry kerfuffle, it's probably best that I pick it out myself."

"At least you're capable of learning from your mistakes," she said.

"You'd better believe it." His smile widened. "So, Barbara Kopczynska, now Alicia Darr, will you marry me?"

"Yes, Jack Kennedy," she said, tears returning to her eyes. "I would love nothing more than to be your wife."

WASHINGTON, D.C.

It was usually around two o'clock in the morning when the panic set in.

Alicia hadn't been a good sleeper since she left Łódź. They were probably all like that, she guessed. Where the war had survivors, it also had millions of twitchy-eyed specters who'd never get a full night's sleep again.

She didn't have to worry about Gestapo raids anymore, at least when her dreams behaved, and Alicia was grateful to fret over more pedestrian concerns. Nonetheless, it was one month until their planned honeymoon and they didn't have a wedding date. How would this all come together?

Alicia slid from the bed, careful not to jostle, for Jack hadn't been sleeping well either. In addition to his usual back ailments, his headaches had worsened. Later in the week, doctors were going to X-ray his skull.

"My greatest wish," he'd said last night, "aside from marrying you, is to experience twenty-four hours free of pain."

Alicia crept downstairs, feeling her way through the unfamiliar darkness. It was her first time in Washington, and the home Jack shared with Eunice, though Eunice was rarely there. She'd been working with juvenile delinquents in Virginia, to her mother's vast chagrin.

In the living room, Alicia slumped in a blue wingback chair and glanced out to the cobblestone streets. Much like her husband-to-be, Georgetown charmed her on sight, with its gas lamps, tree-lined avenues, and rows of federal townhomes, not to mention all those American flags flapping together in the magnolia-scented breeze.

"This city," Alicia had said as they meandered the neighborhood last night. "It's so beautiful and unimposing. Everyone seems happy to be alive."

Jack laughed.

"Give it two weeks," he said. "When summer hits, you'll see this place for the festering, insect-ridden armpit that it is."

But Alicia didn't want to be in Washington in two weeks. She wanted to be in Hyannis Port, preparing to exchange vows. Even a modest affair needed planning, too.

"Everything will be fine, Alicia *Dahr*-ling," Jack promised. "We can change the date, wait until the timing is right."

This was the problem, for the timing was never good. Jack was right then working on a new bill, something about a pine tree quarter, which didn't seem terribly important, but who was a DP to judge? Plus, the Kennedys were scrabbling about, trying to figure out how to deal with Teddy and also accommodate Ethel, due to give birth any day.

Now Jack was talking about going to Korea, to survey the problem firsthand. It needled Alicia, if she might be so selfish. She didn't understand how someone could choose rubbing elbows with the Reds over an outside double cabin on the *Ile de France,* which they'd booked for next month.

As Alicia watched the quiet streets, she sank deeper into the chair. Maybe postponing the nuptials wasn't the worst idea. While she didn't mind the "small affair" they'd discussed, Alicia couldn't help but remember last summer, when the house was abuzz after Bobby's grand celebration. Was it wrong to want the same excitement, at least for Jack?

But, there was the matter of time, and Alicia's mother, who was sicker by the day. Despite the Catholic upbringing, Alicia wasn't convinced on heaven, and she wanted her mom to finally see that Alicia was important, that she was worth something, by and by.

Alicia closed her eyes. She sent a prayer to her mother, and to her father, wherever he might be, if anywhere at all. *Please let these dreams come true, and please let them be able to see.*

Sunlight blasted through the windows, and Alicia woke up kinked and cramped. She sat upright and tried to rub the pain from her tingling neck. Was this what Jack's body felt like, as though he'd slept in an uncomfortable position for nights, weeks, years on end?

With some effort, Alicia stood. She stretched and checked the clock. Seven fifty-three. In front of the house was an empty spot where Jack's convertible had been parked. He was gone, it seemed, working on his twenty-five-cent piece. Alicia wished he'd woken her before he left.

She went upstairs to pack.

That night, Jack was bound for Boston, to speak at yet another dinner, and Alicia was going home. The Cape Cod Art Association opened in a few weeks and she planned to submit a painting, of what, she did not yet know.

As she stepped into Jack's room, Alicia let out a groan. It was an abomination. The bed was a wreck, and clothes were scattered everywhere, like someone had detonated a suitcase bomb. He and Eunice had a maid, but she'd once been Jack's nanny and therefore spent more time mothering Jack than cleaning his home.

After slipping into an aquamarine skirt and terrace blouse, Alicia searched for her stole, which she ultimately found under a shoe. She tossed it over her shoulders and went to grab her handbag, which sat on Jack's paper-covered desk.

"Slob," she muttered.

Purse hooked onto her arm, Alicia collected Jack's letters into a neat pile, along with scads of bills, some unpaid since December. No wonder Jack's friends were always cross with him, and that Dumont's had stopped extending him credit.

As Alicia stepped away from the desk, something caught her eye, a letter with Merchandise Mart on its mast. This was Joe Kennedy's Chicago operation, but it wasn't the charmless office building that made Alicia stop. It was Sarge's name, underlined with two strong strokes. She picked it up.

> *Dear Jack—*
>
> *Here's the bill for the present. Hope it's not too much over your limit. If convenient, your check should be drawn to order of The Merchandise Mart.*
>
> *I hope everything goes well in Washington. When are you getting married? and what of Helena?*
>
> *Best,*
>
> *Sarge*

Alicia's hands began to shake. Though she could be miffed about the involvement of Sarge Shriver in what seemed to be another gift, this was not what socked Alicia in the gut.

What of Helena, Sarge asked.

The name rendered Alicia disoriented, punch-drunk. Was this a reference to Helen Doyle, Jack's smug new secretary? Perhaps, but there was a second option that rattled her more.

She'd been Barbara Kopczynska and Alicia Darr, and Jack knew both of these names. But Alicia hadn't told him that there was also Helena Nowak. Helena was blond and Catholic and attended convent school. Helena was the one who survived.

The front door opened with a thwack. Alicia dropped the letter, then snatched her valise, and tore downstairs. She'd expected to find Jack, but it was Eunice standing there, with her white-tiled grin and ill-fitting dungarees.

"Hiya," Eunice said with a wink. "Didn't know we had guests. Jack never tells me a thing."

"Me neither," Alicia huffed. "But not to worry. I'm on my way out of town."

"You okay?" Eunice asked, and cocked a brow. "You seem a little hot."

Alicia paused, one hand on the door. Oh, what the hell, she thought, sounding oddly like a Kennedy in her own head.

She flipped around.

"Eunice, I have a question," Alicia said, walking back into the room.

"Yowza. This sounds important."

"It's nothing important. Simply a matter of . . . curiosity."

"Sure." Eunice shrugged and threw her lanky, clambering body onto the couch. "Shoot."

"Janet des Rosiers. Your father's secretary. What does your mother think of the situation?"

"What situation could you possibly mean?" Eunice asked, and began flicking through a magazine. "Janet takes care of everything."

"Don't play dumb, Eunice. It doesn't suit you."

Eunice startled, as if slapped.

"I've seen it play out right in front of your mother," Alicia said. "I've seen it in front of you, and your siblings, and party guests whose names I don't know. Explain it to me. Educate this outsider."

Eunice sighed and shook her bushy mop of hair.

"My mother is happy," she said.

"Is she?" Alicia asked. "Do you know that for sure?"

"What on earth would she have to complain about?"

"Okay, so answer this. Your mother is a religious woman. How does she justify what's going on? She didn't ignore one thing, one time. She has to do it over and over again, every day."

Eunice contemplated this, for what Alicia realized was the first time.

"That's a pretty nosy line of questioning, pal," Eunice said. "My mother is dang square with the Church, so it's not anyone else's show to judge."

"What about the Bible?" Alicia pressed. "What about the Ten Commandments? Thou shalt not commit adultery. Thou shalt not covet—"

"Aw, kid," Eunice said with a throaty cackle. "You don't have to recite the commandments. I'm well acquainted with all of them, numbers one through ten. I assume no one's apprised you of the lesser-known eleventh?"

"The *eleventh* commandment?" Alicia said. "And what exactly is that?"

Leave it to the Kennedys to have one more than everybody else.

"Oh, Alicia," Eunice said with another laugh. "The eleventh is my mother's favorite. She recites it all the time. Sweet girl, the eleventh commandment is 'Thou shall not get caught.'"

HYANNIS PORT

Alicia dropped her bags at the Neills' and went straight to the Center.

They were between shows, the next run of *Along the Great Divide* due to start in an hour. That'd be plenty of time to make herself useful, and fish some advice out of George on the side. He had no romantic history to speak of, but Alicia wanted his view. Eleven commandments, of all the Kennedy things.

With great drama, Alicia yanked open the Center door and swept inside, as if the whole of the theater had been biting nails, waiting for her to arrive.

"Hello, everyone!" she trilled.

Alicia's eyes latched on to George, who stood in the corner looking very much like someone who'd just walked off an unseen step.

"I've returned from Washington!" Alicia thumped her handbag onto the counter. "Didn't have time to grab my uniform, but that's never stopped me from pouring a few Cokes!"

Alicia prattled on, ignoring George's quizzical bearing, anxious to busy herself so that she might suffocate the questions that'd plagued her since she left D.C. Mainly: did she want to wed the Kennedys? Because that's how it'd be with them. She wouldn't marry Jack, she'd marry every last one of them, this family that was somehow singularly attractive yet often repellent at the same time.

Then again, Alicia loved Jack, she truly did. And the newspaper clipping would be worth more than all the money she'd sent to her mother so far.

European artist Alicia Darr marries Congressman Jack Kennedy, son of the former Ambassador to Britain's Court of Saint James's.

"Oh, George," she said. "I had such the time. I could use your insight."

The man had a straightforward wisdom, if nothing else.

"I'm telling you," she went on, George oddly quiet, "some woman is going to be very lucky to scoop you up. She won't have to worry about marrying you and a cast of others besides. She'll just get your mother, who is a delight."

Alicia twirled around for a cup and found herself fronting a slight, plain-mugged girl. The two women locked into a flustered immobility as they stood a hand's width apart.

"I'm Doris," the girl said, as if this explained anything.

"Are you?" Alicia said, and looked at George. "And what does being Doris entail?"

She felt a pending sense of doom.

"Doris is Paul's niece," George said, breaking his silence. "She works here now."

"Lovely!"

Alicia smacked her hands together with such force they prickled and stung.

"It's fabulous to meet you!"

For her part, Doris remained pale and quiet as a corpse. Fat chance this girl could upgrade someone to a jumbo. Maybe it was a charity case, as her attributes were slim.

"Welcome to the Center," Alicia said. "I'm so glad you're here! With the season in full swing, it'll be fantastic to have the extra hands. I'm shocked your uncle Paul sprang for the help. He can be rather tight."

"Alicia," George said with an exasperated sigh.

He marched to her side.

"Are you not getting it?"

"Getting what?" she asked.

"You're right. Paul would never hire two concession girls. That's why we have one, and her name is Doris."

Alicia's eyes widened; her heart sped like a train.

She'd been *fired*? From a concession stand? When she was an artist, a painter, someone who'd been offered a shot at the silver screen? Alicia made a brief appraisal of Doris, who was about as compelling as dishwater.

"That can't be right," Alicia said, and tried to laugh.

"I'm sorry," George answered. "I'm afraid that it is."

"And why, exactly, couldn't Paul deliver the news himself? I mean, really! Have some class!"

"Alicia, he tried to fire you. Three times. But it wasn't easy. He never knew when you'd deign to show up for your shift."

They sat on the steps, squinting against the waning sun. Alicia pulled her skirt over her knees.

"Why are you surprised?" George asked, examining his watch for a third time, lest his projectionist duties go neglected. "You're never here. You've been in New York, Boston, and D.C. in the past week alone."

"But look who he replaced me with!"

George scrunched his face.

"Someone reliable and able to work multiple times per week?" he asked.

"No! Well, yes. Doris has that quality about her." Alicia rolled her eyes. "But she's so drab!"

"Oh, she's not so bad. You've been spending too much time with the Kennedys."

"I thought Paul hired me to give this joint some oomph!"

George checked his watch again and stood. He brushed off his pants.

"I think he just wants someone who'll show up," he said. "Come on."

He reached out a hand. Alicia crossed both arms over her chest and shook her head like a defiant child.

"Why are you so teed off?" George asked.

"Because I'm unemployed! I'm an unemployed immigrant refugee from Poland! They could deport me for that!"

"Aren't you getting married next month? To a congressman? I can't really picture a Kennedy shoveling popcorn."

"That is the plan," Alicia said with a snort.

She pushed herself off the ground.

"If I can bring myself to marry Jack," she said. "And Joe and Bobby and Ethel, and the rest of them. If I can bring myself to succumb to their very Kennedy rules."

"Oh, please. It's not the Kennedy rules you have a problem with. It's their stability. *That's* what you can't succumb to, like I've said before."

"You have no idea what I'd be getting into if I married that family. None at all."

"Maybe I don't," George said. "But it seems pretty basic. Either you love Jack enough, or you don't."

"Enough? What's *enough*?"

"Do you love him more than your freedom, Alicia? Enough to override your apparent inability to stay in one place? That's the question you need to answer, not the one at the altar, not 'Will you take this man?'"

With a final shake of the head, George turned and walked inside. Alicia stood slack-jawed beneath the awning as she listened to the swish of the Center Theatre door one last time.

EX-ENVOY KENNEDY BECOMES GRANDFATHER
The Boston Daily Globe, July 6, 1951

HYANNIS PORT

They planned to wed on Labor Day.

Hundreds would be there. A thousand, perhaps. Family. Friends. People Alicia had never known. The Kennedys weren't embarrassed to trot her out, and there was something in that.

"Maybe you should've gone off with that Don Class character," Eunice said. "You're one hell of an actress. I can barely tell you're foreign these days."

Even Joe Kennedy seemed warmer, less apt to visually canvass her body with that combination of lasciviousness and disgust. Or maybe it was what Alicia said to Jack. She did not mention the letter she found, or ask about "Helena," but she aired her reservations all the same.

"I'm not marrying Joe Kennedy," she said. "And if that's what I'm in for, we should end it now."

She didn't believe in extra commandments, or any other slippery Kennedy rules, and she didn't want some old man telling her what to do.

"Not marrying Dad? Well, I should hope not," Jack answered with a teasing glint. "He's already hitched."

"Is he now? Sometimes it's impossible to tell."

"I'll talk to him," Jack promised. "Make sure he understands that we have our own lives. I'm not a kid, or a bachelor anymore. He'll get used to the idea."

Alicia hugged him in thanks, despite the nagging thought that she was something to "get used to," like Jack's back pain or the wet towels he left on the floor.

Now they were gathered at the big house, to celebrate a new family member added to the ranks. Bobby and Ethel's daughter was born days before, on the fourth of July. They'd named her Kathleen, after the departed Kick. She weighed in at nine pounds, six ounces.

Kathleen was beautiful, but she was a Kennedy, so, of course. She was also curious and inquisitive, even at a few days old. She seemed to understand the dynamic, and she basked in the light of the family's adoration as they passed her around the room.

"Here!" Jean said. "Let me hold her!"

"I was next," said Eunice.

"Uh-oh, don't let Sarge see that," Jack said. "Then he'll really start with the heavy sell."

Everyone laughed as Alicia's eyes fell to the ring that now sat on her left hand. Jack swore he picked this out, and he must've, as it was every bit as dazzling and original as he was. It was a "halo ring," with a large center stone, set in platinum, and fourteen round brilliants surrounding it.

"The center is European-cut," Jack said, "just like you."

Alicia twisted the ring once around her finger, then looked up, directly into Irenka's acidic stare. The woman had been slinking about all afternoon, setting her on edge. She spun the ring one more time, and pulled her gaze away.

The family passed Kathleen from one person to the next, bearing grins so broad it almost hurt to watch. Alicia worried for the girl, and about the expectations being splashed onto her like a baptism. For her part, Rose Kennedy sat in the corner, hands clasped as she lobbed scraps of advice into the room.

"Don't give her too much attention," she said. "Or she'll be spoiled. Where's the nurse? Someone should call the nurse."

The warnings stopped no one, and Joe Kennedy snuggled the child, his face years younger thanks to his delight. Times like these Alicia thought that maybe he wasn't so bad.

"You're not supposed to play with babies," Rose called out. "Irenka! Get in here and collect the discarded linens. The baby, too."

"I'm keeping the girl," Pat said.

As Irenka bustled into the room, Alicia tried to catch her eye, to somehow smooth the air between them. They'd been through so much together, it didn't have to be this way.

"You can't play with them," Rose repeated, because no one had yet listened. "With too much attention, babies are made nervous and irritable. They sleep badly and suffer in numerous other respects."

Weeks ago, or perhaps it was a month, Alicia asked Jack if his mother ever touched them. She was picturing a hug, a kissed boo-boo, that sort of thing. Jack deliberated this for a split second and replied, "When she spanked us, she did."

Alicia had taken it for a joke but now she wasn't sure. Rose Kennedy was a strange, hard little woman and her coldness toward her granddaughter was prime proof. Maybe Joe's business with Janet wasn't so outrageous. Maybe it was done in despair and under duress.

Finally, a nurse came to collect the baby. Irenka was on her heels, with a bottle in hand. Joe kissed Kathleen lightly on the head, and the nurse lifted her from his arms. Joe glanced up, face shining.

"Prettiest Kennedy so far," he said. "Sorry, Jack."

The room laughed, and Kathleen jumped, surprised.

Joe swiveled toward Bobby.

"Have you thought about godparents for this magnificent child?" he asked.

"Yes, as a matter of fact, we were thinking of asking Jack—"

"And his bride-to-be!" Joe said. "That is a perfect idea!"

From the edge of the room, Irenka squawked. She dropped the bottle and it clattered to the floor.

"*Her?*" Bobby said, agog.

"Surely one of the aunties would be a better choice," Alicia said, trying to save them all. "Pat? Eunice?"

"You'd be perfect," Joe said again, mystifyingly determined. "Alicia, we are thrilled to have you in this family."

"Thank you, Mr. Kennedy," Alicia said, unblinking.

That must've been some winning speech Jack had given his father. Maybe he was his own man. She twisted the ring, her latest nervous habit.

"The perfect Catholic wife," Joe added.

Again, Irenka made a sound, loud enough that it caused every pair of eyes to swing her way.

"Sounds like quite the idea," Bobby said evenly, not prepared to go up against his father. "I'll talk to Ethel when she's up from her nap."

Everyone tittered their agreement. Irenka gaped, openmouthed, until duties forced her to leave the room.

Without Kathleen as anchor, the party broke up. Jean and Eunice scrambled upstairs. Bobby went, too, no doubt to find his wife and tell her of Joe's demented plan. Jack left to place a phone call, and Joe was off to a conference with Janet. As for Rose, she disappeared, vaporized, probably to her private house by the sea. Meanwhile, Alicia sat alone in the sunroom, wondering what to do next.

"Hiya," someone said, and kicked Alicia's shoe.

She looked up into Pat's pretty face.

"Wanna grab a smoke with me outside?" she asked.

"Sure," Alicia answered with a smile.

She stood, wondering why Pat always thought her keen for a cigarette. Alicia considered it a dirty habit, and the latest health news was grim. Smoking interfered with athletic activities, they said, and it also made you dumb. But Alicia was willing to take the risk for a few moments with Pat.

"Welp, you're a brave girl to lock in with this crew," Pat said as they sat in wicker chairs facing the sea.

"Hmm." Alicia nodded, pressing her lips together. "I've had a few hesitations, but I love Jack."

Alicia was a different person on the porch, beside the sound, with a cigarette in hand. She felt open, relaxed, imbued with the freedom America promised.

"Hesitations because of us?" Pat asked, with a smirk.

Alicia smiled.

"Thankfully, my concerns have been allayed," she said.

"One thing I like about you is that you're impressed by Jack, and Jack alone. Not the rest of it. Half the time, I don't think you're all that impressed by him."

"Oh, it's impressive," Alicia said, and took a drag.

She lowered the cigarette and watched the smoke curl around her sparkling diamond ring.

"Impressive, but best observed from a distance?" Pat guessed.

"It *can* get loud when you're too close," Alicia said. "But I was an only child, and then I lived in a convent, so I'm accustomed to quiet."

"Doll, I'm *not* an only child and it's often too much for me. That's why I live in Hollywood. My kids will grow up in Malibu, not here. Of course, I need to find a husband first."

Pat ground out her cigarette and went to light another.

"You know," she said, "I think you see more than most people do. I can tell you're watching, and that you understand. You distract with the blond hair and the red lipstick, but you're smarter than you let on."

Alicia chuckled tightly.

"I'm not sure whether to take that as a compliment," she said. "Perhaps I'm not so smart after all."

"What I'm saying is, you'll do okay."

Pat stood, cigarette still dangling from her mouth.

"Hey. I'm in the mood for tennis," she said. "Care for a go?"

"Sure," Alicia said, and rose to meet her. "But, fair warning, I'm not very good."

"Eh. None of us are all that hot." Pat thought about this. "Well, Eunice is, I guess. We just *act* like we're good. The trick is to hit hard, be aggressive, and make large movements. You'll fool most people. As any Kennedy knows, it's not about your game, but convincing others how well you play."

Alicia walked downstairs in her tennis costume: white, scalloped-edged shorts with a white, tied-at-the-waist top that showed a hint of stomach. She'd purchased it solely for use in Hyannis Port, the getup heretofore unworn. Tennis was a swell sport, if it involved dressing like this.

As she rounded the stairs and veered toward the kitchen, she heard the staccato beat of a prickly conversation. Alicia slowed her steps. She recognized Joe's large, booming voice. As for the second person, it was impossible to mistake the broken English of an Eastern Pole.

"Those are some hefty accusations," Joe said. "Are you certain?"

Alicia grabbed the banister. Her entire body tensed.

"*Tak*," Irenka barked. "Ya. One hundred of sure."

"If what you say is true . . ."

Alicia didn't wait for Joe to finish. She tore through the hall, to find Jack. Her heart pumped at full pace.

"Jeannette!" Alicia said, almost pummeling her old colleague, who'd been trying to exit a linen closet. "Have you seen Jack?"

"Yes . . ." she said, adjusting herself. "Miss Dee is trimming his hair in the sunroom."

Alicia darted off, heaving when she finally set foot in the green-paneled room. She grabbed her side, which was now wound up and cramped.

Jack was in a chair, back to the door. Chunks of his hair littered the floor, and Janet was rubbing a musky-scented oil into his scalp. The scene seemed like a lie, but whose mistruth, Alicia couldn't discern.

"Alicia, is that you?" he called out.

"Excuse me, Janet, but are you done? I need to discuss something with Jack," Alicia said, her mouth running faster than her heart.

"Yes, we are through," Janet said slowly, sweetly.

She whirled around and wiped her hands on a towel.

"I'll send in someone to clean up the mess."

"I need to tell you something," Alicia said before Janet was out of the room.

Maybe this would be fine. Jack took news of her mother in steady stride. It compelled him to propose. This was probably for the best. A marriage shouldn't start with secrets as big as these.

As Jack rotated toward her, Alicia crouched down and plucked a lock of his reddish-brown hair from the floor. She slipped it into the pocket of her shorts.

"Cute outfit!" he said. "Suddenly tennis is my favorite sport."

"I was thinking," Alicia said, sounding very much like she'd just played a vigorous two or three sets. "About what Bobby . . . your father said about us being godparents. You'll do a fine job. But as for me . . ."

"Really, Alicia, don't worry about it. You don't need to do much. It's more ceremonial than anything. You'll be fine."

"It's not the duties. I'd be honored, no matter what. It's the religious aspect."

"The religious aspect?"

"Yes." She sighed. "You see, a godmother should probably be Catholic. And that's the problem. Because I'm a Jew."

You know that we fled Łódź, and went into hiding in Radom.

You know that my parents kept me safe in a convent school.

You understand that every action my father took, we took, these decisions all came with risk. But the risk was greater than I'd let you believe. Because while we were associated with the intelligentsia, and the resistance, we had a far worse label, in that we were Jews.

The danger started long before we left Łódź, when the Germans descended upon our city and began enforcing their rules. They confiscated family businesses, including ours, and cordoned us into separate living quarters, which were soon walled off. They forced us to wear armbands and expelled all the Jews from school. Father knew his family had to find another way.

Although he understood we were on a list and denial was not enough, when we got to Radom, he burned our armbands and said we were Jewish no more. Mother was horrified, because what did we have if not our faith?

"Our lives," her father answered. "We will have our lives."

In our apartment in Radom, I began to notice things were disappearing: all the valuables Father made us haul through the forest in the dead of night. The crystal, the artwork, the jewels, these things vanished, one by one. At the time, I assumed he sold them to buy food on the black market, as we rarely went hungry. But what happened to these precious items soon became clear.

One night, Father roused me from sleep. The clock read just past midnight. It was 1941. I had recently turned eleven years old.

"Are we moving again?" I asked, groggy from sleep but always with that constant, stinging knowledge that at any second I'd need to be wholly alert.

"A nurse is here to see you," Father said. "You're ill. Your fever is extreme."

I touched my forehead. It seemed cool, normal.

"I'm fine, Father."

"Sit," he instructed, firmer than he'd ever been.

When I elbowed myself up, I noticed the dance of a candle flame on the table. Mother was weeping in her chair. Beside her stood a nun, dressed in head-to-toe black.

"Mamusia?" I said, but Mother would not meet my eyes.

I felt fine but Father was never wrong and Mother looked like someone was about to die.

"This is Sister Anna," he said, and the nun stepped into the light. "She is a nurse, and is going to help."

Before I could blink, the woman jammed a thermometer into my mouth. Father scooted beside me, and placed his arm around my shoulders, firmly, locking me down. His other hand slid beneath his cloak. The nun began speaking loudly about my "illness," and explained that she would take me to see a doctor in the ghetto.

The ghetto!

The thermometer dropped to the floor. The nun frowned, picked it up, and shoved it back in.

Weren't we trying to *avoid* the ghetto? That's what I'd been told. There's one way out of there, Father warned, though he never said what that one way was.

"The money is all here," Father said, and removed a sack from beneath his clothes.

Her face a mask of stone, the nun took the package, and tucked it into her habit.

"And also, this."

Father shook his arm, and removed his gold watch. My heart stopped. He was giving up his *watch*? It was once his own father's, the first luxury purchased when my grandfather achieved business success. He gave the business to Papa, and then the Nazis took it for themselves. All that was left to represent it was the watch.

"In case we cannot make further payment," Father said, and showed her the gift in the palm of his upturned hand.

In that moment and for the first time, my dear father was not strong and proud but shaky and small. I would've cried out again, but I was gripping the thermometer too tightly between my teeth.

"Are you ready to go?" Sister Anna asked me. "To the convent?"

The thermometer fell from my mouth once more.

"A convent!" I said. "I'm not leaving my parents! And if I did, it certainly wouldn't be to go to a convent!"

Now the nun showed alarm. She was used to a bit more compliance, but Father had taught me to speak up.

"*Shhh!*" she hissed.

"*Myszko,* my sweet baby mouse," Father said, and crouched to match my height. "It's time to go. This wonderful, kind sister will take you to a convent school, where you will remain safe until we can be together again."

"I can't go to a convent! I'm a Jew!"

Sister Anna slapped a hand over my lips.

"Never say that again," she growled. "You must be quiet. You must be discreet. And, above all else, you must forget the life you once had. There are a thousand people willing to give you up. It doesn't matter if these people were once your friends."

Tears filled my eyes. Although I was only eleven, I understood my misstep. We were alone in this room, but who might be spying, lurking nearby, could not be known. The government offered five hundred zlotys and a kilogram of sugar for the capture of any Jew. Everybody was needy, wanting in those times. Would you sacrifice another to save your own family? Many did.

"You trust me, don't you, sweet girl?" Father said.

He was crying, too. I bobbed my head, unable to speak.

"We will leave," Anna said, slipping the watch up her arm. "With only the clothes on your back."

She looked at Father.

"The girl will be properly outfitted with her uniform and other essentials once we arrive at the school. You are doing the right thing, Mr. Kopczynski."

I went to protest, but could not speak. I wanted to accuse Father of being a bad parent. He didn't love me if he was sending me to live with Catholics. Through it all, Mamusia sat there, quivering, saying nothing. How could a mother give up her child?

"You are Catholic," Father whispered, and held my hands. "Do you understand that, *myszko?*"

I nodded again, lips trembling, for now I *did* understand. He was sending me away because, for the first time in his life, Father was scared.

"You are a Catholic student," he said, "and—this is very important—you must scratch out the memories from any other religion. Forget the prayers. Forget the synagogue. Forget Yiddish. You know six languages now. Erase the seventh."

From the corner, Mother began to speak. She was convinced this was a malevolent plot by the Catholics, who were trying to make money from the suffering Jews. It didn't help that there were stories from the eighteen hundreds about the church abducting Jewish children and baptizing them without their parents' consent.

"We should accept our fate," Mother said, "along with the rest of our people. It's immoral, what you're trying to do. Using money and lies to secure a better fate. Sacrificing our Jewish souls."

Through it all, Sister Anna stood patiently, knowing that Father would win the day.

"If I can save my daughter," he said, "our only child, then my own soul be damned."

And so, it was decided. Anna wrested me from my parents, and our makeshift home. Although my heart shattered into a million pieces, I was certain this was temporary, that I'd see my family again. Father always had a plan, and his plans always worked.

As we hurried out of the city, the nun took my hand. It was soft, but cold. My chest felt heavy and my eyes watered to the point of near-blindness. Sister Anna told me that if I loved my parents, I shouldn't look back, only forward. I followed her advice.

At the convent, they changed my name to Helena and bleached my hair. They gave me Aryan papers and a baptismal certificate. Eventually, I took my first communion. I lived the life of a Catholic girl.

Though we were not safe from Gestapo raids, and there remained danger at every turn, I found solace in the traditions of the Church, in the rhythm of the hymns and prayers. It was the Catholic Church that sheltered me, the Catholic Church that saved me, with help from my knack for languages. My ability to recite Hail Marys, Glory Bes, and the Apostles' Creed in perfect Latin diverted countless suspicions, and *"In nomine Patris, et Filii, et Spiritus Sancti"* dropped from my tongue so easily it might've been the first sentence I ever spoke.

My feelings about the religion remain addled. I think of myself as Catholic on some days, and in some situations, and at other times decidedly not. In the end, my religious identity is displaced, same as me. I've attended mass many times since leaving the convent, in Europe as well as in the United States. The Church sponsored my passage to America, yet I struggle to balance the sense of being rescued and that which I was rescued from.

"I am Catholic."

This is the truth and a lie at the same time. I am Catholic, and have the papers to prove it. But I suspect I'm not the sort of Catholic you want.

Jack refused to look at her. His mouth was locked in a scowl. It was the same expression he made when battling through the worst of his pain.

"I understand why you're upset," Alicia said. "But where do we go from here?"

"Please. Give me a second."

Alicia nodded, though he couldn't see. She waited, twisting her hands, as Irenka's words wended through her mind.

A filthy Jew.

"I appreciate the expectations of your family," Alicia said, for she could not abide the silence. "And your political position."

"Alicia. Stop. Talking."

She wept silently. Soon came the patter of slippered feet. Alicia glanced up to find Joe, who had in his eyes something more than derision. It was a palpable, spitting hatred. How could this be the same man who so lovingly cradled Kathleen?

"Jack, we need to speak," Joe said, without acknowledging Alicia. "Come to my office."

He turned and walked away.

"You should probably go," Alicia said. "No one refuses Joseph P. Kennedy, right?"

Jack continued with his silence, and rose to his feet. Alicia stood, too, desperate to reach him, her nose and eyes hot with tears. He gave Alicia a slow once-over, then crammed both hands into his pockets, and staggered out of the room.

After Jack had been with his father twenty-seven, twenty-eight minutes, Alicia couldn't wait any longer. They were debating *her* history, the person that *she* was. Surely in this country one had the right to be present at one's own trial. If Alicia waited for them to come to her, she might wait forever.

"A fling is one matter," Alicia heard Joe say as she approached. "But romance is another. Did you learn nothing from dating that Nazi spy? The decision on whom to marry must be made with your brain, and not your groin."

"You think I didn't put a great deal of thought into this? I love her, Dad."

Alicia shivered. She had this, at least, the love of Jack.

"Love is not the point," Joe said. "You think you'll be president by accident? You're not going to even get Lodge's Senate seat with a Jew on your arm. How do you expect to oust an old blue blood without the proper wife? Things don't happen, boy, things are made to happen. Have you not learned that by now?"

"It's a new world, Dad. People don't care so much about religion and background. I'd prefer to get elected on my *ideals*, not who I sleep with."

"Who you sleep with is very much part of your 'ideals.' You almost had me, Jack." Joe released a thin, papery laugh. "You almost had me on board with this girl. Sure, she's Eastern Bloc, but I thought it was workable with her aristocratic pedigree and the fact she speaks so many languages. She went to convent school and your mother saw her at mass. We could've spun it. We could've made people read her the right way. A Viennese artist does have a certain cachet. But now it comes out that she's a *Jew*? You're never marrying this girl."

"I was surprised, too," Jack said. "But Alicia was *raised* Catholic. She knows all the doctrine, and considers herself of the Catholic faith."

Alicia frowned, for she'd told him the opposite, that she didn't see herself as belonging to any particular religion. Was Jack softening the news for his father? Or had he heard what he wanted to, and not what she said?

"She's a Jew," Joe barked. "You cannot marry her."

Jack exhaled loudly.

"I'll talk to her," he said.

Alicia jumped back and at once saw what was to come, a play she'd watched a dozen times. Jack would apologize on his father's behalf. But, not to worry, he was his own man. They'd do their own thing, together. That is, if Jack even dared go to such lengths for a Jew.

Every good intention and bold assurance didn't matter, though, nor did every secret he'd forgiven her for. Sure, Alicia could marry Jack, but he'd remain under Joe Kennedy's command, and therefore so would she. Alicia loved Jack, like nothing she'd known, but she didn't want to marry them all. The Kennedys would never be satisfied, and therefore neither would she.

"Excuse me," Alicia said, and stepped into the room.

Jack rushed toward her, yammering apologies, tripping over his mouth and his two big feet.

"I'm not sure what you heard. . . ." he rambled, or something along those lines.

Alicia tried not to listen.

"I'm leaving," she said. "Your family won't need to worry about Alicia Darr, anymore. Mr. Kennedy, I couldn't agree more. Jack needs a proper wife, someone who meets your standards. To that end, I wish you the best of luck."

"I want to marry *you, Alicier,*" Jack said in his Boston clang.

Oh, how she'd miss that voice.

"You need a good American girl," she said. "A debutante. A social-register type. What about that darling Markie from the party the other night? Or her sister, Alex? Either would be perfect for you, and your family. Of course, whomever you choose . . ."

She stopped, and suppressed a laugh.

"Whomever *you both* choose," she said, "must be willing to live under a plan that's been determined, no room for her own choices, or her own life. I'm sure someone will be more than willing, but I'm not that sort of girl."

She glanced at Jack, her heart tugging as her eyes began to soften.

"I've loved you greatly, Jack Kennedy, and I'll remember you with the fondest of thoughts. I'm going to get my citizenship, fast as I can, so that I can have the honor of voting for you when the time comes."

"Alicia . . ." he said with a whimper.

"Thank you for a magnificent year. I'll remember each moment, every one of your smiles. Our time together was even sweeter, knowing that it wouldn't last. But, as Ulysses says, 'Every hour is saved.'"

Alicia kissed him on the cheek, then sashayed out of the room. But she stopped one last time in the doorway, and peered over her shoulder.

"Oh, and Ambassador?" she said. "There's something I should mention."

"Yes?" he said, both brows spiked.

"I'd like to educate you on the painting you bought. The one that hangs in your bedroom."

"Er, uh, what now . . . ?"

"I was sad to let it go, but I greatly appreciated the twenty dollars. You should know, that's my favorite of all my work. It's the grand synagogue in Łódź, where my family attended services each week."

"It's a synagogue?" he balked.

"Yes. Thank you, Mr. Kennedy, for supporting the Jewish arts."

Alicia stood at the postal counter, the tattered valise at her feet. In the side pocket was a train ticket to Boston. A plane in Boston would take her to Hollywoodland.

She read the letter one more time. Jack deserved a more personal good-bye, but if Alicia saw him face-to-face she'd never find the nerve to leave.

Dearest Jack,

You called twenty-three times last night, and knocked on the door twice. A bit onerous to the sweet Mrs. Neill, who's been nothing short of grace. It's nice to feel loved, but darling, you're not the only person in the world.

Please, don't contact me. I'm sure it's agonizing not to get your way but, rest assured, you'll "win" in the end. I'm letting you off the hook, as the saying goes. Your dad is dead right. You need a Catholic, American wife. Someone who will strike the right pose, and give you gobs of kids to boot. It will all be fine, just as you've always said to me.

And so I am off, to the golden coast. I'll recall nothing but the best of you, dear Jack. Because the best is all you are.

All my love,

Alicia

"I'm about to close up!" called the postmaster. "It's now or never, Miss Darr!"

"Sorry, sorry, give me a second."

She sighed, and folded up the note. She stopped to admire the ring still on her finger, and wondered if she should return that, too.

"You be sure to call with your forwarding information," the man said as she crammed the letter into its envelope. "When you get to California."

"You'll be the first to know."

Alicia teared as she licked the envelope and then pressed it closed. For a second, she let herself picture Jack's face, the very best version of him, at the helm of the *Victura*, sunglasses on, wind stirring his hair.

"We are tied to the ocean," he once said. "Our bodies have the same percentage of salt. Seawater is in our sweat, it's in our tears."

Alicia wiped one last tear of her own, and shuffled toward the postmaster. She reached into her handbag for a pen.

"One last thing," she said.

Smiling, Alicia scribbled two lines from "Ulysses" on the envelope's seal.

Come, my friends,
'Tis not too late to seek a newer world.

"Seems like you're stalling," the postmaster noted. "Maybe whatever that is—" He pointed. "—you should hold on to it for a night or two. I can't tell you how many people walk in here every week, hoping to retrieve some letter or package they'd sent in haste."

Alicia shook her head.

"I'm sure about this," she said. "It has to go out."

She pushed the stamped, sealed letter across the counter. The postmaster smiled, then tipped his hat. He tossed her envelope into a bin, said good-bye, and then slammed the gate closed.

"Let me grab the post," Serena Palmisano says to the tall American boy as she fumbles with her mailbox.

It's odd she does this now. Sometimes she goes days—weeks—without checking. But for some reason, she is compelled. Perhaps it's because of the mail carrier, who materialized from behind a potted plant, giving Serena a minor fright. He seemed similarly alarmed to encounter her. God forbid someone catch an Italian postal worker doing his job.

"*Bella*," he'd said with a nervous twitch before hurrying off.

"Was that a mailman?" the American had asked.

The American's name is Lee Perenchio and they've known each other for one week.

"Yes, of course," she'd answered.

Now Serena slides out her mail. There are a few flyers, a bank statement, and an envelope addressed to her in purple ink. She thinks to throw it out but the bin is overflowing.

"He delivered *one* letter?" Lee asks, still stuck on the postman.

Serena has taught him much about the vagaries of Roman life. Like how traffic lights are suggestions and it's best to follow a nun across the street to avoid being squashed. But the postal system is something else entirely.

"*Allora,*" she says, "the successful delivery of one letter is a banner day in the Italian postal regime. Come, follow me."

She moves toward the stairs.

At the landing, Serena peers through the window, toward the courtyard where the mail carrier is scuttling off. *Lee Perenchio might have a point,* she thinks. The mailman doesn't have a bag. Then again, somebody somewhere is probably on strike.

When they reach the apartment, Serena pulls out her keys and begins to unlock. Lee ogles the nine-bolt system. She explains that crime is rampant, even on Margutta. Lee shakes his head. He will never get used to this city.

Serena opens the door, wondering if she'll regret bringing this stranger to her flat. She hopes he doesn't expect any funny business. Then again, maybe she *wants* funny business, which is why she brought him here.

Meanwhile, Lee is still mulling over the locks. Somehow, he is always one step behind, which is why he's so frequently in danger of being hit by *motorinos.*

When they walk inside, Serena throws her post onto the kitchen table. Her eyes shift toward the letter. It is mangled and much abused. Also: who hand-addresses an envelope these days? Never mind that, who writes a letter and then *posts* it? It's quaint, almost. Like a wartime telegram.

"Your apartment is gorgeous," Lee says, admiring the parquet floors, white walls, and arched doorways.

Serena nods. The home has undeniable charm, even with Nonna's mismatched furniture, French telephones, and quirky objets d'art. One day she'll clear out Nova's things, but Serena can't muster the resolve quite yet. Her grandmother's not been dead that long.

"*Grazie,*" Serena says, stalking back toward her mail. "It's a bit cluttered, especially with the newspaper clippings on the walls. I don't have the heart to take them down."

Again, she regards the funny envelope and finds herself unable to leave it be. As Lee inspects one of her grandmother's paintings—a whipped-candy cat with turquoise eyes—Serena tears into the envelope and begins to read. She squints.

Dear Miss Palmisano,

I am executor of the Estate of Alicia Corning Clark. I'm sad to report that Mrs. Clark passed away in February. She left behind a considerable estate.

It does not take long for Lee to notice her distraction.

"Whatcha got there?" he asks.

"Some very peculiar correspondence," Serena answers, realizing her brows have been stitched together for several minutes.

Her eyes flash to the envelope.

"From a lawyer," she says. "In Los Angeles."

"Don't sound so disgusted," Lee says, and forces a laugh. "At least a few good things come out of that hellhole."

Lee is from Los Angeles, too.

"Mind if I take a gander?" he asks.

She loosens her hold, and Lee slides the letter from her hand. She watches as he reads.

Though I cannot be sure this letter will reach you, I've written to say that you—Serena Palmisano—are potentially a beneficiary to Mrs. Clark's estate. While this means you <u>might</u> be an heir, I cannot guarantee that the courts or probate law will deem you as such. There are many complicating factors, not the least of which is that Mrs. Clark left all legal and financial documentation in a state of bedlam.

"An inheritance?" Lee's face lights up, as if he were a cartoon. "I thought Novella . . ."

He stops himself. *I thought Novella was your last remaining relative* is what he'd started to say.

"She was," Serena snaps, finishing his sentence in her mind. "I'm sure this . . ."

She waggles her hand toward the letter.

"I'm sure it's some sort of swindle," she says. "A Nigerian hustler."

"Oh." He frowns, disappointed. "That's another Roman thing, then? People faking inheritances?"

"Not that I know of," she replies as he scans the paper a second time.

"I'm not an expert," Lee says, "but it looks legit. I've heard of this law firm. It's large, and very well known. Plus, the letter is from America, so we can't chalk it up to squirrelly Roman street moves."

Serena should be offended, but it is a fair characterization.

"There are many non-legit aspects to your culture, as well," she says.

"I don't disagree, but there aren't any red flags in this instance. Like I said, I'm familiar with the firm and we can find out in two seconds if this lawyer really works there. Also, he doesn't ask for money, or your bank account information, or anything like that. He'll pay for any expenses you might incur."

> *Before you can be legally attached to her estate, you will need to come to Los Angeles to discuss the matter in person. You will be reimbursed for your lodging and airfare. You will also receive a per diem of $50, payable out of the estate.*

"Aren't you curious?" he asks. "Don't you want to find out more?"

"Who just gives someone money?"

"Anyone who has assets when they die," he says. "That's why there are wills."

"A con job," she grumbles.

Beautiful, elegant Serena has an edge to her, a certain skepticism usually found in aged and grizzled men. It's no wonder Lee thought that she was older than her twenty-one years when they first met. From the minute Serena spoke—rapidly and with heavy use of hands—he developed a crush on what he thought was an older woman. Then Lee discovered he had her by two years.

"What is that expression, Lee Perenchio?" she says.

"I was thinking about how I'm going to miss you," he answers honestly.

Serena bats the air.

"The letter," he says, redirecting the conversation. "Why are you so skeptical?"

"Look at the scrabbly handwriting." Serena points to the paper. "You can't mail something to Rome and handwrite the address. Everyone knows that."

"I didn't. Though it does seem strange that it was stapled shut."

"That's the least suspicious part! I'm sure it was opened and then reassembled."

Lee makes a face.

"Who would open it?"

"*La posta*, naturally. They take all the good stuff. We're lucky this person didn't send a check." She snorts. "Not that he actually has money to send."

Lee reviews the letter.

I've been Mrs. Corning Clark's lawyer for some fifty years, and have her best interests—financial and emotional—at heart. I want to make sure what's left goes to the right person. I want to make sure her wishes are carried out.

Lee puts down the letter and picks up his cell phone. He begins to type.

"Holy shit!" he yelps, then jabs a finger at the screen. "This woman. She was wealthy, like *crazy* wealthy. Heir to the Singer sewing machine fortune. It's hard to imagine there's still a sewing machine fortune to be had, but apparently there is."

"I am well acquainted with the woman and her sewing machine dollars," Serena says, and rolls her eyes.

"Wait." Lee gawps. "You actually know this person?"

"*Sì, certamente,*" she says. "Of course."

Serena can hear her grandmother's voice from across the years. *Oh, that Alicia! You won't believe what she's up to these days!* Che donna! *What a woman!* On Alicia Corning Clark, Nonna Nova had a lot to say, mostly using words like "*era un disastro,*" "*catastrofe,*" "*sciagura*" . . . peppered with a generous does of "*strabellissima*" for balance. Alicia had always been beautiful.

"She was close with my grandmother," Serena says. "They lived together, right here in this flat, during the fifties, *la dolce vita.*"

"So, you've met her."

Lee is confused, so very confused.

"Yes," she says. "I haven't seen her in many years. Probably close to a decade. But when I was a girl, we spent a week or two each year at her garish estate in the Bahamas."

"My god. Serena!" Lee throws back his head. "That alone should eliminate any questions about the validity of the letter. How would a random swindler make that sort of connection?"

"*Dai,* Alicia . . . she got around."

"According to this article, her estate is worth over seventeen million dollars, possibly as much as forty."

"Is that all?" Serena says with a small snicker. "The way she spoke, you'd think seventeen million is merely what she carried in her purse for emergencies. Or in the pocket of one of her minks."

Che brutta!

"Alicia was very colorful," Serena adds.

"I'll say. Apparently, she dated JFK?"

"Ah. Yes. Among others. Gary Cooper. Ty Power. Name a matinee idol and he was on the register." Serena is quiet for a second. "I don't mean to sound uncharitable. Alicia made a grand life for herself out of a very questionable start, but she could be a handful, 'high maintenance.' Nova was bohemian, so Alicia got on her—how do you say—nerves. She loved and hated her both. What is the term they use in the States? Friend, but also nemesis? Fremesis?"

"Frenemy?" Lee says with a smirk.

He sets down his phone, and the letter. Damn, Serena is cute. He doesn't entirely understand his emotions about her.

"*Avajo!*" Serena says. "Yes. 'Frenemy.' That's the word."

Mere months ago, Serena was living in Washington, D.C., taking classes and attending college parties. She'd fancied herself mostly American, save the matter of her passport and country of birth. Alas, she'd misjudged her own status if the colloquialisms are slipping away. Serena wonders how her Italian—her Romanesco—sounds in the ears of true locals. She is neither one thing, nor the other. It is a distressing thought.

"Frenemy," Lee says. "I thought grandparents were too wise for that sort of nonsense."

"My *nonna* was not a typical grandmother."

"The muse of *la dolce vita*," Lee says, remembering what she'd said. "The world's most famous gadabout."

Serena chortles.

"So, there *is* a possibility this woman left you money?" Lee asks.

"A remote one." Serena nods slowly. "She divorced or outlived all of her husbands and never had children. Her parents died in the war. But it doesn't make sense that she'd leave the money to me, instead of Novella. They died a few weeks apart. I doubt Mrs. Clark knew my grandmother was gone."

"Technically," Lee says, "the letter states that *you* might be a beneficiary. Maybe your grandmother was named, but the lawyers figured out—"

"She's dead," Serena says. "Perhaps."

"You need to pursue this," Lee says. "You must go to Los Angeles."

"Who has time for that?"

And who has the money? Though she's inherited Nova's estate—however grand or insignificant that might be—it will be a great while before the money is in hand, if the Italian legal system has anything to say about it, which of course it will, and for years.

"You have time," Lee says. "You're on leave from college. You're working as a contractor for a tour company."

Serena shoots him a look. He holds up both hands.

"It's not an insult," he says. "The point I'm trying to make is that you have greater freedom now than you'll ever have again."

"Perhaps you've forgotten, but I've received one inheritance this year, and it's more than enough."

Serena glowers and Lee understands.

Thanks to intimate conversations held in front of awe-inspiring canvases or, better yet, over bottles of wine in quaint, brick-walled trattorias, Lee knows that Serena was raised by her grandmother. Her father died, her mother left, and Nonna took charge. She gave Serena the best of everything: a Roman childhood, boarding school and university in the States, plus unconditional love all the way through. Breast cancer took Nova a few months back, and now Serena has no family left. Money is great, but not when it reminds you of what you've lost.

"I'm sorry," Lee says. "I sound like an ass."

"No, you sound Milanese. Which is really the same thing."

Though she is not joking, Lee chuckles. The Rome-Milan rivalry matches anything he's seen in American sports. To accuse a man of being Milanese means he's a rapacious money-grubber, fueled entirely by ego and greed.

"Milanese?" Lee says. "I'd never step foot in that city!"

"Ah, so you have been listening."

Serena sits. She pulls forward her long, thick hair to cover her ears.

"To journey to California seems like a hassle," she says. "Why can't this be conducted via telephone?"

"It's not always that simple," Lee says. "And he's clearly been on the hunt for some time. He tried to contact you at Georgetown. Come on, Serena. You have to at least think about it."

"Why are you so pushy about someone else's affairs?"

Lee joins her at the table.

"You should have the money," he says. "If that's what Alicia Corning Clark wanted."

People inherit things from long-lost friends and quasi aunts all the time. Well, not *all* the time, but it's not unheard of, it's not a Nigerian prince. On the other hand, Lee must acknowledge the fact that he wouldn't push so hard if the letter requested her presence in New York, or Chicago, or some other place. Lee is from Los Angeles and he'll be there until August, when he starts his Silicon Valley job. He'd love to spend the summer with Serena, so the letter feels like a potential windfall for him, instead of for her.

"Are you going to deny a woman her dying wish?" he asks, a pinch desperate.

Serena grunts, then ponders his view. Meanwhile, Lee removes a tube of *burro cacao* from his pocket, the ChapStick that he applies and reapplies, all day long. It's an endearing habit, although Serena should not be thinking about Lee Perenchio's mouth right now.

"I can't leave," she says. "It's prime tourist season."

The rationalization sounds thin in Serena's ears. She's a tour guide. She shuttles people around, through, and below the Colosseum and takes them to her favorite pizzerias. She leads them to Palatine Hill and the Forum and provides lists of the most underrated places in Rome. And if she's not there? Some other person will do these exact things. No one will miss her at all.

The thought rattles Serena. No one will miss her. Exactly zero people, now that Novella is gone.

"I can't leave a job I just started," Serena adds halfheartedly, still thinking of her *nonna*. "To travel to the other side of the world for a chat."

"You wouldn't be going for a *chat*, you'd be going to collect your inheritance!"

"I must tell you," she says, and smiles, "money is the least compelling aspect of the proposed journey. There are better reasons to go."

"Oh really?" Lee wiggles his eyebrows.

He's trying to be playful, to mask his neediness yet still convince this foreign beauty to spend a summer in the California sun.

"Are you referring to a certain charming guy you've recently met?"

"Don't flatter yourself," Serena says.

Can an orphan like her latch on to a handsome American boy? It is probably more dangerous than exciting, she thinks.

"You are very cute," Serena allows. "And you most certainly sweeten the idea. But I must admit, this lawyer . . ."

She sweeps a hand toward the letter.

"He knew Mrs. Clark for fifty years. Nova did too. She told me countless stories, each more fantastical than the last. In my childhood, Alicia loomed like a fairy godmother, or a witch who's both a little bit good, and a little bit bad. Alas, I'll forever have Nonna's side, but suddenly I'm anxious for Alicia Corning Clark's."

PART II

Alicia Darr has Hugh O'Brian breathless.

New York at Night, by Bob Farrell, March 6, 1953

HOLLYWOOD

Alicia slapped the newspaper onto the blue-flecked Formica table.

"I leave Hugh O'Brian breathless," she said, grinning with wonder. "How about that?"

It was her first time in the gossip pages, and she barely had to try. If Mother wasn't impressed by the money Alicia sent, she might find her daughter's rising stardom better compensation.

"Are you going tonight?" asked her housemate, striding into the kitchen as she fluffed her hair.

Poor girl, she could primp and fidget all day long, but it was hard to rectify the flossy orange abomination atop her head.

"Of course I'm going," Alicia said.

She gestured toward her outfit: skintight silver dress, ermine stole, egret feathers in her hair.

"I don't dress like this for fun." She paused. "Or do I?"

"Sheesh, no need to be testy," Fannie said. "It's a fair question. You're a bit of a wild card."

Fannie pried open the metal blinds, scanning the street for Fred and his Caddy. They were due at a party; the usual concoction of Hollywood bigwigs, starlets, and oilnaires. For a fee, Don Class provided window dressing at such events, in the form of Alicia and her roommates. The girls called this "mixing" and it was quite the side job to look pretty and sip champagne for a hundred clams per night. Alicia would do it for fifty, which was what Fannie got.

Though she enjoyed it, the mixing wasn't much of a choice, as the actress business was slow going. Alicia had scored a few B roles, here and there, but California's landscape was drier than she'd anticipated, in more ways than one.

"Obviously," George said, when Alicia called to complain last week. "Fewer movies are made now that studios can't own the theaters. Are you not familiar with the 1948 Supreme Court decision?"

Alicia smirked as she pictured George standing at the pay phone, in the Center lobby, all the way in Hyannis Port. She couldn't believe it'd been almost two years since she'd left.

"The studios can't 'block book' a year's worth of movies because they don't control the theaters anymore," George yammered on. "Which means no guaranteed income, which means fewer movies made. None of this is helped by the inexplicable popularity of television."

"Somehow, George," Alicia said, laughing, "whenever I call for a pep talk, you always make it worse."

Alas, this was George Neill, same as forever. Who else could she say these things to? She had three housemates at Don Class's bungalow in the Hollywood Hills, the orange-haired Fannie, plus Yolanda and Daisy, too. While Alicia liked them well enough, she did not trust them one hundred percent. She'd learned her lesson. Never get too close.

"He's here!" Fannie cried, spotting Fred's Caddy on the graveled drive.

She grabbed her pocketbook and hurried outside.

It was fun to flit from the Bay Club, to the Beach Club, to the Firelight Room at the Bel-Air Hotel. They spent many delicious weekends relaxing at the Polo Lounge, in the Beverly Hills Hotel pool, or all the way out in Palm Springs. All of these places made Alicia count her lucky stars, but it could be exhausting, and she longed for something more.

Fred honked his horn. Sighing, Alicia straggled into the living room and thought maybe she wouldn't go after all. This was probably what Fannie meant when she called her a "wild card." Alicia glanced toward the gossip magazines scattered across the low table and thought she'd rather curl up with one of those versus an oilnaire.

She might've done just that, if Alicia didn't hate being alone in that house of wood: the furniture, the floors, the walls and the roof. It was unsettling, with the brush fires always tearing through the hills.

Someone pounded the front door. Fred, no doubt. Alicia didn't answer, so he jiggled the knob, and let himself through. Another problem: there were no streetlights and the doors didn't lock.

"Are you planning to join us?" he asked, waddling in, smelling of cigarettes and scotch.

Fred was the last person you'd expect in Hollywood, as he was broader than he was tall, sweaty no matter the weather. A former Los Angeles police officer, Fred now spent his time driving around in a chauffeured Cadillac, accompanying girls to parties to make sure they behaved. Don Class didn't pay Fred much for this, he claimed, but he never talked about his "real" job. Yolanda insisted he was a private eye.

"We're headed to the Graham party," he said. "Yolanda is already there, along with half the honchos in this town. You should go. You're certainly dressed for it."

"I don't know, Fred. I'm suddenly not in the mood."

"What's the problem?" he asked. "Hugh O'Brian pulling the jealous act?"

"He's the last person who might control my schedule," Alicia said. "How'd you hear about him?"

"From the paper, like everyone else. Didn't realize you two were so hot and heavy. Couldn't have guessed you left him . . . *breathless*."

"Very funny," Alicia said, and rolled her eyes.

Hugh O'Brian was fine, as beaus went. He was handsome, square-jawed and brooding. At seventeen, he'd been the youngest Marine drill sergeant in United States history, and Alicia appreciated a storied military career. He was a decent actor, too, though sometimes he came across as desperate, the sort of person who would do anything for a role. Alicia didn't object to this necessarily, but he shouldn't be so damned obvious about it.

"So, Hugh's breathless and you're . . . ?"

Fred pulled a flask from his coat, took a sip, and released a throaty *ahhhhhhh*.

"Speechless, is it?" he asked.

Alicia shrugged, as one did in that town. It was something she'd noticed about Los Angeles. Lots of shrugging, the inability to commit and a reluctance to be dazzled.

"You're linked with a famous guy for the first time and now you clam up?" Fred said. "Just so you know, coyness doesn't pay much in this town."

"I'm not being coy," Alicia said. "I enjoy his company, for now."

"And what of Coop?" Fred asked.

Alicia's eyes went wide.

"Coop wasn't in the papers," she said.

"Not yet, but he's been calling around town, inquiring about your 'status.'"

Alicia smiled, flattered by his effort.

"Well, between you and me," she said, "he's been giving the hard sell, trying to get me to join him in Mexico, where he's shooting some film."

"I gotta hand it to you, Alicia," Fred said with a wet sniggle. "You have some balls to cat-and-mouse Gary Cooper."

"It's not like that," Alicia said, but had to wonder. "I don't think I'm allowed to leave the States. Coop's staying out of the U.S. to avoid paying taxes, thus the cat and mouse are stuck in separate countries."

"I'm sure you could find a way to Mexico City, if you really wanted to."

Alicia nodded. She was attracted to Coop, and who wouldn't be? She liked his style, his swagger, the very American maleness of him. After the hours she'd spent ogling him onscreen at the Center, that he was pursuing *her* was worth something, no two ways.

For a second, Alicia contemplated the outcome if it was *his* name linked with hers, instead of Hugh O'Brian's. Coop had been friends with Jack Kennedy, long ago. Jack had traveled to Hollywood expressly to see what made Gary Cooper tick.

"How is he that charismatic?" he'd wondered.

Jack was looking for some tips but in the end found only more questions. Namely, how could a man be so magnetic while also being an utter bore? It drove Jack bonkers that Coop remained a screen god, that people made the sorts of comments Tallulah Bankhead once did:

"The only reason I went to Hollywood," she proclaimed, "was to fuck that divine Gary Cooper."

"We'll have to see about Mexico," Alicia told Fred, then adjusted her dress, which was starting to cling to the wrong places. "Though it sounds better by the minute."

"Lucky guy," Fred said. "Okay, doll, ya coming or not? You can't stay in, you've got some major va-va-voom tonight. Is that dress low-cut enough, do you think? I can almost see to Timbuktu."

"Don't be a wolf."

"And don't be a drip. Let's roll over to Sheilah's for a cocktail and to celebrate the love of Hollywood's newest newlyweds."

"They'll last a year, tops," Alicia said with a snort.

"I'm sure they'd both agree. All the bigwigs will be there. One of them could give you your break."

Alicia checked the mirror above the fireplace. In that low light, the tinctures and lotions she'd applied shimmered and glistened, from her collarbone all the way down. Maybe it *was* a waste not to go. She looked damned fine.

Plus, as Fred reminded her, you never knew who might be at a party, who might be the one to change your life. And Alicia could use the money. Los Angeles living was astoundingly fast and expensive. She earned more here than in Hyannis, but she spent far more.

"You sold me," Alicia said. "Let's go to Sheilah's grand soiree."

"That's my favorite girl."

Alicia reapplied her signature cherry-red lips. She watched in the mirror as Fred belched and then ran a hand over his slicked hair.

As they walked toward the door, Fred stopped at a small, square painting tacked to the wall.

"Whose house is that?" he asked.

"Oh." She sighed. "It's a place I once knew, on Nantucket Sound. I painted it myself, actually."

"You did?" Fred raised a brow.

"Yes. I used to be an artist."

It almost sounded like a lie. Sometimes, it was easy to forget the lives she'd led: schoolgirl, painter, counter clerk, maid. Fiancée of a congressman named Jack.

"Why, Alicia Darr!" Fred said. "That's amazing! I had no idea!"

"Oh, well." She exhaled. "That was a different person. A different life."

A different dream.

Fred offered a good old Southern California shrug.

"Okeydokey, whatever you say, sweetie. Come on, let's hit the road."

Fred was right. Everyone was there.

Along with the bride (Sheilah Graham, gossip columnist) and her new husband (Stan Wojtkiewicz, no stated occupation) were a hodge-podge of stars and moguls and other Hollywood impresarios. Within seconds of walking through the front door, Alicia saw Mike Todd, Evelyn Keyes, Joan Crawford, and Marilyn Monroe, always with her publicity wagon and sack of pills.

"This is a scene," Alicia whispered to Fred as they wandered through.

"I told you. It's Sheilah Graham."

"I cannot accept that she married someone named Bow-Wow."

Sheilah called her new husband "Bow-Wow" because "Wojtkie-wicz" was too Polish and impossible to say. A little odd, Alicia thought, not to know your spouse's name. Then again, Bow-Wow was in his thirties, and Sheilah was almost fifty and had been through several husbands already, not to mention a love affair with the writer F. Scott Fitzgerald, who died in her apartment. To someone like Sheilah Graham, proper pronunciation probably seemed nitpicky and irrelevant.

"Listen, I gotta see a guy about a thing," Fred said, and released Alicia's arm. "You good on your own?"

"Always." She nodded.

"Holler if anyone gives you trouble."

With that, Fred sauntered off.

Alicia snaked through the party, champagne glass in hand, necks straining as she passed. Eventually, Alicia found herself in the living room, where she zeroed in on an attractive couple nestled on a gold brocade sofa. The man was dark-haired and handsome, the woman au-burn and bright. Her shoes were off, bare feet tucked beneath her rear. It was Pat Kennedy. Alicia's heart locked in her throat.

She'd seen Jack's sister often and from a distance these past two years, including at the Beach Club last week. The circles they ran in often touched, and it was a miracle Alicia had gone this long without saying hello. She'd eventually have to, and so, emboldened by the champagne and her ermine stole, Alicia decided this was the night.

"My goodness! Pat Kennedy!" she said, sweeping toward them. "How wonderful to see you!"

Pat smiled, a pop of recognition on her face as her eyes remained curious and searching.

Alicia extended a hand. A diamond bracelet dangled from her wrist. Pat pursed her lips at the sight, and conspicuously assessed the ice. Were the diamonds real? Were they top grade?

"I'm not sure if you remember me," Alicia started, "but I dated your brother. Jack."

Saying his name was a stab in the chest.

"How is your brother these days?" she asked, to get it out of the way. "I haven't thought about him in ages!"

This was a lie. Alicia had tracked him, every step. It was easier now that he was a senator. Jack's increased political clout meant more headlines every week.

KENNEDY WILL SEEK LODGE'S SENATE SEAT.

CAPITOL NEWSMEN VOTE KENNEDY HANDSOMEST.

LODGE REPLACED BY KENNEDY.

KENNEDY VICTORY SMILE.

"Alicia . . ." Pat said, and stood, wobbling on the way up.

Peter gave her a steady arm.

"Peter, this is one of Jack's—"

"We were engaged," Alicia said, curtly. "The name is Alicia Darr. Nice to meet you."

She jutted out a hand.

"Likewise," Peter said. He glanced at Pat. "I didn't know Jack was engaged."

"For a *very* short period of time."

"This is true," Alicia said. "Jack was a wonderful beau, alas, my background and religious inclinations weren't satisfactory in the eyes of dear old Dad."

"Father knows best," Peter answered with his deep laugh, husky and rich, thanks to his British accent and fast-living life.

Alicia had met him a time or two, and heard enough stories to fill a book. She knew the way this fella worked, and Pat would probably do well to stay away. But Pete Lawford was handsome as sin and Alicia appreciated a man worthy of the fuss.

"Can I get you ladies a drink?" Peter asked. "Something with more balls than champagne?"

"I'm fine with this," Alicia said.

"Whatever you're having, babe," Pat said.

As Peter walked off, Pat dropped onto the sofa, and slapped the seat beside her.

"Sit, sit," she said. "Fill me in on what you've been up to since . . . Geez, how long it's been?"

"I left Hyannis Port two years ago in July."

Pat whistled.

"Doesn't feel that long," she said. "So, you're in Hollywood now? Trying to make a go?"

"That's the idea. I've had a few roles, nothing you've seen."

"You certainly have the face for it," Pat said. "Your accent is entirely kaput."

Pat lit a cigarette and passed her silver monogrammed case Alicia's way.

"Do you smoke? I can't recall. . . ."

"I'm fine for now," Alicia said, and shook her head, thinking of the cigarettes they once shared on the porch in Hyannis Port.

"You still with Don Class?" Pat asked. "Living in the bungalow? With the other girls?"

Alicia beamed in awe. Well, look at that. Where she'd tracked

Jack, perhaps Pat had tracked her, too. She wondered if siblings shared confidences about parties they'd attended and the people they'd seen. For a moment Alicia wished Coop were with her, tax authorities be damned.

"Yes, I have three roommates," Alicia said. "Daisy, Yolanda, and Fa—"

"Fannie!" Pat snapped her fingers. "That's the one I was thinking of! Raven-haired?"

"No, actually, her hair is orange. Are you thinking of Yolanda?"

"Yes!" She snapped again. "One of Peter's friends is bonkers for her."

Pat tilted forward. The smoke from her cigarette curled up into Alicia's nose, and through her meticulously styled hair.

"You think you could get him a date?" Pat asked. "With Fannie?"

"Yolanda. That shouldn't be a problem. She's not specifically attached."

"Brilliant! I'll let him know."

Pat leaned closer. She smelled sweet and smoky, her eyes a deeper purple than Alicia remembered.

"It's Frank Sinatra," she whispered. "If you must know."

Pat sprang to her feet.

"If you'll excuse me, I have to go peeps. Are you going to Louella's after this?"

"I'm not sure," Alicia said. "I'm thinking about it."

Pat ground her cigarette into the coffee table. She left the butt sitting there, damp, lipsticked, and smoldering.

"If I don't see you at Louella's," she said, "keep in touch. I've always liked you, which is a compliment, as Jack usually has the worst taste in broads."

The new light in Gary Cooper's blue orbs is caused by Alicia Darr, Viennese starlet.

Hollywood Today, by Sheilah Graham, March 14, 1953

HOLLYWOOD

Alicia convinced Coop to risk his tax situation so that he might woo her in Hollywood.

The gossips took fast notice. Coop offered a lot more prestige than Hugh O'Brian, and Alicia should've lit this fire sooner. From Fairchild's, to the Beverly Wilshire, to coastal excursions in Coop's convertible Mercedes, the papers mentioned it all. Spies were even at the Fish Shanty to capture him playfully dropping toothpicks down the front of Alicia's dress.

Their relationship was pure Hollywood glitz, but with a kick of old-fashioned romance. When Coop returned to set, his director accused him of being too tan, too glowing with happiness, and asked him to please tone it down.

At over fifty years old, Coop was not a young man, but he was as stouthearted and red-blooded as they came. Alicia adored the cowboyness of him, his pure American verve. Once she overheard him tell a scriptwriter to "just make me the hero," and Alicia thought, yes, that was his perfect role. Not that any role wasn't perfect for Coop. He had won an Academy Award the previous week.

Now he was in Mexico City, filming *Blowing Wild*. He'd begged
Alicia to join him but she was shooting a scene for *Brady's Bunch*, plus
she still didn't know what was required of a displaced person wanting
to travel abroad. Something about an "Affidavit of Identity in Lieu of
Passport," but Alicia didn't have the time, or the funds, to hassle with
that sort of paperwork. Not to mention, which identity would she use?

Also, she was expected at a luncheon, in the Sun Lounge of the Beverly Hills Hotel. The event was hosted by Enrique "Heini" Schön-
dube, a Mexican playboy and industrial heir. Alicia questioned why a
"Mexican" might have such a German last name, but Heini was ada-
mant about his heritage. He paid a mariachi band to follow him around.

Heini's table decorations were as repugnant as the mariachi band,
with red and white carnation centerpieces and pink glassware. It was
almost enough to distract Alicia from her mission, which was to be delightful and bright.

"That's the best thing about you," Don Class had said. "Anyone can
be pretty, but your ability to string together more than five words makes
you stand out."

At the luncheon, Alicia listlessly sipped her champagne. Beside her,
Kay Spreckles prattled on about her divorce from the sugar magnate.
She was dubbed a gold digger; he beat her with a shoe. Now Adolph
planned to marry his twenty-four-year-old nurse.

Alicia answered with the usual. Nods. Frowns. "What a dirtbag!"
She'd heard this story a dozen times before. It could all get so very tire-
some.

With another sip of champagne, Alicia's eyes flicked down the table,
toward Jerry Lewis, Nancy Davis, and Ronald Reagan. She saw her
roommate flirting with Heini, and good for her. Daisy didn't get the
same attention as the others. She hadn't even gotten a movie role yet.

Once the dessert plates were cleared, and Kay rotated to harass some
other sap, Alicia took the opportunity to sneak off. She didn't say good-
bye to the host, or his pack of trucklers, or any other guest. No one
would miss her, as there were plenty of starlets to go around.

After snagging her coat from the coat-check girl, Alicia strode out the hotel's front doors. When she reached the end of the porte cochere, Alicia glanced at the bold stripes overhead. She closed her eyes and remembered what it was like to walk inside the Beverly Hills Hotel for the first time: as though she were stepping into a candy box. Maybe life wasn't so ordinary after all.

Alicia opened her eyes. With a firm shake of the head, she reminded herself that *this* was what she came for. Days like these, sunny and champagne-filled. An actor to her right, a sheikh to her left, all of it inside a grand, pink hotel.

Although it often felt like she'd been in Los Angeles a decade or more, Alicia understood that time was an illusion, like happiness and success. Unlike so many others in this town, she was not some battle-weary starlet dragging her tail. Alicia Darr was just getting started and the best was yet to come.

"Really, Alicia?"

She froze in her driveway. Goose bumps scattered across her skin.

"Who's there?" she asked as her stomach dropped clear to the floor.

A figure moved, near the porch.

"I couldn't believe my fucking eyes," the man said. "Of all the bastahds in Hollywood, you picked goddamned Gary Cooper."

"Jack."

She gasped. Her mouth was drier than a Palm Springs afternoon.

"In the flesh," he said.

Jack Kennedy hopped down from a bougainvillea-covered wall and stepped out into the full sunlight, grinning his high-voltage smile. He was beautiful, golden almost. Alicia struggled to catch her breath.

"You need to be careful," she said, her voice thin.

Alicia pointed to the pink flowers, and their prickly vines.

"Bougainvillea is beautiful," she said, "but it has thorns."

"That's one helluva metaphor."

He let out one of his deep and gutty Jack Kennedy laughs. Alicia's heart swelled. Her eyes watered and she had to turn away. It was too much to take him in. You didn't stare at the sun. You didn't eat a full cake in one sitting.

She hadn't seen him in nearly two years. On first blush, he looked every bit the same, but on the second and third, Jack Kennedy seemed bigger somehow. He took up more space. A happy fact, she supposed, given the newspaper photos of him on crutches. She'd been worried about his health.

"What are you doing here?" she asked.

"I came to see you, of course," Jack said, looping his thumbs into the waistband of his baggy, wrinkled pants. "Jesus, Alicia. Gary Cooper. You really know how to break a guy's heart."

"What do you have against Coop?" she asked, pretending not to recall. "He's a swell guy. Just won an Academy Award, in case you didn't see the news. It was his second."

"I saw the news all right." He rolled his eyes. "What a feat, beating out a *dog* for best actor."

"Rin Tin Tin is very talented."

"Are you upset he's dating a 'Viennese starlet' as well as you?" Jack asked.

"I see your wit is still intact."

"What do you see in the guy?" he said. "Do you know I once sat beside him at a dinner party and he said exactly three words the entire evening?"

"Still waters run deep," Alicia sniffed. "He's not one of those types who likes to hear his own voice. He's not a Kennedy."

"Right, right. I'm sure his brain is boiling over with the world's most important thoughts."

"You'd be surprised. And, he has other charms. You know what Tallulah Bankhead said about him, and why she went to Hollywood."

Jack grunted.

"Yeah. And there was that vaudevillian actress who accused him of lacking proper *thrust*."

"The exact quote was that Coop 'has the biggest organ in Hollywood but not the ass to push it in well.' Pardon the rough language," Alicia said, and fanned herself, as if she were blushing. "You're hardly in a position to criticize someone's flat ass. And, as for the first part of the statement, I've found it to be true, though I've not sampled all available choices."

Jack's features dropped, and with it, Alicia's heart. Scoring a verbal victory against the whip-smart, impossibly droll Jack Kennedy didn't feel half as good as she'd presumed.

"I'm sorry," she said, and sighed, eyes fixed on the ground.

A lizard skittered by.

"I didn't mean that," she said. "I'm just thrown off. You're the last person I expected to see. Why aren't you off doing senatorial things, or finding your perfect wife? You always said you'd marry, if you won Lodge's seat."

"I did find my perfect wife," he said. "But she ran away, dumped me via the Hyannis Port post."

Alicia looked up. Jack stepped forward, and wrapped both arms around her waist. Then he dipped in for the softest, lightest, most patient of kisses, a kiss so tender it almost stopped her heart. Normally, Jack would've had her naked and up against a wall ninety seconds after he said hello.

"I didn't run away," she whispered, taking in the scent of his shampoo, his aftershave, his clothes. "I finally accepted what I should've long before, that you and I could never be."

"Alicia *Dahr*-ling, you never gave me a chance to fix anything."

Jack rested his chin on her head. Alicia ran her hands across his bony, ramrod back. She felt for his brace. It was bulkier than she remembered.

"I've missed you so much," she said. "Nothing is the same. No one is the same. Not even 'that divine Gary Cooper.'"

He kissed the tip of her ear. Alicia smiled, for suddenly she felt something familiar, occurring on the front side of his pants.

"Same old Jack," she said, and pushed her pelvis into his.

"We'd better get inside," he said. "Before I screw you right here and ruin your reputation. I don't care about mine."

She laughed, feeling like herself for the first time in years.

"That's not true at all," she said.

"I've waited twenty months, Alicia Darr. And I can't stand one second more."

They woke at four o'clock in the afternoon.

Alicia's mouth was sweet and dry thanks to the champagne luncheon, a nap, and, of course, Jack.

They'd gotten to the sex briskly, in the typical Jack Kennedy sprinting fashion. Not two steps through the front door and Jack had yanked down his khakis. He took Alicia up against the bar cart, metal clanging and whisky spilling onto the rug.

When it came to lovemaking, Jack had all the grace of a runaway freight train, and while Alicia guessed some girls might find it offputting, she liked it, because it was so very him. In all things, Jack was cerebral and quick, and she loved his urgent, pleading way.

Now they were lingering in bed. Any of the girls might walk in at any time, but Alicia didn't mind if they saw the wreck. She was proud of it, in some way.

"I've missed you, kid," Jack said, his right leg hooked over her left.

His hairs scratched against her skin as he squirmed in search of a more comfortable spot.

"You haven't had the time to miss me," she said.

"It's not about time. You're always . . . there. Tell me, Alicia . . ." He flipped onto his side. "What are you doing, hanging around here?"

"I'm trying to make it as an actress, you know that."

"Like everybody else in this town. What about your art?" Jack inched closer. "What have you painted lately?"

"I'm not doing that anymore," she said.

"Why not? Anyone can be beautiful, but to have your talent is something truly worthwhile."

"My so-called talent didn't get me anywhere before," she said, thinking of her failed gallery show, and the painting of the synagogue hanging on Joe Kennedy's wall.

That wretched thing.

Alicia turned toward the window, and the sunlight coming through the trees. California was a funny place. Beautiful and temperate, yet also harsh. She wondered about the rattlesnakes and coyotes and skunks outside.

"What are you doing here, Jack?" she asked.

"What do you mean? I've come to rescue you."

Alicia gave him a once-over.

"Who says I need rescuing?" she said.

"You're palling around with Gary fucking Cooper, to start."

"If I'd known you'd be this upset about Coop, I would've started dating him sooner."

"Come with me," Jack blurted. "To Washington."

Alicia laughed.

"Jack Kennedy, don't say things you don't mean."

"I'm serious. Come. Be with me."

Alicia clamped her lips together, trying to suppress the fantasy, the vision of a charming brick town house with white trim and black shutters, its house number written in script:

One Thirty-Five

"I can't go to Washington," Alicia said. "I need to make a living. I've finally found a hospital for my mother that I can afford."

"Your mother's still alive?" Jack said. "How about that? Terrific!

And I'll pay for the hospital. Hell, I can have her outta there by to-morrow. Tell me who to call."

"It's not that easy. And what would I do in Washington?"

"Paint." He shrugged against the bed. "Attend art school. Make love to me."

"Hmmm. This sounds familiar. And where does Papa Joe fit in?"

"It's different now. I've distanced myself from him. I got elected with *no* wife, didn't I? Dad can't argue with victory, or my winning smile."

"Good grief."

Alicia lurched out of bed. Her behind jiggled as she walked. She'd been eating out too much these days, thanks to Coop.

"You don't believe me, do you?" Jack sniffed. "I'm hurt."

"You'll get over it."

Alicia rummaged through her closet. The flowered, gathered-waist dress she'd worn to the luncheon was much too much for that time of day.

"I'll prove it," Jack said. "You'll be my date to Eunice's wedding in May. What can anyone say to that? Surely Dad will have to zip it, and more so, you."

"Eunice's wedding. Really."

Alicia glanced over her shoulder, then zipped her sheath halfway up, as far as she could reach. Jack made no move from the bed. He was not the sort to help a lady get her clothes *on*.

"So, she finally agreed to marry Sarge?" Alicia said.

She never understood his pursuit, nor Eunice's reluctance, as Sarge was a handsome man.

"Yeah, she's marrying the bastard," Jack said. "As she says, 'I searched all my life for someone like my father, and Sarge came closest.'"

"I'm sure he gave her a nice rock," Alicia said with a smirk. "Given his experience in selecting gems."

"I chose your engagement ring," Jack said, eyes darting toward her left hand. "Guess I shouldn't have expected you to still be wearing it."

"I sold that long ago. A girl has to eat."

She reached back and pushed her zipper ninety percent to the top.

"You'll come with me," Jack said. "To the wedding. It'll be fun. I'll parade you across the dance floor, proud as can be."

Alicia smiled and closed the closet behind her. She walked several steps toward the bed, her feet padding against the cool tile floors.

"Well?" he said, grinning wide as the world. "Whatcha think?"

She sighed, and shook her head.

"I'll think about it, Jack. But I question your ability to keep that sort of plan."

KENNEDY'S DAUGHTER WED AMONG SPLENDOR

The Philadelphia Inquirer, May 24, 1953

NEW YORK

Alicia held the card in her right hand. *Admittance to church,* it read.

At the wedding of Eunice Mary Shriver, Alicia felt every bit as fraudulent and on guard as she did at the convent posing as a Catholic girl. But Alicia pushed away the thoughts. This wasn't the same. For one, her life was not in danger. Also, the Kennedys already knew that she was a Jew.

In the last row at St. Patrick's Cathedral, Alicia sat jittery, all tumbling belly and shaky hands. Had she worn the right dress? Would she say the right things? More importantly, would Jack?

Tonight would be their seventh time together since his unexpected appearance amid the bougainvillea. Their relationship was solidifying, settling into some kind of normalcy, though they lived on opposite coasts. The arrangement suited Alicia, for now. Keeping Gary Cooper on a string helped, though he was increasingly suspicious of the senator.

"I know how that guy works," he'd said, when he called from Mexico. "And he doesn't want to be your *friend.*"

These past few months, Jack paid regular visits to Los Angeles. He and Alicia dined and danced and attended all the good parties, sipped all the best champagne. Although, it was not glamour all the time. One night, Jack insisted on the Malibu Cottage, a dreadful bar with tattered stools and sawdust on the floor. Alicia preferred the Mocambo, and its live parakeets and macaws, but down-at-the-heels places were a novelty for Jack.

They played tennis in Palm Springs and sunned themselves at the Beach Club. They hung around his sister Pat, and Peter Lawford, too. Sometimes Jack brought a friend to California, like Dave, or Kenny, or Torb, or Red Fay. Her roommates kept the men entertained as Alicia remained perplexed about who was married, who was free, and who enjoyed an "understanding" with his wife.

Alicia and Jack had their rhythm in California, but now they'd need to find footing in New York. Because of this, Alicia was drunk with nerves from the minute she stepped off the plane.

"Maybe I won't let you go back to California," Jack had said. "Maybe I'll kidnap you, and take you to Washington."

Alicia brushed it off, but the truth was, she was thinking about it. She was considering a move to D.C.

Inside St. Patrick's, Alicia watched, insides brimming, as Eunice glided down the aisle in an off-the-shoulder dress and twenty-foot train.

"Christian Dior," Jean would later say, to everyone, to make sure they knew.

The gown was magnificent, but the veil was longer and more dramatic, as was her seven-carat sapphire ring.

Pat was the maid of honor, and all ten bridesmaids wore strapless white organza sheaths topped off with boleros. The ushers totaled twenty, Jack the handsomest of the bunch.

After the ceremony, Alicia hurried through the church's heavy bronze doors. She didn't wait for the wedding party and instead followed a cluster of guests along Fiftieth toward the Waldorf Astoria, where a luncheon awaited on the Starlight Roof.

When Alicia walked into the reception, she was instantly taken with the art deco ceiling and the lantern stars dangling overhead. White flowers had been brought in by the truckload, and an eight-tiered cake sat in the corner.

Alicia recognized many of the guests who trickled in: Truman, Hearst, Harriman, and several men she'd seen on television delivering the news. She also saw the full complement of Jack's cronies and friends.

"Ken said he was bringing you, but I didn't believe him."

Alicia whirled around to find Lem Billings. She smiled. He'd grown on her, the toothy, asthmatic lug. Compared to Jack's other pals, he had a gentler side, and wasn't nearly such a wolf.

"Lem," she said, and kissed each cheek. "Terrific to see you."

"For you," he said, and passed her a flute of champagne. "Cheers."

They clinked glasses. Alicia would never tire of the taste of champagne, and the joyful, dry hum it created in her throat. To think, she once preferred beer.

"Eunice looks beautiful," Alicia said. "Not even Rose could complain."

"Oh, I'm sure Mrs. K could come up with something."

The two chuckled, though there was nothing untrue about what Lem said.

"So, where have you been these days?" Alicia asked. "I haven't seen you in Los Angeles in ages."

Lem was dopey, awkward, and prone to overindulge in booze. But he was also sweet, and loyal to Jack, and Alicia got the sense he didn't approve of the randiness of his other friends. If Lem were married, he'd never sit naked in a hot tub with Fannie, or Yolanda, and definitely not both.

"Work's been busy," he said. "I got a promotion, actually."

"Congratulations!" Alicia said as they touched glasses a second time.

"Plus, California isn't really me. I don't have much interest in hunting expeditions."

Alicia nodded, not sure what he meant.

"I'm glad you and Jack are seeing each other again," Lem said. "He's happier now. The Gary Cooper move was smart. Jack's a jealous bastard."

"I wondered if Coop got his attention," Alicia said with a laugh. "But it wasn't calculated at all."

Lem regarded Alicia, wincing.

"I heard about what happened," he said, "before you left Hyannis Port, with Mr. Kennedy."

"I'm surprised Jack told you. He's always anxious to get past unpleasantness. We've had squabbles in the morning that he can't remember by sundown."

"That's Jack all right," Lem said. "It was Pat who told me, actually. If it's any consolation, she was mortified."

Alicia bobbed her head. Was it any consolation? A little, but it'd never erase the sting, or the heartbreak of that night.

"I'm sorry it went down like that," Lem said. "It's just . . . Jack's their golden boy, so the whole thing was a shock. They thought you were Catholic."

"The Church itself thinks I'm Catholic, so . . ." Alicia rolled her eyes. "For people so intent on moving forward, they sure care a lot about a person's past."

"Mr. Kennedy had all kinds of problems with Jews in his Hollywood days. So, there's a history there."

"Mmmm-hmmm. I've heard all about it. He also thought Hitler was an impressive man."

Alicia tersely sipped her champagne.

"You have to understand," Lem said, "they were stunned. You don't *look* Jewish. I mean, your nose is slightly prominent, but other than that . . ."

Alicia frowned. Her nose was prominent? Lem's profile wasn't exactly one for the ages and she could say much worse things about the man.

I don't look Jewish? That's funny because you don't look like a faggot, yet people swear that you are.

"I hope you don't take offense," he said. "Mr. Kennedy has very big ideas about where Jack is going, and who with."

Alicia examined him for a minute, wondering if Lem liked her because he knew that she and Jack would never last, and she'd therefore never supplant him in Jack's heart.

Don't worry, Alicia, Red or Dave Powers had once said. *When you're not there, Jack has Lem suck him off, so he doesn't get one of his "head-aches."*

"I've always known Joe's ambition spelled bad news for me," Alicia said now, and smiled tightly.

"The thing is," Lem said, "Jack swears he's his own man. And every once in a great while, when it comes to you, I actually believe that it's true."

"Kid!" said that wonderful voice.

Alicia had been chatting with a Supreme Court justice when a person whooshed up and took her by the waist.

"At last!" he said. "You're gorgeous!"

Jack pulled her away from Justice So-and-So and kissed her briefly, on the lips. Alicia blushed to her toes. A modest gesture, but the most publicly affectionate Jack had ever been, and he'd done it right there on the Starlight Roof, amid the orchids and in full view of his family and friends.

"Oh, Jack," Alicia said, happy tears gathering. "What took you so long?"

She meant this about so many things.

"The receiving line lasted almost two hours. It was pure misery."

He ran both hands through his bushy, auburn hair.

"I'm beat," Jack said, and snatched her champagne.

He polished it off in one gulp and set the glass on a nearby table.

"Why are you so damned gorgeous?" he asked, scanning her up and down. "I know a few bridesmaids who are going to be chapped. Maybe even the bride."

Alicia smiled, blushing still. She hadn't been sure about the dress: a pale blue, silk shantung sheath. The style and color were perfect, but she worried that the rhinestones at the neckline were too avant-garde. Sparkle in the daytime was the latest fashion, but these folks might not have heard.

"Thank you," she said. "I don't mind bugging a bridesmaid or two. Now, if someone ever asks me to be one, I'll weep, knowing I've lost my looks."

As Jack chuckled, Alicia took a chance to study him. He was handsome as ever, the tanned golden boy, but the man was skinny, too reedy and frail. If Joe Kennedy weighed the same, they'd probably send him straight to Polyclinic.

"Do you need to sit?" Alicia asked. "Your back must be a mess after standing for so long."

"Nope!" he said with a clap and what could be described as a small leap.

Sometimes she marveled at Jack's energy, his get-up-and-go. If Alicia hadn't met his similarly charged siblings, she might think Jack was on Dexamyl. She'd seen the pills in action, with actresses and friends. While it kept a person perky and thin, it likewise kept them up for days. Alicia was grateful she didn't have to resort to such tricks.

"Come on!" Jack said, and took Alicia's hand.

He took her hand! Right there in public! Under the art deco sky!

"It's time to reintroduce you to my parents."

"Are you sure?" Alicia said, heart rattling like a parakeet trying to escape its cage. "Aren't they too busy with guests?"

"Now or never, kid. It's been a year."

"Almost two," she said.

Jack tugged her arm and Alicia's eyes found Joe and Rose Kennedy, holding court on the other side of the room. It was odd to see them here, far from wicker chairs, sailboats, and the Nantucket Sound.

"Hey, Pops!" Jack called out.

As Joe and Rose began to close in, Alicia's heart flapped beyond control.

She saw that the Ambassador was still the tall, confident patriarch, albeit with marginally less hair. Rose, as always, was pinched and grumpy. When they stepped forward to greet their son and his date, Joe Kennedy did not glower or sulk. If anything, he brightened by noticeable degrees.

"Miss Darr! How lovely to see you!"

Joe clasped both hands around hers. His were clammy and warm. Alicia swallowed, hard.

"You look ravishing!" he said.

Alicia nodded her thanks. She never understood this term: "ravishing." As if he intended to devour her whole.

"Mother, do you remember Jack's friend, Alicia Darr?" Joe asked, and glanced at his wife.

"Yeeees," Rose said in her squeaky hiss.

The women shook hands as Alicia pushed her face into the biggest smile she could find. These two almost seemed happy to see her. Alicia checked Jack, and he winked.

"My dear," Joe said, "I hear you've had great success in Hollywood."

"I don't know about 'great' but I've found a few roles."

"Don't discount the bit parts. We all have to start somewhere. Right, Jack?"

Joe walloped his son, and the men cackled lightly. Alicia's belly loosened. The Kennedys didn't seem bothered by her at all. She thought of Joe's words from two summers ago.

How do you expect to oust an old blue blood without the proper wife?

Jack did oust the blue blood, all on his own, no wife necessary. Why would he need one, being so thoroughly magnetic and smart? Maybe Joe Kennedy finally understood this, and trusted Senator John F. Kennedy more than the congressman of the same name.

"Well, Dad, Mother," Jack said, "I hate to break up the reunion, but I'd like to take this beautiful creature onto the dance floor."

"Fine idea," Joe said. "I might follow your lead."

"I don't care to dance," Rose snipped.

"Of course not, Mother. I'll just cut in with Jack and Alicia."

Alicia smiled meekly, her stomach tumbling once again. After bidding his parents adieu, she followed Jack onto the parquet floor, sighing as he took her into his arms.

"What do you think about the French Riviera?" Jack asked as the band played.

Don't let the stars get in your eyes

"The French Riviera?" Alicia said with a laugh. "I'm sure it's lovely this time of year."

"No, I mean, what do you think about going?"

Alicia laughed again.

"I'm still trying to decide about Washington."

"Do both!" Jack said, limping along.

Jack was doing a hero's job at the reception, dancing and shaking hands and treating each person like an old friend. But the night was long and he'd become increasingly rigid and tight with pain.

"France is worked out," he said. "The plan is to leave in July. Two weeks on a yacht. Gourmet meals, sunbathing, skinny-dipping, whatever we please. The boys are all signed up. What about you?"

"Sounds very romantic, what with all 'the boys,'" Alicia said. "But, Jack, I can't go to the French Riviera."

She wondered if he remembered. She wondered if he recalled the tickets they'd bought, an outside cabin on the *Ile de France*, for the honeymoon they never had.

"And why not?" he asked.

"Because," she said, "I'm still noodling on Washington, and that's a big enough decision for now."

Plus, Alicia didn't know if she could. She wasn't a citizen, and leaving the country was tempting fate, especially given how desperate she was to get in the first time. It would've been different on a honeymoon, traveling as husband and wife.

"I should be glad that you're still contemplating D.C.," Jack said. "I thought you might string this out for years."

"I am considering it, but only because you're such a convincing man."

By the time Eunice cut the cake—the last event before the newlyweds took off for Spain—Alicia resolved that yes, she would join Jack in Washington. Some might say she was giving up her Hollywood dreams, but Hollywood was never Alicia's dream, not really. America was her dream, art was her dream, and Jack was, too. Acting was a hobby she picked up along the way. Sort of like Coop.

"Wow," Alicia said as someone wheeled Eunice's cake onto the dance floor. "I've never seen a dessert that requires a ladder."

"Especially since Eunice has often been mistaken for one."

The bride ascended slowly, but assuredly and with her customary athleticism. At the top, Eunice radiated over her adoring, tipsy guests. She cocked a hip, hoisted her lily-of-the-valley bouquet, and then chucked it straight at Pat. Everyone roared with applause as Pat did a victory dance. Meanwhile, Peter was slumped against the wall, bearing the demeanor of a man who'd traveled a very stormy sea.

"Looks like Pat will be the next Kennedy to wed," Alicia said.

Jack gave one of his sly, sideways grins.

"Maybe," he said, and hooked an arm over her shoulders.

Alicia felt his breath in her hair, on her neck.

"But you never know, kid," he said. "It could just as easily be someone else."

Serena is in seat 32E, hurtling over the Atlantic toward California, where she'll stay with a boy she's known for ten days. Technically, she's trying to claim an inheritance, but really, it's about the boy.

"You need to pursue this," Lee Perenchio said, when they read the letter together for a tenth time, a twentieth. "The universe wants you in L.A."

"*L'universo*," she'd muttered, with a snort.

"You received a letter inviting you to Los Angeles, when you were with a person *from Los Angeles*. It couldn't be more perfect. We can go together!"

"Together?" she'd demurred, despite the tickling thrill. "You and me? *Che palle!*"

What balls!

They'd met a mere week before the letter arrived. Lee's family booked a tour of the Colosseum, and Serena was their guide. When she first saw them, Serena thought: what an interesting amalgam of persons.

There was a well-heeled, older man with slick silver hair and a massive gold Rolex. Lee's dad. Beside him, two middle-aged women. Lee's half sisters, all of them from different moms. Behind these people stood Lee himself.

This stranger wasn't a boy, though neither was he a man, exactly. He was tall (two meters, at least), wavy-haired, and attractive in an indisputable but artless way—like a Labrador or a loquacious woodland animal from an animated film. Though he seemed so boyish, Lee Perenchio was a recent Stanford graduate and twenty-three years old.

Serena earned her money that morning, thanks to one sister in Lucite heels, and the other put off by graffiti, hobos, and what she called "the general smell of Rome." When Lee showed up the next day, Serena assumed it was to lodge a complaint. Alas, he was there for another tour. He'd go on to book a tour every day, for the next seven days.

"I want to see this city without my sisters," he'd said.

"There are other guides," Serena replied.

"You're the best one. I like the way you talk with your hands."

Serena could not help but be charmed.

By the end of the week, she'd run out of sights, and so she took Lee to the famous Via Margutta, a street that told a thousand stories. It is home to the Roman art scene, she explained, and was the setting of *Roman Holiday*.

Everything about Margutta is quintessential Rome, with its cobblestones and planter boxes and ivy-festooned buildings of orange and yellow and pink. The avenue is open to foot traffic only, a good thing as Lee had demonstrated himself susceptible to oncoming automobiles. Margutta is also Serena's home, which is how they ended up in her flat. In her flat, they read the attorney's letter, and now she is on a plane.

"We've known each other a week!" Serena reminded Lee as he tried to coax her into California.

"I know that," he answered. "But it seems like a lot longer. You're one of the people I'm closest to."

"*Santo Cielo!*"

Serena threw up her hands.

"*Nun te stai a regolà!*" she said. "Don't get mushy and romantic on me!"

"I'm starting to think Italian men are unfairly singled out as lotharios," he groused. "No one ever mentions the women."

As he reddened, Serena reached over and squeezed his hand. Oh, but this puppy dog of a boy made her happy, after a scant seven days.

"If you want to know the truth," she said, "I returned to Rome two months ago, and you're the best thing about it so far."

It's possible the letter is a fraud, Serena thinks as she sails across the sky. But, real or fake, does it matter? Either she travels to Los Angeles and inherits many millions of dollars, or she travels to Los Angeles and spends the summer with Lee.

On the other hand, the trip is an absurd idea, especially for someone so fantastically low on cash. But Serena is twenty-one years old. She has no boyfriend or husband or family of any kind. Her only pet is a cat on the wall. Nonna Nova herself would tell Serena that it's okay to be impetuous, foolish every once in a while. You make mistakes while you're young.

All that and Serena wants to find out about the money and what happened to Alicia Corning Clark. She wants to see Los Angeles because she's never been. And she wants to do these things with Lee because—all-American as he may be—there is something original about him. The way Serena sees it, she has nothing to lose.

HOLLYWOOD

Alicia staggered through a Beverly Hills mansion, champagne in hand. Fred followed, to make sure she didn't fall through a window, or knock into something too valuable to replace.

"Let's get you out of here," he said, as she careened away from him.

"Get out of here? I'm working, in case you hadn't noticed."

She went farther down the hall, Fred stuck on her heels. She couldn't lose the bastard, this bodyguard she never hired but who always seemed to be around.

"You were paid to meander drunk in a producer's house?" he said. "That's a new arrangement."

"Fuck you."

Alicia stopped and peered into a room. She flicked on the lights.

"Holy shit!" she said, and burped. "Look at this place. Can you imagine having an art gallery in your home? There's a Renoir in here. A Picasso! Over there is a . . . what's-his-name. You know. The one?"

"I don't know what the fuck you're talking about," Fred said, "but the owner is a renowned collector of art, and women. I can't speak for his taste in art, but his taste in women is shit."

Alicia thwacked him in the chest with the back of her hand.

"Ouch!" Fred yelped. "What's your deal tonight? I've never seen you so loaded. Romance problems? The breakup with Coop, perhaps?"

Alicia shrugged, as a tear slipped down her cheek. "Romance problems" was one way to put it, but of course it had nothing to do with Gary Cooper.

The wedding was scheduled for September. "The tall, hatless Kennedy," the "personable and dashing young Democrat," was getting married, despite being heretofore "pictured as impervious to romance."

But, John F. Kennedy had been snagged, by a debutante no less, a so-called artist. Alicia could've stomached any other career, and they had plenty to choose from. Jacqueline Bouvier was alternately described as a photographer, heiress, socialite, and general "career gal." She had attended George Washington University, Vassar, and the Sorbonne. A perfect goddamned match, probably handpicked by Joe himself.

The couple had known each other for one year, some reports said, while others pegged it at two. Where had this *Jacqueline* been these past few months, she wondered, when Jack was so often at Alicia's side?

Miss Bouvier was probably the very reason Joe had been so pleasant at Eunice's wedding. His son was set to marry the ideal woman and already had a piece on the side, just like Pop. Jews were dandy behind closed doors, as long as they were good in bed. Alicia felt like the world's biggest fool.

Was Jacqueline pretty? Mostly. She had a dark and haunting air about her, but her face was somewhat flat, her eyes too far apart, like a shark's. She had the perfect nose but, if Alicia wasn't mistaken, beneath it was the suggestion of a mustache. Her hair was kinky and Alicia's friend Zsa Zsa recently sat beside her on a plane and disclosed that the girl had terrible skin and a very grating personality.

But what had really gotten to Alicia, what really sent her entire spirit plummeting, was the four-page spread in *Life* magazine. "Senator

Kennedy Goes A-Courting," the cover announced. It featured the new couple sailing on the *Victura*.

The photographs were mostly staged. Whenever in his life had Jack Kennedy "chatted on the lawn" wearing a sport coat and shoes shinier than the pearls around Jacqueline's neck? But the cover was real. On it, Jacqueline gripped the mast of the *Victura*, her forearm muscles straining. Jack sat on the bow, relaxed and shoeless, arms wrapped around his knees as the boat tipped toward the sea.

With a shake of the head and tears in her eyes, Alicia strolled the art gallery, heels clacking on the floor. Had she waited too long to agree to Washington? What if she'd said yes to France?

No matter. Jack was getting married and it was probably for the best. Part of the Kennedy contract was to produce kids. Ethel was pregnant with their third. Doubtless Jack was expected to catch up and Alicia couldn't help him with that. Last week, she'd gone to the doctor, fretting that she'd been knocked up. He gave her even worse news.

"It's unlikely you'll ever be able to conceive," he said.

There'd been a surgery, back in Germany, performed hastily and without the proper aftercare. Such was the way in the camps, especially with former Nazi doctors at the helm. Alicia's monthlies had always been sporadic, so she'd never taken this as a sign, until the doctor told her that it was.

The question was, where would Alicia go from here? She'd convinced herself that she was tired of the parties and the bit roles that were an unholy union of long hours and low pay. Giving this up for Jack was easy. Going back was not.

Alicia rubbed her eyes with the base of her palms, makeup be damned. Suddenly, she felt someone else's presence and glanced up, expecting Fred. When she saw it was the owner of the house, she let out a puff of surprise.

"Sorry!" the man said, holding up both hands. "I didn't mean to startle you."

He was attractive, in the vein of a silver fox, but Alicia couldn't muster the energy to flirt. They'd met before, though Alicia didn't recall his name.

"Someone told me there was an artist in here," he said, scratching the bald patch at the crown of his head. "A woman with a good eye."

"I don't know about my eye. I simply like what I like."

"And what is that?" he asked.

"My taste is somewhat varied," she said, and ambled toward a Toulouse-Lautrec. "As is yours, I see. Assuming you picked these out yourself."

"Of course! No curator here. Otherwise, this isn't an art gallery, but a way to show off."

Alicia chuckled flatly.

"No one in Hollywood would fault you for that."

Alicia took a few more steps, scanning the paintings on the easternmost wall. She was starting to sober up, probably thanks to the incessant crying.

"I didn't know there were so many Picassos in private collections," she said. "In *one* collection, at that."

"He's my favorite."

"Don't say that too loudly." Alicia smiled over her shoulder. "He's a Communist, you know. You can't have anyone thinking you're sympathetic to the Reds."

The man laughed through his nose.

Alicia walked a few more paces, past more paintings, before stopping beside one she hadn't seen. With a single glimpse, she concluded it was her favorite in the room.

"Who did this?" she asked.

It was a swirling, pastel nude woman with a feline's face and large, balloon-like breasts. The subject was somehow cartoonish and serious, playful and evocative, all at the same time.

"An Italian artist," the man said. "Novella Palmisano. Famous in Europe for her surreal nudes, but she's virtually unknown here. I picked it up last time I was in Rome, visiting the art galleries on Margutta. The piece caught my attention."

Alicia inched closer and fought the pulsing temptation to reach out.

"It's magnificent," she whispered.

"The artist herself is even more colorful," the man said. "She's four feet, nine inches of pure hellfire and lust. I've never met anyone quite like her. Actually, now that I think about it, you two would get along like gangbusters."

"How's that?" Alicia asked with a smirk. "I'm not that short. Or lusty."

"You have a similar devil-may-care attitude."

"What makes you think that about me?"

"You were scheduled to be at two dinners of mine last month, and you showed up to neither."

"Sorry about that, I was . . ."

Indisposed? Involved? On her way out of town?

"Don't worry," the man said. "It can be a good trait. Novella's like that. She lives life, does what she wants, and views nothing as an obligation. And you have very similar laughs. Deep. True. From the belly."

Alicia nodded. It was the laugh she found with Jack. More tears welled and she looked away, so that the man would not see.

"You're both European," he continued, "and artists. And—heck— I think you've dated the same men. Weren't you with Kirk Douglas?"

"I've spent some time with Kirk," Alicia confessed. "You must've done your homework."

She fixed her concentration on the nude. Alicia last painted in Hyannis Port and had long since stopped calling herself an artist. But maybe she should start up again, and this time paint people, not places from a past now dead. Alicia wondered what the *debutante* painted. Endless seascapes, no doubt. Portraits of her grandparents. Depictions of her two homes.

Alicia pivoted toward the door, her chest heavy with sorrow, her mind thick with melancholy, the rest of her body filled with too many sensations to name.

"Your home is lovely," she said to the man. "But not as lovely as your art. I'm honored to have seen it firsthand."

The man screwed up his face. This was not the kind of buttering up he usually received.

"Do you want to . . ." he started.

"I'm a tad light-headed," Alicia said, and swished by him, skimming his arm with her fingertips as she passed. "I should call it a night. Thank you for introducing me to Novella Palmisano. I'm inspired."

Alicia left the gallery and made her way to the rocked foyer at the front of the house. She wondered which of the departing guests might give her a lift home, as she lacked the energy to find Fred.

Anxious to kick off her shoes and slip into her pink nightie, Alicia trailed an acquaintance who was walking to his car. Then she heard a noise, a veritable racket. Her stomach dropped. She'd know it anywhere, that guffaw. Patented, probably trademarked, and identifiable as one hundred percent Kennedy.

She hightailed it back into the house. A flash of auburn whizzed past and Alicia draggled after Pat Kennedy, until she caught up with her on the lanai.

"I hear congratulations are in order!" Alicia said as she strutted outside, feeling none of the swagger she tried to project.

Also, she was a tad winded.

"Alicia!" Pat said with a genuine smile. "I didn't know you were at this party! What are you congratulating me for? He hasn't proposed. Yet."

Her eyes skipped toward Peter, who was trying to light a cigar on the other side of the sliding glass door.

"Anyway," Pat continued, "you're not supposed to say 'Congratulations' to a woman. The appropriate response is 'Best wishes.'"

"Thank you for the lesson," Alicia said. "But I was referring to your brother's engagement."

Pat blinked and took a drag of her cigarette.

"What now?" she said.

"Jack's engagement?" Alicia said. "To Jacqueline Bouvier?"

"Oh. Her." Pat blew a stream of smoke more or less into Alicia's face. "It's pronounced Jack-*leen*. Rhymes with 'queen.' Just how she likes it, the brat. Ugh, she's such a bore."

Alicia's body pinged with glee. Whatever Joe Kennedy thought, at least Pat didn't like Jacqueline, and she had exceptional taste.

"It's funny," Pat said, "when Jack rang with the news, I offered my best wishes, felicitations, the whole nine. I hung up and told Pete. His first question was 'Who's the girl?' And the thing was, I had no idea! I called him back. I said, 'Jack, have you picked the bride and, if so, might you also tell me her name?' "

Pat howled and howled. Alicia didn't find it as funny as all that but pushed out a laugh all the same. Did she want Jack to love this Jacqueline? Or would she prefer that the wide-eyed woman was no better than an actress, playing a lead role in Joe Kennedy's finest achievement? The first option cast a poor light on Alicia, the second on Jack.

"Sounds like a match made in heaven," Alicia said.

"Ha." Pat grunted and then stomped her cigarette into the floor. "He proposed via *telegram*, which is goddamned perfect. What she's getting out of the situation, I haven't the faintest. The one thing I do know is that my brother may be getting married, but Jack Kennedy will never settle down."

Hollywood beauty Alicia Darr had her nose bobbed.

Behind the Scenes in Hollywood, by Harrison Carroll, September 28, 1953

HOLLYWOOD

Alicia stood on the front steps of the Wilshire Country Club. After a sweep of the premises to make sure she was alone, she flipped open her compact and held up the mirror.

She pressed on her skin. The caverns beneath her eyes had been bruised for longer than she'd anticipated. Damn it. It looked okay in the bathroom at home, not so out in the sunshine, enhanced by the glare from the white stucco clubhouse behind her.

Alicia clicked her compact shut and pulled out a pair of cat-eyed shades. These would have to stay on, lest she be forced to answer any questions about the state of her face. As she latched her pocketbook, a wild-haired figure stomped out from the club's front doors.

"You know, golfing is a sport!" yelled this person—a woman. "Not sure why it's a problem to wear shorts. Raúl! Fetch my car!"

Alicia gaped for she recognized the shorts-clad golfer on sight. It was the one and only Katharine Hepburn.

"Miss Hepburn . . ." Alicia said, and walked down the stairs to join her.

"Oh hiya," Katharine said, like they'd met a hundred times before.

"I didn't see you there. Ignore my tantrum. I'm just chapped because they kicked me off the course for wearing shorts. For Christ's sake."

She gestured toward the baggy, wrinkled Bermudas that might as well have been cut for a man.

"I adore the shorts," Alicia said, though she would've chosen something more flattering, a light wool gabardine, perhaps. "Forget your attire, I can't conceive of any club that would eject Katharine Hepburn! I'd let you play in your birthday suit!"

The woman laughed in her throaty way.

"No one wants to see that," she said, and pulled off her kid leather gloves. "Please, call me Kate."

She traded her gloves for a package of cigarettes.

"It's a lovely day for golf, in any case," Katharine—Kate—said. "Are you coming or going?"

Alicia squinted at the red-roofed building.

"Coming. I think. I'm supposed to play with a group of men who are in town for a convention. The American Dietetic Association, I think."

Alicia sighed. A locker room attendant was probably right then propping her bag up on the driving range, its gold tag glinting in the sunlight. Of Don Class's girls, Alicia was the athletic one, capable of playing a solid eighteen or a few sets on the tennis court. Whether this was to her advantage or detriment was as yet undetermined. She liked tennis and golf fine, but chatting with dietitians less so.

"I'm not sure if I'm up for playing," Alicia said. "You think they'd miss me if I skipped?"

"They'd miss you all right," Kate said with a snort. "What'd you say your name was?"

"Alicia." She extended a hand. "Alicia Darr."

"*Enchantée*," Kate replied. "I've seen you before. You're with Don Class."

"Yes. I am," Alicia said, eyes fluttering against her great shock.

"Hollywood's a tiny town, you know," Kate said, gauging Alicia's surprise. "It's part of its lack of charm."

Alicia nodded. Hollywood was small, and Alicia wasn't exactly a wallflower. She went to auditions. She attended parties. She'd filmed a bit part in *Miss Baker's Dozen* with Greer Garson a while back.

"You should get a better agent," Kate said.

"Don seems fine, but if you have any suggestions—"

"What you really need, kiddo, is to get to New York. Hollywood is too one-dimensional. I arrived three days ago and already it's making me batty. They're trying to talk me into television of all things, to play the part of a spinstery career gal who's a shoulder to cry on for everyone else."

Alicia was bewildered by this woman's presence, and the way she spoke. Kate talked briskly, each sentence sticking to the last like a gathering avalanche. They were strangers, but there was a certain familiarity to her, a comfort one might find with an old friend.

"I'd get a piece of the action," Kate rambled on, "but who cares about that. I've got other things going on. I'm working on an adaptation of *The Millionairess*, which I performed last summer, in the West End."

At once, Alicia understood why she wasn't cowering despite being in close proximity to the world's biggest star. It was Katharine's countenance—that gangly nature and bounding personality, as well as her fluffy, auburn hair, grayish eyes, and haphazard dress. Also, it was her speech: that rat-a-tat New England beat. She reminded Alicia of Jack.

The valet drove up in a white convertible two-seat Corvette. Alicia gawped at the sparkling paint job and red leather interior.

"Gorgeous," she said.

"Ya think?" Kate said, and waved a ten-dollar bill at Raúl. "Why don't you hop behind the wheel?"

"Oh, Miss Hepburn," Alicia said, her heart beating so fast that she felt sick. "I can't drive your car. I don't have a license! Some church ladies in Oklahoma gave me lessons years ago, but . . . goodness . . . I can't fathom the outrage if I killed Kate the Great in an automobile crash."

"I don't want you to drive me. I want you to have it."

"Have it?"

Kate shrugged.

"Why not? I'm going to New York tomorrow, and I have a car there. I don't plan to return for a long, long time."

"I can't," Alicia stuttered even as she moved closer to the glittering white car. "How would you get home?"

"I'll just pop inside and call George to come pick me up."

"George?" Alicia said, with a jerk of her head.

With one word, Alicia was thrust back to another year, another coast, back to a time when *she* used to call George to pick her up.

"George Cukor?" Kate said, meaning the famed director.

Because of course it would not be George Neill, goofy projectionist who'd never left the Cape. An unexpected sadness shot through her.

"Go on," Kate said. "Take it. It's yours."

"Are you sure? This seems extravagant."

"More than sure! At least someone will get use out of it. I'd ask you to drive me"—Kate winked—"but, to your point, right now would not be a good time to die."

Alicia regarded the car, and then Kate, and then took a glimpse of the eleventh green.

"I don't think I'm golfing today," she said.

"I guess that makes two of us," Kate answered with a laugh. "Go on, take the car. Rest assured, I never offer anything that I don't truly mean to give."

Before Katharine Hepburn could reconsider, Alicia shook hands with her new friend, hopped into the running car, and bombed it out of the parking lot. This driving thing was easier than she remembered.

An hour later, hair tangled from a high-speed jaunt up the coast, Alicia blasted into the bungalow's driveway. She leapt from the car and exploded through the front door.

"Fannie!" she called. "Yolanda! Daisy? Hello?"

The home was quiet for that time of day, nothing but the whir of the fans. Where was everyone? Damn it, if Katharine Hepburn gave you a convertible, you wanted someone to tell.

Alicia picked up the house phone and began to dial, only to remember that George—*her* George, not Cukor—wouldn't answer. He was in Niagara Falls with his new wife, Doris, Paul's niece, the girl who replaced Alicia at the candy counter. *Weddings were quite the trend nowadays,* Alicia thought grimly, but at least George's had been small, instead of an over-the-top display described by newspapers as "one of the most lavish weddings Newport has seen in recent years."

Jack *hated* Newport.

"Why isn't anyone home to take my call?" Alicia wailed.

As if on cue, Fred pushed through the front door.

"Fred!" she squealed, running his way.

He looked behind him, as if expecting some other man. Alicia was usually a dash cooler, less effusive, never more animated than "hello."

"Are you on something?" he asked.

"Did you see the car out front? Isn't it gorgeous?"

"I did notice and was wondering—"

"It's mine!" she sang. "Someone gave it to me! You'll never guess who."

"It's a present?" He removed his hat. "Whoa. That's quite the score. One of the golfing fellas?"

"Forget golf," Alicia said.

"Oh geez." He groaned. "Don't tell me that you actually did *forget golf.*"

"I chose not to go. Now, listen to this. I was walking into the club and there she was, right there in the flesh. Katharine Hepburn! She asked me to call her Kate. We gabbed for a bit, and then she gave me her car. For keeps!"

"That's Kate Hepburn's?" he asked, jacking his thumb toward the window.

"Isn't it exciting?" Alicia lifted onto her tiptoes and clung to his shirt. "Isn't it the best?"

"It's something all right," he said, and shook her off. "But Don's not gonna care about a Corvette. He'll be pissed that you didn't golf with those men."

"Oh, Don is mad at me all the time." She slapped the air.

"Can't argue there. Christ, Alicia. I like you. I like you a lot. And hanging round Katharine Hepburn isn't the worst idea. I mean, she's a dyke—"

"Fred!"

"It's true. And at least she won't rough you up, or knock you up."

"No one can knock me up," she said.

"Yeah. That's what they all think." He rolled his eyes.

Alicia didn't explain that this was plain fact. Of course, no man wanted to hear about a lady's medical problems, not even someone as uncouth as Fred.

"What are you going to do?" he asked. "When Don kicks you out? Never mind an income, where are you going to live?"

Alicia pursed her lips and glanced outside.

"I have a car," she said.

"You're going to live in a car?!"

"Of course not!"

"So instead you'll sell a gift from Katharine Hepburn?"

Alicia frowned.

"No," she said. "I could, if I got desperate. Not that I'd want to."

Alicia was so weary of this feeling, of always being thin on cash. For two years she'd imagined her big break as being just around the corner, and with it her money problems gone. But, so far, her career had been made of many minor breaks, and Alicia only ever had enough to squeak by in between. She'd have to be more penurious when it came to the latest fashions, and not so prone to impulse buys. But certain Newport newlyweds needed a pair of cold meat forks from Cartier. They really did.

"Is this what you want?" Fred asked, sweeping his hand, meaning the house they stood in, but also more. "Because it seems like you don't."

"I don't plan to live here forever, if that's what you're asking."

"It's not. Don Class makes stars. Isn't that why you're here? Isn't that why any pretty blonde comes to Hollywood?"

"So, I'm merely another blonde?" Alicia sniffed, and crossed her arms.

"No. That's my point. You're special, and you have a talent the others don't. I can never figure out whether you're on the brink of something great, or about to lose it all. You could be the next Marilyn Monroe, if you wanted to."

"I do not want that at all."

Fred shook his head. He reached into his jacket and pulled out a stack of business cards. Sighing, he shuffled through them.

"Until you figure out what the hell you're doing . . ."

He flicked a card at her, which Alicia caught before it hit the floor.

"*Confidential* magazine," he said, and then tossed another. "Hedda Hopper. She writes a gossip column for the *Los Angeles Times*."

"You know I read Hedda's column every day."

"When I want to pick up extra cash," he said. "I sell some stories. They have to be true, mind you, otherwise don't bother."

Fred cleared his throat.

"'Gary Cooper continues to get around at high speed. His latest darling: Alicia Darr, a Viennese actress . . .'"

"That was you?" Alicia said as her mouth fell open.

"You're welcome on the 'Viennese' bit."

"Oh, Fred." She sighed. "You have no idea how much trouble that caused me."

"I have some idea," he said. "I won't name names, but we can *congress* about it later."

Alicia swallowed the lump that'd risen in her throat. How did Fred know about Jack? He'd never said a thing. Though, she supposed, that was very much Fred's style.

"Well," Alicia said, "I hope you weren't the one who told the papers about my nose job."

"Wasn't me," he swore. "Cross my heart."

Alicia pored over the cards.

"So, this is your job?" she asked. "How you get by?"

"Nah. It's more of a side gig."

"Side gig to what?" Alicia looked up. "I've always wondered."

"It's hard to explain," he said. "Mostly I'm the guy who sorts out personal problems for the rich and famous."

Fred put on his hat.

"If you call," he said, "tell them you work for me. It will give you credibility."

"Go figure," Alicia said with a smirk.

"Now, if you'll excuse me. I have to fetch Daisy from the Beach Club. She's gotten into some mix-up with two sheikhs and a shah."

Alicia nodded, half listening, as she stared at the cards. Peddling gossip was a seedy endeavor but Alicia was in dire need of cash. Plus, she had a nose for details, and this might give her something to do when dinners or dates went stale.

Within minutes, Alicia found herself in the kitchen, phone in hand, dialing straight through to Hedda Hopper, the best in the biz.

"Yes, hello," she said to the person who picked up. "I'd like to report a sighting. Katharine Hepburn was kicked out of the Wilshire Country Club for wearing shorts."

Serena and Lee sit in the dining room of a Spanish-style beach home in Southern California. A lawyer named Leonard is across from them.

"Thank you for coming all this way," he says.

Leonard explains that he's semiretired. His office is in New York, but he prefers California this time of year; any time of year, really. Another stroke of luck, Lee thinks. If the directive was for New York, Serena would be there, if not still in Rome.

"Shall we get to it?" Leonard asks. "Angela is going to take notes."

Leonard's personal secretary is at the table, too. She wears a diamond ring, which is too big for her finger. It slips with the slightest movement and she's constantly returning it to faceup. Each time she does, Leonard's eyes flit in her direction.

"I'm relieved the letter made it to you," Leonard says. "We had a hell of a time tracking you down."

"*Allora*, it's quite the miracle," Serena says. "Especially with the Italian mail system."

"Yes, I've read about that."

The girl surprises Leonard. He expected someone blonder, lighter. Her hair is very, very dark—black almost—and her skin is olive-toned. Then he notices her uniquely colored eyes, framed in thick black lashes, and has to wonder.

"It was opened," Serena says. "Your letter. Probably because you addressed it in purple ink."

Leonard glares at Angela. Why'd he spend hours researching the vagaries of the Italian postal system if she wasn't going to follow his instructions? Angela smiles and shrugs. It all turned out fine.

"Well, back to business," Leonard says.

He asks Serena how much she knows about the deceased, Alicia Darr Purdom Corning Clark. Angela holds a (purple) pen hovered above a notepad. Her ring slips again.

"Mostly the headlines," Serena says. "She was a friend of my grandmother's. They lived together in Rome for several years. When I was young, we visited her in the Bahamas, and sometimes she came to see us."

"What about her background?" Leonard asks. "How much information did Ms. Palmisano provide there?"

Serena blinks. Miss Palmisano?

"Novella," Leonard qualifies. "Your grandmother."

"Oh. Yes. Well, I know that Mrs. Corning Clark married three times. Her most recent husband was a Bahamian bodybuilder. She was Polish, a displaced person from the war who emigrated to the States in 1950, or so. My grandmother said she was quite social. She had a lot of boyfriends."

"Yes, all of those things are true," Leonard says.

True, but not enough. How will he ever explain the full extent of Alicia? Entire books could be written about the woman and still never come close to addressing her complex life.

He pushes a brown scrapbook across the table.

"For your amusement," he says. "She saved most press written about her."

Serena glances at but does not touch the book. Lee opens to a random page and flips through several more. Serena catches some headlines. Gary Cooper. Ty Power. Edmund Purdom. Warren Beatty. Roberto Rossellini. JFK.

"To be as direct as possible," Leonard says, "we have reason to suspect that you are related to Alicia Corning Clark."

"Related?" Serena wrinkles her nose. "Were she and my grandmother siblings?"

It's the first thing that comes to mind. Nonna did often say Alicia was "like a sister."

"Siblings?" Leonard frowns. "No. We think you're Mrs. Clark's granddaughter."

He drops the news on her, like a weight.

"On my father's side?" Serena says, unable to work out the equation. "It's possible, but he was Persian, not Polish."

"On your maternal side," Leonard says. "Benedetta Palmisano. That is your mother's name, correct?"

"That's her given name, yes. She's been married many times, and has changed her first name and her last. I haven't spoken to her in years."

She gives Lee a weak smile. Last night she'd told him the full story. When Serena was two, her mother left her in the care of Novella, in order to "find herself," which involved sampling the various communes, cults, and drug dens of the world.

"She was never settled," Nova used to say. "From the minute she was born."

At first, her mother called on holidays, and Serena's birthday, too. Then the calls became letters, and then postcards, and soon faded to nothing at all.

"Don't be sad," Serena said to Lee when he'd gotten teary. "I don't remember her. I had a wonderful life with Nonna and I never wanted for more."

"So, you haven't been in touch with your mother recently?" Leonard asks, drumming his fingers on the table.

"No." Serena shakes her head. "There's a strong possibility she's dead. She was a bit of a risk taker. *Is* a risk taker?"

Then she pauses, thinks for a second. Did Leonard say that Alicia Corning Clark was her *maternal grandmother*? That must mean . . .

"You are wrong," Serena says. "Novella Palmisano is my grandmother."

"I understand that's what you've been told, and it might even be true."

"Of course it's true. I don't know what Mrs. Clark might've claimed, but she was half mad, at least according to my *nonna*."

Serena looks at Lee as if he could confirm. He nods dutifully, his show of support.

"Alicia had a very energetic imagination," Serena says, making a hand motion, like something exploding overhead. "It's likely she made it up."

Alicia Corning Clark was nothing but antics. To wit, the scrapbook is open to an article that references a bar brawl. There are also a "strip club scandal," home invasions, and numerous arrests.

"Perhaps she *claimed* my mother was her daughter," Serena says, "and not Nova's. But it cannot be true."

"I'm confused," Lee interjects. "I thought you flew us—I mean *her*—to California because she was named in the will."

Leonard stands and tugs on his slacks, which are struggling to stay up over his belly. He pads over to the window, and gazes toward the street.

"Mrs. Corning Clark named the doorman and bellman in her will," he says. "And an elevator operator, too, as well as the caretaker of her Bahamian estate and multiple charities. As I mentioned, she had several wills, most of them undated, all conflicting."

Sounds like you're a top-notch lawyer, Lee thinks to himself.

"Then what do I have to do with this?" Serena asks. "If I'm not mentioned?"

Leonard returns to the table.

"Before we can address the various others," he says, "we must first determine whether she has blood heirs."

"But Alicia never had children."

"We'd like to confirm," he says. "Which is why you'll need a DNA test."

"What?" Serena scoffs. "I will not do that."

"It's the only way to sort this out, the only way to know for sure."

Serena sits with the information, and what he's asked her to do. Why doesn't she want a DNA test? What is she afraid of? Lee looks at her, curiously.

The lawyer's stomach grumbles. Why is the girl being so difficult? Just take the damned test, and maybe become rich. Jesus, he doesn't have time for this. It's eleven minutes past noon.

"Listen, we can go round and round about Mrs. Corning Clark's wild imagination or what she's said to me and others. But what is more convincing than DNA? It's not too often I get to use science to solve a legal problem."

"And who would my supposed grandfather be?" Serena asks.

She's never had a grandfather. Novella's pregnancy with Benedetta made the papers, as she had to announce her retirement from café society. Nova refused to name the father, until divorce was legalized in Italy. When it finally was, *la dolce vita* had ended, and everyone scattered to other countries, to other lives. There was no one left to care.

"Miss Palmisano," Leonard says. "Let's not speculate about any grandfather until we get this test out of the way."

He places both hands on the table.

"I've arranged an appointment for you at a lab," he says, "the day after next. Angela, hand her the card."

Angela hands her the card. Oh dear, the boss is getting hungry. This will all come to a very terse end.

"We can meet again after the test," Leonard says. "Feel free to take the scrapbook, acquaint yourself with Alicia Darr Purdom Corning Clark. Angela, please show them the door."

Angela hastily ushers them from the room. Serena walks like a drunk, unbalanced and befuddled. Lee scuffles along, scrapbook beneath his arm. As they enter the foyer, Leonard calls out to Serena one last time.

"Good luck," he says. "I have to admit, I hope you're Alicia's granddaughter. I knew the woman fifty years and despite the furs and the diamonds and the fabulous life, there was always something sad about her. I think she would've wanted a granddaughter. Lord knows she never had that kind of uncomplicated love."

Also ringsiding: Prince Mahmoud Pahley, brother of the shah of Iran, with Mr. and Mrs. Roy Davis and Alicia Darr.

The Daily Reporter, March 4, 1954

HOLLYWOOD

At Ciro's, Alicia sat at a four-top beside the stage with the Roy Davises and her date, a prince and the brother of the shah of Iran. Already she was envisioning how she might report this to Hedda, or Harrison Carroll. She'd mention they were ringsiding, of course.

The crowd was pretty namey that night. A sweep of the joint revealed Nicky Hilton, Harry Rothschild, and Esther Williams teaching the mambo to anyone who cared to learn. Meanwhile, Marlon Brando roved the room with that hungry look of his.

Brando was hot news lately, thanks to the two-million-dollar lawsuit filed after he walked off the set of *The Egyptian*. His agent called him a "very sick and mentally confused boy." Alicia felt sorry for the kid, but he'd provided her enough fodder to pay the next two rents. A good thing, as it was expensive living on her own. Her Doheny Drive apartment was bare bones, and on the unfashionable side of Sunset, but it was still a stretch to afford. At least the Corvette had its own parking space, and was no longer subject to housemates begging to take it for a spin.

As the music played, Alicia gently tapped the cylindrical candle in time with the beat. Meanwhile, Mahmoud chattered with Roy Davis, who was some sort of oil magnate, by Alicia's best guess.

Sighing, Alicia accidentally caught eyes with Shelley Winters, who waved animatedly from across the room. Although Shelley was every gossip's dream, Alicia was happy to leave her stories to other reporters.

Alicia cranked her head away and straight into the chiseled face of a man so handsome her breath snagged with one glimpse. He had wavy, dense hair and a dark and moody stare. His lips were full and red, his squint flirtatious and wry. Here was the thinking woman's James Dean. James Dean, if we here sexier.

Alicia excused herself to the ladies' so that she might assess the intriguing newcomer at closer range. Unfortunately, she only encountered Marlon Brando, who was muttering "I'm all right, I'm all right" to no one in particular.

"Alicia!" called a voice, high-pitched and ringing.

Alicia looked at her table and saw that the prince and the Roy Davises had decamped, and were replaced by Miss Winters. Of all the blasted luck.

"Oh, hello, Shelley," Alicia said, approaching the table.

She forced a smile and sat down.

"Aren't you supposed to be in Rome?"

"Yes, I'm very much supposed to be in Rome," Shelley said with a huff. "*Everyone's* in Rome these days."

"That's what they say," Alicia responded flatly, well aware that "everyone" included Shelley's soon-to-be-ex-husband Vittorio and his seventeen-year-old-fiancée. "*Roman Holiday* has generated a raging case of Roman fever."

"I'm missing out!" Shelley cried. "I'm only in the States to get my damned divorce."

"Hmmmm," Alicia said, and polished off her gin and sin.

"Vittorio's acting difficult on purpose." Shelley flicked a lock of hair off her forehead. "I wish he'd worked this hard at our marriage. Every girl dreams of the kind of man she'll marry, but she never thinks about the sort of man she wants to divorce."

Alicia sniggered, thinking this was actually a decent point.

Then, over Shelley's right shoulder, Alicia spotted her dark stranger reentering the room.

"Hey, Shelley," she said. "See that man? White shirt? Gobs of hair?"

Shelley craned to get a gander.

"You mean Ed?" she asked.

"Ed? That's his name? That doesn't seem right."

"Edmund Purdom." Shelley turned toward Alicia. "He's a British actor. Rumored to be the next big thing."

"The name is familiar," Alicia said. "I must've read about him somewhere."

"I'm sure you did," Shelley said. "He has five movies coming out this year and just landed the lead role in *The Prodigal*, working with none other than my jerk of a husband. It's a religious movie, to be filmed in the Holy Land, of all the impossibilities. The entire place will probably go up in flames."

"Come on, Vittorio's not that bad," Alicia said.

Aside from the seventeen-year-old, of course. A few lines formed in Alicia's mind.

What Shelley Winters told reporters about her estranged groom told a great deal more about Shelley, a very unhappy girl. . . .

"Vittorio is the worst." Shelley shook her head. "The very worst. Also, Edmund Purdom is about to replace Brando in *The Egyptian*."

"I thought Marlon was trying to win his part back?" Alicia said.

It's what she'd told James Copp, in any case.

"A day late and a dollar short," Shelley said. "Isn't it crazy how Hollywood works? Brando might win an Academy Award for playing Mark Antony, and Edmund Purdom had a bit part in the same movie. Now the bit player is supplanting the marquee star."

Alicia's gaze shifted toward Edmund. He was more attractive than Marlon, more magnetic, too. Alicia was struck with the odd sense that within days he'd be plastered all over the press.

EDMUND PURDOM NEW SENSATION IN HOLLYWOOD.

EDMUND PURDOM IS HOTTEST NEW ACTOR IN HOLLYWOOD.

"I recognize that look," Shelley said, and nudged Alicia with her elbow. "And it's about to burn a hole in the drapes. Sorry to break the news, but Purdom is married. He has one kid, and another on the way. His wife fancies herself a playwright or some such nonsense."

She batted the air.

"What a shame," Alicia said. "He is certainly . . . handsome."

She pulled her eyes away.

"Tell me about Rome," she said.

"You'd love it! They're calling it the new Hollywood, but it's better than that. The Cinecittà. The shops on Via Serviti. The Via Veneto scene. It's Parisian café society, but bigger and more decadent!"

"Sounds grand," Alicia said, and signaled the waiter for another cocktail. "I wish I could see it."

She did wish this, very much, for Alicia was getting restless in Los Angeles. Everyone buzzed about Rome, even Kate Hepburn, who rarely buzzed about anything, as a rule. But neither Alicia's bank account nor her displaced status allowed for such a trip.

"Oh, Alicia, you should go!" Shelley said, and grasped Alicia's forearm with a rather strong hold. "You're an artist, aren't you?"

Alicia chuckled.

"I have been," she said. "At various times."

"Rome is the *only* place for art these days. Paris is so passé. You'd adore Via Margutta! There are artists behind every door. Fellini has a place there. Picasso, too! My dear friend Novella is a painter and she says—"

"Wait," Alicia snapped. "Novella? As in Palmisano? The painter of nudes?"

"Yes! That's her! She's the toast of Rome."

"I saw one of her pieces," Alicia said, "in a private collection. I'd love to see more but I'm not in a position to travel abroad right now."

"Then I have great news!" Shelley said with a grin. "In a few weeks, Novella will be in the States for the first time *ever*. She has a show at the Karnig gallery in New York."

"Really? New York? When?"

"Oh . . ." Shelley thought about this. "Mid-April, I believe? I'm sure you can call the gallery to find out the details. Might I have a sip of your drink? I'm quite parched."

"Sure, go ahead," Alicia said.

Alicia performed a quick mental calculation. Perhaps New York could cure her fitful, wandering mind. She would only have to spring for the plane ticket, as she had a permanent invitation to Kate's.

"Listen, you need to get out of that rathole," Kate had said, just last week. "I can hear it in your voice. You're bored. Come to New York and stay in my townhome. I'm hardly there with all this back-and-forth to London."

"Maybe soon," Alicia replied.

But she was suddenly overcome with the intense desire—no, the compulsion—to see Novella's show, and spend a few weeks in New York. Alicia could find some work there. Like Hollywood, Manhattan was chock-full of fame and glamour and good-looking people behaving in horrible ways.

And in April this would be truer than ever. Imagine the types who'd descend upon the city to drink, carouse, and witness the spectacular wedding of Peter Lawford and his bride-to-be, an ambassador's daughter named Pat Kennedy.

PRETTY GIRL IS LOOKING FOR PERFECT U.S. MAN—TO PAINT

Statesville Record & Landmark, April 16, 1954

NEW YORK

Alicia had to breach a wall of semi-nude men in order to reach the Sixty-second Street gallery. This was not what she expected when she thought "New York."

"Hello?" Alicia called as she walked into the Karnig. "There's supposed to be an artist showing? Am I expected to wait in line?"

"An artist showing," repeated a man—the gallery owner, as it happened. "It's a damned show all right. If you're looking for Novella Palmisano, she's over there and, please, take her with you."

"*Signor*," said another man, sweaty with desperation. "*Perdonami, scusami tanto* . . . my client, you must excuse zee behavior. Zis highly temperamental nature drives zee art. But mostly zee problem is . . . er . . . uh . . . *gli uomini*?"

" 'Woe-many'?!" the owner bellowed. "I don't know what that means!"

"The men," Alicia piped in, noticing a female reporter nearby.

She offered a smile, as the poor girl appeared quite puzzled.

"This gentleman," Alicia said, "claims the problem is with the line of men, not the artist. And he has a point. I don't see Novella on the premises."

"She's down there," the owner said. "On the ground. Taking her sweet time, measuring the unmentionables. This is not what I signed up for."

Alicia peered around the handsome, brawny assemblage, to find Novella crouched on the floor. She was an elfish thing with tousled little-boy hair, dramatic eye makeup, and a nude mouth. Her shiny black-and-white-striped blouse was unbuttoned to great depths.

"Excuse me!" Alicia hollered. "Miss Palmisano!"

"Don't bother," the owner said. "She only speaks four words of English: 'Thank you very much.'"

"That's okay. I speak Italian." She looked at the man. "I thought Miss Palmisano was scheduled to have an exhibit? Are these men the art?"

"Evidently, she doesn't plan to exhibit any art until the end of the month. Instead, she's put out a bulletin asking all able-bodied, red-blooded American men under thirty to show up. She plans to paint one of them. *In the nude*. She is really quite the pill."

"Miss?" said the reporter.

She walked up to Alicia, carrying a notepad, a camera dangling from her neck.

"Hi. Hello," the woman said. "If you speak Italian, may I ask what Miss Palmisano means by *'non troppo muscolos'*?"

"Not too brawny," Alicia said, pleased with her nimble translation.

Novella stood. With a tip of the hand, she dismissed the current specimen and signaled for a new candidate. Alicia watched a tall, dark-haired man strut up. He wore a fig leaf, as if he were a Greek statue.

"How many men are outside?" the reporter asked, pen poised. "Best guess?"

"I counted seventy-five an hour ago," said the owner, "but more have arrived."

The reporter scribbled something down.

"This is disastrous," he ranted on. "We've been open less than four months and I don't want to give people the wrong impression. Can someone please tell her to hurry up?"

Everyone glanced about, until their eyes zeroed in on the one person capable of communicating with everybody in the room. Exhaling, Alicia stepped forward and explained to Novella Palmisano that the man was concerned with his reputation, and wanted to clear the streets of men.

Novella didn't acknowledge her request and instead continued to inspect one man's loins with the diligence of a scholar. After a while, she paused, hand on hip. The room held its breath. Then, she erupted into a chicken-scrabble torrent of words.

Alicia snickered, and gave the woman a wink. She turned toward the gallery owner.

"Miss Palmisano said, 'It is what he does. For he is right now doing it and he should be glad of the publicity.'"

"Doing 'it'?" the man said, and threw up his hands. "Doing *what*? And this is not the publicity I want!"

"Can you ask Miss Palmisano," the reporter said, "why she's come to America? I thought Italian men were the tops?"

Alicia relayed the message, wondering if she might be paid for this translation work.

"According to Miss Palmisano," Alicia said, once Novella answered, "Italian men are terrible models. She needs a rugged, tough American."

The best sort there was, Alicia could not help but think.

"*Vieni qui!*" Novella yipped, gesturing toward Alicia. "*Chi sei?*"

"*Ciao bella. Sono Alicia Darr. Sono il più grande ammiratore!*"

"*Ah! Anvedi!*"

The gallery owner broke into a sweat. Who had time for chitchat when there were partially clothed men two blocks deep? Someone would call the authorities, before long.

"I saw one of your pieces at a friend's place," Alicia told Novella in Italian, "in Beverly Hills. I've been anxious to meet you ever since."

"Beverly Hills. *Ahò!*"

"*Conosco alcuni dei tuoi amici. Kirk Douglas e Shelley Winters.*"

Novella made a face.

"*Sì,*" Alicia agreed.

Through it all, the current specimen stood patiently, his commendable-sized penis dangling unperturbed by the studio's chill.

"What do you think of this one?" Novella said, and nodded toward the man.

"He's very handsome," Alicia answered with a shrug. "But too much like the others."

If anything, he was too laden with *muscolos,* not that Alicia was a good judge. Her favorite physique was gangly, jaundiced, and broken most of the time.

"Get this one out!" Novella yelled, and cracked the measuring tape like a whip. "Bring me someone new!"

Next up was Don Armand, a twenty-seven-year-old unemployed dancer from Cloverdale.

"*Perfetto,*" Novella whispered, and pressed both hands against his stomach. "*Il vincitore dei fisicos.*"

Alicia swiveled toward the gallery owner.

"Good news, you can tell the others to leave," she said. "Miss Palmisano has chosen her man."

The man giggled, then clapped wildly.

"Miss Palmisano," the reporter said, "of the hundred-plus men, how'd you settle on this one?"

"He's got the body harmonious," Novella said in Italian, for Alicia to translate. "He's not overdeveloped like so many of the boys, and he's got a classic profile. Now, everybody leave."

As the scantily clad contestants filed out, Novella kicked her supplies into the corner and then grabbed her knapsack.

"*Andiamo,*" she said, taking Alicia's hand.

And then, in English, she added:

"I can tell we will be friends."

Novella's English was stronger than she'd let on. The problem, she explained, was that most men weren't worth more than four words.

"Kate!" Alicia called as they walked through the door of Katharine's Forty-ninth Street town house. "I've brought a friend for you to meet!"

A man stopped them in the hallway—one of Kate's employees. Wei Fung had no official title but made a full-time job of waving gloved hands and issuing orders in Chinese.

"Wei Fung, excuse me, but I'd like to see Kate."

Charles, the stocky bodyguard-handyman-chauffeur, waddled in upon hearing Alicia's voice. As he greeted them, Novella whispered to Alicia in Italian, a comment on the unflattering nature of his military-style buzz cut.

"She's in a mood," Charles said, right off the bat. "The damned Sturges project."

Alicia cringed. The screenplay Kate wrote had been killed due to "money problems." She couldn't find anyone to underwrite the film because, as she put it, Sturges was a "truly brilliant man, unfortunately a terrible drinker." Kate offered to work for free and pay the director's fee out of pocket, but that didn't bring any takers, either. Alicia suggested she should move on, but Kate was not apt to listen.

"This is the project I want to do," Kate had said. "If I wavered every time people asked me to, I'd forever be playing whores or discontented wives who always wonder whether they should go to bed with some bore."

"Emily can make you a sandwich," Charles said. "If you want to wait in the kitchen."

"I'm not really hungry. . . ."

"I hear a familiar voice!" someone trilled. "Leesy, have you returned? How was the show? Did you get your nude?"

Kate appeared in the entryway, eyebrows arched in hand-drawn precision. She propped herself up against the doorjamb and swirled her glass, ice shifting in the amber booze.

"Oh dear, what sort of trouble have you gotten yourself into?" she asked in a voice more Katharine Hepburn than Alicia had previously known. "Hello, Novella, nice to see you again. *Ciao*. Et cetera."

Alicia blinked.

"You two know each other?" she asked.

"Sure. We've met a few times, in Rome."

"I can't believe you never told me this."

"I told ya I'd heard of her," Kate said. "And *everyone's* met in Rome. Where'd the wee one go? She seems to have vanished."

Alicia glanced around.

"What on earth? She was here a minute ago. . . ."

"She's tricky," Kate said with a wink. "God love her, but you have to watch out for that one. Come. Let's see where your new friend's gone."

The two pattered down the hallway and, after investigating several locations, found Novella sitting cross-legged on the library floor. She'd hauled in a cushion from some other room.

"So, kittens," Kate said, and sprawled herself across the rug, her typical position that time of day.

It helped with digestion, she alleged. Alicia was in a skirt, so she took a seat on a green velvet settee.

"Shall we get to the dirt?" Kate asked. "Tell us, Nova, what's new in Rome?"

The way Novella (and Kate) described it, Rome was everything the jet set insisted, the very start and end to it all.

The city was filled, absolutely engorged, with all manner of models and actresses and royalty. In any given hour, one might run into Errol Flynn, Anthony Quinn, and Rock Hudson, all on the same block.

"Novella's right about all of it," Kate said. "Mark my words. Soon it won't be Hollywood for film, and Paris for art. It will be Rome for everything."

Alicia was frantic to see the city, more so by the day, or the minute, now that Novella was with them, telling her stories, adding new layers to Rome's endless tales. Kate was due to film *The Window* there in the fall, which made Alicia all the grumblier that she'd have to stay behind.

"Just fill out the damned forms," Kate said. "Why do I keep telling you this?"

"It's not that easy," Alicia answered, as she had so many times before.

"This one can't handle a little paperwork," Kate said, and jerked a thumb in Alicia's direction.

Novella smiled blandly and Alicia wondered if her English comprehension extended that far.

"If you're not going to use the proper channels," Kate said, "then you'll have to find some poor sucker to marry. You've probably had too many aliases to do it on your own."

Kate knew Alicia's complete story, from Łódź to Radom to Germany and beyond. She knew the girl who went from Jewish to Catholic to whatever she was now. And Kate understood that her friend Alicia Darr was nothing more than a concoction, a dream of who she wanted to be.

"I thought you didn't believe in marriage?" Alicia said.

"I don't, for myself, or any serious actor. But for you, it'd be fine."

"Thank God I'm not serious, then."

Alicia crossed both arms across her chest.

"Actors are too involved with themselves," Kate said. "The work is too demanding. You can't give the necessary amount of consideration to both acting and another human being. It's the same reason an actress shouldn't be a mother."

"I don't believe in marriage either," Novella chirped. "Because in Italy, no divorce."

"Not to worry, a gal can get divorced here, no problem," Kate said with a cackle. "And I know firsthand. Leesy, you should do it. Then I don't have to listen to you bitch about your damned lack of a passport."

"Maybe I will," Alicia said with a sniff.

She hadn't known Kate was so put off by her being displaced.

"I'll get married, and go to Rome."

"Terrific," Kate said. "Anyone but that horrible Edmund Purdom." Alicia looked up.

"What's wrong with Edmund?" she asked. "He's very handsome."

"And married."

"I read that he's separated from his wife."

Had she read that? It sounded like it could be true, which did not necessarily mean that it was.

"Please." Kate snorted. "Which venerable gossip columnist said that? Or did you make it up?"

"No, no, no," Novella said, steering them to a conversation she might be able to follow. "Marrying is terrible idea if you want to go to Rome. Catholic Church. Tyrants."

"Shelley Winters seems to have no trouble getting divorced in Italy," Alicia said, not really joking, but the other women laughed, all the same.

The three gabbed until nearly dawn. After they said their overdue good-nights, Alicia went to bed in the blue guest room on Kate's third floor. As she slipped between the sheets, Alicia felt happy, full, and a stitch drunk. The night had been more fun than most dates. Alicia took a deep breath. Her eyes fluttered and her worries began to fade. She was so calm, and so at peace, that Alicia could nearly forget that somewhere in the city, Jack Kennedy and his new wife slumbered, side by side.

NEW YORK

Alicia left the Turtle Bay townhome in the early afternoon, still groggy though it was late in the day. She'd probably had too much wine the night before, and mornings at Kate's were never peaceful. Phones and doorbells rang constantly as the cook and Wei Fung scuttled to and fro. The front door slammed every sixty minutes when Charles went outside to make sure no one had ticketed the car.

In no shape to hoof it the thirty-some-odd blocks uptown, Alicia hailed a cab. The driver dropped her in front of the Met, though Alicia had no plans to see the new Medieval gallery, or the Renoirs on loan. Though it probably would've been the more prudent idea.

Alicia headed toward Eighty-ninth Street. Nearing Madison, she saw that roads were blocked, and the streets were packed. Policemen held signs and blew whistles. Alicia's heart quickened as she pushed through the increasingly dense throng.

So many people for Pat Kennedy was Alicia's first thought, before she took in the preponderance of twinsets and taffeta skirts. Bobby-soxers: which meant they were there for Peter. Sometimes a Kennedy finished in second place. It felt like a victory of some kind.

Alicia fought through the girls, and the police and barricades, too, until she reached the wrought-iron fence of St. Thomas More. She stared up at the gray Gothic building and visualized the organ playing inside. She'd never be able to hear it, on account of all the squealing.

Shortly after four o'clock, the doors flew open. The crowd released a cheer as Pat stepped out. The late sun shot between the buildings, landing perfectly to illuminate her broad and cheerful face. Pat was glorious in her white satin gown, a single strand of pearls around her neck. She carried a bouquet of white orchids. Alicia formed a small, appreciative smile. Pat was truly the most beautiful of the Kennedy sisters.

Suddenly, one girl collapsed, and a swarm of hundreds broke through a police barrier. The authorities lost control as the girls rushed the couple, knocking off Pat's veil. It took almost thirty policemen to usher the couple safely to their car, which itself could not move for another half hour.

As the policemen cleared a path, Alicia pivoted and walked off, the pandemonium ringing behind her. She looked back one final time, as if to say good-bye.

At that moment, Jack stepped out of the church.

In Alicia's mind, the crowd hushed and all the sun's rays fell on him. Jack lifted his head, and caught eyes with her. He jolted, then offered a wave, followed by a quick salute, and his droll Jack smile.

Alicia started to raise her hand, but then lowered it again. She'd already given Jack Kennedy more than he deserved. He continued to stare with a laser-like heat and Alicia allowed not a twitch to her face as she pivoted and strode away, shoving through the dwindling crowd as tears rolled down her cheeks.

"Tell Jimmy what's wrong."

Alicia was at the town house, sobbing, as Kate, known only to herself as "Jimmy," rubbed her back.

"I've never seen you in such a state. You survived the Nazis. Surely you can't be howling about something that occurred on the Upper East Side."

"I'm sorry," Alicia sniffled. "I don't know what's come over me."

"Of course you do."

"It's about a man."

"A goodly number of stories start that way, don't they?" Kate said with a cluck. "Stop your moping. A broken heart is common as a cold. And you've shattered plenty yourself. Hugh O'Brian. Coop. I'm sure there're others."

Alicia released a quivery sigh.

"I didn't break their hearts," she said. "Cracked their egos, maybe. But they didn't love me, and I didn't love them. Especially not in the way I've known."

"Oh, dear, here we go. . . ."

"I've tried to distance myself," Alicia went on. "There are a million more suitable men in this world."

"There are a million men, yes, until there is one. Oh, sugar."

Kate inched closer and slung an arm around Alicia's shoulders.

"Look at your big heart," she said. "Jimmy thought you were a bit of a cold fish, a tad impenetrable, almost clueless at times."

Alicia shook her head as tears dripped off her chin, landing on her clasped hands.

"This man," Kate said, "did you rendezvous with him today?"

"Not really. I saw him from afar, and he saw me. We didn't speak. I don't know why I went. We were in love once, but he's married now."

Kate nodded, but her expression was pinched in Hepburn-style disapproval. Alicia gave a toss of the eyes. Katharine Hepburn was in no position to judge the coveting of a married man, as Mrs. Spencer Tracy would doubtless concur. At least Alicia hadn't acted on her desires. Meanwhile, Kate couldn't use the bathroom without checking Spence's schedule first.

"He wasn't married when I met him," Alicia added. "And the kicker is, in some ways I feel badly for the woman. He can be so self-centered and has the grace of an untrained monkey. He's also unreliable, and riddled with all manner of physical ailments. Also, I'd be remiss not to mention his efficient lovemaking. *Too* efficient, if you ask me."

"Sounds like you have quite the list."

"And that's not all!"

Alicia twisted herself toward Kate, and tucked one leg beneath her. These things, they were all true, and that was the very problem. Jack invoked such a complex set of emotions, competing waves of rage and longing, that he was impossible to figure out.

"He's not even that handsome!" Alicia said. "He's too skinny, for one. His hair's a mess and sometimes he's less tan and more . . . jaundiced. I mean, compare him to Edmund Purdom, and it's not close."

"Good Lord, here we go with *The Egyptian* again." Kate gave Alicia a thumbs-down. "I don't know why you're so fixated on the man. His ego is as big as the moon. His poor wife. Did you know that with his first big paycheck, he didn't get her jewelry, or a car, but a nose bob?"

"He did?" Alicia said, touching her own nose, on reflex.

"Jack Kennedy is far more appealing than Ed Purdom, and is also far less of an ass."

"What?" Alicia rattled in surprise. "What do you mean? Who said anything about Jack Kennedy?"

"So, you're not in love with the senator from Massachusetts?" Kate said. "That's not the 'John' character who romanced you on the Cape?"

Alicia exhaled so long and with such force, it was a wonder there was any breath left inside of her.

"Fine," she said. "You've figured me out. The man I told you about was Jack Kennedy. I'm not going to ask how you know."

She sighed again and was hit with the strong, swift relief of speaking his name. The last time Alicia had copped to Jack, she was wearing a Center Theatre tuxedo, and the listener was George.

"Sweet Leesy," Kate said. "I won't dissuade you from your feelings, and I certainly understand the appeal of auburn-haired Irishmen, though Spence is now mostly gray."

"I want you to dissuade me," Alicia said. "Jack is hopeless. Never mind that he's married, his poor wife is married to him, and twenty other people, like his siblings and all those lackeys, each more kowtowing than the last. To speak nothing of that dreadful father."

"His interests and demands would always come first," Kate said, in a flat, almost weary tone. "That is true."

Her gaze drifted toward the window.

"Sometimes I wonder," Alicia said, "how I can love him so much when he gives me so little in return?"

Kate nodded, eyes fixed outside.

"When you love someone, what you get varies." She regarded Alicia. "But you give because you love, not because you expect something. If you're lucky, you may be loved back, which is a wonderful thing, but there is no guarantee."

"That is a very depressing view of romance."

"Is it?" Kate furrowed her brows. "True love is total devotion. And sometimes you really have to give all of yourself, every last miserable piece."

"I don't want that sort of relationship," Alicia said, thinking of Kate following Spencer, fixing his hair, and his clothes, and every mess he ever made. "Love should be the story of two people, both devoted, with a cast of bit players on the side. I wouldn't want the life that goes with Jack. I didn't want that life, which is why I left."

Kate let out a quick laugh.

"Is there something funny?" Alicia asked.

"Did you say that you left?"

"Not this most recent time, of course, what with Jacqueline Bouvier and all. I'm referring to when I left Hyannis Port. We were engaged, and then . . . a moment of clarity. I realized Jack's life was not his own, and if I stayed with him, mine couldn't be either."

"You left," Kate said again.

"I packed up my things, posted a letter, and took the next bus out of town. Luckily, I had somewhere to go thanks to a chance meeting with Don Class. I recognize your distaste for the man, but he was an escape route when I needed one, and I'm forever grateful."

"You didn't know about Don?" Kate said.

Alicia squinted.

"Do you mean that he's a talent scout? I'd never heard of him until we met, so couldn't compare him to Charles Feldman or any other agent you deem superior. But I was just a Polish girl on the Cape, selling popcorn, and dreaming big. Why, that sounds rather cinematic, doesn't it? I should write it down."

"No, I mean"—Kate shook her head again—"how is it you don't know this? Everyone knows this, even people who have nothing to do with you."

"What are you talking about?" Alicia asked, her hands going clammy. "Everyone knows what?"

"Oh, Alicia." Kate chuckled sadly, both eyes closed. "Sweet girl, that was no 'chance meeting.' Joe Kennedy sent Class to find you, at your movie theater."

"To find me? Why?"

Her heart pounded.

"The Ambassador paid Don Class thirty grand to get you out of Hyannis Port, and away from his boy."

At first, Serena resisted Lee's invitation to stay at his house. A hotel would suit fine, and shacking up with a stranger is ill-advised, the one lesson a girl might learn from a mother who leaves.

But Lee promised her something better than a hotel, even more private, in the form of a two-bedroom guesthouse located beside a pool. The amenities impressed, certainly as compared to whatever grimy budget motel she would've been able to afford. Serena is to be reimbursed by the estate, but that implies she has money to spend. She maxed out her credit card for plane fare, and unless Leonard the lawyer can front her cash, the promise of reimbursement is beside the point.

With little choice, Serena accepted Lee's offer and immediately realized his wealth was greater than suspected. She'd guessed at the Perenchios' status, thanks to Big Jim Perenchio's Rolex and Italian leather shoes, not to mention Lee's inattention to the cost of things. Also, his sisters had an irritating propensity to broadcast their wealth, as if they were being paid for advertising space.

"Jim Perenchio! The world's cheapest billionaire!"

They used the word "billionaire" so frequently, Serena assumed they were exaggerating. But Lee's house tells her: not so.

"I don't know," Lee said, blushing, mumbling when Serena probed for details, "eight thousand square feet, give or take."

Lee's home has a pool, and a pool *house*. A tennis court. An art gallery. A room entirely for hanging the book bags of children who'd grown. It's located in Brentwood, the fancy neighborhood where O. J. Simpson stabbed his ex-wife. Serena would've expected someone with that much money would live on the ocean. Later she'd learn about the house on Kauai and the beach riddle would be solved.

It's the day after their meeting with the lawyer, and it takes Serena some time to find Lee. He's in the sunroom, sipping coffee and pecking on his computer.

"I thought I asked you to start wearing a tracking device?" Serena halfway jokes as she saunters in.

"Hilarious," he replies, barely looking up from the screen.

As Lee is between his Stanford graduation and Silicon Valley job, Serena wonders what this clicking and clacking is about. She leans over his shoulder. The ends of her hair tickle his collarbone, giving him chills.

"What are you working on?" she asks, thinking that Lee smells like a shower.

"Googling Alicia Corning Clark," he says. "To see if there are any mentions of her having a kid. There's nothing in the scrapbook. I've subscribed to, like, eleventy million newspaper sites—"

"Eleventy million?" Serena makes a face. "What kind of number is that?"

"It's made up," he says. "For emphasis. You know what I mean."

She does, sort of. But why not use a real figure?

"*Anyhow,*" he says, eyes narrowing, a mite bearish. "I'm trying to pin down Alicia and it's not easy. Her name was Barbara first. Then it was Alicia and Alicja—with a *j*—and Alice Marie and plain Alice, on occasion. Her last name is no easier. She's had five of them, and often uses two or more at the same time, in any order."

She had several occupations, too, Lee goes on to say, and newspapers mention varying birth years and homes. She is reportedly Polish but, every so often, is inexplicably "Viennese." And then there are her paramours, coming quickly and in large numbers. Somehow Alicia has Hugh O'Brian "breathless" on the sixth and is "getting around at high speed" with Gary Cooper by the twelfth. The articles seem to be in clusters, a flurry of antics, and then Alicia disappears for months or years at a time. Lee is tracking the information on a spreadsheet. Alicia Clark: a mathematical problem to solve.

"This woman was nuts," he says. "All the men, the fighting in bars, the breaking and entering and bouncing of checks."

Serena nods, thinking it's not so outlandish that Alicia might be her grandmother, considering her mother's temperament. Not that Novella was any sort of schoolmarm. After all, she was a key player in many peccadilloes—stripteases, love affairs, what have you.

"She brags about something one day," Lee goes on, "then denies it the next. So, who the hell knows about any of it?"

He claps his computer shut.

"I should wait until after you take the test to start spinning my wheels," he says. "Because if you're not related, then Alicia Corning Clark is moot."

"Moot?" Serena gives a startle. "I don't think my connection to the woman determines whether her life mattered."

"That's not what I meant."

Lee thinks about this.

"Then again, if she went from party to party, man to man, what's the point?"

"For shame, Lee Perenchio!" Serena gives him a swat. "Perhaps she would look at you, young, rich American, taking rich, American job, and say what is the point?"

"Pretty sure rich Americans were in her wheelhouse," Lee mutters.

Serena laughs. Really, it is more of a guffaw, somewhat horselike. Lee loves every note of it.

"*Grazie a dio,* is that my problem?" she says. "Have I inherited this abysmal trait? Spoiled Americans? *Ahò!*"

Lee pinches her mischievously in the side. Serena squirms but he reels her in and pulls her onto his lap.

"I think you should take the test," he says into her hair. "Find out if it's true."

"I don't know." Serena sighs. "I don't want to know."

"But wouldn't you always wonder? You can return to Rome, and to your life, but this possibility will go with you. Refusing the information does nothing for your relationship with Novella. It won't strengthen it. It can't bring her back. Come on, Serena, aren't you curious?"

"Yes, I'm curious, but let's not forget that many cats are killed by such sentiment."

"I think you should do it," he says again.

"Maybe, but only because I need the money."

"Fine." He exhales, then tosses his head, to remove his still-damp hair from his eyes. "But if you don't do it for the money, then at least do it for me."

It is getting so a column with no mention of ex-Ambassador to Britain Joseph Kennedy's family is rare indeed.

Skylarking, by James Copp, August 7, 1954

HOLLYWOOD

When Alicia returned to Los Angeles, the city seemed small, impossibly claustrophobic. Manhattan had a way of lessening other places, an effect magnified by what she'd learned about Don Class.

"Don't worry about it," Kate said, in New York, as Alicia wailed. "The story gives you intrigue. You're so alluring that a wealthy diplomat paid great sums to have you vanquished."

"Thirty thousand isn't 'great,' to Joe Kennedy."

"Doesn't matter. And you have something worth more than cash. Why, you have a fabulous story," Kate said, almost giddy. "You could destroy lives."

"I don't want to destroy anything. I only ever wanted to be with Jack."

Now Alicia was on the West Coast, straggling around Los Angeles, sick with the news and flinching with each set of eyes that passed her way. Kate said that "everyone" knew about the arrangement. Did "everyone" mean Lana Turner, and Mel Tormé, and Betty Grable, too? What about Harpo and Chico Marx? Or the maharaja of Baroda?

On the other hand, maybe Alicia flattered herself to think that these people remembered, or cared. It'd been three years since Joe Kennedy's slithery deal. Thanks to a heavy supply of booze and pills, half the people in that town couldn't recall last week. With no end to parties and crack-ups and sexual scandals, would anyone bother to think about her twice?

"I can't believe you never told me," she said to Fred, despite knowing his very existence in Hollywood was predicated on his ability to keep secrets.

Fred never gave up confidences. Not to a friend, a lover, or a priest. He drank scotch by the gallon, and smoked five packs of cigarettes a day, but you could trust the man to hold your secrets like money in a vault.

"I thought you knew" was Fred's response. "I thought that's why you barely tolerated Don and his demands. Plus, there's your . . . yanno . . . *thing*. How you're so goddamned smart and sly, but you play dumb as a rock."

"That's some compliment, especially in this town."

"Don't take offense," he said, and burped. "Sometimes playing dumb is a smart fuckin' move. I don't need to tell you that. You've mastered the game."

Occasionally Alicia *did* look the other way, pretending not to see something smack in front of her face. But she liked to think the best of people, and sometimes that required a splash of willful ignorance, in order to get by.

Alicia struggled to settle back into Hollywood life. From Ciro's to the Mocambo to Café Deauville, and every other joint on the Sunset Strip, Alicia brandished her red-lipped smile, flirted gaily, and accepted dinner invitations two, three at a time. Ty Power was the latest to put on the charms, but there was also Edmund Purdom, frequently appearing in his sly, sexy way.

Alicia and Ed hadn't officially met, but there was *something* brewing between them, even though, so far, the entirety of their relationship was comprised of roguish grins, sideways glances, and a single toast they'd shared at Romanoff's the day his wife gave birth. Alicia was almost starting to forget Jack, when a full compendium of Kennedys descended upon Los Angeles to ruin her good time.

Jean started the parade, arriving for what gossips dubbed a "Hollywood frolic." Teddy then joined, followed by Eunice. Pat showed them around, and soon Alicia couldn't get through a day without seeing a set of Kennedy teeth or hearing a clacky "Terrific, kid!" flare up somewhere. By the end of the week, Alicia knew every back door in town.

One afternoon, as Alicia wandered the Chateau Marmont grounds after a champagne brunch, Joe Kennedy emerged from one of the bungalows. Alicia stopped dead and watched in horror as he lowered himself into a small, oval pool, his white belly and pink nipples droopy and petered out. The vision so disgusted her that Alicia took a three-day resting cure in Palm Springs.

When she called Harrison Carroll with the latest scoop from the desert—a girl had to make a living—he tipped her off that Jack and Bobby were on their way to California, too. Would Alicia kindly give *him* any news first, before Hedda, or Cholly, or someone else? And, for the love of God, news more interesting than the state of Joe Kennedy's tits.

Enough was enough. It was time to call Kate.

"I'm returning to New York!" Alicia sang. "This time, for good! I'm done with L.A."

Kate applauded the decision but, darling, couldn't talk right now. Spence had purchased an island off the coast of Italy and she needed to understand what it was all about.

"You can stay at my place," Kate said. "Though, I wish you'd join us here."

She and Spence were in Venice, where Kate was shooting *The Time of the Cuckoo*. They were having a ball, of course, as positively *everyone* was in Italy these days. Why, they'd had dinner with Novella just last week!

"But I don't dare ask you to come," Kate said. "Lest I subject myself to more whining about your immigration status."

"It's a real problem, Kate."

"It does sound like a problem. Imagine if you tried to do something about it."

On her final night in California, Alicia attended a house party at the home of Charles Feldman, the most renowned agent in the business. He represented John Wayne, Ava Gardner, and Marilyn Monroe, to name a few.

As she parked her Corvette outside Feldman's European-style villa, Alicia realized how much she'd miss that gleaming hunk of chrome. Forget sassy dresses or her signature red lipstick, this car was a surefire beauty trick, every time. With one roar of the engine, she'd feel instantly glamorous, hangovers and sunburns and nose jobs be damned. Her landlord had graciously offered to watch the vehicle, as long as needed while she was away. He'd ogled that car far more than he'd ever ogled Alicia's sleek legs or singular carriage.

She rang the bell and a housekeeper answered. The woman took Alicia's handbag and gestured outside. Alicia made her way along the sun-filled corridor, as shadows from the eucalyptus trees danced on the walls.

When she stepped outside, Alicia caught sight of Marilyn Monroe, who lived (unhappily, they said) with Joe DiMaggio directly across the road. Feldman got the house for her because he liked to keep a close watch on his volatile, moneymaking star.

"Alicia!" Feldman called when he spotted her across the flag-stone.

He whispered something to Marilyn and touched her back firmly, as if pressing her into place. Marilyn beamed into the air.

"Delighted you could come," Feldman said as he walked over.

The two exchanged kisses and Alicia flashed her best, most-practiced smile. Feldman looked the same as always: big nose, wispy mustache, sweating more than a few drops.

"Can I get you something to sip on?" he asked. "I'm having a Tom Collins."

"Sure, that sounds neat," Alicia said without really thinking about it. "Only one, though. I'm not staying long."

"It breaks my heart that you're leaving us," he clucked. "The beautiful Alicia Darr. We've scarcely had any time together at all."

Charles Feldman always seemed pleased to see her, forever friendly, never wolfish or unkind. The most successful agent in Hollywood made Alicia believe she mattered, but he'd never offered to take her on.

"I've enjoyed California," Alicia said, "but it's time for me to go. This city . . ."

Her eyes darted toward Marilyn, and then across the pool to Ty Power and Jack Palance.

"It's become too crowded," she said.

"You're just noticing that now?" Feldman chortled. "Even I think that. So, what will you do in New York?"

"Paint a little. Maybe, er, see about journalism."

There were gossip items to be found in Manhattan, so Alicia didn't anticipate being short of work. Plus, she had phone numbers for all the car attendants on the Sunset Strip. They were loyal, and with a few calls on any night, Alicia could find out who left in what car.

"No stab at Broadway?" Feldman asked.

Alicia shook her head.

"I don't think I'm meant to be an actress."

"Really?" he said, as the pool danced and glittered behind him. "You're quitting the biz?"

"That seems to be the shape of it. Three years in Hollywood and I've come to realize that you have to really want the job to endure the hassle of having it."

Feldman laughed and took out a handkerchief to dab his hairline.

"Indeed," he said. "It takes a special sort of soul."

Alicia made her last rounds in Hollywood, still hanging on to that first drink. She understood that a second cocktail would lead to a third, and then a fourth, and suddenly it'd be midnight at the Mocambo. Then the night would end, and the week, and the year, and soon she'd find herself buying a burial plot at Forest Lawn.

When she polished off her good-bye drink, Alicia set down her glass, said farewell to Chuck Feldman, and strolled toward the foyer. Two steps from freedom, the front door swooshed open to reveal Edmund Purdom, looking tousled, out-of-breath, and oddly victorious, as if he'd minutes ago won some sort of duel.

"Oh. Hello," she said.

Alicia tucked a piece of hair behind her right ear and began to perspire. What was it about Edmund that so unnerved her? Nothing had happened between them, but there was a ting, a tension, a knowledge that they'd been thinking of one another, seeking each other out in crowded rooms.

"Alicia Darr," he said, and wiggled his thick brows. "Leaving already?"

"The party started hours ago."

"Nothing really begins or ends in Hollywood," Edmund said in his smoky British accent. "There are no rules. You should stay."

Alicia gave him, she hoped, a good pout. Edmund was sexy as hell, but she had to move on.

"I can't stay," she said. "I'm going to New York."

"New York?" His eyes darkened. "When? And for how long?"

"I leave Monday," she said. "And indefinitely is the idea. Perhaps you can visit one day. I'd love to see you the next time you're in town. You could bring Tita?"

Ed laughed bitterly.

"Tita? My wife won't be visiting New York, at least not with me. The only place she wants to go is the bank or an estate agent's. That's the worst thing about this 'stardom,' I should think. It was a thrill to get my possessions out of hock, but hell to find out who's really on my side. Or, rather, who's not."

"Oh, Edmund," Alicia said. "You've taken on so much this year. I'm sure everything will seem clearer, very soon."

"Here's hoping."

Edmund kissed Alicia gently on the head, and a chill shot through her. She was tempted to stay but sometimes it was best to keep a fantasy untouched. Everyone knew Edmund Purdom was temperamental, self-indulgent, and prone to fits.

"Good-bye, Edmund," Alicia called out. "I can't wait to see what you do next."

As she moved through the open doorway, Alicia felt his eyes roam from her neck, to her shoulders, down to her rear. In the distance, a car door slammed. Alicia hurried, to avoid being waylaid by another guest.

Then, she heard a peculiar sound.

Clump. Clump. Clump.

Not footsteps, exactly. Something else.

Clump. Clump. Clump.

Alicia's stomach clenched as she made out the apparition before her: one man, two crutches, a bushy head of hair.

"Jesus, kid, you've been hell to find."

Jack Kennedy hobbled a few steps closer.

"Absolute *hell*," he said.

"Jack," she gasped, her heart rate doubling. "What are you doing? You look terrible."

The words slipped out but Jack *did* look awful, worse than before. In addition to being sweaty and twitchy, he was also minus at least forty pounds. This was not the man she'd seen on the steps of St. Thomas More.

"Not exactly the reaction I was hoping for, kid," he said with a laugh. "I've practically killed myself trying to find you. So, are you going to introduce me to your friend?"

Alicia peeked over her shoulder to find Ed standing there still. Surely, he should be on the lanai by now, partway into a Tom Collins.

"Hello, there." Jack balanced on one crutch, and extended a hand toward Edmund. "The name's Jack Kennedy."

"Purdom," he muttered.

"So, just the one name then?"

Alicia shook her head. Jack was sickly and yellow and had all the pluck of a ninety-year-old hemophiliac, yet he managed to put himself immediately in charge.

"First name's Edmund."

"Ah," Jack said. "The movie star."

Ed nodded with satisfaction.

"I read about you in the paper."

"Yes, I'm getting favorable reviews for—"

"Nope," Jack said. "It was Tijuana. You left a bullfight because it was too grisly? Am I right?"

"The gore and violence was unnecessarily over the top," Edmund groused.

"Pal, what'd you think was going to happen? Senoritas and margaritas and flowers thrown into the ring? Now, if you'll excuse us, I'd like some time alone with my favorite girl."

Purdom glowered first at Jack, and then at Alicia. She wanted to grab him, but she didn't have the strength, or the reach.

"Fucking tease," Ed grumbled, and then pattered into the house.

Alicia swung around to face Jack.

"That was rude," she said.

"Yeah, what a prick. I can't believe he called you a tease."

"You're the prick." She looked at him, tears in her eyes, the full weight of everything bearing down on her chest. "Was it really necessary to bring up the bullfighting incident?"

"I thought so," he said with a shrug.

"Why are you here, Jack?"

"I came to see you."

He crutched closer. Alicia put up a hand to push him away.

"Wow, that's a frosty reception, considering."

"Considering what?" she said. "That I haven't seen you in a year? That we were together one minute, and the next you were married to some girl I'd never heard of?"

"I had nothing to do with that."

"Same old story," Alicia said.

"Don't you see?" he said. "I had to get married, or people would start thinking I was a queer. It's not what it seems."

"I know it's not what it seems," Alicia scoffed. "And I was right. You're incapable of being your own person."

"Listen here, you don't know the first thing . . ."

"Spare me."

Alicia flicked her hand, and started to walk off.

"I thought I could do it," he called.

Jack tried to give chase, but only made it a meter or two before he tripped and lost a crutch. Alicia rescued it, though she should've left the damned thing in the gravel for Jack to figure out for himself.

"I thought I could find someone who'd make us both happy," he said, hopping back into place. "Dad and me. I knew I'd never be able to say good-bye to you, so I didn't. Instead I tried to shut out that part of my life and play the good husband. But I haven't been able to forget you, not for one goddamned second."

"You left without a word," Alicia said. "You owed me an explanation. To see it in the papers . . ."

She struggled to get the words out.

"It was devastating," Alicia went on. "I would think you'd appreciate that, given your reaction to Gary Cooper. Sometimes I think you're the world's biggest hypocrite."

"Don't you understand? That was the only way I *could* leave. And I had to get married. My father, he's done so much for me, and he's been right about everything. I was convinced he'd be right about this, too."

"She seems like a lovely girl," Alicia said with a huff.

"*Dahr*-ling. My father was wrong. It's not working. We're getting divorced."

Alicia laughed, she actually *laughed*. It did not feel good at all.

"We're separated."

"A good Catholic wouldn't divorce in a million years," Alicia said.

"I'm far from a good Catholic, you know that."

"Forget the pope, then, and let's talk about the pop. Your father would disown you before he'd let you divorce."

"He doesn't have a say. Not if I want it, not if she does too."

"Don't lie, Jack," Alicia said, voice trembling. "Please. Don't lie."

"I'm telling the hand-to-Bible truth," he insisted. "She has exactly no interest in me, or in our marriage. She's in Europe right now, for god's sake, and she's agreed to a meeting with Mac."

Mac was Jay McInerney, former attorney turned official payoff flunky. Over the years, he'd set up many financial arrangements for the Kennedys. He was probably the guy who paid Don Class.

"A settlement will be reached," Jack said. "And it's best for everyone. Her mother's on marriage number two, and has done quite well. Plus, she *hates* politics. She'd rather stay inside and read a book."

"I can't fathom anyone wanting to divorce you, I honestly can't."

"Aw, shucks, kid."

"I say that with great regret."

"Make no mistake, we both understood that this was an arranged marriage. Now we're miserable as hell."

Dizzy, Alicia steadied herself on a stucco wall. Surely this exceptionally bright and handsome couple would survive more than one measly year, especially when supported by all that Kennedy grit.

"I'm going into the hospital," Jack said. "For major surgery, on my spine. They're finally gonna fix this broken back."

"I'm glad you're getting help . . ."

"Yeah, we'll see. Who knows, I could end up dead."

"Jack." Alicia rolled her eyes. "Fatalistic as ever. I'm sure you'll have the best surgeons money can buy."

"That's no guarantee. I don't know, because of this upcoming appointment, I've had an overwhelming urge to set things straight. With her, with you. Life is too short to live without passion. But no one understands that better than you and me. You're the one person who gets it. You're the only other person in this whole damned world."

Jack crutched past her and then whirled around. He extended a hand, best he could.

"Come with me," he said.

"Where?" she asked.

"Everywhere. But for now, upstairs."

"I'm not going upstairs with you."

Alicia crossed her arms.

"Sweetheart, I'm in agony. I've got to get off these feet. Feldman's an old friend and has a terrific tub upstairs. It's heaven for my back, and big enough for two."

"Jack . . ." Alicia said with a wilting sigh.

"I miss us. Don't you? Let's be together again, starting right now. Just us, Alicia and Jack."

Again, he extended a hand. His nails were in dire need of a trim.

"I can't hold your hand while you're on crutches," she said, still glaring.

But, she followed him inside.

"Can you make it up?" she asked, once they reached the bottom of the stairs.

"I can make it up all right," he said with a snigger. "Four, five times at least."

Alicia shook her head and laughed.

"What am I getting myself into?" she said. "Again?"

Then something darted in her periphery, a snag in the corner of her eye. Alicia looked over to see a dark and handsome face scowling through a sliding glass door. *Shit,* she thought, *Edmund.* This wasn't the impression Alicia hoped to make, but when it came to Jack . . . well, when it came to Jack there was simply nothing and no one else in the world.

Kennedy is also rich which sometimes is an advantage.

These Days, by George E. Sokolsky, November 26, 1955

NEW YORK

Alicia had been in New York eighteen months.

The days were getting shorter. The seasons turned with greater speed. In a few weeks, it'd be 1956—ten years since she reunited with her mother at the camp.

Alicia had a twenty-fifth-birthday party earlier that year, despite swearing she'd never celebrate a birthday again. The event might've made Alicia weepy, if it hadn't made her feel so very middle-aged. By twenty-five, her mother was married, with a toddler underfoot.

"Be glad you're not me," Marilyn Monroe said at Alicia's birthday soiree. "I'm going to be thirty soon."

Sixty people came to El Morocco to celebrate. They dined and danced and went through eighty bottles of Sortilège, the tab picked up by Alicia's friend Aly Khan. She might've felt guilty about the price tag, but Alicia knew the renowned playboy threw it mostly so that he might seem like the sort of person who did such things.

The party was months ago, but twenty-five was something Alicia thought about every day. It was a milepost, a turning point, though toward what she didn't know. Now it was December again, time to meet a whole new year.

Alicia rolled over in bed and checked the clock. Quarter past eight. She slid from the sheets, and ran a hand through the hair of the man beside her.

As horns blared and trucks revved outside, Alicia tiptoed across the room to fetch a discarded silk robe. She exited the bedroom. The door clicked and she plodded out into the living room of their penthouse suite.

Alicia picked up the phone.

"Yes, I'll hold," she said, winding the cord around her finger as she peered out the window toward the glittering Christmas decorations on the streets below. "Yes, thank you. Coffee service for one, please. And tea for another."

She hung up and glanced toward the door, under which someone had slipped a white envelope. Alicia rolled her eyes, but let out a small smile, for she knew its sender. Jack Kennedy usually went about things in this manner. The minute she took to ignoring him, he swept back in.

Alicia unfolded the note.

Miss you violently, it read. *I need to see you, or I could die. Again.*

The joke was getting tired, and Alicia still didn't know how much was truth. She'd last seen him in California, in Feldman's bathtub. Then she left for New York, and Jack went dark like he had so many times before. There'd been no divorce, and Alicia spent weeks kicking herself for being such a fool. Fred was wrong. She didn't "play dumb," she was dumb in fact.

And then, last December, almost one year ago, a letter arrived for her at Katharine's place. It was from Torb Macdonald.

You must come to Palm Beach. Call Powers—he's set up a hotel room in your name. I'll explain everything when you arrive. Literally a matter of life and death.

Alicia didn't go to Palm Beach, but she spoke to Dave Powers, who said that Jack was gravely ill following his October surgery. On death's door, he declared, when Alicia seemed unmoved. She didn't believe him. It all sounded very ordinary in the press.

SENATOR'S CONDITION GOOD was the first report.

CONDITION IS EXCELLENT, they swore.

But, as the weeks passed, the descriptions began to temper.

KENNEDY OKAY AFTER OPERATION.

KENNEDY CALLED FAIR.

KENNEDY STILL BEDRIDDEN.

KENNEDY GETS WIRE FROM POPE.

Then Alicia saw the picture of Jack being wheeled into his parents' Floridian compound. He looked more corpse than live man, and Mrs. Kennedy stood beside his stretcher, flinty and tired.

Alicia called Dave Powers a second time.

"What you said was true?" she'd asked. "He's really dying?"

"Jesus, Alicia, have you ever known me to lie?"

"Yes. Often."

"Oh, don't worry, it's nothing major. He was merely in a *coma.* They administered last rites. Twice."

"Twice?" Alicia wheezed.

"Can't you come?" he pleaded. "He's desperate to see you. You'd lift his spirits."

"Isn't his wife better suited for that?"

"While I avoid agreeing with Lem Billings as a rule, on the venerable *Mrs. Kennedy,* we're of the same mind. She's never here. Ever. She put up a poster of Marilyn Monroe over Jack's bed, to stand in her stead."

"Marilyn?" Alicia said, gagging the slightest bit.

"I'll tell ya what," Dave said. "Jackie Kennedy looks great in the papers, but she's a terrible wife."

"Then why are they still married? Jack told me they're getting divorced. Yet, so far, nothing."

"A LITTLE HARD TO GET DIVORCED WHILE IN A COMA, DON'T YOU THINK?" Dave shouted into the phone, so loud that Alicia had to hold the receiver from her ear.

But what could Alicia do? Jackie was his wife and hurrying to Jack's bedside benefited no one. He needed rest, not the mayhem her presence would bring.

"I'm sorry, Dave, I can't do it," Alicia said. "It'd upset too many, and I don't want to subject Jack to that."

In February, Jack's condition worsened and he went in for another surgery, and several more to follow. He didn't return to the Senate until May. May! Seven months after he'd gone in the first time. The newspapers published photos of his triumphant arrival, Jacqueline by his side, her head bowed, face hollowed out beneath the eyes.

Finally, Alicia relented and called Jack in his Washington office. She had to know how he was really doing, without the Dave Powers take.

"So, you don't want me dead," Jack said when his secretary Evelyn put her straight through. "By the way, it wasn't my spine. They were actually repairing my broken heart."

All that summer, Jack wrote, he called, he promised his separation was pending, any day. Plans were delayed as Jack fought for his life. This sounded well and good, plausible even, but it also had a ring of familiarity. She'd been watching a similar scene firsthand.

Kate Hepburn had a lot of opinions, rendered on a great many people and things, but as for Spencer Tracy she had only excuses. Kate didn't want to get married, but that didn't explain why her boyfriend still was.

"He can't leave his child," Kate explained, referring to Spencer's son, who was born deaf. "Spence loves John, and he's riddled with good ol' Catholic guilt. I can't very well demand he step away from that."

This boy John was now in his thirties, and married.

And while convalescence explained Jack's delayed divorce, soon he had Spence's excuse, too. He called Alicia before the news hit the papers, but etiquette was no salve for the crushing pain.

"She's pregnant?" Alicia said, agog. "How is that possible? Haven't you been hospitalized for the better part of a year?"

Then again, Jack never let infirmity get in the way of a good screw.

Jack promised that the divorce was still on, but a baby meant revisions to the original terms. She'd be asking for a lot more now. She, being Jacqueline, not the baby, though Jack rarely said his wife's name.

But then Mrs. Kennedy lost the baby, and surely Jack couldn't leave her after that. If rumors were true, he was also gunning for the vice presidency, which was more reason to keep the debutante. She'd probably be pregnant again soon, Alicia reasoned. Mrs. Kennedy didn't seem like the type to give up.

As Alicia folded Jack's latest note, the suite's buzzer rang. She placed the letter in a drawer and showed the waiter inside. After he prepared the coffee and tea service and bid farewell, Alicia took out her stationery and sat down to write.

Dear Kate, she began.

The shower came on, and within seconds Alicia heard the pipes groan with water. She imagined Edmund's strong, chiseled body stepping inside. He really was the finest example of a male specimen. Alicia was glad she'd convinced him to come to New York.

The city misses the Great Kate, she wrote, *but I'm sure you and Spence are living it up.*

They hadn't seen each other in six months, Alicia realized with a frown. Kate spent the summer touring Australia with the Old Vic, while Spencer remained Stateside, making headlines of his own. There'd been too much screwing (Grace Kelly) and too much screwballing (in the form of booze), and Spencer had unraveled the goodwill he'd built these last few years.

METRO WORRIED OVER TRACY'S RECOVERY.

SPENCER TRACY FORCED TO QUIT MOVIE.

SPENCER TRACY'S MEDICS HAVE BEEN BEGGING HIM TO
JOIN AA.

Spencer blamed his behavior on altitude, which didn't jibe with his upcoming plans to film in the French Alps. Naturally, Kate slingshotted to his side.

"I know that Spence has to help himself," she said. "But I also know that I can help him too, now that I've been fortified by the stage."

The couple was in London, preparing for a big New Year's party at the Berkeley Hotel.

I wish I could join you, Alicia continued. *I can't for the party, but maybe soon! Have you heard from Novella? She tells me she's switched to fluorescent paints so her work will glow in the dark. She's also dating a Ringling Brother although, frankly, when I saw that picture of Rock Hudson carrying her across St. Mark's Square in the rain, I thought she should focus on him instead.*

Of course, anyone with an ear to Hollywood understood that Novella was not the sort to excite Rock.

Life with Edmund remains fun. He's still not over The Egyptian *and* The Prodigal *bombing so spectacularly, but there'll be a new turkey soon, and everyone will forget about his.*

Alicia went on to describe the city's Christmas landscape, and asked when Kate planned to return to the States. As for Alicia's mother, she was recently transferred to the Catholic House for the Aged in Munich. Her mind continued to disintegrate while her body soldiered on.

When she finished the letter, Alicia signed and then sealed it, her thoughts still on the note from Jack. It was somehow poetic that Alicia's last hurrah in Hollywood was likewise her last hurrah with him. Then again, Alicia wasn't one to revisit something, once she was well and truly done.

"When are you going to come meet my son?" George Neill asked, for now he and Doris had chosen to breed.

Alicia promised "soon," even as she understood that she'd never see

Hyannis Port again, just as she'd never see Oklahoma, or Germany, or Radom. Once she left Łódź, Alicia was never going back to any place. There was no use in revisiting Hyannis Port and there was no point in returning to Jack.

Hollywood's Edmund Purdom, a study in melancholy.

On Broadway, by Walter Winchell, May 1, 1956

NEW YORK

He begged her to meet him, Friday for lunch.

This was a first. Jack was coming to her, at a specified time, instead of materializing in the shrubbery, or in someone's else drive.

"You can't ignore me forever," he said.

Yes, I can, Alicia thought, before realizing that he was right.

It was possible he'd heard about Edmund. Sweet, sexy Edmund Purdom, a man with countless attributes, not the least of which was his ability to follow through on a divorce.

When it came time to leave, Kate was on the phone, badgering some producer with her Spencer Tracy demands. As her rapid-fire voice echoed through the stairwell, Alicia put on a pair of iridescent crystal earrings and a light-colored silk dress. Fashion editors were saying, "Blondes are back," so she grabbed a blond Balenciaga coat and crept downstairs, shoes in hand, and quietly asked Charles for a lift.

He dropped her at the Plaza's Fifth Avenue entrance. In the opulent lobby, Alicia paused to catch her breath. She watched as the bejeweled maidens, highly coiffed dowagers, and spoiled poodles paraded past. Standing under the hotel's grand chandelier, Alicia got a little hot.

"Why are you here?" she asked herself. "What good could possibly come?"

She glanced at the clock. Twenty after, and she was therefore later than a missed taxi or an ill-timed light. Alicia shuffled toward the Oak Room, a dark-wooded, iron-wrought monstrosity built to resemble a British men's club. Why hadn't she requested the less oppressive Palm Court?

She spotted Jack instantly, and her heart sighed. How she missed the bastard, through it all. But Alicia did not go to him right away and instead watched as he read the newspaper, feeding that delicious brain. He appeared much healthier than he had at their prior meeting, in Chuck Feldman's tub.

Alicia examined him for a few more minutes, as he turned from one page to the next, brows furrowed over his reading glasses. Nostalgia washed over her to imagine Jack in this very position, in Hyannis Port, five years before.

He had aged in the last two years, and probably so had she. But Jack still carried the hint of a rascal, the scamp that'd weaken her defenses with a smirk or a pinch. Every once in a while, he'd look up from his paper, a shot of insecurity passing across his face when he noticed the time.

Alicia wiped her eyes as a waiter approached. Jack motioned, indicating he would continue to wait. That's when she saw his wedding ring, shiny even in that dim and smoky light. Nothing had changed, really. And with Jack, nothing ever would. Alicia inhaled, pivoted, and walked out of the room.

As much as she wanted to talk to him, to touch him, to hear that voice, she could not keep this date. Unlike Kate, she was not strong (or rich) enough to keep circling, to run the same track time and again. For once and for all, she had to leave Jack behind, to the life *he'd* picked, no matter how much he blamed it on his dad.

Alicia rapped on the door. She waited, listening for any sound.

"Edmund!" she called, pounding harder. "It's Alicia! Open up!"

Generally, Alicia avoided scenes in hotel hallways, as she was not keen on visits from the vice squad. But, in this case, dramatics were in order and Ed would appreciate it fully.

"Eddie!" she hollered again. "Edmund Purdom!"

Finally, the door swung open. Eddie stood before her in his skivvies, his face creased from the sheets and his hair a mess of thick black waves. Damn, the man was gorgeous. Jack Kennedy was not the sole game in town.

"What are you doing in bed this time of day?" Alicia asked, and sashayed into his room, the tail of her blond coat wafting out behind her.

"I'm a bit knackered," he said. "Question is, what are *you* doing? I thought you had a luncheon date, and I wouldn't get to see you before I left."

"The date was canceled." Alicia flipped around. "Eddie. I want you to stay."

At once, Edmund perked up, no longer looking like a naughty child sent to his room.

"Your . . . business." She waggled her fingers. "The bit about going to Europe with Linda Christian. Is that true?"

He'd been saying it to the press for weeks. Edmund Purdom was done in America. What did he need with Hollywood, or, indeed, New York? London, Rome, these cities were more fashionable than anything Stateside. Besides, the timing was right, as he'd recently left his studio (mostly) of his own volition. He had the reputation of being hotheaded and childish but, unlike Spence, at least Eddie wasn't a drunk.

"Are you really leaving?" Alicia asked. "Or are you trying to get back at me for the rejected proposals?"

"A bit of both. I have to milk the publicity, doll, you know that." He reached out for her. "This scandal's been the best thing to happen to my career."

In Alicia's estimation, the best thing to happen to his career was getting cast in Brando's role. Although, Edmund *was* in the paper a lot more now thanks to the rumors. Alicia didn't care for Linda Christian, or her brand of overly solicitous sexpot, but was glad everyone blamed Miss Christian for the dissolution of the Purdom marriage, instead of her.

"I thought Linda bored you."

Alicia took off one glove, and then another.

"I don't think of her much, one way or another," Edmund said. "But if they're going to put us onscreen to sell tickets, I'll gladly accept the money."

Alicia flung her gloves onto the dresser. She slipped the coat from her shoulders, and let it fall to the floor.

"I don't want you to go to Europe," she said. "Because I can't, not with my MoMA internship starting next week."

"Also, your immigration status."

He rolled his eyes, as fed up as Kate was with the excuse. They had this one thing—and only one thing—in common.

"Please, Edmund. Stay. Stay in the States with me."

"And you'll be . . . what? Showering me with attention one minute, and then poof—gone—the next? Doing whatever it is you do when you vanish . . . gallivanting, painting, nattering about Communists with that horrible Jack Kennedy?"

Alicia's stomach went squirrely from hearing Jack's name.

"I really don't like that man," Edmund said.

"I'm aware," she replied, a little tartly given she'd previously flaunted Jack directly in his face.

It'd been two years, but that sort of thing stuck with a man.

"Jack's not part of my life," Alicia said. "Not anymore. But you are."

"You want us to be together?" Eddie asked. "Like a proper couple?"

"Exactly like that." She smiled.

"No more Jack Kennedy?"

"No more Jack."

"Good," Edmund said. "Because I don't want to see that jowly mug ever again. I don't want to hear his bloody name."

"My sentiments exactly," she said. "Although you *are* the one who brought him up."

Edmund nodded, and looked at the ground, as he lightly bit his bottom lip. Then he lifted his gaze, and wielded that sexy, snaggletoothed grin.

"Well, Alicia Darr. In addition to being the steamiest bird I've ever seen, you cut a convincing argument."

"That's a yes?"

"Of course it's a yes. All you had to do was ask."

Edmund Purdom and Alicia Darr are expected to elope any edition.
On Broadway, by Walter Winchell, November 18, 1956

NEW YORK

When Edmund walked into their room at the Warwick Hotel, Alicia was huddled in a chair by the window.

He'd just returned from his second appearance in *Child of Fortune*, a dramatization of the Henry James novel *The Wings of the Dove*. The critics had panned the performance, calling it a "bloodless affair" and Eddie himself "dull in a dull role." Alicia went to opening night and found both the plot and Ed more than adequate. Even the catty Walter Winchell "enjoyed every moment of it." Alas, she was an art student, and he a gossip columnist, so what did they know?

"Bloody hell," Eddie murmured, staggering in. "The audience booed. I've put everything into this performance, my absolute all. People don't appreciate good theater these days. A sodding tragedy, is what it is. No culture, no class."

Alicia glanced up.

"Edmund," she whimpered, "I can't, with the . . ."

Ego, she wanted to say.

"I can't do it," she mumbled instead. "Not tonight."

"Apparently neither can I," he said with a snort.

He dropped onto the bed, took off his shoes, and then finally noticed Alicia's sad eyes, anemic face, and the piece of paper wadded up in her fist.

"Did something happen, love?" he asked, propping himself up on both knees.

There were many things one could say about Edmund Purdom, but if nothing else, he understood women. He was attuned to their moods and varying degrees. Kate argued it was because Eddie was a bit of a woman himself.

"My mother died," Alicia said, and opened her hand to reveal a telegram.

WE REGRET TO INFORM YOU THAT AFTER A LONG
ILLNESS . . .

"A long illness" was one way to put it. Mother had been dying for ten years, probably longer with everything she'd gone through before setting foot in the camp.

"Aw, shit," Edmund said. "Are you sure?"

"If you can't trust a priest, who can you?" Alicia said, and again brandished the telegram. "I've spoken to the chaplain. They've prepared the body and will lay her to rest in a cemetery beside the hospital. I wish it could be somewhere in Poland, but mailing bodies around Europe is frowned upon and I have nowhere to bury her anyhow."

"You're not going back?" he asked. "To say good-bye?"

"Oh, Eddie." She sighed. "Say good-bye to what? A corpse? I don't have a passport and it'd take weeks, months, to get the paperwork in order."

"Right, right," Eddie said, nodding.

Even Edmund Purdom knew not to tease Alicia about her immigration problems that day.

"I'm sorry," he said. "That is crap news."

"Crap news" was better than anything she might've come up with. Alicia was upset, yet not. Shocked. A touch relieved. Filled with remorse. In the end, these reactions had all combined into a dull flatness, a tired, ugly gray.

"Doll, I wish you'd say something." Edmund crouched beside her. "What can I do to make this better?"

He ran a hand along her shin, then peered up at her, imploring.

"There's nothing to do, really," Alicia said. "Not now. It's probably for the best. She was in pain, and her mind was gone, and she was furious that she was in a *Catholic* hospital. Plus, she wasn't exactly missing me. She told the priest I died in a convent."

Alicia chucked the balled-up telegram across the room.

"I have an idea." Edmund lifted her to standing. "Let's get out of here, have a night on the town. I'm thinking the Harwyn sounds nice?"

"Eddie, I'm not in the mood."

"What are you going to do instead?" he asked. "Sit by the window moping all night?"

He jerked her forward. Alicia let herself be pulled.

"Look at you," Eddie said, indicating her dress, a black crepe number with a side drape. "You're dressed, beautiful as ever, despite your despair."

He gently fingered the black pearls resting on her collarbone.

"I went to church," she said.

"Now that's something you don't hear every day," he joked.

"I lit a candle at St. Pat's. Can you believe it? Catholic Church for a Jew. Even in death, I can't do right by her."

"Bollocks. You did everything you could."

Eddie gave her another tug, and Alicia followed, resigned. As he opened the door, Alicia grabbed her mink, then retrieved her pointy-toed heels from beneath the console, the only ones unpacked. Most of Alicia's things were still in the suitcases stacked in the corner. Last week they'd had to downgrade from a suite to a regular room, as Eddie hadn't been paid for his most recent work. There was also his greedy ex-wife, who kept demanding more.

"Are you ready?" he asked.

"Not really. But let's go."

"That's the spirit. If I know my pretty bird, she'll perk up when the flashbulbs burst and the first drink is poured. Fame and adoration." He chuckled, and shook his head. "The best medicine. I don't know why everyone bothers with all the bloody pills."

The Harwyn was a mistake.

The club was too garish, too cheerful with its pink and black decor, and the crush of people dancing and spilling champagne.

"This way, my love," Eddie said. "They've saved us a spot."

As they wended through the tables, Alicia spied gossip columnist Cholly Knickerbocker, otherwise known as Igor Cassini. She shot him a glare. He'd been writing about her lately, though they'd long ago agreed that he would not.

"Igor," Alicia seethed.

She arced toward him, but Eddie was quick with the grab.

"No, no, no," he said, clutching her arm, dragging Alicia to the table he'd picked over the phone. "Harass the poor bastard later. Gossip is his job, which you know best as anyone."

"Yes, but we had a deal. I'd give him the freshest scoop and he wouldn't write about me."

"Oh, love," Eddie said. "A deal is just another script, bound to be changed."

They sat down.

For a few minutes, everything seemed okay. Alicia sipped her champagne, Eddie his whisky, and they danced exactly twice. Then, Elvis came on—"Heartbreak Hotel"—and Alicia found her chest locked up, nose quivering. She slipped on sunglasses so no one would see the tears.

"What's with the glam business?" Eddie asked. "People will think I've been rough with you and that you're covering a black eye."

He looked over to see her push away a tear.

"Are you crying?" he asked, aghast.

"I'm sorry," she said. "Not even I understand what's wrong with me. I mourned Mother years ago. She was miserable, and ill, and no matter what I did, I couldn't make her happy or healthy. I couldn't make her proud. I always thought I'd have another chance at both of these things."

"I'm not especially healthy." He winked. "But you make me immensely proud."

"Maybe she was right. What have I done with my life, really?" She gestured toward the now-empty bottle of champagne. "Aside from attend parties and visit dance clubs?"

"What about the money you've sent over the years?"

"I should've gone to see her. I always intended to, but I never did. My parents gave me a second chance, and I took it and ran."

"But you couldn't leave the country, lest you not be able to get back in. You've told me yourself, a hundred times."

Alicia nodded, though that wasn't exactly true, was it?

She supposed it could be, using the strictest interpretation of immigration law. Really, though, she'd had her chances. Like when Jack wanted to take her to the French Riviera, soon after Eunice's wedding. Or, any of the times Kate invited her to London, or to Rome. Hell, Alicia could've finished the paperwork she started six years ago in Oklahoma. She'd be a citizen by now.

"I have to stop making this same excuse," she said. "Over and over again."

Alicia set down her glass and stared at the bubbles popping in the light.

"Rome," she said, then looked up.

"Um, what's that?" Eddie squinched his eyes.

"Let's go to Rome," she said. "I've been dying to and *everyone's* there now. I have an open invitation, you know, to Novella's studio on Margutta."

"That sounds splendid, my love. But won't you have to wait until the paperwork is in order?"

"Perhaps." Alicia twisted her mouth. "Or, I could get married. That'd be more expeditious."

"Married?" he said, his eyes now wide. "Any specific chap?"

"Why, yes. I'm thinking of a seductive, spicy Brit. He's asked for my hand seven times already."

Seven and a half. Most recently, Alicia stopped him right before the "will you," to save them both the embarrassment and the inevitable fight. Edmund was so frantic to marry her, he almost always carried a ring in his jacket, in case she changed her mind.

"Whaddya say?" Alicia asked. "Care to make an honest woman out of me?"

Just as she reckoned he might, and as she'd seen eight times before, Edmund fell onto one knee.

He flipped open the lid of the red velvet box. The hinge no longer creaked, thanks to overuse. Alicia took a second to admire the art deco masterpiece, with its tiered diamond steps that led to a three-carat, square-cut emerald at the peak.

"It's *tsavorite*," Eddie clarified. "Which is sturdier and far more radiant than an emerald. Alicia Darr, for the last time, will you marry me?"

The tsavorite glittered in the club's darkness.

"The *last* time?" Alicia said with a spark in her eye.

Eddie Purdom was such a handsome devil, the rare star who was every drop as sexy as his reputation. He wasn't like so many of the leading men, who were either weak in character, or attracted to the same sex. Plus, Eddie made his own decisions, to hell with the opinions of agents or managers or tyrannical fathers. His choices weren't always the best, but they were always his.

"The last time," Eddie said. His grin expanded. "But you are damned hard to resist, so it's likely I'll be fighting for you the rest of my days."

Alicia leaned forward. The candlelight warmed and illuminated her cheeks.

"Yes," she whispered.

Eddie sprang to his feet and began hopping about.

"She said yes! She said yes!"

"Shhhh!" Alicia said, laughing, tears seeping. "Igor is looking our way."

Eddie sat, and pulled Alicia onto his lap. She giggled, feeling as though a heavy weight had been cut. This was the start of a new story. She didn't need her mother, or Jack, or even Kate Hepburn. Alicia could be his completely.

"Next week," Eddie said, and threw a full glass of whisky down his gullet. "Let's get married next week!"

"Why the rush, Mr. Purdom? Are you in a family way?"

"No. I am simply in love."

"I'm not an expert on American divorce laws," Alicia said. "But doesn't yours still need to be approved by the courts before you are officially free?"

"You're right." He blubbered his lips. "You'd think they'd speed it up. Tita and I have agreed to everything."

"Is that why she's trying to take you to court again?" Alicia rubbed his arm. "Oh, sweetheart. We have plenty of time to be married, plenty of years as man and wife. And, we should let the excitement of our engagement sit for a while. Give our big news the chance to spread."

"To spread?" Eddie blinked.

"I meant . . ." She smiled. "A chance to sink in. I can't wait for everyone to find out."

PURDOM TO WED AGAIN; POLISH GIRL TO BE BRIDE

The Cincinnati Enquirer, April 8, 1957

NEW YORK

Their pre-wedding party was set for a Sunday night, at the Living Room. Alicia wore a blue silk dress with a matching belt. Eddie put on his favorite ascot, which was red. She asked him to please change it to navy blue.

The guests arrived early. Alicia and Eddie skated through the room, showing off her ring and discussing Eddie's latest project, the television show *Marco the Magnificent,* to be filmed in London next month. Alicia smiled brightly and often, despite being somewhat on the brink of tears thanks to Kate, who'd elected not to come.

Alicia could picture her friend lounging diagonally across the bed at the Warwick, in her ratty, white cardigan and loose-fitting trousers, suede boots propped up on the nightstand. She wore a floppy felt hat, though they were indoors.

Kate had just wrapped *Desk Set* with Spence. Rumors had them starring in *Ten North Frederick* next, and strictly with each other from then on. *Until death do us part,* Hepburn-Tracy style.

"That's why you can't come," Alicia huffed when Kate delivered the bad news. "Because of Spence."

"He's part of it. Also, this whole thing is nonsense. Why are you marrying him, Alicia? You still haven't explained."

"What's there to explain? Eddie is handsome and interesting. He's kind."

"Is he?"

"I realize you did not have a good marital experience, but I'm a different woman. For you, it was a cage. For me, it's freedom."

"Freedom!" Kate cawed. "Oh, sister, you're in for it."

She began to howl, hardily. Alicia grew ill from the cruel sound of Kate's laugh.

"Freedom," she cackled on. "That's rich. So damned rich, it could buy its own island and aero-plane."

"It's really quite direct. I love Eddie, and marrying him gives me the freedom to be Alicia Darr."

"And where does 'Purdom' fit in? Oh, Alicia." Kate gave a long and drawn-out sigh. "You're marrying him because you want to escape, and you think Rome is the answer, now that Europe is finally safe."

"What do you mean 'finally safe'? The war ended a decade ago!"

"I mean, Europe is finally safe for *you*. It poses no danger for Barbara Kopczynska, or Alicia Darr, or whatever you're calling yourself later today or next week. Europe is safe, now that your mother is dead."

Now that your mother is dead.

As Alicia remembered Kate's words, the tears formed again. Her lips quivered. Eddie sensed the change in her right away.

"Are you all right, love?" he asked, pulling her from the crowd. "You seem upset."

Alicia smiled, grateful to be marrying this man.

"I'm so happy," she said. "But I'm missing the people who aren't here."

Edmund frowned, probably assuming that Alicia meant her mother, when actually she was thinking of Kate.

"Might I make a toast?" he asked. "I've been planning it for weeks."

"We decided on this party a few days ago."

"Exactly," he said, that sneaky glint in his eyes.

Eddie smacked Alicia's rear and hopped up onto the table.

"Ladies and gents!" he called out, and clanged a dessert fork against his glass. "If you'd allow me to say a few words. Don't worry, I won't go on too long. I would hate for some theater critic to give me yet another bad review."

Laughter rippled across the room, everyone astounded that Edmund Purdom could joke about this already. Maybe his ego wasn't as bloated as they all thought.

"If you know my beautiful Alicia," he said, "my wife-to-be, then you know she came here as an immigrant, a castoff from the war. She carried nothing but a suitcase, her good looks, and her brains, the latter two of which should not be underestimated."

Eddie winked. Alicia smiled out into crowd.

"But Alicia is an enterprising sort," he went on. "Soon she was scoring roles, turning out canvasses, and hobnobbing with the elite. She's consorted with princes and sheikhs and Oscar impresarios, even an up-and-coming politician or two. She's friends with the biggest names in the business. All this to say, I don't know how *I'm* the one lucky enough to get her for keeps."

The crowd "ahhhh"ed, right on time. Alicia placed a hand over her heart to show Eddie that she was touched.

"And, so, let's raise a glass to my stunning bride. I promise to love you, and to serve you, from tomorrow at . . ." He checked his watch. "Three o'clock, until the end of time."

Three o'clock? Alicia's neck felt squeezed, as if in a vise. Dear God, she was to be married tomorrow, from sixteen hours hence "until the end of time." She swallowed several times, but the saliva would not go down.

"Cheers!" Eddie trilled.

"Cheers!" everyone returned.

All eyes shifted Alicia's way. She held up a glass but said nothing, her throat still clenched by some invisible force. Meanwhile, Eddie beamed, reveling in the admiration of the crowd.

"Cheers!" he said one more time.

Eddie gulped his champagne, cocked his arm, and hurled his glass against the wall. For a second, the room held its breath, and then all manner of glassware began whizzing past as people whooped and hollered. When Alicia realized she was the only one still holding a glass, she threw hers, too, with as much force as she could find.

"*Na zdrowie!*" she shouted, the first words that came out.

Eddie jumped down.

"That went well," he said, a pat on his own back.

"You're the star of the show," Alicia agreed.

They were getting married. Tomorrow. And then it was London after that.

What would she do while Eddie was filming? Play housewife? Cater to his whims? Would he expect Alicia to get pregnant? With Tita, he'd had two kids in three years, so Eddie was a proven quick shot. She'd never told him that pregnancy, for her, was not to be.

"Alicia, are you listening?" Eddie shouted directly into her ear.

"We can't get married tomorrow," she blurted.

Eddie's eyes bugged, and Alicia nodded, for she was equally surprised by the words she'd said.

"Have you lost the plot? Everything's arranged."

"Not everything," Alicia said. "We haven't found a judge to perform the rites. Also, I'm still trying to convince Kate and Spence to come."

"Kate Hepburn?" Edmund said, and snorted. "For fuck's sake. The clackety old dame strikes again."

"And the dress." Alicia scooted closer, and pressed her body to his. "The seamstress says it'll be done by tomorrow, but it fit like a paper bag six hours ago!"

"A *dress*?" Edmund scoffed. "You want to postpone our marriage because of a frock?"

"I've been dreaming of it my whole life!"

Her "whole life" was a bit of a stretch. Alicia hadn't been the sort of child who fantasized about weddings. As a teen, she couldn't afford to ruminate on the future at all. Alicia had only been dreaming of it since last month, when she saw *Funny Face* and determined Audrey Hepburn's wedding dress would be even better on her. Alicia located the best seamstress in New York, and had it copied, to the last seam.

"Please, darling?" Alicia said, and batted her eyes. "We have time. You're not expected in London until the end of April."

"Fine," he said. "But the license is good for another two weeks, and I'm not standing in that bloody line again to get it renewed."

"Very well." She shuddered in relief. "I promise. I won't make you suffer the bureaucrats a second time."

She popped up onto her toes to give him a kiss.

"I love you, Edmund Purdom," she said. "Thank you for making my dreams come true."

A week later, Alicia and Edmund were still unmarried.

Their license remained valid, and Alicia's dress hung in the closet. Alas, there was no wedding date and the two barely broached the topic. Edmund brooded silently while Alicia carried on, blithe to promises and expiration dates. Maybe if she did this for long enough, everything would turn out okay, whatever "okay" meant.

Working hard at her good cheer, Alicia pranced into El Morocco, Eddie straggling morosely behind. The second they were through the doors, friends waved them over, and thank God for that. Alicia took Eddie's hand and they went to join the couple, who were themselves recently hitched. Liz and Mike wed on the beach in Acapulco two months ago, and in one move, Elizabeth Taylor became both a wife and a grandmother at the age of twenty-four.

"It's the merry lovebirds," Alicia said as they sauntered up.

Liz smiled, gorgeous as forever, the lone person who could make Alicia ponder life as a brunette.

"Merry indeed," Liz said, and patted the seat beside her. "Come sit next to me, Eddie. Oh, Alicia, how do you get more beautiful by the day?"

"High praise, coming from La Liz."

"Speaking of merry lovebirds," said the handsome and tanned Mike Todd.

It was hard to accept that he and Spence were nearly the same age. They seemed like two entirely different cuts of meat. Mike was a fine steak as opposed to Spencer's chewy, aged gristle.

"I've heard that you two are following us down the aisle," Mike said. "Are the rumors true?"

"Indeed, we'll be married any day," Alicia said quickly. "We're quite excited!"

She whipped her head toward Liz.

"Please explain why you aren't on the dance floor?" she asked. "You're not one to shirk in the corners."

"My dear Liz is feeling poorly," Mike Todd said, and kissed his wife. "We expect this to continue for some time. Nine months, perhaps?"

He smirked, giving them all a clue.

"Liz!" Alicia clapped. "You're pregnant?"

Liz lit up, her answer clear as day.

"What wonderful news!" Alicia sang. "When are you due? I thought you looked especially lovely tonight. I was seconds from grilling you about your skin-care regime!"

"The baby is expected in late summer," she said with a dewy blush. "Which seems like ages from now."

"Fabulous news," Eddie said.

He lifted his glass.

"A toast," he said. "May the baby have all of your talent, Liz, and none of Mike's looks."

"Hear, hear," Mike said with a laugh.

"Is it really that awful?" Alicia asked. "Being pregnant?"

"Jesus, Alicia, what a question," Edmund said.

"It's fine, Eddie," Liz said. "And yes! I'm exhausted! And nauseated all of the time. I'm not sure why we're here tonight, other than my husband wanted to see some friends. And they had the nerve not to show!"

"Sorry, babe," Mike said, and kissed her again, this time on the head. "I'm a shit husband. We'll stay in, the next three nights, and I'll spend it all rubbing your feet."

"If only." Liz sighed. "Don't forget, dear, we have the ball on Thursday."

She bent toward Alicia.

"The April in Paris gala," she said. "Are you going?"

Alicia shook her head. April in Paris was New York's biggest social event of the season. This year's party commemorated the two hundredth birthday of the Marquis de Lafayette, and its purpose was to raise money for various Franco-American charities, such as the French Students Fund and an organization that aided refugees from the First World War. Why not the second, Alicia wanted to know.

"It's the day after tomorrow," Liz said. "I'm sure it will be spectacular but it sounds like agony to me."

"Fuck the ball," Mike said. "We're not going."

"Now it makes sense," Alicia said. "This morning a mysterious woman rang my room. She offered to pay a hundred dollars for the hair appointment I have at Bergdorf's tomorrow. I declined, but maybe I should put it on the auction block."

"Keep the appointment!" Liz said, violet eyes wide. "Keep the appointment and take our place at the gala!"

"A fabulous idea," Mike agreed.

"Please say yes!" Liz begged. "You'd solve *all* my problems. The tickets were quite dear, one twenty-five each, and I'd have awful guilt about throwing them out. You'll love it. French clothes and French people. The Paris Opera will be performing!"

"The Paris Opera?" Alicia said, her interest now piqued.

She wasn't sure about stuffy, prim-nosed affairs with New York's best and brightest, but French clothes and opera were two things Alicia could get behind.

"The lists are closed, so you couldn't get in if you wanted to," Liz said. "All the biggest names will be there, a once-in-a-lifetime event. It was so clever, they sent the invitations in red-and-white-striped hat boxes."

"It does sound fun," Alicia said, and looked at Ed. "What do you think?"

"Mike will call it in tomorrow!" Liz said. "Have them replace the Mike Todds with the Edmund Purdoms."

"They're not married yet, dear."

"Hold up," Edmund said. "Perhaps we can fix that."

He swung his gaze toward Alicia.

"Let's get married tomorrow night," he said.

"Tomorrow? But we can't," Alicia said.

"We can. We have the license, and the dress, and the requisite hair appointment, too. Now or never, babe."

"So, that's it?" Liz said. "You'll get hitched tomorrow?"

"I won't wait another day," Edmund said, then gave Alicia a triumphant smile while she sat slack-jawed and clammy.

"You romantic son of a gun."

Mike Todd reached around to ruffle Eddie's hair.

"What do you say, Alicia?" he asked. "Are you ready to be married? Is tomorrow finally the day?"

Alicia nodded, because what else could she say? Her dress was ready. Kate wasn't coming to New York "any time this year." And, there was the hair appointment, too. Really, she had no reason to wait.

"We'll take your tickets," Alicia said with an exhale. "Please tell the organizers to expect the Edmund Purdoms."

NEW YORK

Alicia Darr, or Barbara Kopczynska if you'd rather, and Edmund Purdom married on Wednesday, the tenth of April, at the Hampshire House, in a rose-embossed wallpapered room overlooking Central Park.

A city court judge presided over the vows, which were witnessed by twenty-five of their closest and most readily available friends. Liz and Mike attended. Likewise, Dean Martin, Esther Williams, and the Milton Berles. Lucy and Desi stopped in for a post-ceremony toast.

Alicia wore a white satin dress that, like Audrey's in *Funny Face,* had a boatneck and a flared, tea-length ballerina-style skirt. On her head was a delicate tiara made of platinum, diamonds, and pearls. The night floated past as a dream, or a trance, somehow like a picture Alicia might paint, yet not what she expected at all.

The next morning, Alicia woke with the sun. She threw a fur coat over her nightclothes and rushed to the newsstand, to see if she and Eddie had made the cut.

When she saw that they did, Alicia was at first thrilled, and then her stomach turned to stone. The photograph. Dear God. In it, Alicia's chin was tilted upward, away from her new husband, an arm held against her stomach, as if she might be sick. Eddie stood awkwardly behind her, and appeared to be suckling her right eyelid.

Alicia whimpered, then sprinted upstairs to wake Eddie, who was sipping tea and smoking languidly.

"You won't believe what they printed!" she cried. "It's a disaster!"

Eddie gave the photo a scan, then returned to his teacup, unmoved.

"It's fine," he said, a bizarrely indifferent response given his phenomenal vanity. "You're always far too worried about your image."

Kate had a similar reaction when called. As did Fred, in L.A.

"I don't care about the damned picture," he said. "Why'd you marry the bastard in the first place?"

Alicia would have to double down at the April in Paris ball, work to get in the papers for *that*. She'd chosen a red strapless sheath taken straight from *Funny Face*, like her wedding gown. When she'd spotted it at Bergdorf's, she remembered Audrey dancing on the steps of the Louvre, arms outstretched, a red chiffon scarf fluttering in her wake.

As they rode to the Waldorf, Alicia worried that her getup was overdone. The dress code called for red, white, or blue, to match the French flag, but Alicia's red was so bright, it seemed like another color altogether. But, when they stepped into the Grand Ballroom, Alicia's concerns evaporated.

"Wow," she said, gaping at the elaborate bunting, dramatic ostrich plumes, and tricolored drapes. "I hadn't expected this."

"Remarkable," Edmund agreed, and took his new wife's hand.

The tables were set in rows and adorned with blue tablecloths, silver candelabras, and flowers shipped from France. Gilt armor was stationed throughout the room. On the stage, a statue of the Marquis de Lafayette was flanked by fountains lit in red, white, and blue. Alicia would be lucky to be noticed at all, in a room like this.

The program listed performances by the Rockettes and Paris Opera, followed by a reenactment of Lafayette's wedding to his fourteen-year-old bride. Later in the evening, guests would be treated to a demonstration of Parisian fashion (Dior, Balmain, Dessès) and French jewels (one million dollars' worth, provided by Cartier).

A waiter handed Alicia a glass of French champagne, and the Purdoms sat for a seven-course meal modeled after Lafayette's wedding feast, beginning with *la procession royale des brioches au fromage*, the royal procession of cheese and buns.

They were midway through the fourth course when an unexpected performance sprang up on the far side of the room. It was Marilyn Monroe, making a late entrance in a dramatic sequined gown.

"Jesus," Eddie muttered.

Alicia gawked. She'd never seen a dress that skintight, or low-cut. Papers would later describe it as "mostly skirt held up by a couple of rather wide shoulder straps." Marilyn wore no jewelry and her hair was twisted into a sloppy chignon. Her latest husband, the bespectacled playwright Arthur Miller, walked several paces behind.

"Great timing," Eddie griped. "Who arrives when dinner is halfway through?"

"You can't expect La Marilyn to wear a wristwatch," Alicia said. "Or the requested colors, apparently."

Marilyn was in black.

As the Arthur Millers took their seats, no less than thirty people decamped from the Duchess of Windsor's table and rushed toward them, programs in hand, hoping for an autograph. The photographers likewise flew to her side, followed by several dozen self-proclaimed "old friends." If this party were on a ship, they'd capsize.

Thirty minutes passed. The waiters couldn't get in to serve the next course, so they hung back, waiting, as the food cooled. Nearby, the Duchess of Windsor clucked and clacked, furious that she'd been upstaged in this way. *She* was supposed to be the guest of honor, and therefore the center of attention, not Marilyn Monroe.

"If you ever throw a party for me," Alicia said, one eye still on the duchess, "make sure that Marilyn Monroe is not on the guest list."

She looked at her husband.

"Unless I'm trying to lose weight," she said.

Alicia's eyes darted back to the duchess's table. That was when she noticed the duke, who was speaking to a man in a tuxedo. His companion was tall and gangly. He was slightly hunched over, using a chair for support.

Alicia's heart stopped.

"You okay, love?" Edmund asked.

"Yes, yes, fine." She sprang to her feet. "But my throat is very dry all of a sudden. Please excuse me while I step out for a sip of water."

Alicia's throat *was* dry, and she was light-headed, too. From the champagne, and the night, and the prickling realization that *I am married*. The prickling realization that *Jack is still around*.

As his telltale laugh rippled across the room, Alicia took off, and sprinted through the double doors. She paused outside the ladies' room, gripping a marble table as she sputtered and gasped. A thousand people in one room—it was too many. Especially where Jack or Marilyn was involved.

Soon, Alicia heard footsteps. She glanced up, a joke on her tongue. Something about how they didn't need Broadway, when Marilyn made for such great theater.

"Oh!" she yelped, then jumped.

Jacqueline Kennedy. The last person she expected or wanted to see.

"Hello there!" Alicia said.

Jacqueline was lovely in person. Hers was not a classic beauty, but something dark and alluring, like she might hail from a small but cultured country you'd never heard of. That said, Alicia found some comfort in her lack of breasts and canoe-sized feet.

"What are you doing out here, all alone?" Mrs. Kennedy asked, in what could only be described as an exaggerated whisper. "Scheming and plotting and trysting?"

"Nope," Alicia chirped. "I'm not the scheming sort."

Jacqueline tossed her eyes slightly to the right and lit a cigarette. Alicia noticed that her fingernails were bitten to the quick.

"I'm, er, waiting for the Marilyn excitement to die down," Alicia said. "The woman sure knows how to steal the show."

Jackie snorted.

"I, for one, will never understand the fuss," she said. "Marilyn is pretty but, as they say, 'There is no there there.' I can't imagine conversing with her for longer than ninety seconds."

She blew a stream of smoke over her shoulder.

"She is a little hard to talk to," Alicia agreed. "But she is sweet and it can't be fun to be Marilyn Monroe."

"Hmmm." Jacqueline blew another stream of smoke. "It would be quite miserable."

"I'm Alicia Darr—Purdom as of yesterday—I don't know if we've previously met."

They hadn't met, but Alicia was in the tricky position of acknowledging familiarity with the Kennedys, while avoiding the fact of her intimacy with Jack. Mrs. Kennedy did not reply and instead sucked on her cigarette interminably, leaving Alicia to become quite damp beneath the arms.

"Are you having fun tonight?" Alicia asked. "I haven't been before."

"Lovely. Yes." Jacqueline shook her head. "Poor Jack. My husband hates these stuffy functions."

Her attention floated away, to some distant place.

"I can't blame him," she continued. "I know he'd much rather be sailing on the French Riviera with his ridiculous friends and whatever sluts they've brought on board. If not the French Riviera, then lying on the beach in Malibu, or hanging out at a Hollywood producer's house with some starlet or another."

Jacqueline's eyes narrowed.

"Even a lunch meeting at the Oak Room would be better than this," she said.

"I've never been to the Oak Room," Alicia answered, chin lifted.

Jacqueline dropped her cigarette and ground it into the floor.

"Alas," she said, "life can't be all sunny days and blondes in bikinis. I always tell Jack, *enjoy it while you can*. I like to make life as comfortable as possible for him, but he'll have to grow up someday, although it's his youthfulness that makes him so damned fun . . . and it'll make him a terrific father."

She touched her belly. Alicia thought she might be sick.

"Jackie!" said a voice, a cloying, nasally voice that could only belong to Bobby Kennedy.

Alicia put a hand to her mouth. Oh, this was about to end quite horrifically.

"Jackie, is this bimbo bothering you?" he said, and buzzed to her side.

Bobby shot daggers at her with his steely blues. Alicia didn't know whether to be flattered or alarmed that he'd recognized her on sight.

"Leave Mrs. Kennedy alone," he said. "If you keep being such a pest—"

"A pest?" Alicia scoffed. "I've done nothing. Mrs. Kennedy and I ran into each other outside the ladies' room. I think she is quite capable of handling herself in ordinary conversation, don't you?"

"I'll have you deported," Bobby said.

She blinked, stunned that he'd sink so low, not to mention signal to Mrs. Kennedy that Alicia was not some anonymous "bimbo."

She hadn't met Jack in the Oak Room that day, and she'd not seen him since, until tonight. But he'd called, and telegrammed, and again invited her to the French Riviera, doubtless as one of the "sluts" mentioned by his wife.

"I can do it," Bobby said. "I can have you sent to Germany. Deportation due to moral turpitude. Happens all the time. Look it up."

Alicia held her expression steady, though her heart beat with force. Jacqueline watched it all with a dead-eyed smirk.

"It was nice speaking with you, Mrs. Kennedy," Alicia said. "Enjoy the rest of your evening. Please tell Jack that I said hello."

With that, Alicia walked off, heels clacking on the floor.

She didn't reenter the ballroom that night. Alicia concocted some excuse; she'd torn her dress, gotten sick in a planter. Eddie would be angry at first, but not for long. You couldn't hate your wife on the second day of marriage. It wasn't fair.

The bell rang early the next morning. Startled, Alicia took a minute to orient herself. She was in a room, with her husband, who was himself in a dead sleep. A gift box from the ball sat on the desk.

When the visitor rang a second time, Alicia slipped into her robe and plodded toward the door. This was rather aggressive, for half past ten.

"Whatever is so important that you must ring twice?" Alicia said as she thrust open the door.

"Mrs. Purdom."

It was the manager.

"This is for you," he said, holding a tightly wrapped white gift.

At first, Alicia thought it was another souvenir from the ball. Then she noticed the thin, red satin ribbon—a telltale wrap job by Cartier.

Alicia's hands trembled as she took the gift.

"This was dropped off this morning," the manager said. "I was told it was urgent."

"Thank you," Alicia said, her voice as shaky as her hands.

"Have a nice rest of the day, Mrs. Purdom," the manager said.

Without good-byes, Alicia whisked off the ribbon and peeled back the thick, white paper to reveal a red Cartier box. Inside the box sat a set of cold meat forks. The same wedding present she'd given Jack.

Congratulations on your marriage, the card read. *I would've given this to you in person, but you're always running the other way.*

> The recently wed Edmund Purdoms (Alicia Darr) have problems already.
>
> Gotham Gossip, by Dorothy Kilgallen, July 26, 1957

NEW YORK

LIST OF PASSENGERS
Name of passenger (Surname first): PURDOM, Barbara K.
Class of Travel: FIRST
Address in the United Kingdom: Stafford Hotel, London
Occupation: Housewife
Country of which a citizen: ~~USA~~ STATELESS
Intended duration of stay in U.K.: Indefinitely

Alicia boarded the ship, heart in throat, head filled with thoughts of what lay ahead, and what remained behind. As with the last time she traveled by ship, Alicia carried but one suitcase. Of course, she'd also shipped two boxes of clothes to London in advance.

Alicia could offer many excuses for spending her honeymoon in New York, by herself, while Eddie was abroad. Paperwork. Finishing her internship at the Museum of Modern Art. The ever-present "problem with immigration authorities," the problem being that she hadn't contacted them.

"You don't have to stay married," Fred said. "In fact, you shouldn't. You belong in Hollywood, not playing housewife in London. As soon as this trial is over, I'm flying you home."

Fred was embroiled in a libel lawsuit, thanks to his association with *Confidential* and *Whisper*. He'd let Alicia know not to expect business from either magazine until this mess was fixed.

"I knew you weren't serious about him" was Kate's take. "Come stay with us, we're at John Barrymore's place in Los Angeles."

Even George Neill found the decision suspect.

"I thought the one thing you wanted in life was to *leave* Europe?" he'd said.

Unlike the others, George did not offer that Alicia might stay with him. She didn't especially want to, but it would've been nice to have been asked.

"I could revisit the Cape," Alicia said, pressing him on the matter. "Reconnect with that beautiful town and the best time of my life."

George laughed, quite boisterously given he was such a taciturn man.

"What would you do in Hyannis?" he said between fits. "Sell candy?"

The man had a point and Alicia didn't really want to go back anyhow. Returning to California wasn't an option and neither was staying in New York. The grand, expansive United States seemed cramped and inadequate now. Her sole choice was to move forward, to confront the decisions she'd made. Plus, the Warwick had kicked them out, so Alicia needed to go somewhere.

"I'm on my way!" she announced to Ed, who was nothing short of shocked.

He'd been suspicious of her "immigration issues," but was in no position to comment on slippery dealings, as their eviction was on account of his unpaid bills. Alicia asked Fred to please get rid of what she'd left at her old apartment, so that she could pay Edmund's debts before she left. Alicia didn't want to sell the Corvette, but Kate insisted.

"The thing's in rotten shape," she said. "Thanks to your poor driving. And you can't leave New York without squaring up."

Alicia sold the car. It gave her enough to pay Eddie's bills, with not a penny left over. Finally, a slate wiped clean.

As the SS *United States* glided out of the New York harbor, blaring its horns, Alicia stood on the upper deck, heavy with memories of the last time she crossed the Atlantic. Alicia felt every bit the same girl as then, though this ship was fancier with its sleek hull and red, white, and blue smokestacks. Of course, the *Sturgis* had been designed for utility, not luxury. Back then, Alicia slept in a hammock, in a windowless cabin with five other girls. Now she traveled first class.

Although her hair was blonder now, and her clothes were more fashionable, she toted the same valise, for reasons only nostalgia might explain. But this suitcase was now packed with silks and crepes instead of itchy, rough wool. Wrapped inside a cashmere scarf was a bottle of Chanel No. 5. Wrapped in two scarves was a cigar box filled with letters, photographs, and other reminders of the States. Most of these were memories of Jack.

Maybe London would give Alicia the physical distance she craved. Jack was in newspapers and on magazine covers with a jarring frequency, and simply opening *The New York Times* was an act of courage these days. Perhaps Jack passed a piece of legislation, or was fighting for a bill. Bobby or Pat had another child. Jacqueline was expecting, due that fall.

Before Alicia set sail, she removed one item from her keepsake box, a photo of Jack she'd snapped on the streets of D.C. years ago. She scribbled in blue ink:

The Next President of the U.S.

And sent it his way. This was her good-bye.

Alicia thought of Jack as she strolled the upper deck, where the mood was joyful and buoyant. Only the truly privileged would be so excited by the prospect of *leaving* American shores. Of course, most would peg her as a woman of undeniable privilege, someone for whom life was smooth. But where a person might find Alicia Darr in the first-class dining room, on the passenger manifest she was Barbara K. Purdom: housewife, stateless, expected to remain in London indefinitely.

As they passed the Statue of Liberty, Alicia's stomach flipped. She looked straight into the woman's steadfast face, tears tumbling down her own cheeks. The city receded, and before Alicia thought to wave farewell, America vanished completely from view.

It's amazing the problems Alicia Corning Clark causes, even in her death, Leonard thinks.

First, the young Italian woman, *Serena* as she's called, flew all this way for an inheritance, yet she continues to resist the DNA test. I ask you, is there an easier process through which one might secure a fortune? The answer is no, there is not. Even Alicia's way of acquiring the money in the first place necessitated some effort, expeditious as it was.

And now, this call from the doorman, one of the people doubtless praying Serena will be ruled out as heir.

"I have to tell you something," William said when he rang Leonard, the day before.

No good conversation starts with these six words.

"Felix found a letter," he went on, Felix being the elevator operator of the same building. "He's been holding on to it but his conscience got the best of him."

Alicia had written the letter in 1977, William explained. It was addressed to someone named Andrew Quigley, but never mailed. Leonard recognizes the name. Mr. Quigley was a state senator and publishing impresario, one of Alicia's close friends.

Leonard pours himself two fingers of scotch and totters out onto the patio into the cool, damp California evening. As he watches a seagull peck along the sand, Leonard replays the contents of the letter—now memorized—in his head. Could this be right? Could it actually be correct? William swears it's Alicia's handwriting and he has no reason to lie. Rather, he has a reason to lie, but this is not the lie he'd tell.

The thing is, this letter matches what Alicia said one night, late in her illness, when she was prone to telling stories with no beginning or end.

"I had a child once, Leonard, did I ever say?"

Using uniquely coherent speech for that stage in her life, Alicia told him when it happened, and with whom, and why she'd left the child for someone else to raise. Leonard nodded dutifully, though he pegged it as a fairy tale, something conjured from her thinning mind. But she wrote in 1977 the same thing she told him forty years later.

What to do, what to do. Leonard rests against the patio railing. He has to show the girl, doesn't he? Damn, he wants to seal this can of worms. Why couldn't Alicia Corning Clark die like a normal person? With a signed and notarized will, like he'd advised?

"Stop writing codicils on napkins and paper scraps," he'd said. "You'll save everyone a lot of hassle if you formalize the thing."

She didn't listen, of course, because she never did. Maybe it runs in the family. Leonard shakes his head. These women. He is entirely too old for this shit.

PART III

MRS. PURDOM INVOLVED IN ROME BRAWL

Los Angeles Times, September 26, 1959

ROME

Alicia didn't last six months in London.

Edmund was selfish, a prima donna, his self-worth bound entirely in what others thought of him. He could be insufferable when his career was going well, subhuman when it wasn't, and "going well" was in Edmund Purdom's rearview mirror.

Their daily squabbles often escalated to hurricane-grade brawls, during which Edmund would tear apart their flat, then lock himself in the bedroom for days, refusing to eat, refusing to speak.

Alicia said he was a baby. He called her verbally abusive, and a slut.

"You're fucking that bastard Kennedy," he sneered.

"How can I be having an affair with Jack, when he's an ocean away?"

Edmund was in no position to talk affairs, and the press was on to his assignations. He was, they reported, anxious to divorce Alicia and marry Linda Christian. When Alicia's first thought was that this sounded like a genuinely good idea, she realized their relationship was over. She'd done many things she wasn't proud of, but the greatest of these was marrying him.

"I'm not angry with Edmund," she told Harrison Carroll when he called for comment. "But his behavior is impossible. I believe he should go to a psychiatrist."

She *wasn't* angry; Alicia merely wanted to be rid of the man. But this wasn't basic subtraction, given Edmund's nature, and Bobby Kennedy's deportation threats. The grand irony was that Alicia was actually safer *before* she got married. A person couldn't be deported without somewhere to go. Now she was married to a resident of the U.K.

"You need to finalize your citizenship," her lawyer advised, "before you finalize the divorce."

The documents were mostly in order, but Alicia wasn't going to stick around dreary London while they finished the rest, and so she absconded to Rome. That was over a year ago, and nothing much had changed in the meantime.

"Are you going to send me the signed paperwork?" her lawyer wanted to know. "You can't wait forever."

"Soon, soon," she promised, though the United States didn't seem like such a prize these days.

The minute Alicia laid eyes on Rome, her heart had leapt, skipped several beats. It was everything they said it'd be, this golden city on a hill. The colors, the people, the piazzas lit and humming at night. Rome was ancient, but it seemed alive and new.

Alicia stayed with Novella, in her flat on Via Margutta, a narrow, cobblestoned street lined with buildings the color of a sunrise. The studio sat mere blocks from the Spanish Steps yet felt days from the bustle and crowds.

Each morning, they'd throw open the shutters, set up their easels, and paint in the saffron light as Novella's herd of twenty or so cats stalked about. Often, they'd entertain a guest or three, as Novella was the so-called most specialized tourist attraction in Rome.

"Name a famous man who has come to Rome," she said, "and hasn't looked me up—and down."

In the afternoons, they prowled Via Veneto, that glorious avenue with its red and blue sun umbrellas and dozens of Jaguars, MGs, and Rolls-Royces lining its manicured curbs.

At any moment, one might stumble upon Ava Gardner, Ernest Hemingway, or Jayne Mansfield. Clark Gable or Sophia Loren, to name two more. But Rome was about more than its stars. Its streets were thick with Hollywood defectors, yes, but the rest of humanity, too. Gigolos and dope fiends, kings and princes, stars rising and stars after the fall.

Café de Paris was Alicia's favorite spot. After closing time, she and Novella would turn on a transistor radio and dance in the street. Later, they might take target practice on the Tiber before stopping by a masquerade ball, where they'd revel until dawn. This was ordinary life in Rome. They called it *la dolce vita*, and Fellini was making a film about them all.

It was almost October. The latest crop of comers had vamoosed. Still recovering from a raucous summer—in Rome and on Capri— Alicia and Novella were tucked away in the relatively mellow Bricktop's, a basement jazz club owned by a husky-voiced, red-headed Negress from Harlem.

As a singer belted out "*Ciao, Ciao, bambino,*" Bricktop herself sidled up to the table, cheroot cigar in mouth, a two-finger tumbler of rye whisky in hand.

"Hiya, girlies," she said, and sat. "What's the shakes?"

"Ciao, Bricky," Novella said.

"How are you two this evening? Staying out of trouble, I hope," Bricktop said with a wink. "I plan to sing in a few, and I don't wanna have to stop midset to kick you out on your tails."

"Cause trouble?" Alicia said, and batted her eyes. "Have you met two more innocent girls?"

"Humph," Bricktop said, and blew three smoke rings.

She gave Novella the once-over.

"You're teensy as a bug," she said. Then, to Alicia: "And you're a skinny thang. But I read the papers, honey luv. What's this about you getting arrested last week? In Capri?"

"Utter nonsense," Alicia said, and batted the air. "It's Edmund. Again. He is the reason for all my problems."

"She broke into ze villa," Novella clarified, in her thick, Italian accent.

Alicia shot her a glare. Sometimes she regretted teaching her friend so much English. Novella had become irritatingly fluent.

"Burglary?" Bricktop said with a hoarse chuckle. "Who's the victim?"

"There's no victim. . . ."

"Rich *Americana*," Novella piped in. "Norma Clark. I told Alicia, zis is fun, but you get to jail."

"It wasn't the least bit fun." Alicia looked at Bricktop. "I did it for my divorce. I needed evidence of Edmund's adultery and can't afford a private investigator."

Bricktop tittered and shook her head.

"Honey chile, I've been rich and poor, rich and poor, so many times. . . ."

She ran both hands over her thick belly and fluffed her red-now-graying hair.

"But I never committed a dang crime."

"I didn't commit a crime," Alicia said. "It was an *investigation*."

These were the words Fred told her to use. Of course, Fred was enmeshed in his own legal troubles. This time he'd been indicted for race fixing. A misunderstanding, he swore.

"I have no ill will toward Norma Clark," Alicia said. "I don't even know her."

"Isn't she sleeping with your husband?"

"I don't care about that." Alicia flicked her hand. "She's welcome to him, but she will have to wait in line. I've named seven women in my petition. Along with adultery, I'm also charging Edmund with concubinage, assault, and associating with vulgar low-type characters."

"He does make questionable relationships," Bricktop said.

Alicia rolled her eyes.

"I found what I needed. A pair of Edmund's underwear. One sock. Shavings from his beard. It's all going in the dossier."

"She wants to be citizen," Novella said. "Zen she acts like zis. She is too crazy for United States."

Bricktop downed her whisky.

"You'd better be careful," she said. "Or you'll end up like Charlie Chaplin. Uncle Sam canceled his reentry permit while he was abroad and for the last seven years he's been . . ." She waved. "Locked out. Probably for good."

"Getting stuck in Rome wouldn't be the worst outcome," Alicia sniffed.

She couldn't wait much longer to divorce Edmund, as Alicia needed the settlement more than she needed citizenship. Purdom was known to be a shoddy payer-of-alimonies, but it remained her best hope.

Money was again thin, with bit roles at Cinecittà barely covering her paints. As for the gossip trade, Alicia maintained her network of spies in lingerie departments, psychiatric wards, and AA meetings nationwide, but Hollywood news traveled ten thousand miles to reach Rome, and ten thousand miles to reverse, and her information lagged behind the hundreds of tips columnists received each day. There was some appetite for Via Veneto scoop, but not enough to keep Alicia in nice dresses and the occasional fur.

"Well, girlies." Bricktop smacked the table. "It's been nice squawking with ya."

She pointed at Alicia with her stamped-out cigar.

"Don't get yourself into any more tussles, sister. I know it's tough, with that body, and that face, but antics get tired, even in Rome."

With that, Bricktop sashayed off.

"Goodness," Alicia said. "One tiny fracas, and suddenly it's 'antics.' I'm no crazier than anyone else in this city. Compared to you, I'm a nun!"

"Ha!" Novella squawked. "I am quiet artist."

"And your paintings get the most press of all," Alicia said, as that old jealousy crept in.

She took a sip of bourbon as Bricky slid behind the mike. With a distant smile, she closed her eyes and began to sway. The song was Cole Porter, Bricktop's "favorite person who's ever lived."

"Novella," Alicia whispered, stretching across the table. "Let's go. I'm not feeling well."

There was something disquieting about the way Bricky sang, how she dipped into each note with her full body, and with such passion and despair. It was too intimate, too stirring almost.

The thrill when we meet
Is so bittersweet

"Please?" Alicia pleaded, for she was ten seconds from tears.

Novella grunted and swiped her handbag from the floor. Alicia gave Bricktop a good-bye wave, but the woman didn't notice. When Bricky sang, it was only ever her, and the music, and maybe Cole Porter, too.

They stepped outside. The air was cool. As they walked, Alicia cinched her coat tighter, thinking how drastically the temperature had changed in a few weeks. The days were still warm, but at night you could no longer smell summer in the air. A new season had begun.

The two women tottered a few steps, until Novella's heel slipped into a crack, and she launched right out of her shoe. Gripping each other in a fit of giggles, they hopped backward to fetch the lost pump.

"One cocktail too many," Novella said.

"I'm less concerned with what we drank than the fact you could've slipped through that crack. An Italian *Alice in Wonderland*."

"I am short, but you are zee person skee-ny enough to fit."

Novella began to sing.

"'*Ciao, ciao, bambina! Un bacio ancora. . . .*'"

"'*E poi per sempre . . .*'" Alicia gave a little burp.

"Hello, ladies, we are merry tonight," said a thick, molasses voice.

Alicia glanced up to see Mario, *Prince* Ruspoli, if you please. And Alicia did please, for she and Mario had recently started dating. He'd been impressed and not put off by her Capri escapades. Most Romans felt the same.

Novella continued to sing.

"'*Ciao, ciao, bambina!*'"

"*No, no, no!*" Mario said. "*No 'Ciao, ciao, bambina.' Bambina* stay. *Ti voglio bene da morire!*"

He clutched his heart and Alicia snorted.

"*Boh!* So much you could die? Really, Prince Ruspoli."

Mario offered one of his wolfish smiles.

"I've come all this way to see you," he said, "but it seems the fun's been had."

"Yep," Alicia said with a hiccup.

"Fancy another cocktail?"

"I must decline," she said. "I'm trying to be good. One more drink and I could accidentally get myself involved in another striptease scandal!"

"Rome should be so lucky."

Laughing, Alicia looked toward Bricktop's and noticed a modest-sized group walking toward the entrance, led by a man with jet-black hair.

"*Stronzo,*" Alicia growled.

She rotated away from her friends and marched toward the club. Novella called out, but Alicia didn't listen. Instead she picked up her pace.

"Purdom!" she screamed, wielding her handbag as if she might strike.

"Ah! Brilliant! It's my lovely wife!"

"The judge told you to stay away from me during our separation," she said. "Away from Rome. And, aren't you supposed to be in the States with your daughters? You're a worse father than you are a spouse."

"Relax, darling, just having a bit of a holiday," he said, cool as forever.

"*Bella*, Alicia," said a member of Edmund's party, coffee heir Manuel Miranda. "You look lovely."

"*Grazie*," Alicia grumbled.

She scanned the others. French actor Pierre Brice. A busty, nameless blonde. And—of course—Linda Christian, smugger than a Fifth Avenue child after a Christmas feast.

"Hello, Alicia," Linda said in a genuine attempt at politeness.

"*Ciao, ciao.*" Alicia faced Edmund again. "I have all the evidence I need to compel the most generous of divorce settlements. But if you don't behave, the price will go up."

"Your threats, like a fly buzzing in my ear," he said, and rolled his eyes.

"I have evidence," she said again.

"You've stolen some possessions belonging to Norma Clark." Edmund shrugged. "What does that mean? You and I are estranged and free to date whomever we please. You've been with a bevy of men yourself. The parade of boring, charmless princes, to start."

"Hey," said Prince Ruspoli, halfheartedly.

"And let's not forget your multiyear affair with an official of the United States government."

"How many times do I have to say it? I haven't seen the man in years."

"But you've spoken with him. He's sent you telegrams, asking to meet."

"You're making it all up."

"Have you looked, Alicia?" Edmund said, and shot up a brow. "Have you looked for that box you toted from the States to London, and then to Rome?" He snickered. "There are some gems in there. Movie tickets and telegrams and love letters galore. Some were pretty steamy, my dear."

Alicia's heart beat quickly, like the patter of hooves on turf.

"What did you do, Edmund?"

"Just had a little fire. The weather's getting chilly, my love."

Alicia gasped.

"Not to worry," he said, "I didn't burn *all* of it. Had to keep a few things for personal use. A bloke never knows when he might need an erotic letter, or a lock of hair."

Alicia cried out again. If this was all true, she'd lost more than her memories of Jack.

"You snake," she said. "My citizenship papers are in there!"

"*Were* in there, in any case."

Alicia lunged at him. He fell into a bush and she jumped on top and lashed at his chest and face. Before long, Manuel pulled her off and Alicia accidentally punched him, too.

"Those are the only mementos I have," she said, hot tears rushing, "of my entire life, and you took them, along with my chance to be an American. Your ex-wife was right, everything she said."

Edmund lit a cigarette. He blew a stream of smoke from the left side of his mouth.

"I'm debating whether to hand some of it over to the press," he said, and wiped a drip of blood from his cheek.

Alicia checked her hands and found scraps of skin beneath her nails.

"Who's going to care about some senator?" she asked, flicking parts of Edmund's face onto the pavement. "Politicians are the dregs of the gossip pages, the very end of interesting information."

"Perhaps they won't care about a senator," Edmund agreed, "but they will when he runs for president."

"President? Where did you hear such bunk?"

"It's in all the papers. John Kennedy has many assets, but no one knows about his greatest liability—you. How very un-American to bed an immigrant, from a Communist country, no less, a woman so inconsequential she doesn't have a real name. A woman who, it must be stated, is completely made up."

Alicia sprang toward him a second time, but Manuel was agile, and got to her first. As he held both of her arms behind her back, she lifted one foot and kicked Edmund Purdom square in the nuts.

Behind her, a camera went click.

She struggled to twist around and give the *scattini* a kick of his own, but Manuel was too strong. The man snapped one more photo and then hopped into his shiny red car. A Fiat, of all the injustices. Maybe Rome wasn't so great. The damned *scattini* had stature now.

"Enjoy your evening, Alicia," Edmund said, and took Linda's hand as he limped away.

"*Arrivederci, stronzino!*" Novella called out.

She was resting on a fountain, smoking a cigarette and watching the show.

"*Vaffanculo!*" she added. "How you say in English? Ah . . . go fuck yourself!"

"You can let go of me now," Alicia told Manuel as she squirmed free. "Your friends are inside."

Manuel whistled for a taxi. Novella tossed her cigarette into the fountain and then made her way back to the curb. A wave of sorrow washed over Alicia. She began to cry.

"Ay, Alicia, he is not worz zee tears," Novella said, and slung an arm across her shoulders.

"He's a despicable person," Alicia snuffled.

"*Sì*. But we know zis for always."

"I'll never understand what ladies see in Purdom," Manuel said, as he pushed the women into a taxi. "He's a cad, no more than three-quarters a man."

"Perhaps you should alert your pal Linda Christian," Alicia said.

Manuel slammed the door, then poked his head through the open window.

"Oh, I wouldn't worry about Linda," he said. "She thinks he's a good lay, but nothing more. He wants to marry her, but the sentiment isn't shared. The girl is *praying* for a long divorce so that she might be let off the hook. I hope you're not the one stuck with him for good."

ROME, HOLLYWOOD ON TIBER, IS PLACING EMPHASIS ON SEX
The Petersburg–Colonial Heights *Progress-Index*, November 22, 1959

ROME

As Rome buzzed with the so-called Purdom squabble, Alicia locked herself in the studio to paint. When she first landed in Hollywood, she was desperate to be in the papers. Now she couldn't stay out of them.

"I thought you were going to cool it," Kate said after reading the latest in the *Los Angeles Times*. "But I see your name more than Kennedy's. Are you running for president, too?"

Regarding him, Alicia called Jack five or six times, using the numbers she still had. She also sent two telegrams and tried the Senate switchboard, all to no success.

She didn't know that Edmund would really go public. The man was unpredictable, but lazy to the core. Alicia prayed that exposing Jack would prove too taxing and that he'd eventually forget. It was her only hope, since Jack hadn't returned her calls.

Edmund's material felt like a ticking bomb, and Alicia grew more agitated by the day. Thanks to Gestapo visits and air raids, her sleep had long been fitful, but it'd gotten even worse. She was like a difficult baby, napping in ten-minute increments, only to wake up fussy and unsatisfied.

One night, after Nova and a gaggle of others left for the clubs, Alicia lay in bed, hands crossed over her chest, as she beseeched the heavens for the sweet release of sleep. But all she could think of was Jack, and Edmund, and her citizenship papers, now gone. Alicia claimed that she didn't care if she ever returned to the States, but that wasn't true. If nothing else, she'd promised to vote for Jack.

After two o'clock in the morning, Alicia gave up. She kicked off her blanket and charged toward the phone.

"For fuck's sake, Alicia," Fred said when he heard her voice. "I told you not to go to Europe with Edmund Purdom."

"It's a tad late for I-told-you-so's, don't you think?" Alicia said. "And he tricked me."

"Tricked you, how?"

"The bastard drew me in with his dusky handsomeness. I mistook his tantrums for passion, his tendency to sulk for broodiness. He was supposed to be the next big thing, and then he wasn't. I never truly appreciated that he's a shit actor, so wooden and boring."

"'Boring' doesn't seem like the word for either of you these days," Fred pointed out.

"It's all being blown out of proportion."

"I read that you slapped his face and pulled his beard."

"I *scratched* his face, and I'd never touch that nasty beard," she said. "He provoked me! He stole my citizenship papers!"

"I didn't realize you had those."

"Very droll, Fred. I was the person wronged here, not Edmund."

"Linda Christian is telling people that you threatened to punch her in the mouth."

"She wishes. Then she'd have reason for more plastic surgery."

"Do you *not* want to come back to the States?" Fred asked. "Is that it? I mean, if Jack Kennedy is going to be president, I can see that."

"Of course I want to!" Alicia said, tears brimming. "That's why I called. I must reach Jack. Edmund says he'll expose everything about our relationship and I need to warn him."

"What are you so worried about?"

"Fred, you know that at times our—um—communications have overlapped with his marriage."

"That's one way to put it," Fred said with a chortle.

Alicia could tell from the wet, thick sound of his laugh that Fred had gotten fatter since she'd been away.

"I tried to call him," she said, "numerous times, but he hasn't responded."

"And you want me to help you find him," Fred guessed.

"Yes," she answered softly.

Fred sighed deeply, and blubbered his lips.

"I am working with the family on a few things," he said.

The "family" was Peter Lawford, no doubt, though he scarcely qualified. Alicia had seen his wife on Ari's yacht over the summer, and Pat made it clear theirs was a marriage solely in name. Alicia hadn't gotten around to prying for details, as she was too distracted by the eight types of caviar, two hairdressers, and world-class masseuse aboard the *Christina*.

"There's an event in New York," Fred told her. "The first week of December. It's a jubilee in honor of Eleanor Roosevelt, and Jack is scheduled to attend."

"Great. Perfect."

Alicia's body slackened in relief. She closed her eyes.

"Thank you, Fred."

"I'll send you the information, free of charge."

She opened her eyes again. The phone line crackled.

"How are things with his wife?" Alicia asked, barely able to get the words out. "Has their relationship improved, now that they have Caroline?"

"Oh, Alicia," he said, voice rumbling. "That's such a loaded question.

He loves being a dad, and *that's* no photo op. As for the wife, he's more interested in her now that the rest of the world is, too."

Alicia nodded, her chest shaky. She refused to let herself cry.

"I really thought he'd leave," she said, voice quavering. "I thought he was different from other men, above that sort of lie."

"No man is, Alicia. But, they have come close to divorce more than once. Hell, Jackie was o-u-t out a few years ago, and Joe paid her to stay."

"To stay?" Alicia straightened. "I thought the settlement was for—"

"One million for each baby she squirts out," Fred said, "plus a pile for Jackie herself. The arrangement was made before she had Caroline, which caused Ethel to bitch to the high heavens. At that point, she and Bobby had five kids and Ethel hadn't seen a motherfucking dime."

"That poor woman should get paid twice the sum, for suffering Bobby's sexual advances." Alicia shook her head. "Thank you, Fred. You've been helpful. As always."

"I don't know why I keep coming to your rescue. I must be a sucker for your particular brand of crazy."

"Hey!" Alicia sniped. "The only crazy thing I've done is marry Edmund."

"I can think of a few other examples." Fred snorted. "But, let me ask. Can you afford the ticket to see Jack?"

"I'm fine," she said, a pat answer, though not necessarily true.

She could pay for the trip, strictly speaking, though it wouldn't be easy and she'd be left on a very slim ledge. While she could probably weasel some cash from the hard-nosed, salty-but-sweet Fred, she did not want to be indebted to him.

"I'll figure it out," she said. "One way or another."

After they hung up, Alicia rushed to her bureau and slid open the bottom drawer. She sifted through her white silk panties to find a package wrapped in a pair of nylons.

As she unwound the stockings, her stomach rolled. Edmund had the keepsake box but at least she had this, her diamond engagement ring. She'd told Jack it was sold long ago, but Alicia kept it so that she might always have one more option, a final crumb of hope. Once it was gone, the picture of them dancing at the firemen's ball would be the only thing left of Jack.

PURDOM'S SPOUSE STILL IRRITATED, FILES FOUR SUITS

The Desert Sun, November 27, 1959

NEW YORK

Alicia took a room at the Great Northern Hotel on West Fifty-seventh Street, near Carnegie Hall.

Kate offered her place for Alicia's "proposed misadventure of folly and doom," but famed artist and stage director Oliver Messel was staying at the townhome while he prepared for a much-heralded show. There was more than enough room for both of them, but Alicia didn't wish to suffer the indignity of some artist trotting around, gleaming with success.

Alicia arrived a few days before the party, to meet with her lawyer. She was now suing Edmund for adultery and assault in Naples, and in Rome, as well as for stealing her citizenship papers in New York. She'd already filed for separation in London, bringing the total legal actions to four.

The morning of the ball, Alicia lolled about her hotel room, and caught up on news from the States. Sure enough, Jack was expected to announce his candidacy any day. But almost more famous than Jack was his wife. Alicia found herself oddly drawn to Jackie Kennedy and her wide face, that smug smile, and the headlines she snagged all on her own.

WIFE A VOTE CHARMER.

JACKIE KENNEDY GIVES ADVICE TO OTHER WIVES.

GLAMOUR GIRL AND SPOUSE.

Alas, the stories about Jackie were as unrevealing as they were dull, comprised mostly of "I don't mind" and "I plan around it" and "whatever Jack wants." Sometimes, she brought him "a hot meal from home in the baby's warming plate." She still painted . . . "a little."

"Watercolors because they are less trouble," she explained.

JACKIE KENNEDY—A GIRL WITH EVERYTHING.

"She is nothing like they portray her in the papers," Fred assured Alicia. "She's the cattiest woman I've ever met."

This made her feel better, for a minute or two.

After cramming the newspapers into a lobby trash can, Alicia visited the hotel's twenty-four-hour beauty salon, where a stylist fashioned her hair into a beehive, and secured it with a jeweled clip. By sundown, Alicia looked perfect and poised, but her insides were racked with nerves, despite three glasses of champagne.

Soon, she was ready to go. Alicia stood before the mirror and pirouetted twice, watching the skirt of her blue-black iridescent dress change color as she moved. She inspected herself from the side. Alicia was thinner than ever, thanks to the lean times in Rome. Thinner than Mrs. Kennedy, who "weighs a slim 125 pounds; is 5'7" tall."

Alicia took one last swig of champagne and grabbed her mink. She exited the elevator and strode through the salmon-colored marble lobby, swishing past its potted palms.

Though the Waldorf was close, Alicia hailed a taxi, her legs too wobbly to walk. The ride was brief, and she considered asking the man to circle the block, so she could drum up her nerve. But she was too poor to buy this kind of time, and so she stepped out of the cab, smiled, and steeled herself against the emotions percolating inside.

"Who do you like for president?" a statesman named Max asked as he and Alicia waltzed well into the night.

They'd already exhausted other topics, including travel, the upcoming holidays, and what his fifteen-year-old daughter might like as a gift.

"For president?" Alicia said, scanning the room, wondering when Jack might show.

How quick she'd been to forget that America's handsomest politician was also its least reliable guest.

"All the candidates haven't declared," she added.

"That's true, but we know who *will*."

That's when she finally spotted him, *her* candidate, standing by a table near the dance floor. Alicia's body tensed; a thrill shot up her chest.

"Ow," Max said.

She'd accidentally squashed his hand.

"Sorry." She blushed.

Alicia appraised the situation. Around the table were three men, plus Jack, but no Mrs. Kennedy in sight. Perhaps she was upstairs, heating food in the baby warmer, or playing tennis to keep herself trim.

"Personally, I like Kennedy's chances," Max said. "He's a young buck but you can't beat that boyish charm. Or, the pretty wife."

"Yes," Alicia replied, through her teeth.

As the song began to fade, she met eyes with Max.

"Speak of the devil," she said. "Mr. Kennedy is over there. I'd like to see the president-to-be. Dance me over to him. I know him very well."

Max led her across the floor, in what seemed like a thousand tiny steps. God, what would Jack think of the Edmund business? What would he think of her?

When they reached the group, handshakes were exchanged. The men pulled back and Alicia stepped out from behind Max. She smiled, unable to speak, because she had too much to say. The moment Jack's gaze locked on to hers, he grinned big as the room.

"Kid . . ." he said, one word, and took her in his arms.

Did she say good-bye to Max? Or Jack to his assortment of friends? She would never remember, because at that second, there was Alicia, and there was Jack, and that was all.

"God, I've missed you every damned day," he said, gliding her across the floor.

Alicia couldn't hear the music anymore.

"I've missed you, too," she said, biting her lip, turning away.

It'd do no good to flirt with nostalgia, to think about this tanned, handsome man and the intimate ways in which she knew him. Alicia was there to warn him and to finally say good-bye.

"Look at you," he said. "You're beautiful. Stunning. I need a damned speechwriter for the things I want to say."

"A speechwriter, how romantic."

"You sparkle. Everything from your face, to that dress, to the jewels in your hair."

She nodded, wondering what he might say if he knew she traded a far more glittering prize to acquire the dress, her fake gems, and a chance to talk to him.

"December '59," Jack said, running his hand along her spine. "The end of a decade. Hey. Look at me."

She lifted her chin.

"That's better. Kid. Don't cry. . . . What's wrong?" He frowned.

"It's just—I'm overwhelmed."

"My sentiments exactly. Jesus." He shook his head. "Seeing you here, right now, before everything changes . . . it's a lot to take in."

"Before 'everything changes'?" She lifted a brow. "Are you referring to your candidacy, Mr. President?"

"No comment."

He grinned, then spun her once beneath his arm.

"The end of a decade always seems so seminal," he said, pulling her back in. "It's only another year, but somehow not. We're defined by these chunks of time. The roaring twenties. The threadbare thirties."

"What do you know about any threadbare thirties?" she said, then added, "The fighting forties."

"And now the furious fifties," he said. "I wonder what the sixties will bring?"

"A dashing new president, I'd guess."

"Nice try, kid." He winked. "Right now, it feels like I'm at the end of something, instead of at the beginning."

"This life," she said, "is what you wanted. It's what you've been working toward for so many years."

"That's true. Tell me, how is Italy? I'm green with envy. I can't articulate how grueling these past few months have been. Fifty thousand miles and twenty-three states. Rome sounds like a dream."

Alicia smiled. So, Jack knew where she'd been, which was either a compliment or a sign that her antics were as publicized as Kate claimed.

"Well, Rome is Rome," she said evenly.

A bit of a nonanswer, but not untrue. Rome *was* Rome. There was no other word with enough guts.

"Are you painting?" he asked.

"I've sold a few pieces. Nothing to earn a living by, but enough to give me hope. I can't decide if being around Novella Palmisano is inspirational, or a repeated bludgeoning to my pride."

Laughing, Jack twirled her again, and then a third time. Already Alicia's nerves had broken up, her worries were released. At that moment, they might've been nine years younger and at the firemen's ball, when it didn't seem outrageous that she might become his wife.

"And what about your acting?" he asked. "You were on a hot streak in L.A. I can still picture your face on the screen, and see your name in lights."

Alicia chuckled. This boy with the tallest aspirations still got stars in his eyes about Hollywood.

"I'm doing some film work in Rome," she said, "but, in Italy, everything is dubbed. Acting is added to the film *after* it's made."

One Italian director told Alicia that she needed but two expressions: horizontal and vertical. Her bedroom eyes, traffic-stopping chassis, and the film editors would take care of the rest.

"At least you get to be in Rome," Jack said.

"Yes, a small price to pay," she agreed, then wondered.

They swayed in silence, Alicia puzzling over how long they'd been dancing, and through how many songs. They didn't have a lot of time left that night, or in general.

"I called you," Alicia said. "And wrote countless letters. Though if I did count, I'd say two dozen, at least."

"*Letters?*" Jack snorted. "Kid, I get seven hundred pieces of mail *per day*."

"Okay, but I also sent telegrams. And, like I said, I called."

"Alicia *Dahr*-ling, then you were one of eighteen phone lines lighting up the switchboard. My secretaries don't have time to get to them all. And you know me. I'm rarely in the office. I'm out on the road or running around, trying to get a bill passed."

Alicia blinked, the explanation so eminently reasonable yet empty at the same time.

"I need to talk to you about something," she said.

"Okay, lay it on me."

"Can we go somewhere? It'll only take a few minutes, but it's important."

"Hell, you're not dying on me, are you, kid?"

"No, nothing like that."

"Phew. Come on."

He pulled her off the dance floor, and then to a nearby table, where they ducked behind a centerpiece.

"Here," he said, reaching into the pocket of his tuxedo. "This is the key to my room. I'm in the Presidential Suite—don't say it!"

Together, they laughed.

"I need to bid farewell to some folks," he said. "Can I meet you up there in . . . ?" He checked his watch. "About twenty minutes?"

Alicia took the key, which was cool in her nervous little palm. Jack squeezed his hands around hers.

"You okay, kid?" he asked, and leaned closer.

"Yes, I think I'll be okay."

Alicia hadn't intended to go to bed with Jack, but he walked into the hotel room hot with purpose and resolve. Within twenty seconds, he was tugging the shoulder of her one-shouldered dress.

"The need to speak with you was not code for something else," Alicia said, making a halfhearted show of wiggling free.

She hadn't "intended" to have sex with Jack, but she wanted to all the same.

"You can't *literally* waltz into my life," he said, "looking like that, and not understand that I'll *have* to take you by the end of the night. I had the worst damned headache when we were dancing. I'm surprised you didn't notice my boner through my pants."

"Jesus, Jack," she said with a forced laugh.

He yanked on her dress and Alicia heard the zipper rip from its seam.

"You're paying for that," she said.

"Oh, I'll pay for it. I'll pay for it all night long."

Jack ran his lips down Alicia's neck, across her chest, and to her belly. He kissed all these places and others, too, but did not kiss her once on the mouth. After mere seconds, he slid inside her and began grinding his hips. She shuddered as if it were her first time. Jack Kennedy was not the best lover she'd had, but he was the one she loved best.

Then, it was over, like the slamming of a door. His lovemaking was brusquer than she recalled.

"The best thirty seconds of my life," she'd later tell friends.

She'd also forgotten that he never lingered. Jack couldn't stay in bed for more than (another) thirty seconds, at which point he'd be up on his feet, charging toward the bathroom for a shower or a bath.

"That's right," Alicia whispered as she watched Jack's pale, flat bottom retreat.

The water turned on and Alicia sat in the dark, eyes open and glassy. It was so overwhelming. Jack. The night. The enormous suite she was lying in and the evidence of him all around. Piles of clothes. Discarded shoes. The remnants of newspapers, folded lengthwise. They were in the nicest room of the fanciest hotel in New York, yet Alicia was reminded of Hyannis Port and its shabby furniture, sandy floors, and views of the sea.

Fifteen minutes passed. Alicia threw on a robe and padded toward the bathroom. She cracked open the door to find Jack in the tub, lying so still he might have been dead.

"Jack?" she said.

He startled, causing a tiny splash. Then his face fell into a soft smile.

"Hiya, kid. Was drifting off there." He patted the side of the tub. "Here. Have a seat."

Alicia hiked up the robe and sat on the cool, slick marble. She swung her legs into the water, then scooted behind Jack. He rested against her shins as she massaged his shoulders and neck.

"Ahhhh," he said. "I could stay here for a year."

"I hope you're planning to give yourself a rest," Alicia said, the muscles in his back spasming against her legs. "Palm Beach for the holidays?"

"Mmmm," he said.

"Did you know I got married?" Alicia asked. "Two and a half, almost three years ago?"

"I heard something about that," he said.

"Now I'm trying to get divorced." She sighed. "I actually . . . I need to talk to you about that. You see, my husband is a real—"

"Prick?" Jack guessed.

"Yes. On his best day. As I was saying, I have no shortage of charges on which to file this divorce, but because Edmund doesn't want to pay me a dime, he's trying to find dirt on me." Alicia sucked in her breath, trying to rouse enough brass to go on. "For example, he's threatened to go to the press about my relations with a certain presidential candidate."

She expected Jack to jump, or groan, or display some alarm. But he carried on as before, floating in the water, in his semilucid state. It was nice to see him like this—relaxed, not drumming his fingers, or tapping his teeth.

"Jack?" Alicia said. "Did you hear me?"

"Relations with a presidential candidate, huh? Are you screwing Nixon, too?"

"Don't be vile. Anyhow, I've filed four lawsuits against Edmund, but he's threatened to name you in a countersuit. I haven't told him anything, it's what he's . . . inferred over the years."

"I don't give two shits about Edmund Purdom," he said. "And you shouldn't either. He's an ass. Get divorced as quickly as possible and move on."

"I do have my citizenship to keep in mind . . ."

"Fuck it," he said. "Listen, I'll help you with whatever you need. Like I told you, get rid of the bastard. If Edmund causes any trouble, I'll have someone take care of it."

"Oh. Um. Okay."

She did not expect it to go this easily. Jack had a reputation to uphold, and he was easily set off. Once he yelled at her for sending his favorite shirt to the wrong cleaner.

"You're not upset?" Alicia said.

"Fuck no."

Jack cranked his neck to peer up at her.

"That's what you wanted to talk about?" he said. "*That* pissant is why you flew to New York?"

"Yes, well," Alicia said, reddening, feeling foolish.

What had she been worried about? Edmund *was* a pissant, wasn't he? How could a twerp like him do anything to someone like Jack?

"I didn't want him to ruin your candidacy," Alicia said. "And you didn't return my calls . . ."

"Aw, kid, that's swell of you to worry about me." He turned around and sank deeper into the bathwater. "Edmund Purdom can say whatever he wants. The only person he'll hurt is himself."

So. Alicia had done what she needed to and Jack was more reasonable than she might've predicted. Still, she felt empty somehow, deflated, a leftover balloon from a party that didn't need decorations to start. She wondered if he was on some sort of pill, to make him this calm.

"I'm glad it's not a problem," Alicia said. "I wanted to be sensitive. People get quite hot about the concept of adultery, if you haven't noticed."

"That's true. Alas, you're married too."

"Yes . . . I am . . ." Alicia said, head swimming.

She was married, wasn't she? Alicia never thought about it that way. Now that one bad decision, that one night, trailed her like a foul smell.

"I'll tell you this," he said. "If I don't win, we'll also have divorce in common."

"Oh, Jack, that's ridiculous. First of all, you've predicted divorce half a dozen times. Second, of course you're going to win."

"Who knows," he said. "Sometimes I ask myself whether this is what I want. You and me, we're so much alike. I knew it the first time we talked, outside the Hyannis."

"The Center," she said. "We met at the Center."

"Oh. That's right. How can I keep track? You're always moving. You're *compelled* to move, same as me."

"That's how I grew up," she said softly, though Jack did not seem to hear.

"When I see you, I think of the line from 'Ulysses.' 'For always roaming with a hungry heart . . .'"

"'Much have I seen and known,'" she answered, pleased she could still recall the lines; "'cities of men . . .'"

Jack exhaled loudly. He reached around and looped his arms through her legs. He sighed again.

"We're the same, Alicia."

"I don't know about that."

"It doesn't matter what city we're in. When I see you, it's like coming home."

Alicia stayed until the next morning.

Jack had an early flight but, before he left, he ran out to Bergdorf's to pick up something for Alicia to wear to her hotel. The getup was frowsy, a shapeless slacks-and-sweater combination, but it was a kind gesture, and Alicia was grateful for it.

He walked her to the lobby. Alicia offered to accompany him to the airport, but Jack didn't want to put her out.

"I'll see you soon, kid," he said.

Alicia went in for a hug but he pulled away, which was not a surprise but still stung. There was always a barrier between them. Jack Kennedy wasn't made for one person, he was made for the world, and Alicia would never reach him all the way.

"Good-bye, Jack," she said, and smiled sadly, an acknowledgment that this was the end of them.

It was possible, she supposed, that Jack would leave his wife if the election didn't go his way. But losing was a more fantastical concept than the notion of a Kennedy divorce. Jack would become president because Kennedys always won. The "furious fifties" were nearly over, and Alicia had to accept that Jack was, too.

ADULTERY DENIED BY ACTRESS
The Long Beach *Independent*, April 15, 1960

ROME

The sun was loud that day, the city quiet. Novella was out of the studio, entertaining a visiting actress by the name of Tina Louise.

A hush had fallen over the city. It began with the death of Errol Flynn, which came like a warning shot. From that point on, parties were sporadic and rarely lasted until dawn. Everyone gathered for the Roman premiere of *La Dolce Vita*, but then disbanded as soon as the lights came on, like cockroaches scrambling back into the walls.

Even the Orsini cousins, "the world's most famous playboys," had tempered their antics. Prince Filippo and Belinda Lee canceled their suicide pact and Filippo returned to his wife. Raimondo stopped buying so many drugs. By the time *La Dolce Vita* premiered, the buzz surrounding the film was far more scandalous than anything actually occurring in Rome.

For Alicia, there'd been no better time for the dawn of a more tempered city. It was a new decade. If only Alicia could rid herself of the last vestige of the fifties, Edmund Purdom.

To his credit, he'd not yet come out with anything about Jack, whose candidacy was now real instead of assumed. Alas, Edmund was a snake, and Alicia had been trailing him around the globe pleading for a divorce. So far, she'd followed him from New York to Munich, back to Rome. In Switzerland, he gave her the slip. Alicia stayed to ski in St. Moritz and had to write a bad check to cover her stay.

The Purdoms were due in court next Thursday. Alicia was practicing her testimony when someone knocked on the studio's door. She'd expected another artist, or maybe Tina Louise looking for Novella, who was often lost due to her shortness and propensity to scrabble about.

But when Alicia opened the door, she saw not a redheaded star but a doughy, plain American. She'd met this man before.

"Alicia Darr," he said, and helped himself inside.

It was Jay McInerney, or Mac as he was called in the Kennedy camp. He was an "attorney" by trade, but mostly they used him to grease wheels and ease roads.

"Get Mac to handle it," Jack said when some "slut" accused Joe of coming on to her too aggressively. "She'll shut up for a couple thousand bucks."

"Get Mac to push the paperwork through," she'd overheard another time. "Using a heavy sack of cash."

Mac was the family's payoff guy, which did not explain why he was in Rome.

"Excuse me, Mr. McInerney," Alicia said, showing that she knew his name. "You cannot just walk into a woman's home uninvited."

Alicia adjusted her painting smock and crossed both arms over her stomach.

"This is a matter of national security," he said.

"National security?" Alicia's voice caught. "Is Jack okay?"

"He is splendid. No thanks to you."

"To me?"

Mac slid a hand into the breast pocket of his coat and extracted a paper. He snapped it straight.

"You've been a busy girl, Barbara Kopczynska. Alicia Purdom. Whoever you are."

"I've not been busy at all." She nodded toward her easel. "Painting, as you can see. Alone in my studio."

"Ah, yes, I'm sure you're quite busy with your artistic endeavors," he said. "When you're not trying to extort money from the Johnson camp."

Alicia wrinkled her nose.

"Who are the Johnsons?" she asked. "Oil people?"

"Lyndon Johnson?" he said with a toss of the eyes. "He's running for the Democratic ticket against John F. Kennedy?"

Alicia snorted. Long ago, Jack confessed that he used the "F" for one reason: it'd be shortened to JFK, thereby linking him to FDR in voters' heads. Never mind the middle initial, even the "John" sounded off to Alicia.

"You can call him Jack," she said. "I already think he's greater than FDR."

"Come again?"

"Why are you here, Mac?"

His brows popped up at the casual use of his name.

"I don't have anything on the Johnsons," she said. "I don't know the first thing about them, other than Jack told me Lyndon is a real prick."

"Don't play dumb with me." Mac batted the paper still in his hand. "You don't have dirt on *him*, you have dirt on Senator Kennedy. Alleged dirt, I should say, about a supposed affair."

"It wasn't supposed," Alicia sniffed. "But I'd never sell information on Jack. I wouldn't trade that part of my life for anything."

"Then how do you explain this?"

Mac passed the paper to Alicia. Before she'd read a single word, her eyes fell to Jack's harried scrawl at the bottom of the page.

I talked today with Bobby Baker. He informed me that three weeks ago an attorney he knew named Mickey Wiener from

Newark (?) Hudson Co. called him. Wiener states that if Sen. Johnson would give him 150,000 to the wife of 'a well known movie actor' (Baker did not know her name or who the actor was), she would file an affidavit that she had had an affair with me. Baker said he thought it was blackmail, and did not inform Johnson of the matter. He did tell Joe Alsop that he was concerned about an attempt at blackmail of me but did not go into the details.

John Kennedy/April 8
Sealed by
Pierre Salinger
April 11, 1960
Witnessed by Lenore Ostrow 4-11-60

"That's an affidavit signed by Senator Kennedy," Mac said, as Alicia read it a third and a fourth time. "And he's talking about you."

"I don't see my name here," she said.

Her voice went thin and scratchy.

"Your name's all over this, Miss Darr," Mac said. "Even if it's not on the page. I was there when he signed it. You came up then, and several more times after, with Jack, Bobby, and the FBI."

"The FBI?" Alicia yipped. "What?"

"I tend to agree with Bobby," Mac went on, "in that you're nothing more than a 'half-assed hooker,' but you need to be dealt with all the same."

Alicia looked at the paper, stomach sloshing.

"This is why you believe I'm a matter of 'national security'?" she asked. "Because I once slept with Jack?"

"That's the gist, yes."

"I don't know anyone named Mickey Wiener." She returned the paper. "My attorney in the States is called Simon. Also, I'd think the 'wife of a well-known movie actor' would eliminate Mrs. Edmund Purdom from consideration."

Alicia pondered this. It could've been Edmund himself who called.

He'd certainly speak of himself in such lauded terms, but she would've expected him to indiscriminately vomit information all over the media. To blackmail took foresight and ingenuity. She was momentarily impressed.

"Mrs. Purdom," Mac said, and slipped the affidavit into his jacket. "I'd be very careful if I were you."

"I have nothing but fondness and respect for Jack," Alicia said. "And I'd never do anything to jeopardize his candidacy. I flew to New York in December to tell him that Edmund might talk. Jack told me not to worry."

"It's time to worry."

"It's probably him." Alicia tilted her head toward the spot Mac had put the letter. "Edmund is a horrible man, but ultimately harmless and easily done in by his own stupidity."

"You're pinning this on your estranged husband?"

"It's the only reasonable explanation. Why would I want to ruin Jack's life?"

"Why does anyone do anything?" he said. "Money. You are in a precarious financial state, are you not?"

Alicia stiffened as Mac smirked.

"According to whom?" she said.

"Divorce lawyers. Various shopkeepers throughout Europe. Your bank balance."

"My *bank balance*? I have plenty of money, and multiple sources of income. In fact, Edmund is seeking spousal support from *me*."

Alicia said this with her chin held high. It wasn't trembling, she didn't think.

"I'd be very careful," Mac said, unswayed. "You're a problem. The family has very powerful friends and while the Kennedys are straight as arrows, their friends don't always play by the rules."

With that, Mac pivoted to leave. Alicia slammed the door before he was wholly out of the way and then pressed herself against the wall, winded. Had she just been threatened? Fear tingled along her spine.

"The affair," she reminded herself. "He only mentioned the affair."

Maybe the Kennedys weren't so powerful and all-knowing, if their biggest fear was that she might tell Lyndon Johnson a few stories about sex. Alicia would have to be careful not to give them anything else. She had information far more ruinous to their presidential hopes.

To that end, Alicia had a few things in her favor, like Novella's tucked-away studio and the timing of Mac's visit. Most fortunate of all was the smock she wore, and how easily it hid a pregnant swell.

PEPPER FLIES IN CAFE DISPUTE

Orlando Sentinel, November 16, 1960

NEW YORK   •

Alicia glanced at the hospital band, which hung loosely on her thin wrist.

For the second time that year, she found herself alone, in an antiseptic room, staring at a plastic strip with *Purdom, B* scribbled in blue ink. She'd wanted the divorce for three years, and Alicia was still a damned Purdom.

It was a few minutes after two, the official start to visiting hours. A nurse knocked and asked if she was ready for a guest. Alicia grinned, for she wasn't merely "ready" for a guest, but desperate for one.

"Well, this is a fuckin' mess," said a booming voice.

"Oh, Fred."

She collapsed into tears as he lumbered toward her.

"You really had no one else to call?" he said. "In the whole world? I'm honored, in a way."

"You were the best choice."

Kate was in Hawaii, and Alicia wasn't in the mood for a lecture anyhow. Nova couldn't come for one very important reason. That left Fred. Sure, he was every bit as unctuous and crude as people said. But Alicia had a soft spot for the brute. He was always there when she needed him and now she needed him in a very specific way.

"So, what happened?" Fred asked.

He lowered himself onto the bed. Alicia envisioned herself being flung across the room.

"By the way, you look terrible," he told her.

"You should've seen me yesterday," she said. "I couldn't open my eyes. My entire face was swollen."

She explained the situation.

Two nights before, as Alicia walked through La Fontanella, she spotted a handsome, dark-haired man dining alone. She gave him a smile. In a flash, the man was up on his feet, hurling a fistful of something directly into her face. Alicia crumpled in agony and was rushed to the hospital.

The papers said the substance was pepper, and that Edmund had thrown it, but neither were true. The man was a stranger and, according to doctors, he'd thrown Mace.

Thanks to Edmund, Alicia was accustomed to light harassment, but this was a different case. In the past few months, she and Novella had suffered five break-ins, when there'd been none in the five previous years. Phone lines clicked, doorbells rang, and suspicious cars idled outside. One van advertised television repairs, but when Alicia tried to call, the number was out of service.

"Mobsters!" Nova said, a smidge gleefully for Alicia's taste. "You have mobsters!"

Nova was dramatic and Alicia didn't necessarily agree, but something was amiss.

"It's possible that I'm paranoid," she told Fred. "But at this point, I'm relieved to stay here for observation. Someone's following me. I'm absolutely sure of it."

"Following you?" Fred said, and narrowed his eyes.

"It might be the Kennedys," she whispered. "I'm sure you think I'm a loon, but I had this visit a while ago . . ."

"Alicia . . ."

"I know, I know, it's probably in my imagination. Not enough going on in Rome these days. Jack is the *president-elect*. Why would the Kennedys ever bother with me? Thank you, Fred, I feel loads better."

"You're exactly right," Fred said, nodding vigorously. "It's them."

"What!?" She choked. "Are you sure, or are you just guessing?"

Her eyes began to sting, or maybe it was the Mace.

"I'm sure," Fred confirmed. "I've overheard some stuff. Lawford's been paying me to surveil his wife. He's convinced Pat is having an affair."

"Peter Lawford is worried about his *wife* running around?" Alicia said. "Good grief, he's lucky she's not surveilling *him*."

"Oh, she is."

"Jesus Christ," she muttered. "Why are they wasting time with me? Shouldn't Jack be preparing his cabinet? Figuring out what to do when he finally takes office? This is all so petty."

"The Kennedys are petty as hell. They're also assholes."

"They're not that bad."

"Why do you think I flew halfway across the globe to talk to you?" he asked.

"Because I asked you to, and you enjoy my company?"

Also, Novella was convinced that Fred had the hots for her.

"I enjoy your company sometimes," he said. "But I'm here because you called, and we can't talk on the phone. You're being bugged. I suggest you negotiate an agreement."

"An agreement? What do you mean?"

She scooted up in the bed.

"Say you'll keep your mouth closed, if they pay up."

"Fred!" she yelped. "I couldn't do that to Jack. Never in a million years."

"Don't you want them off your ass?"

"Wouldn't blackmailing them put me in more danger?"

"I don't *think* they'd have you killed, if that's what you're asking."

"They wouldn't resort to that," she said. "The family is obnoxiously ambitious, sure, but they're not frightening. Well, Rose Kennedy is scary. I've never met anyone that cold, not even in Germany. But they'd never do anything to risk a lawsuit, or jail."

"You know Joe Kennedy started as a bootlegger, right?"

"Say what you will, but the man has a good nose for business."

"And they bought the election for Jack."

"Bought the election?" Alicia laughed. "That's preposterous. Jack wouldn't need to buy votes! Women probably lined up for blocks just for the chance to ogle his name."

"Don't you find it strange that he won by the narrowest possible margin? Isn't it peculiar that he got Texas of all places? They despise Kennedy there."

"Lyndon Johnson is from Texas. That's probably the reason Jack picked him as a running mate."

"Wake up, Alicia," he said. "Joe Kennedy hired Sam Giancana, Chicago Mafia boss, to make sure Jack won. Giancana knows all the union leaders and spread Papa Joe's millions among his underworld to produce votes. They stuffed the ballot boxes in Illinois *and* in Texas, and probably a few other places for kicks. The Kennedys are so tight with the Mafia, they're basically mobsters themselves."

"Have you been talking to Novella? She thinks the Kennedys have 'given us mobsters,' as if they're fleas." Alicia sighed, and studied her hands. "What are they so concerned about?" She looked up. "Is it still the affair with Jack? Because I haven't gone public."

"They think you're waiting until he takes office, and it's stressing them out."

"Just tell them I won't blackmail Jack, or anyone else in that family. What can they do if I don't say anything?"

"What can they do?" Fred scoffed. "Have you noticed that the president-elect hasn't nominated the attorney general yet?"

"Presidential appointments are not something I've kept up on," Alicia said, though this was not entirely true.

"He's hesitating because he knows the press will explode when it's Bobby."

"That can't be right," she said. "How can Jack have an attorney general who's never practiced law, who's never seen the inside of a courtroom?"

"It's a fuckin' joke," Fred agreed. "But it's happening all the same. Not sure if you're up on the details, but the attorney general is in charge of the FBI, and in charge of who gets into the country, and who's kept out."

"Shit . . ."

"Yup. There's one person who can revoke a reentry permit for no reason, and it's the AG of the U.S. Something tells me he'll keep you out."

Alicia didn't know what to say. She lowered her gaze and stared again at her bony, white hands. Fred scooted closer.

"They're ruthless. They got into bed with Giancana, a man who hangs people on meat hooks. They're also super fucking ambitious and super fucking paranoid. A chilling combination." Fred cleared his throat. "You should know, Alicia, that they think you've given birth to Jack's child. They believe you popped out some bastard baby over the summer, and put it up for adoption. Gave it to a friend or some shit."

"That's not true," Alicia said, face tingling as the blood drained from it.

"I didn't think so." Fred nodded, and the whole bed shook. "You told me years ago you couldn't have kids. Plus, if you hadn't gotten yourself knocked up by now . . . Everyone knows Jack never uses a condom and I confirmed that you've never visited any of the three doctors the Hollywood girls use."

"You checked to see if I had an abortion?"

"I'm very thorough."

"Well, they're wrong," Alicia said, shaking her head. "I didn't put her up for adoption."

"*Her?*" Fred's mouth dropped. He drooled a little on his shirt. "What the fuck are you talking about, *her?*"

"There is a baby," Alicia said, starting to weep. "And she is Jack's. Novella helps take care of her, but she is all mine."

Her name was Benedetta Maria Kopczynska.

She was born on the sixth of August, in the morning, after a brief labor supervised by Novella.

"You must give zee correct drugs!" she demanded, bracing against Alicia's screams. "Zis is a crime what you do to her!"

Kate couldn't be there. She wanted to but was busy working in Connecticut, where she was depicting the Queen of Egypt onstage.

"Another jam for Alicia Darr!" she said, but sent Alicia a gift nonetheless.

Five thousand dollars, in hard cash.

Benny was born gorgeous, but Alicia expected nothing less. Her head was perfectly round, almost cartoonishly so. Atop this glorious head was a spray of black hair. She had Jack Kennedy's eyes. It was both poetic and heartbreaking that the sole man Alicia found to love was the one man who could get her pregnant. Rather, the second man, if the soldier at the camp counted. But it was the aftermath of that pregnancy, and Alicia's attempt to end it, that made childbearing a lost cause. Or so she'd been told.

The three left the hospital together—Novella, Alicia, and Benny, too. It was an odd sort of family, but for the first time since those days with Jack in Hyannis Port, Alicia was hopeful, filled with wonder. It was true what they said about motherhood. One glance and she loved that baby with every cell.

The women walked down Margutta with their new prize, Alicia so overcome she couldn't feel the pain from the labor she'd endured. She swelled with joyful tears as they chatted, hatching big plans for this brand-new girl.

As they approached the studio, Alicia spotted something peculiar on their doorstep. They shuffled a few steps closer and that's when Alicia saw what'd been left. Two dead cats. A mother and a kitten, gutted and lying side by side.

She cried out, and threw up in a nearby pot.

"Do you think they'll hurt my baby?" Alicia said, once they were in the apartment, the locks all latched.

"Until we escape mobsters," Novella said, "we tell zat Benny is mine."

"We'll say that Benny is *yours*?" Alicia gasped, horrified.

"Is gud plan," Nova said with a definitive nod. "Keep her safe."

"No," Alicia said, though she understood that was exactly what they had to do.

Alicia loved Benny fully and from the start and would do anything to keep her safe. But for all the heartbreak that came with Novella's idea, the anguish was doubled because Alicia couldn't help but think of her parents. She couldn't help but *feel* them, through the wide swath of time and place. In Alicia's mind, it'd been Father who saved her. She never gave Mamusia credit for the pain she must've suffered when she let her daughter go.

"Oh, Mamusia," she whispered into the Roman sky. "I wish I'd done a better job loving you."

Within hours, the women worked out the details. Soon, Nova announced her pregnancy, the father's name withheld.

"I will never marry in Italy until it's legal to divorce!" she said, always a flair for the dramatic.

Over the next few months, Novella invited reporters to the studio, to photograph her knitting baby booties, in case doubters needed proof.

"Where's your roommate? That painter?"

"She's off with another of her princes. You know . . ."

Meanwhile, Alicia sat in the water closet, nursing Benny.

They kept the baby mostly indoors. If they wished to leave the studio while Nova was still "pregnant," they hid Benny in a pram full of kittens. Neighbors were long since accustomed to seeing Novella Palmisano push a cartful of cats around, so no one looked twice.

As the plot played out, Alicia was careful with her emotions. She didn't want to love Benny with too much force, but she couldn't help but fall. A person! She'd created a human being! The power and responsibility scared Alicia, and her sleep worsened by the day.

How come no one ever told her about this? About the awful intensity of this sort of love? No wonder Kate never wanted children. What a fierce, consuming situation to bring upon yourself. It was all too painful, too brilliant to bear.

Fred left Rome the next day, and Alicia returned home two days after that, under strict instructions to wear sunglasses for the next four months.

Nova was cuddling Benny when Alicia walked in. She called out her daughter's name, but for the first time, the baby did not look up at the sound of her voice. Alicia's heart cratered, but what had she expected, having been gone for days?

Alicia realized she needed to get Benny back. They'd been living this charade for months now, and nothing had changed. Alicia was still being followed. She'd been assaulted in a well-lit restaurant, in front of dozens of patrons, and the man hadn't been caught.

"I suggest you negotiate an agreement," Fred told her. "You'll get money, and they'll get peace of mind. Everybody wins. And remember, although he'll be president, you're the one with power."

Well past midnight, Alicia was lying in bed debating these things when she heard a rustling outside. Because her defenses were down, and she was worn to the point of pain, Alicia threw on a mink and went outside. She crept around to the alley. Near the window outside her bedroom, Alicia found a man rummaging through their trash.

He paused, and made a quarter turn. Alicia drew in a sharp breath. It was him, the man from La Fontanella. He gave her a menacing glower, then cocked back, as if loading before a pounce.

In that moment, Alicia was surprised to find she wasn't scared. Her heart was beating at a reasonable pace.

"I'm not afraid of you," she said.

Alicia lifted her shoulders. She used Fred's words to fortify her courage.

"You can't hurt me," she said. "I'm the one with the power. I've been quiet, minding my own business, but you've forced me out of my shell. Tell Jack that I need to speak to him. Before it's too late."

NEW YORK

They'd arranged to meet at one o'clock, Le Pavillon.

Alicia chose a corner table, seated with her back toward the mirrored wall. She watched as the front door opened and closed. When someone of Jack's build darkened the doorway, Alicia lifted her chin in anticipation, her insides a tangle of nerves.

When she spotted a familiar face that wasn't Jack's, Alicia's first thought was *Of all the luck.* This was a favored Kennedy haunt but she hadn't expected anyone else, especially not Bobby, shifty and ratlike as always. Alicia considered sliding under the table as he cut a path in her direction.

"Hello, Madam Purdom."

He tossed his briefcase onto the floor and sat.

Alicia narrowed her eyes. *Madam,* he'd said, not *madame.* She did not miss the innuendo. He'd blame it on his clunky accent, but she knew better. Bobby missed no opportunity to call her a whore.

"Hello," she replied coolly, and extended a hand.

Perhaps Jack sent his brother in to clear out the room. The

president-elect couldn't take any chances, being weeks from his in-auguration.

"What is it I should be calling you these days, Mr. Attorney General?" Alicia said, as her eyes bounced about. "Congratulations on your most unexpected appointment. We heard about it in Rome."

"I wouldn't call it 'unexpected,' " he grumbled.

"Really?" Alicia returned her attention to the table. "Everyone else did."

A waiter darted over. He plunked down two glasses and filled them with Alicia's favorite white burgundy, Château de Puligny-Montrachet.

"Nothing for me," Bobby said.

"I'll have the shrimp," Alicia said, though she was not hungry.

"Shrimp" was his longtime nickname, an inside joke among his siblings, and appropriate since he was such a dirty, writhing arthropod. Alicia wanted to remind him that she was once privy to familial intimacies, thus wasn't the two-bit slut he claimed.

"You look well," Bobby said, without actually looking at her.

"Thank you," she said. "I *feel* well."

Alicia ran her fingers along the beveled grooves of the Baccarat glass.

"You look the same," she added.

This was true, though not a compliment necessarily. Those beady blue eyes, the angry, gnawing teeth. In the ten years she'd known Bobby, Alicia's view had not changed a speck. Lyndon Johnson called him a "little fart" and she couldn't agree more.

"When does your brother arrive?" she asked.

"My brother?" he said, reaching around by his feet.

He whomped the suitcase on the table.

"You thought Jack would be here? Sorry, but ridding himself of old hassles is at the bottom of the president's priority list. To that end." Bobby tapped the suitcase. "Five hundred."

"Five hundred *what*?" Alicia said, wondering if it was possible Jack really wouldn't come see her that day.

"Five hundred thousand dollars," Bobby said, exasperated.

"I really need to speak with Jack."

"Five hundred is more than fair and is also all I'm authorized to offer. You wouldn't get more out of him."

Alicia's stomach coiled. It was both an ungodly sum and somehow not enough. She needed the money, but money wasn't why she came. Though her request to see him was mildly threatening, Alicia hadn't planned to ask for a cent. She simply wanted to see Jack, and tell him about Benny, before he was swallowed up by the world.

"I don't want your money," she said, mouth dry. "I want Jack."

So. This was what her life and a decade-long relationship had been reduced to: a suitcase of money. Alicia thought to the days when a suitcase was all she had, when she carried it off the bus in Hyannis Port, hoping her life would change but never picturing in this particular way.

"Is this not what you wanted?" Bobby asked.

It was, and it wasn't. What she truly wanted could not be had, yet Alicia took a second to contemplate his offer. She thought about the checks she'd bounced in Rome, and in Switzerland. Police visited the studio last week.

"Any hooker in town would be thrilled with a fraction of this amount."

"I'm not a prostitute," she seethed.

"Hmmm, well, I do know that you're a woman who can be bought."

"No," Alicia said. "I don't want your money. Not a penny of it."

Her jaw was set in steely resolve, but Alicia's insides quivered. Jack was paying her off, like one of the mobsters who fixed his election. The soon-to-be most powerful man in the world deemed her complicity worth a fortune. Yet, it was the very specificity of the price tag that made her feel worthless.

"I don't want it," she repeated, as much to herself as to him.

"Don't you *need* the money?" Bobby asked, sweat collecting at his hairline. "From what I hear, you're flat broke."

"You've heard wrong."

Alicia wrapped her fur tighter. It was far too warm in the restaurant to keep it on, but she was trying to make a point.

"Look here, Mrs. Purdom—"

"Enough of the 'Mrs. Purdom' nonsense," Alicia said. "I'm getting divorced."

"I don't care about your personal life. Are you gonna take the money or not?"

"I will not," she said.

Alicia stood. She tucked her crocodile purse beneath her arm.

"You are welcome to pay for my meal and the wine, however," she said.

Alicia's nose tightened. Tears prickled.

"Give my best to your family," she said. "And send your brother my sincerest congratulations. He will do great things for this country."

"And where are you off to now? Planning to raise more hell?"

She gave a watery smile.

"I'm not planning on it," she said. "Though, I guess, one never knows."

"Where are you *going*?" he asked again.

"To my hotel. And after that, probably Rome."

"In other words, you'll continue to be a problem for us."

"A problem?" She shrugged. "That depends on your definition. But don't worry about me. I'll make my way, somehow. Surviving is what I do best."

"I'm sorry I haven't taken the test," Serena Palmisano says as she walks into Leonard's study.

She assumes this is why Leonard's summoned her to his home. He's complained enough about wanting to return to New York, and that her indecision is holding him up.

"Who let you in?" Leonard asks.

He is confounded. No one gave him any warning and though he'd asked Serena to stop by, he did not expect her to show up so early. Lee follows closely behind. He's wearing jeans and a button-down shirt, untucked.

"The man . . ." she says. "With the hair?"

Serena acts like she's brushing something off her shoulders.

"He let us in."

Ah, his would-be son-in-law. He is not Leonard's favorite, but it's nice to know he is capable of waking up before ten o'clock.

"Well, you're here," he says, unnecessarily. "Let's talk."

As Leonard sits, he remembers that he's wearing sweatpants.

There'd been plans to try a yoga class but he chickened out, after googling the poses. Yoga is supposed to be relaxing, but what is so relaxing about standing on one's head?

"The reason I did not take the test," Serena says, though he's not asked, "is that I currently lack the . . ." She looks at Lee. "The guts. Novella—my *nonna*—was my life. I don't want to change my past."

"I understand completely," Leonard says.

He should've given this girl credit, for valuing her history over a pile of cash.

"No one can force you," he adds.

Serena's thick lashes flutter. Lee fiddles with a thread on his shirt.

"Take the test, or don't," Leonard says. "It really makes no difference to me."

"But . . . is that not why you asked us over?" she says with a squint. "To complain that I haven't taken it?"

"No, actually. I called because another matter has come to light."

Leonard ponders how he might address this prickly topic. He could give her the letter, to read for herself, but that feels like a sneak attack.

"Listen," he says. "How much do you know about Alicia's romantic past?"

"She was never short of lovers," Serena answers. "I know that."

"We've spent hours combing through old newspapers," the boy pipes in. "From the scrapbook, and things we've found online."

"How far have you gotten?" Leonard asks. "All the way up to her death?"

"No, not that far," the boy says. "There are thousands of articles mentioning her name, or *names*. Barbara. Alicia. Alic-ja with a *j*. Alice. And her last names: Kopczynska and Darr and Purdom and Clark and Corning Clark and Gay. Twenty-four different combinations we've found, so far."

"The early 1960s or so," Serena says, answering the question her boyfriend cannot. "That's where we are."

"So, you did not see the news from 1977?"

Serena makes a face.

"What happened in 1977?"

"Have you ever heard of the Freedom of Information Act?"

She shakes her head.

"It allows government documents to be declassified," Lee says before Leonard has the chance. "After enough time has passed, certain information is made public."

"That's the gist," Leonard says.

He swivels toward the walnut credenza behind him and lifts a piece of paper from its gleaming, polished top.

"In 1977, J. Edgar Hoover's files were declassified," he says. "The man had a thing for JFK."

A hard-on for the guy is what Leonard is thinking, but will not say in this company.

"Hoover had been in charge of the FBI for thirty years by the time JFK took office," Leonard continues. "He started a file on John Kennedy in 1941, and on Joe Kennedy much earlier. This is an article that discusses the more titillating aspects of his files."

Leonard slides the paper toward Serena. It's an article from *The New York Times*.

"Kennedy's file was thick," Leonard says. "Most of the documents were threats made against the president, or letters from outraged citizens accusing him of treason, or being a pawn of the pope. The files also discuss his link to mob boss Sam Giancana, as well as the mob doll Judith Campbell Exner. You probably know this. Kennedy's dalliance with her has been highly documented."

"It has?" Serena says.

"Yes, but there are other revelations," Leonard says. "Please, why don't you take a minute."

Serena regards the article, from late 1977.

F.B.I. FILES DISCLOSE LETTER ON KENNEDY

WASHINGTON, Dec.14—J. Edgar Hoover told Attorney General Robert F. Kennedy in 1963 that the Federal Bureau of Investigation had information that Mr. Kennedy had paid a $500,000 settlement and had had court records sealed in a lawsuit brought by a woman who said she had been engaged to marry his brother, John F. Kennedy, in 1951.

"Why am I looking at this?" Serena asks.

"Keep reading," Leonard says.

Her eyes move down the page. In 1963, Hoover wrote to Bobby Kennedy, informing him that he was aware of the payoff, and that it'd been settled "out of court for $500,000," just prior to the president assuming office. The journalist notes that the letter could be taken as friendly, loyal, ingratiating, or as "veiled blackmail."

"I still don't see . . ." Serena starts, and then a name leaps out.

Alicia Purdom, the wife of actor Edmund Purdom . . .

Serena glances up.

"Alicia blackmailed the president of the United States?" she says.

"According to Hoover, she did," Leonard answers.

Lee pulls the paper from Serena's hands.

"This gets better and better," he mutters, scanning the article. "I don't understand. The supposed five hundred thousand was paid in 1961, but the affair was ten years earlier, before JFK was president, or even married?"

"This talks about an interview she did with an Italian magazine," Serena says. "Perhaps they were angry about that?"

"They were," Leonard says. "But the article was written *after* Jack's inauguration, and therefore after the alleged blackmail. I have another document that might provide some answers."

He rolls back in his chair and pulls a light blue envelope from a drawer. The letter is addressed in elegant handwriting, written out to a person called Andrew Quigley. There is no postmark.

"This letter was found in Alicia's bedroom, after she died," Leonard says. "She never sent it."

"It'd been sitting there, unmailed, for nearly forty years?" Lee asks.

"It appears that way."

Leonard gives the letter to Serena. Her hands are trembling.

"Andrew Quigley was a friend of Alicia's," Leonard says, "and also of JFK's. In the letter, Alicia is trying to explain herself, and refute the information from the Hoover files. She admits that she met with Bobby, but insists she did not take a bribe." He nods toward the envelope. "It's all right there."

Serena's mouth is suddenly tacky. According to this document, Alicia Corning Clark had a baby in 1960—John F. Kennedy's baby. But more alarming than the speculated paternity of the child is the baby's name, and her date of birth, which both belong to Serena's mom.

"You might be JFK's *granddaughter*?" Lee shouts in disbelief.

His voice echoes off the walls and Spanish tile floors. Leonard sighs. Finally, these two are getting it.

"But the article says nothing about a baby," Serena sputters.

It's not possible. She cannot be an orphan and also related to one of the most famous families in the known world. How can a person be Italian yet so utterly American at the same time?

"You're correct about the article," Leonard says. "But she is quite unwavering in her letter."

"Maybe she's making it up? I know she relished the spotlight."

"She did like fame." Leonard ruminates on this. "But I always got the sense it was a yearning for something else. She seemed happiest at her estate in the Bahamas, where she was alone, unbothered, not chasing one thing, or running from another."

"Plus, the article says," Lee butts in, "that 'Mrs. Alicia Corning Clark of Manhattan could not be reached for comment today.' If she was trying to get attention, I'm sure she would've taken an interview."

"Yes," Serena says, dazed, "I thought she was always able to be reached for comment."

"Serena?" Lee says, puppy eyes wide. "Do you know what this could mean?"

"No, no, no." Serena flaps her hands around. "This is Alicia craziness. We can't be so quick to take her word."

"Perhaps," Leonard concedes. "But any devil's advocate should also ask if it might be true. Last night, I found an interview with Edmund Purdom, conducted shortly before his death. He said that Alicia had been pregnant with JFK's child, and that he used this information against her in their divorce."

"I got the impression that Edmund Purdom was vindictive," Serena says.

"Alicia certainly thought so. However, he gave this interview in 2009. It's hard to imagine he'd still be angry half a century after their divorce. Mrs. Corning Clark told others this same story, over the years. She told the various employees of her building, like the doorman, bellman, and lift operator. She even told me."

"She told you?" Lee balks. "And you haven't mentioned this?"

"It was when she was very ill," Leonard says, blushing in spite of himself. "I thought she was delirious."

They are all quiet for two, three minutes.

"We did see that article." The boy nudges Serena. "Where she mentions your mom?"

She nods and reads the rest of the letter, tears welling. Leonard squirms with discomfort. Serena's eyes are almost completely clouded over by the time she reaches the last line:

And that is what happened to my baby girl.

Serena sets the paper on her lap, tears dripping down her cheeks and onto her chin. Lee gently rubs her back. *This is heartbreaking, if what Alicia wrote is true*, Serena thinks.

"Where is this Andrew Quigley now?" Lee asks. "Can we talk to him?"

"He's been dead twenty-six years," Leonard says.

"Damn." Lee shakes his head. "That would've been useful."

"I can see if the building employees are willing to speak?"

"No," Serena says, her gaze like glass. "We don't need the bellman, or the lift operator, or Andrew Quigley's ghost. We don't need any of these people." She looks up. "There's one way to know for sure, and we can do it on our own."

Alicia Purdom avrebbe dovuto sposare John Kennedy, il nuovo presidente degli Stati Uniti.

Le Ore, February 1961

ROME

One more night in New York was all it took.

Taps on the door. Scratching on the windows. Floorboards creaking all night long. Around midnight, room service delivered an elaborate feast that Alicia never ordered.

"Are you certain, *madame*? It's been prepared especially for you."

She booked the next flight out of town.

"They'll never let you back in the country now!" Kate cried.

This was probably true, but Alicia preferred to live in Italy than to die on American soil.

"Smart," Fred said, "very smart. Not that they can't follow you to Rome—more dead cats and whatnot—but in New York, you're a sitting duck. Damn, Alicia, you really should've taken the money."

"My pride is bigger than my fear, it seems," she'd replied.

Bigger than her financial anguish, too.

Alicia spent the flight to Europe anxious, just south of sick. Although excitement to see Benny could account for this in part, the feeling had an edge to it, the gnawing sense of regret. Had she accepted the bribe, it would've solved so much. Now she returned to Rome, still poor, still in danger, and feeling worse about Jack.

"*Il giornale?*" another passenger offered, when they were somewhere over Greenland.

The woman had finished an issue of *Le Ore* and detected that the saucer-eyed girl beside her was desperate for distraction. Alicia smiled, grateful for the gift, and the chance to catch up on Italy's latest political and cultural debacles. As she turned the pages and beheld the faces of the risen, fallen, and aggrieved, Alicia heard Kate's voice.

You have something worth more than cash . . . you have a fabulous story.

Maybe she could have both. An interview would offer her the two things she needed most: money *and* protection. The Kennedys were worried about Alicia going public, but she could do it kindly, giving Jack nothing but praise. They'd have to leave her alone after that. Their names would be permanently linked.

At the Rome airport, Alicia found a pay phone and rang *Le Ore*. They were game for the story, and everything fell into place. Alicia cashed her check and paid her bills. She stayed up all night before the issue's release.

When she heard the slap of the magazine on the studio's front steps, Alicia raced outside. Robe on and hair tousled, she plopped down in the courtyard to read. They'd given her a multipage spread.

Alicia Purdom ha svelata di essere stata il primo amore di John Kennedy.

Alicia Purdom has revealed that she was the first love of John Kennedy.

Alicia smiled through the first few lines, and the details about how they met. The writer exaggerated at times, asserting that she might've been "*la prima signora d'America*" if not for her Polish-Jewish roots, but Alicia didn't mind.

Then, she flipped the page, and was struck with horror upon seeing Edmund's name. They'd interviewed him, too.

To his credit, the writer called Edmund "an unbelievable actor who assumed incorrect attitudes in public" and also revealed that he was disrespectful, penniless, and a notorious lover of females young and old. Yet, these things didn't read like an indictment of Edmund, but instead of his nagging wife. Plus, she was herself *"non esente da peccatucci d'infedelta,"* not without her infidelity peccadilloes.

A sentire lei, Alicia, merita la palma del martirio coniugale e l'Oscar della sopportazione.

We hear you, Alicia, you deserve the prize for marriage martyrdom and the Oscar for endurance.

With a sour lump in her throat, Alicia turned another page, to the pictures of her reading Jack's Pulitzer Prize–winning book, *Profiles in Courage.* At the time, Alicia fancied that she came across as sensuous and smart, but in print she was cheesecake all the way.

Reading in the bathtub.

Lying on the bed with her cleavage exposed.

In a girdle, powdering her nose.

Crouched on her knees, in a satin nightie, rear aimed at the camera.

Hot with shame, Alicia slapped the magazine shut, and rushed inside to find Nova. She'd sue the magazine, first thing.

"Novella!" she yelled, barreling through the door. "Wait until you see what they wrote about me!"

Alicia stopped next to Benny, who was on the floor, midcrawl. The girl's face was frozen, aside from a quiver in her bottom lip and her glistening green-gray eyes.

"Is everything all right?" Novella called from the kitchen.

Alicia shook her head, then ran to the bathroom and locked herself in for a good sob. Nova knocked several times, and then went away.

"Oh, is not so bad," she would later claim. "You very sexy. And no one cares of zee silly Italian magazine."

It was a fair point. She'd never known anyone in America to read *Le Ore*, and so Alicia grasped this straw and distracted herself by playing with Benny and counting bank notes. Alas, both women underestimated the international interest in Jack and the intensity of "Jackie Fever." To most, Alicia's story seemed like an unwarranted attack on them both.

"Alicia Purdom Says She Was JFK's Fiancée" was the heading of Walter Winchell's column.

He wrote, "Europe is buzzing and so am I over the interview in a Milan magazine quoting Edmund Purdom's estranged wife, Alicia, as stating she could have been America's First Lady. She was quoted as saying she was engaged to JFK before he married Jacqueline. She blames Joe Kennedy for the break-up. . . ."

"MEMO TO EDMUND PURDOM'S ESTRANGED WIFE: Stop Those Fairy Tales About Your 'Romance' With JFK!" ordered *Confidential* magazine, a publication that'd bought hundreds of stories from Alicia over the years.

Edmund Purdom's wife. They hadn't even used her first name.

Other magazines ran similar "memos," sometimes accompanied by pictures of Alicia looking bedeviled or deranged. One rag called her oversexed and off-colored. Another said she made "Picasso look like a piker in the art of purposeful distortion."

"Her poor painting is rivaled only by her poor taste."

"Stay away from this country for good!"

Alicia was heartbroken, bruised with each new insult.

"You can't worry about what people print," Kate advised. "How many times have they crowned me the 'Most Uncooperative Actress of the Year'?"

"Much better to be difficult than oversexed and of poor taste," Alicia replied.

It wasn't merely her reputation that was decimated, but also her career. Within weeks, columnists and magazines refused to take her leaks. They scarcely deigned to cover her antics at all. If someone did bring her up—Hollywood was slow that week—it was only to diminish her further.

"That uninhibited little blonde."

"The little Mittel-European blonde."

Little, blond, barely European. She was left with these scant things.

After the *Le Ore* firestorm died down, the press would never again connect Alicia with Jack, never again mention him among her illustrious loves. But they always put his name close to hers, as if to tease.

"Such loot at El Morocco: Bobo Rockefeller, Bob Hope, Alicia Purdom, and JFK's brother Ted Kennedy," wrote Earl Wilson.

Alicia hadn't known "Ted" was in the room.

"Bobby Kennedy's power-scheme has him backing the 'reform' candidate for N.Y. . . . Alicia Purdom Clark and actor James Fox Have It Bad and that's good," The Voice of Broadway's Jack O'Brian alleged.

Jack's sisters were likewise part of the game:

"President Kennedy's sisters, Eunice Shriver, wife of the Peace Corps director, and Jean Smith, whose husband works in the State Department, will leave Washington Sunday for a European vacation that includes a trip to Poland, Yugoslavia and the Riviera. Alicia Darr filed for divorce in Juarez, Mexico, from British actor Edmund Purdom," said the *Star-Tribune*.

Sometimes these mentions and near-connections felt like the only proof that Alicia hadn't imagined it all, like Cholly and Hedda and Harrison and so many others said.

The *Le Ore* interview solved a few problems, for a time, but the money didn't last and neither did it come close to filling that scooped-out part of Alicia's soul. All that and Benny, her *daughter,* seemed to share the sentiments of the American press. She screamed whenever Alicia got near.

Stay away from this country for good!

"She is fussy *bambina,*" Nova insisted. "Very demanding. Cries, cries, cries. It is not you."

Novella was kind but Alicia saw quite plainly that Benny always cooed in Nova's arms, suddenly the least demanding creature on earth. She was a different baby than the one Alicia left a month ago and didn't feel like hers anymore. It was almost as though this tiny, sweet girl was trying to prove the same point as everyone else.

You see? Nothing important happened between you and Jack. It was all in your mind.

NEW YORK

In early July, as a blanket of damp heat settled across southern Italy, Alicia was in New York to finalize her divorce and also because things were boiling over in Rome in ways unrelated to temperature.

She'd been arrested twice for passing bad checks and there were rumors of more warrants issued. At least the police—not the Kennedys—were trailing her this time, but this didn't compel Novella to release Benny into her care.

"Zings are too unstable," she said. "Not good for *bambina*."

Alicia wondered how she'd ended up in a custody dispute with her closest friend. On the other hand, Novella was not wrong.

When Alicia landed in New York, immigration authorities waved her through, no problem, which wasn't the relief she expected. It only confirmed how inconsequential she was to Jack.

But then, on her third day in the city, Alicia had the sense of being followed, this time by a woman. When she spotted her well-dressed tail slip into a bathroom stall at El Morocco, she kicked open the door to confront the dark-haired woman crouched atop the toilet seat.

"You're following me," Alicia said. "And I'd like to know why."

"Thank God." The woman hopped down.

She extended a hand.

"Jean Sinclair Clark," she said.

"Okay . . ." Alicia reciprocated the handshake. "So, you *have* been trailing me. By the way, you're much prettier up close."

Indeed, if someone said Jean Sinclair Clark was Elizabeth Taylor's chubbier older sister, Alicia would've bought it. She had a certain sweetness, helped by her round cheeks and the endearing pinprick mole beside her right eye.

"Why thank you!" Jean giggled, her laugh like a handbell. "And, yes, I've been following you. Guilty as charged! I'm not very skilled at clandestine activities, I'm afraid."

"No. You're not. Who sent you? Bobby? Jack?"

Jean screwed up her face.

"No," she said. "My ex-husband, Alfred Corning Clark."

Alicia stared blankly. Was this one of Jack's henchmen? Another hanger-on?

"You met him on a recent overseas voyage?" Jean tried. "He's a stately man? Midforties?"

Alicia nodded absently, for first class on any ship was primarily comprised of such types.

"I see you don't remember," Jean said. "But for him, it was love at first sight! He's been positively lovesick, a fever he can't quell. When he heard you were in New York, Al was intent on tracking you down. I offered to help, lest he be mistaken for a prowler or a Peeping Tom."

"You're assisting your *ex*-husband in finding a date?"

"We're on very good terms, always have been. Probably too good, given that during our marriage we were more friends than lovers!" She giggled again. "I stuck with it for the balls and luncheons and

Yves St. Laurent. I must've chaired a hundred events in my day. Child Cancer Fund, Arthritis and Rheumatism Foundation, the National Association of Retarded Children."

"Of course," Alicia muttered, still perplexed.

"And Polo for Polio! I could go on and on, and according to Alfred I often do! I adore being in charge of so many people, and you can't beat the weight loss. Stress is better than a shot in the rear, I'll tell you what."

Alicia blinked, unsure what to make of this woman and her do-gooding, status-seeking, and propensity to overshare.

"Also," Jean prattled on, "Alfred didn't want more children. Step-mother was the perfect role for me! Kids without the hassle of actual mothering. Just ship 'em off to Mum when they get to be too much!"

"What did Alfred get out of all this?" Alicia could not help but ask.

"The usual." Jean wiggled her brows. "Also, a reputation for philanthropy. Before that, he was a rich-wastrel type. Anyhow. Might I play matchmaker? It'd be such an honor!"

She clapped. Meanwhile, the bathroom attendant stood at strict attention.

"I don't know," Alicia said, wondering if this attendant was being paid by any gossip rags. "I live in Rome and am in the States temporarily, to renew my traveling papers. I'm not a U.S. citizen."

"If you married Alfred, you could be."

Jean winked and Alicia chuckled nervously.

"That's true," she said. "But I've already traveled such a road, to disastrous consequences. Speaking of, I'm also in New York to finalize my divorce."

"Well, hop to it!" Jean said, and snapped. "Rid yourself of the old one, to make room for the new."

"I'm trying. But after agreeing to sign the papers last week, he's skipped town again. I'm rather envious of your friendship with Alfred, and that you have an ex-husband in the first place. I've been trying to get one for years!"

"A testament to your allure, no doubt!" Jean said. "My guess? He doesn't want to let you go."

"Ha!" Alicia scoffed. "I assure you, it's nothing like that. Edmund is doing his best to be an ass, and he is very skilled in that regard."

"Which is why you deserve a gentleman like Alfred. Here." Jean grasped her arm. "I'll tell you all about him."

She dragged Alicia through the bathroom door and to the seating area just outside. Alicia reminded herself to leave a tip for the attendant when they were done.

"The first thing you should know," Jean began, "is that Alfred is heir to the Singer sewing machine fortune. His father started the Baseball Hall of Fame."

Jean went on to describe Alfred's looks, the extent of his fortune, and the particulars of each of his first four wives. Jean was his most recent ex-wife, and had been married to him the longest.

"Wife number three is an interesting case," Jean said, then stopped and laughed, again. "I don't need to tell you that! You know Norma!"

"I do?" Alicia wrinkled her forehead. "I don't recall any Normas. . . ."

"Didn't you burglarize her villa on Capri?"

Alicia startled, jarred to have her Italian life dragged onto American shores. In some ways, these were like two separate existences, happening to two different people at roughly the same time.

"It wasn't a break-in," Alicia stuttered. "I was gathering evidence for my divorce."

She couldn't believe it: Norma Clark. Had Jean not said anything, Alicia never would've put the names together and the revelation might've resulted in an unfortunate surprise if she decided to meet Alfred. Then again, it was Edmund's fault that she was repeatedly forced to commit petty crimes.

"Alfred thought it was hilarious," Jean said. "They were only married for a few months and Norma was awful. Why do you think he bought her that villa, on a craggy, rocky island, on the other side of the world? Have I told you how much he likes to buy gifts? And he has no nose for budgets."

After Jean wrapped up a sell job that rivaled anything ever performed in the hat box at Brown's, Alicia agreed to a date with Alfred Corning Clark. Any misgivings she had about his multiple divorces were overshadowed by the enthusiasm of his very likable fifth wife.

Alfred was everything Jean described. He was attractive, in his way, with dark, slicked hair, and a perpetual five-o'clock shadow. He wore bow ties, and smelled like cinnamon. Jean called him sweet, highly educated, and a stitch spoiled, and Alicia saw nothing to contradict these claims. Alfred worshiped her, and Alicia felt at home with him from the start.

"Beware," Jean said, "he's quick to propose!"

Indeed, after six weeks, Alfred presented Alicia with a ninety-five-thousand-dollar Cartier ring. Alicia said yes. Jean threw a party for them at the Harwyn.

Alicia didn't love Alfred, necessarily, but she didn't *not* love him either. That she might one day feel strongly toward him was not outside the realm of possibility. He had a thousand good qualities, not the least of which was his heart. He'd solve her citizenship problems, too, and even seemed jazzed about the prospect of a baby girl in the house. All these things and he'd be able to give Alicia what no one else could. He paid Edmund Purdom one hundred thousand dollars to go through with the divorce.

Edmund swiped the money as soon as they offered it. His career was sagging and he and Linda Christian planned to marry next month. Good luck to them both, Alicia thought. She didn't know who needed it more.

But once Edmund cashed the check, he resumed his slithery ways. They'd agreed to Juarez, but Edmund changed his mind.

"Mexican divorces aren't recognized in Britain," he alleged.

Plus, he was filming in Italy. How about a Swiss split?

Alicia was willing to undergo any hassle to rid herself of the man, so she flew to Switzerland to spend a week with Edmund, for an "attempted reconciliation," as required by Swiss law. But midway through, authorities came knocking, thanks to the bad checks Alicia had written in St. Moritz last winter. They locked her up for the night and the arrest earned Alicia yet another three-page spread, this time in the Italian gossip magazine *Oggi*.

Edmund bailed her out, using money Alfred wired. Kate sent a rash of admonishing telegrams that Alicia partially skimmed. On the upside, getting arrested was easier the fourth time, especially now that she had Alfred to post her bail.

"I'm glad to know that life with you will never be dull," he said. "But let's make a list of all your creditors and pay them off. There are only so many times I can tell my family that my wife is in jail."

Because of the arrest, Alicia and Edmund's "reconciliation" did not meet Swiss standards. After another dip into Alfred's piggy bank, Edmund finally agreed to Juarez, though he managed to drag what should've taken two days into three solid weeks. Edmund Purdom, the one person capable of making a "quickie divorce" seem long.

But it happened. The decree was signed, four years overdue.

ALICIA DARR TO DIVORCE PURDOM, WED SINGER HEIR.

Alicia wept when the papers were stamped and sealed. She took to her bed, sick with relief. Oh, how she wished she could erase their marriage. If not for Benny, Alicia would've considered these past four years a total waste. But soon she'd marry Alfred and become everything at once: a mother, a millionaire, a citizen of the United States.

Alfred and Alicia wed on the sixteenth of September, at his country home in Cooperstown, near the Baseball Hall of Fame. It was a modest ceremony, a cheerful sprinkle of family and friends. Alicia cried as they traded vows, overwhelmed with gratitude and a hundred other sensations she could not name. Alicia clipped the articles about their wedding, and kept the stories in an envelope, as if she planned to mail them one day.

In the years to follow, Alicia was mostly silent on the topic of

Alfred Corning Clark. When people asked why she never spoke his name, Alicia told them there was nothing to say.

"He was always generous and kind," she'd explain. "Our marriage was a honeymoon, a brief but satisfying dream. What possible dirt could I have on the man? We were only married thirteen days."

The widowed Mrs. Alfred Corning Clark (Alicia Purdom, to you cats) was at the Four Seasons looking like a million which isn't odd considering that she now has $10,000,000 or $20,000,000, as the case may be.

The Smart Set, by Cholly Knickerbocker, December 17, 1961

NEW YORK

Alicia didn't know why she did it.

She didn't know why she nudged the dollar figure upward when the inheritance was immense. It niggled at Alicia for days until she concluded it was this—its sheer size—that led to the gaffe. Anything over a million dollars seemed like funny money, something that couldn't be true.

Plus, the pot was close to $20 million when one included the money she received outright, as well as the various homes, personal effects, and guaranteed annual income for life.

The will went to probate but was never contested, and the day after Thanksgiving, Alicia was officially declared the beneficiary of Alfred's estate. It'd been easier to become a millionaire than to get divorced. Alicia wished it could've been Alfred, not Edmund, who received those four years. But Alfred got less than two weeks.

The butler found his body. He'd gone to check on Al, who'd not yet taken his morning coffee. That's when he discovered the "society millionaire" dead, a victim of natural causes. He was only forty-five. Alicia had been apartment hunting in New York, and heard the news several hours after the fact.

Friends now called her Cinderella, in seriousness and in jest, but they always neglected that the original Cinderella gained a husband instead of lost one. Shouldn't the fairy tale have ended at her wedding? Bride or widow, Alicia came into millions either way, and she would've preferred to have Al around.

It could've gone sideways. He had five ex-wives, after all. But she missed Alfred despite the short time she'd known him. He made her comfortable with who she was and where she wanted to go. She told him everything and he questioned no part of her.

"You've lived ten lives already," he'd said. "It's time for you to be indulged, to have it all."

As a wedding present, Al bought her a home on the beach in the Bahamas. They'd also planned to purchase an apartment on Fifth Avenue, but Alicia pulled the contract after he died.

Now, a week before Christmas, Alicia was throwing a party at the Four Seasons for her friends. It was easier to socialize than it was to stare out the window of the Great Northern Hotel, pondering what might've been. Robert Lowell had written a poem about his friend Al, and she couldn't get it out of her head.

"You were alive. You are dead."

It went that fast, in what felt like one line.

Alicia sat at the head of the table, diamonds dangling from her ears and neck. She watched as her guests tittered and howled. Someone made a joke. Alicia laughed, but her smile felt empty, like she was in a foreign country and didn't know the language. She caught eyes with Jean Sinclair Clark, who offered a wink of solidarity. Jean had been glum, too, now that all of her ex-husbands were dead.

Meanwhile, Alicia's attorney was making his way through Europe, clearing up her old debts. Bobby Kennedy couldn't keep her out of the country now, and once Simon paid her creditors, other countries couldn't put her in jail. It wouldn't be long until she could see Benny. Novella had no reason to withhold the girl now.

Alicia missed Benny's second birthday. Was there a party? What gifts did she receive? Alicia didn't know, because she couldn't ask. Any answer would've been too painful to hear.

She had to get to Rome. Nova was loving, and she was fun, but this arrangement had gone on too long. It was possible—likely—that Benny wouldn't remember Alicia at all. That was the problem of time. "Soon" could be a week, it could be a year or more. Each morning was one day closer to Benny, yet also one day farther away.

"It won't be much longer," Alicia assured herself, though she understood that too many days had passed.

Because while Alicia was desperate to see her little girl, she had the unwavering confidence, the absolute certainty, that Benny wanted for nothing. Benedetta Palmisano lived a lovely Roman childhood, with no worries and no familiarity with sadness or regret.

Wealthy widow Alicia Purdom Clark of the Singer Sewing Machine inheritance is talking on the transatlantic phone to perfume prince Bernard Lanvin. She will fly to Paris next month to meet him.

The Smart Set, by Cholly Knickerbocker, May 27, 1962

NEW YORK

Fred asked to meet at Sardi's.

Alicia debated not going. She was leaving for Europe the next day, and had much to do beforehand. But Fred rarely made social calls, and never in New York. He had something to say, and though the very thought tickled her nerves, Alicia understood she couldn't avoid him. Fred was born to tail.

Alicia strolled into Sardi's at quarter past seven, in gold lamé pants and kid boots, sunglasses on. She found Fred in the corner, smoking and drinking scotch beneath a cartoon portrait of Joan Crawford.

"Hello, darling," Alicia said, and slid into the booth. "How are you?"

"Sunglasses?" He raised his forehead. "At night?"

"I'm trying to be discreet."

"There's nothing discreet about those pants, or the dead animal on your back."

Alicia rolled her eyes, though he could not see them. With a huff, she removed her sunglasses and flung them onto the table. She fluffed her hair.

"Why dontcha take that off and stay awhile?" Fred said, and bobbed his head toward her mink.

Alicia exhaled. She summoned the waiter to take it to the coat check.

"A warm night for chinchilla," Fred noted.

"I've grown accustomed to wearing fur."

"Yeah, no shit."

"Well, what is it?" Alicia asked. "What am I worrying about now?"

"Alicia Darr," he said with a laugh, "I can't tell if you're the best or worst lay ever. If only Alfred lived longer, I could've gotten the real scoop."

"Yes, if only." Alicia glared.

"Are you aware that Purdom is saying that you're still married? Because the Brits don't recognize Mexican divorces?"

"I heard something like that," Alicia said with a sigh. "He just wants more money. Al gave him some last summer to hasten the divorce, but he doesn't get a penny more. He should be paying *me* for the torture I endured."

"Purdom's an issue for you. You realize that, yes?"

"The stuff about my marriage being illegal is nonsense. We anticipated such antics, so in his will, Alfred specifically—"

"This isn't about your dead husband," Fred barked. "It's about you. Purdom's a loose cannon and you must do something about him."

" 'Do something about him'?" She snorted. "In case you haven't noticed, I've spent the last four years trying to 'do something' about Edmund Purdom. We're divorced. He's not my problem anymore."

"He's called the White House three times, dangling threats about 'bombshell' information he has on the president."

"Only three times? Edmund is usually a tad more relentless. Sounds like the prez is getting off easy. Give me a cigarette."

She reached out a palm.

"You don't smoke," Fred said.

"I do now."

As he hesitated, Alicia stuck out her hand with greater insistence. Fred lit a cigarette and passed it her way.

"How many times are you going to piss off the Kennedys before something bad happens?" he asked. "You're only going to stay lucky for so long."

"Yes, my life's been nothing but luck. And 'piss off the Kennedys'? What have I done? Nothing!"

"Except have a baby. The FBI is following you. Did you know that?"

"The FBI?" Alicia said, and blinked hard.

It wasn't the mob, it wasn't a dead cat, but, according to Jack, Hoover wasn't exactly a choirboy.

"The FBI," Fred repeated. "They've alerted the attachés in Paris, and in Rome, that you're on your way."

"But how do they—"

"Forget the feds, this family is ruthless. They've gone to bed with so many wiseguys I'm surprised Hoffa's not knocked up. But now Bobby Kennedy's given up the romance and is straight trying to fuck Hoffa in the ass. That is, when he's not attempting to rid the world of Hoover. These people are not afraid to go after their own government, they're not afraid of the mob."

Alicia inhaled on her cigarette, the smoke hot and rough on the way down.

"I'm shocked Jack has time to think about me," she said, "when he has a country to run. His ratings are in the toilet and he just got all those poor people killed in Cuba. Why would he care about old loves or Edmund Purdom?"

"Sweetie, you wouldn't believe the shit they care about."

Fred leaned over the table, candlelight flickering against his face. He ran a stubby finger along his hairline.

"See this? The hair loss? The goddamned streaks of silver? That's sprung up in the last six weeks, thanks to them."

Fred pulled away and took a swig of scotch, sucking it through his teeth.

"Jack doesn't scare me," Alicia said. "And he's the one calling the shots."

Alicia didn't mean by virtue of his office. Joe had a stroke in December, the same night as her party at the Four Seasons. When Alicia heard the news, she felt a familiar ping of hope. Finally! Jack was free from his father's will! Then she remembered that of all the plans Joe laid out for his son, Jack achieved every goal. He wasn't going to jeopardize that now.

"Jack might not scare you," Fred said. "But he and Bobby have pissed off so many people, they have targets on their backs, and on their big, fat heads. You, my friend, are at the center of it all between the bastard baby—"

"Don't call her that."

"And the fact your phone book could take down half the government."

"My phone book? What's that have to do with anything?"

"Bobby's convinced everyone you ran a whorehouse in Los Angeles."

"Oh my God!" Alicia said, and laughed. "Bobby would say anything to make me look bad."

"I dunno, Alicia. Have you forgotten about your cozy place, way up in the Hollywood Hills? Don Class's bungalow, the cutest cathouse around?"

"Fred," she gasped, eyes welling. "Did you just call me a whore? I thought we were friends. I thought you cared about me."

"Why do you think I'm sitting here right now? Come on, don't play innocent. Everyone knows Don Class is the biggest gigolo in town."

"Lies," Alicia said, between her teeth.

"Did you, or did you not, get paid to go on dates?"

"That's different. We were actresses, and 'starlet companion' was merely a role."

"In other words, you were an escort."

"We didn't have to put out."

"Yeah. I'll bet you girls kept your virtues intact." Fred rolled his eyes. "How many times did you set up Jack's friends and family with one of your roommates? A dozen? Two dozen? More?"

Alicia dropped her chin. Her head throbbed. She wasn't a madam, or a workaday whore for that matter, but she could see how Bobby might paint it as such. It didn't help that her roommates had been so loose.

"Christ," she said.

"People would *kill* for dirt on the Kennedys, literally kill, and the Kennedys would do anything to stop that dirt from coming out. Between Don Class and the baby . . . Do you see where I'm going with this?"

"Should I talk to law enforcement?" Alicia asked. "I don't mind calling. I'm—er—no longer on their radar."

There were no longer warrants for her unpaid bills was what she meant.

"The police?" Fred snickered. "You're cute. Peter Lawford's name is in every goddamned trick book of every whore ever busted by the L.A. *and* N.Y. PDs. Yet, he's never been picked up. Have you ever asked yourself why?"

"What do you suggest, Fred? You seem to be giving me a lot of problems and no answers. Can't you tell whomever it is . . ." She waved a hand. ". . . whatever shifty person you're doing business with, that I just want to live my life, and be left alone? I'd never do anything to hurt Jack. I wish him the best."

"But, you see, you've already proven that you're willing to talk."

"Last year I needed the money," Alicia said. "I don't anymore. And that article was far more damaging to me than it was to him."

"I can't disagree. The problem is, you still have information. And anyone can be bought, or otherwise coerced to spill the beans."

Fred polished off his whisky, his third since Alicia had arrived.

"Here's my suggestion," he said. "Don't go to Rome."

"Don't go to Rome?" she said, raising her voice. "Are you kidding me? I have to get—"

"Shhh!" he said, and smacked his glass on the table. "Keep it the fuck down."

"I'll keep it the fuck down when you start being *helpful*."

"I'd be careful," he said. "Very careful. The word is out that you and Jack were engaged, but if you show up talking about your baby, then you're good as dead."

"Don't you think that's a stitch dramatic?"

"Nope. You're good as dead. And so is she."

Alicia Corning Clark, once married to Edmund Purdom before she was briefly wed to the late sewing machine heir, wants to adopt Benedetta, the small daughter of the Italian artist Novella Palmisano, in Rome, where she's recently resumed residence.

Keeping Up with Hollywood, by Louella Parsons, October 4, 1962

ROME

In Paris, Alicia rented a full floor at the Lancaster and dined, traveled, and sunbathed through the summer. She dated heirs, and painted gardens, and said yes to everything at Givenchy. Her days were glorious, her nights passionate, but mostly Alicia was passing time until she could return to Rome.

In mid-September her lawyer called. The time had come.

"You are permitted to travel worldwide," he said. "No more risk of arrest."

Just like that, Alicia was free, liberated from her old debts and past mistakes, even her biggest mistake, Edmund Purdom. He'd married Linda Christian several months before.

"That's the nicest thing he could have done for me," Alicia told the papers.

Now, Alicia was in Rome, in a suite at the Excelsior Hotel. She'd spent the past three days decorating for Benny, assisted by the hotel's chief concierge.

"Why are you wasting time?" Nova asked over the phone. "*Bambina* does not need zee fancy zings."

"A few more days," Alicia said, "and I'll be ready."

She was racked with nerves, positively riddled with jumps and jitters. It'd been so long since she'd seen Benny. Would the girl remember her? Would she willingly fall into Alicia's arms?

There was another hesitation, too. Alicia didn't think she was being followed—there'd been no signs, no strange vans, no hairs lifting on her neck—but Fred's words were ominous and his information a very faithful definition of "inside." He had bugs in multiple Kennedy homes.

Alas, the world had changed since their spring meeting at Sardi's. Soviet missiles were parked in Cuba, China was developing an atomic device, and, on a landing strip between East and West Berlin, Allied planes sat, armed with nukes. Potential world collapse was a much scarier prospect than a supposed madam and her love child. Alicia decided: she couldn't hesitate a second later. Too much time had passed.

With a fluttering heart, she dressed in a shirred-waist, sleeveless wool shift and a pair of knee-high cavalry boots. After throwing on a suede trench and fox stole, she ventured down to the lobby and then past the bright pink chrysanthemums outside the Excelsior's polished brass doors.

Via Veneto was lively that time of night—ten o'clock—and Alicia could hear the revelers long after the clubs and restaurants disappeared from sight. She wondered what it was like these days, without Novella holding court.

She wound her way toward Margutta, the crowd thinning as she went. Looping around a corner, Alicia heard footsteps but found nothing behind her but the dark, chilled night. She picked up her pace. Margutta sat dead ahead.

Again, footsteps. She whipped back, this time to see a large figure move into an alley. Her heart raced. No. This couldn't be, not seconds from Benny. She broke into a light jog, wishing she'd taken time to develop an exercise regime. Apparently, Jackie Kennedy bounced on a trampoline, up to three hours per day.

With no other choice, Alicia rushed past the turn to Margutta and leapt through the front door of the first café she reached.

"I'm being followed," Alicia said to the hostess, hunched over, pain shooting through her stomach.

The woman patted her back haltingly.

"*Va bene, va bene,*" she said.

Suddenly, the woman stopped.

"There is a man," she whispered. Then she called out, "Can I help you, sir?"

The hostess's voice sounded far off, drowned out by the pounding of Alicia's heart. The fox began to smell like the animal it'd once been.

"I'm here for her," said a gruff voice.

Alicia lifted her gaze.

"Jesus Christ," Fred said, "I thought I told you, don't fuckin' go to Rome."

The hostess seated them at a table in the corner. She asked several times if Alicia was okay.

"Yes, fine," she insisted, though she understood the woman's confusion.

Alicia had sprinted into the restaurant in a panic, and Fred was sweaty, poorly dressed, and looking as though he'd recently committed a crime. In other words, his usual self.

"Next time, ring why don't ya?" Alicia said, sipping Pernod, waiting for her pulse to normalize.

"I did call. Thirty fucking times."

Alicia shrugged. He left a few messages at the hotel, but not thirty. Three, at most. She'd been too busy to answer his calls.

"Jesus Christ," he said for the tenth or eleventh time. "I cannot fuckin' deal with this. I told myself, 'Fred, you don't need to babysit Alicia, she'll be okay.' Then I read that you are in Rome, *and* you're making noises about adopting Novella's baby. Seriously, what the fuck? Do you listen to a word I say?"

"I listen to every word. That's why I made sure, in the papers, to specify *Novella's* baby, so people wouldn't think she's mine."

"Oh, smart. Real slick."

"Can we hurry this up?" Alicia said. "I have somewhere to be."

She glanced out the window and imagined Novella and Benny in the studio. She pictured Benny standing by the door, in bobby socks, a suitcase at her feet.

"Half the time, I can't tell if you're smart as a fox or plain moronic," Fred said. "If you don't care about your own life, that's fine, but how can you bring a kid into it? A kid who, it must be said, looks dangerously like a certain politician, especially with that mop of hair."

"You've seen her?" Alicia gulped.

"I can't believe you put it in the damned paper," Fred ranted on. "I can't fuckin' believe it. Or maybe I can. You're a piece of work."

"No one bothered me in Paris," she said. "Who cares about a baby girl? Aren't we on the verge of nuclear annihilation?"

"Only for Alicia Darr would a nuclear war be a positive scenario." He snorted and shook his head.

"Alicia Corning Clark," she corrected him. "And that's not what I meant. Things have been calmer. I haven't felt the heat."

"Bully for you. If only Marilyn Monroe were alive to offer congratulations."

"Marilyn? What does she—"

"Fuckin' hell!" Fred pounded his fist on the table. "Do not pull this naive bullshit on me. You know they killed Marilyn. You *have* to understand that."

"Shhhh!" Alicia hissed, eyes darting about the restaurant.

The hostess stared nervously from her station.

"Zip it," she said. "Marilyn died of an overdose, no news there. The woman was constantly high on pills."

"Very convenient for her murderers."

"Fred, I say this with affection." She reached for his meaty hand. "Maybe you should dry out somewhere? I think the scotch is making you paranoid."

He yanked his hand away.

"They killed her," he said.

"Why would anyone kill her? She's harmless. Incapable of having an orgasm, apparently, but harmless."

"You know she was screwing both of them, right? Bobby *and* Jack?"

"What?" Alicia said, her lungs feeling like they might collapse. "That can't be right. Bobby is too religious. And Jack? Marilyn is— was—a drip. She'd bore him in two seconds flat."

"I don't think her noggin is what ol' J. F. Kennedy was after. You saw that birthday song, did you not?"

Alicia nodded, head swimming.

"Do you have any proof?" she said, evenly. "Or is it just some wild theory?"

"I don't know, Alicia. Do you count audio recordings as 'proof'? The Kennedys murdered Marilyn Monroe, and I have it all on tape."

"About a year ago," Fred explained, "the FBI hired me to wiretap Marilyn's house, and Peter Lawford's beach pad, too. Jimmy Hoffa called with the same request. Hoffa planned to use Marilyn to blackmail Bobby, and get the Justice Department off his back. I took both jobs, which was pretty fuckin' convenient since all of these jokers were surveilling each other already, and I was the person running the tapes.

"Two days before Marilyn died, mobster Johnny Roselli showed up at my door, claiming to be a 'representative' of the Kennedys. He— shall we say—*physically encouraged* me to cancel the FBI contract. I agreed, but all other arrangements remained intact."

"You kept the bugs?" Alicia said. "And you think *I'm* the risk taker?"

"I did exactly what Roselli asked: cut loose the FBI."

Then, Fred told Alicia what was on the tape the night Marilyn died, when she drank too much and decided she'd finally had enough. First, she called the Justice Department, and Bobby's San Francisco hotel. After fifteen attempts to reach Bobby, Marilyn called her psychiatrist, and the White House, and then Peter Lawford, growing more unhinged with each dial. Thirty minutes after she rang Peter, there was a knock on the door. It was Peter and Bobby.

"People began to yell," Fred explained. "Marilyn screamed that she was tired of being passed around the group like a piece of meat."

She threatened Bobby with the information she had: written records, photographs, tapes.

"Where is it?" Bobby demanded. "Where the fuck is it?"

Next came doors slamming, papers ruffling, and clothes hangers being slid and thrown as Bobby ransacked the house for bugs.

"Calm down, calm down," Peter called out impotently.

"We have to know," Bobby said. "It's important to the family. We can make any arrangements you want, but we must find it."

Marilyn started yelling again, louder this time. Now Bobby was the one saying, "Calm down, calm down."

Then, there was a large thump, like the sound of a body being thrown onto a bed. Marilyn screamed out again. Then her voice was diminished, muffled, until it finally stopped. The tape went silent for seventy seconds.

Then one word: "Fuck."

There was more, but Fred stopped there.

"Now do you believe me?" he asked.

Alicia rubbed her eyes. She should probably *hear* the tapes before she took Fred's word. He'd been on the payroll of the FBI, the mob, and a family he deemed more unscrupulous than both. But although Fred could be sleazy and sordid, Alicia had never known him to lie. Plus, she wasn't keen to listen to a woman's death firsthand.

"I don't know what to say," she told Fred.

"Later that night," he continued, "Peter asked me to clean up the

mess. I told him that it sure as hell sounded like somebody was suffo-
cated. He confessed that Bobby smothered Marilyn with a pillow, to
get her to calm down. She died later, he claimed."

Alicia couldn't take it anymore. She stood, her legs tottering. She
tucked her purse under her arm.

"Leaving already?" he asked with an arched brow.

"I'm expected somewhere," she answered in a weak voice, a whisper almost.

"Jesus, woman! Have you not listened to a damned thing I've said?"
He put up both hands. "I'm done giving a shit. What can I do with a
person who insists on making the same fuckin' mistakes over and over
again?"

Alicia gently rubbed his hand.

"I wasn't sure what to think of you when we first met," she said,
"but now I regard you as a dear friend."

"I don't do *friends*," he said.

Alicia smiled sadly. She thought of what Novella always insisted,
that Fred was in love with her.

"I care for you deeply," she said. "And I value your advice. But this
is a risk I have to take. I must do right by Benny. Anyhow, I feel braver
knowing that you're on my trail."

"Braver?! That's rich. Stupider, more like."

"Good-bye, sweet friend. Thank you for trying to keep me safe."

She gave Fred one last blue smile, then turned and walked away.

The studio was ablaze with light. Nova was splattered in pinks and
greens and purples, from her mussed hair to her petite, childlike feet.
Benny looked just like her.

"Oh, Benedetta," Alicia said, and fell to her knees, sobbing.

Nova said nothing and took to stroking Alicia's hair. When Alicia
glanced up, she saw that Benny was focused on Novella, searching for
answers from the person she trusted most.

Years ago, Kate asked Alicia when she'd fallen in love with Jack, and the answer was "right away." Alicia felt the same about Benny, though this child in no way resembled the baby she left behind.

"Mama?" Benny said, to Nova.

Nausea pooled deep inside Alicia.

"Der, der," Nova said, gesturing. "Come, tell Nova what zee problem."

She hoisted Alicia from the ground, which was quite a feat given her diminutive frame. After ushering her to a sofa covered in old newspapers, Nova prepared tea. She dropped in a glug of whisky before bringing it to Alicia, who took the drink because she didn't know what else to do.

"Mama, what's Auntie Leesy doing?" Benny asked, prancing on her tiptoes.

Auntie. Another dagger to Alicia's heart.

"Resting, sweetheart," Nova said. "It's been a long journey."

"What's America like, Leesy?" Benny asked.

"Oh, well, it's—"

"How is Paris? Weren't you just in Paris? Mama used to have a cabaret act there."

Hearing the way Benny spoke filled Alicia with ever more love for the girl, and for Nova. Was there a more darling creature on the planet? Novella had done a splendid job.

"I never saw Novella's act," Alicia said. "But I'm sure it was grand, like everything she does."

Alicia beamed at her friend over the cup of tea.

"Do you like music?" Benny asked. "What kind of songs?"

Benny continued to pepper her with questions, hardly waiting for one answer before spitting out the next. *Not unlike her father*, Alicia thought with fondness, and a few more tears.

"Okay I go to bed now," the girl said. "Benny is tired. Night night."

"Good night, sweet thing," Alicia said.

Oh, precious Benny. Alicia would die if something happened to her.

At once, a vision hit her, with swiftness and with force. A picture. Her mother's face. In a flash, Alicia realized she'd never forgiven Mamusia for handing her off to the Church.

Father was different. Dads were practical. Mothers were supposed to want you at their side. He might've paid vast sums and brokered unconscionable deals, but Father wasn't the only person who sacrificed to keep Alicia safe.

"*Przepraszam, Mamusia,*" she whispered.

I'm sorry, Mother.

"Novella," Alicia said hoarsely after Benny wandered up to the loft. "We need to talk about Benedetta."

Nova bit her bottom lip.

"I must tell you . . ." Alicia said, chest aching, eyesight blurry. "You've done a magnificent job raising your daughter."

"*My* daughter?" Novella said, her voice high.

Alicia nodded, for it hurt too much to speak. All around, the cats on Nova's walls stared at her with contempt.

A mother's job was to keep her child loved and protected, and Alicia had already done this, thanks to Novella. Fred had his warnings, but her daughter's safety was about so much more. Benny was three years old. She had a personality, memories, a life. How could Alicia rip a happy, colorful girl from the only home she'd ever known? It would break Benny's heart.

"She is my daughter?" Novella asked, to be sure.

"Has been from the start."

"Oh, Alicia!" Novella leapt at her, smothering her in a hug. "I was hoping you say zat!"

"You wanted her all along?" Alicia asked, unsure whether this made her feel better or worse.

"Yes! Of course!" Novella said. Then added, "But she was not mine."

"She is yours. I wish it could be another way, but this is for the best."

It was astounding to see how much Benny had changed the woman.

No longer the belle of café society, Novella Palmisano was now off the Via Veneto map. She avoided clubs, and newspapers couldn't claim she was the most common factor in Roman scandals. To think, this loving woman once sued a reporter for calling her a "good girl at heart."

"What will you do now?" Novella asked.

Alicia shrugged, and offered half a smile.

"I'll always be Benny's auntie."

"Yes! Of course!"

"Aside from that, I'll try to press on," Alicia said. "I have no choice but to live my next life."

They sit near the sidewalk, mimicking any other brunching couple, with their sunglasses and coffee and unwashed hair.

Serena Palmisano feels hungover, though she didn't finish the glass of wine she poured last night. Across from her is Lee Perenchio. His hair is chaotic and disordered, made worse as he repeatedly rakes his fingers through it. They've been in Los Angeles five days. It is as though they haven't slept since Rome.

Serena scrutinizes the others who are eating and laughing, when they're not staring into their phones. She wonders if anyone else is contemplating their DNA. Her grandmother might not be Nova. As for her potential grandfather, it's too much to consider.

"This whole thing is nuts," Lee says, tapping his straw on the table before sliding it from its wrapper.

The JFK possibility *is* nuts, but mostly his mind is on Serena, and how she'll soon be gone.

"I don't know what to think." Serena grabs her head with both hands. "Do I want to be related to Alicia Corning Clark? Or your John Kennedy?"

"He's not *my* John Kennedy."

Serena shrugs, stumped. Doesn't JFK belong to all Americans? Isn't this why the country loves him so? The Camelot business, one brief shining moment, and all that?

"If Alicia Corning Clark was your grandmother," Lee says, and stabs at his eggs, "how would you feel about it, and the fact she left your mother?"

"According to that letter, it was to keep her safe. Same reason Jackie O married that ugly, unpopular Greek. Alicia wanted to give her child the best life, and she left her with the best person."

Serena does not miss the parallels to Alicia's own childhood. She looked it up last night. Before the war, there were one million Jews in Poland, and five thousand survived. In Alicia's hometown of Łódź, only a few hundred lived out of several hundred thousand. It was a miracle that Alicia was one of them.

"I can't believe you came all this way," Lee says, "to meet with the lawyer, and take a DNA test, and now you don't want the results?"

"Who says I came for those reasons?" she asks with a grin.

Lee blushes and takes to aggressively stirring his orange juice with the straw.

"That's very sweet," he says, "but I still don't understand why you'd give up this chance."

"Why are you so bothered that I don't care to be rich?" Serena asks, picking up on his sentiments, as she's taught herself to do.

They haven't known each other long, but they know each other well, which is a different and much better thing.

"I didn't have the money to start," she continues. "Why do I need it now? Of course, I *need* money, but not to that degree."

And if she is Alicia's heir, and accepts the estate, then William the doorman and the others will be left with nothing. They were there for Alicia every day. They took her to appointments and tended to her needs. William found Alicia's body splayed across the floor. Alicia promised these men that she would change their lives. Who is Serena to take that away?

"While I admire your integrity——" Lee starts.

"Integrity?" Serena snorts. "Not being a greedy bastard isn't an admirable trait. Maybe in Milan."

Lee rolls his eyes.

"What about your lineage?" he asks. "Nothing could replace your grandmother, but you could be part of an enormous family, *the* family, at least here in the States."

Lee had been surprised that it was possible to determine Serena's potential link to JFK. He'd been dead some fifty years but, apparently, this is not so long. A few years ago, DNA was used to prove that Thomas Jefferson sired children with Sally Hemings, one of his slaves.

"Serena," he says. "You might be a *Kennedy*."

"That's a downside." She sniggers. "One gets the impression that sometimes not even the Kennedys want to be Kennedys."

"What about finding out if you're related to Alicia Corning Clark?"

"I'm not sure I have the willpower to find out one and not the other," she says. "Then I think of the hassle . . ."

She blubbers her lips.

"Surely, they'd need to find my mother first, and then inform the other people named, and what a disaster it'd become."

This one decision could spider into ten more, and probably four times the problems. The judge can't simply say, "You're the heir, here's your money." Alicia Corning Clark's death, and her history with JFK, was in the news. Some sources mentioned the possibility of a "love child" and the doorman, bellman, and lift operator have spoken to the press. If Serena receives the estate, certain people will be mad, and others will demand to know, is she also related to JFK?

Serena imagines blog posts and gossip columns and people knocking on her door. She thinks about the thousands of things written about Alicia, and the people who trailed her for years. What a miserable way to live.

"I don't need a test to tell me who I am," she says. "I'm Serena Palmisano, raised by her grandmother. Serena, a Roman who needs to complete her university degree. A girl who has a strange penchant for tall American boys."

"Serena," Lee mumbles, then exhales slowly. "So, this is it? This is where the story of Alicia Corning Clark ends?"

The story of us, he does not add. For when she's done with Alicia, Serena will be done with him.

"I'll take a few more days to think about it," Serena says. "But, I don't need a big life, only a happy one."

Lee closes his mouth and nods as Serena rips off one end of her croissant. As she chews, Lee looks up and they lock eyes.

"About this life . . ." he wants to know, undertaking what feels like the largest possible risk. "How do I factor in?"

Serena is glad he's asked, because she wonders the same.

"You're an American." She swats at the air, as Lee knew she would. "Surely you will devise a plan to push your way into my existence. Loud and grumbly, like a bulldozer."

"Just so you know, I've signed up for an Italian class," he says. "I hope to be fluent inside three months."

Serena smiles, tilts her head. This man knows how to play her in the perfect way.

"I'll have *you* know I contacted Georgetown this morning," she says, and stares at her plate. "To figure out what I need to start again. I should probably graduate at some point, don't you think?"

"I think that. I think that very much."

"Who knows, perhaps my credits will transfer somewhere more exciting." She grins. "Stanford? Is that close to Silicon Valley?"

"It's pronounced *sili-ken*, not *sili-cone*. Tell me, who shall I bribe to make that happen?"

"*Aho*, you've been ruminating on Kennedys too long if you're thinking bribes."

He chuckles. Serena feels his laughter on her. How she adores this sunny California boy.

"Well, Serena Palmisano," Lee says, for he never lets a moment get too still. "Sounds like we'll be meeting somewhere in the middle. A good thing, too, since that's my favorite place to be."

NEW YORK

Two men wait for their lawyer in a conference room, on the twentieth floor of a nondescript building in Midtown.

William, a doorman by trade, has on a suit purchased in some prior decade. He is large, and has a walrus mustache. Felix, the elevator operator, wears a blue work shirt, with his name and the building stitched in navy. He is bald. They both have glasses. They once knew the same woman, Mrs. Clark.

Her first name was Alicia and she was the heir to a sewing machine fortune, courtesy of her second husband, who died in his sleep thirteen days after they wed. Before him was a British actor, Edmund Purdom. After was a Bahamian bodybuilder turned health minister whom Mrs. Clark divorced in the eighties. Between and among these three was a hit parade of actors, celebrities, and heads of state. Mrs. Clark spared no detail when relaying her antics to William and Felix and the third man, George Rodriguez, retired four years ago and difficult to locate. He is called "George the Bellman" in Mrs. Clark's will.

"I've always adored men named George," she used to say, although none of them could think of an old-time star she'd dated with the name. "They have the best hearts."

Sometimes it was hard to believe her stories, and they'd heard a lot of them in their decades working at 955 Fifth, an exclusive co-op close to the Met, where Robert Redford once lived. A real-estate agent said they planned to list Mrs. Clark's place for a cool five million.

William works the graveyard shift, and Mrs. Clark was a terrible sleeper, and this is how they became friends. For the better part of three decades, she visited him in the dead of night and told her madcap tales.

Mrs. Clark talked about the famous people she loved, names from yesteryear like William Holden, Gary Cooper, and Tyrone Power. Omar Sharif. Roberto Rossellini. Major-league pitcher Bo Belinsky. Warren Beatty. Katharine Hepburn. Various princes and kings.

She spoke of her first husband and their nasty divorce, and her third husband, whom she was married to the longest. Curiously, she never mentioned the second. Mostly, she spoke of John F. Kennedy, the man she loved above all.

"You should write a book," William used to say, "with the life you've lived."

"Are you kidding?" Mrs. Clark would scoff. "I'd have to leave out the best parts, lest the *you-know-whos* have me killed."

She meant the Kennedys, and her bouts of paranoia were not infrequent. She often thought people were following her. God forbid she see some member of their family in Bergdorf's. She'd hide in her apartment for a week.

"They killed Marilyn Monroe," she said.

William assured her that they'd all heard that conspiracy theory, and many others besides. Just because people said it, did not make it true.

"It's on tape," Mrs. Clark swore. "And, sure, they all talk about Marilyn, but no one mentions Mac, the family payoff guy. He died in a mysterious car crash a few weeks before Jack was killed.

"Did you know Frank Sinatra's son was kidnapped because of them?

And what about the socialite Mary Meyer? Friend of Jackie's, lover of Jack's. Mary planned to write a book but was murdered, in broad daylight, while jogging near her Georgetown home. They never found her killer, or her manuscript. Also, have you heard of the gossip columnist Cholly Knickerbocker?"

"Only from you," William would say.

She could go on like this for hours, outlining a veritable dossier of Kennedy comrades who'd met mysterious ends.

"Knickerbocker's real name was Igor Cassini. He and his wife Charlene were pals of the Kennedys, until Bobby got his panties in a twist and indicted Igor for failing to register as a resident alien. Charlene wrote a scathing letter to Jack, and Jackie exiled them from social relevance. She made life so miserable for the woman, Charlene downed thirty sleeping pills to end it all. Though many think she was forced."

There was another gossip columnist, too: Dorothy Kilgallen. She was murdered while investigating the truth behind the JFK assassination. Ms. Kilgallen had an entire folder filled with support for her allegations. Like Mary Meyer's would-be book, it vanished when she died.

Every once in a while, when it was very late, or she'd had too much Pernod, Mrs. Clark would say there'd been a child, a little girl fathered by JFK and given to someone else to raise. If William asked her about it the next morning, she'd panic and take it all back.

Mrs. Clark had one picture of her and the president, which she kept on the nightstand beside her bed.

"There were dozens more," she said. "Plus, letters that'd make your heart skip a beat. But my idiot first husband torched it all in a fit of fury and lust."

Felix had no patience for her stories of romance. To him, Mrs. Clark described her childhood, probably because she recognized a fellow foreigner. She grew up as a well-off Jew in Poland, content until the Nazis unleashed. As a girl, she went into hiding and her parents went into concentration camps. Her mother survived, but came out a fragment of herself. This was, William and Felix both assumed, why Mrs. Clark was so convinced people wanted to cause her harm.

Felix didn't care to have so many details. He wanted to do good work and keep his job. He'd been warned not to get too friendly with the residents, but Mrs. Clark didn't let him keep his distance.

"Felix, don't worry," she'd say. "You're going to be blessed."

She was going to put him in the will, was what she meant.

William deemed himself Mrs. Clark's closest friend. Felix thinks he makes too much of it, but facts are facts. When Mrs. Clark became too weak to travel to the Bahamas, and there was no one left in her life, William stepped in. He escorted Mrs. Clark to her appointments, and on shopping trips to Bergdorf's and Saks. Sometimes, Felix came. George the Bellman carried her bags.

In 2001, Mrs. Clark wrote a will, leaving a million dollars to each of them, and the rest to the Humane Society—odd, since they'd never known her to own a pet. She had a real thing against cats.

"When I'm gone," she used to say, "make sure they know I was important."

"You're not going anywhere," William responded, unsure who she meant by "they." "You're too stubborn."

Once, William asked if she'd gotten what she wanted out of life. Mrs. Clark thought about this for some time.

"I have a beautiful home," she said. "And more money than I could ever spend. But before all of this, there was one year in Hyannis Port, when, for one bright shining moment, I had it all."

In 2011, William took Mrs. Clark to the hospital after finding her incoherent on the floor. Lenox Hill wanted to appoint a guardian, and for a time they discussed it being William or his wife, but somewhere along the way they all forgot. Official guardian or not, William checked on her daily, joking that he was a doorman and a "home health aide" on the side.

A few years ago, Mrs. Clark stopped letting him into her apartment.

"It's a mess!" she'd say. "I haven't had a minute to clean!"

They offered to take care of this—well, William and Felix did—but she refused.

"You have enough tasks in this place without having to clean up after an old lady."

They continued to drop by, but never made it past the threshold.

It was William who found her. She hadn't been to see him in two days, which might as well have been a year. He used his keys to let himself inside and there she was, sprawled across the floor. On her right was the photograph of JFK she'd kept at her bedside. On the left, a surrealistic painting of a cat.

Her apartment was trashed; William had never witnessed anything like it, and in thirty years he'd seen some stuff. She'd become one of those hoarders from TV. He wept, overcome with sadness, because of her death, and because of the way she lived those last few years: alone, surrounded by memories, and inundated by all that junk.

As promised, Mrs. Clark named them in her will. The problem was, she had more than one, and now the lawyers were involved. Even they struggled to parse out what she really desired.

In her bedroom, Felix found a letter addressed to someone named Andrew. He showed it to William, and William gave it to Mrs. Clark's attorney. It was written in 1977, but contained possible information about Mrs. Clark's heirs. Good news for squirrelly estates. Bad news for the doorman, bellman, and lift operator.

"She wanted us to have the million dollars!" Felix insisted when William told him the news. "Not someone she almost wrote a letter to in 1977!"

William agrees. Mrs. Clark did want them to have the money. Still, he couldn't hide the letter.

Now, the men wait for news from their own lawyer. There is talk of a granddaughter. The trick is finding out if this person is really an heir, or if she's in the same boat as the three employees of 955 Fifth.

"Hello, gentlemen," their lawyer says, breezing in at last. "I have some news."

He plunks himself onto a chair. Felix exhales audibly.

"The lead we had on an heir didn't pan out," he says.

"She wasn't related to Mrs. Clark?" William asks, surprised.

"The results were 'inconclusive,' whatever that means. She declined the DNA test. Apparently."

"Yes!" Felix claps.

"Don't get too excited," the lawyer cautions. "There are still hurdles to cross. We haven't been able to establish whether the will was actually in her handwriting, or if it succeeds the one she filed in the Bahamas. All in due time."

He cracks open a miniature bottle of water and takes it down in one gulp.

"This is so wild," he says. "A million here, a million there, the indiscriminate tossing around of cash. No offense, I'm sure you two are the world's best doormen."

"Elevator operator," Felix clarifies.

"Fine, fine." The lawyer holds up both hands. "But you have to admit that's a lot of money for people she didn't know that well."

"I'd say I knew her pretty well," William offers.

"Okay, but the third guy . . . she didn't even remember his full name."

William and Felix trade looks, the tension loosening between them. Felix shrugs. He is not one to question. He wants the money, because she promised. His plans are bigger than to work as an elevator operator for the rest of his life. He has what Mrs. Clark used to call "that intense immigrant's drive."

"She never explained why she planned to leave us the money," William says to their lawyer. "But I saw her almost every day. She had no family. We were her family, the people she counted on. Mrs. Clark wanted to take care of us, but I think she also wanted to make sure that, when she was gone, there was someone to remember that she lived."

"Being remembered is worth millions?" the lawyer says. "If that's the case, why not donate to a school, or a zoo, or something? She could've had her name etched in stone."

"That's not the same," William says. "A plaque isn't a person. It can't tell a story. Isn't that what we all want? To be loved, and then to be remembered?"

"I guess," their lawyer says. "But, seriously, *millions*?"

William considers this.

"Honestly?" he says. "I think she would've given a whole lot more."

Serena Palmisano stands in the foyer of the Perenchio manse, beside two men who've lugged in an oversized crate. She's just returned from Rome, to see Lee before he starts his job. She is working on getting her credits transferred, and securing enough funds to finish her degree.

There is a woman beside Serena. She carries a clipboard. Lee has ambled into another room. Under the woman's direction, the men pull apart the crate to reveal portraits by the unknown artist Alicia Darr. The estate isn't settled but Alicia had gifted these to her doorman over the years, and he's gifted them to Serena, perhaps as some sort of thanks.

The patter of Lee's feet echoes in the hallway. He appears beside Serena and ticks through the pile. He's chosen a favorite. It's a surrealistic portrait of a man. He is bigger than life-sized, and his shadow is made of a hundred other figures. These men have hats. The subject does not.

"Are you sure?" he asks. "Don't you want it?"

"I can't have Alicia's work in my flat," Serena says with a laugh. "Nova would be incensed."

Lee tilts toward the clipboard woman and gestures at the painting. He directs the movers to the art gallery, because an in-home gallery is a normal occurrence for hedge fund impresarios, apparently. There is a Miró, and a Dali. His father even has one Picasso, known to Serena as a friend of Nonna's, a resident of Margutta.

"Hang it here," Lee says, pointing to a spot. "I don't know if this is the most logical artistic sequence . . ."

"Definitely not." Serena grins.

"But I think it fits."

Lee slaps the wall.

"All right," he says to the curator, and the men. "Up it goes."

As the woman measures, Serena has a knot in her throat, and tears in her eyes. She stares at the piece, wondering how it could be that Alicia Corning Clark loved one of the most famous men to ever live, but ended up anonymous and alone.

Now, at least, Alicia will have her immortality beside Picasso, next to Miró. Serena sniffles and Lee takes her hand. Maybe falling for charming, rich Americans is in the blood. Serena will never know.

"I see you, Alicia Darr Purdom Corning Clark," she says, studying the painting that now leans against the wall. "Barbara Kopczysnka. Every person that you were or hoped to be. I know that you were here."

John F. Kennedy was the second of nine children born to Rose and Joseph P. Kennedy. He was the thirty-fifth president of the United States.

Jack was six feet tall and had bushy, reddish-brown hair and greenish-gray eyes. He hated hats, wore the same gray suit, and changed his shirt up to six times per day. Jack was fanatical about maintaining a suntan, but his Addison's disease often made him appear yellow. His wife teased him for being vain.

Despite his good looks and reputation for vigor, Jack Kennedy was not especially athletic and was sickly from the moment he was born. He told friends he would never be more than eighty percent healthy, or live past age forty-five. He died at forty-six.

Jack rarely complained. He hated when people sulked. His wife cried easily, which baffled and annoyed him.

Throughout his adulthood, Jack relied on exercise, hot baths, heating pads, massages, back braces, and crutches to combat his physical pain. He also wore corrective shoes, slept with his head elevated, and had sex with the woman on top. Toward the end of his life, he and his wife had had frequent methamphetamine injections.

Jack's favorite sibling was Kathleen, known as Kick. She met a tragic end, at twenty-eight years old. Jack thought about her often, and believed he could speak to her in his dreams.

Though he was not athletic, Jack was an excellent golfer. He shot in the high seventies, but tried to keep his prowess under wraps, lest voters get the wrong idea. Jack was terrible at poker and foreign languages. His favorite cocktail was a daiquiri, though he wasn't a big drinker overall.

Because of his health issues, Jack tried to live each day to its fullest. He had an incessant need to be loved, especially by women, perhaps because his mother was so cold.

Jack ate briskly, as if someone were about to take his plate. He was a horrible slob, and always late. He was easily bored and fidgeted constantly, forever tapping his teeth, drumming his fingers.

Jack was a captivating conversationalist. He was always hungry for knowledge and read several papers each morning. He had a quick wit, though was also quick to temper. His favorite swear words were "prick," "fuck," "nuts," "bastard," and "son of a bitch."

Though he ascended in the political ranks, it was not necessarily due to his policy making. As Tip O'Neill said, "I've never seen a congressman get so much press while doing so little work." As a senator, he rarely ate in the Senate Dining Room. He took minimal interest in lobbying, or in the work of getting legislation drafted and passed. However, he cared deeply about civil rights and was an early advocate of federal funding for medical research.

Girls loved Jack, and vice versa. He preferred worldly, upper-class women, especially Europeans. But his power over men was just as strong. He was almost always followed by a group of friends, the closest of whom was said to be in love with him.

Jack got married because, if he didn't, people might've thought he was a "queer." Jackie was the woman for the job, and he proposed via telegram. Though Jack wasn't the best husband, he genuinely loved being a father.

John F. Kennedy was many things. He had countless admirable qualities, not to mention a long list of personal foibles. Above all, Jack was charming and charismatic and capable of taking over a room. He might've been a product of his father's ambition, but the magnetism, heart, and dazzling smile were pure Jack.

ACKNOWLEDGMENTS

DID JFK AND ALICIA CORNING CLARK HAVE A SECRET LOVE
CHILD?

In July 2016, while I was supposed to be writing an entirely different book, my editor sent me a link with the above headline. She copied my agent on the email and within minutes it was decided: Alicia
Darr Purdom Corning Clark would be the protagonist of my next
novel.

So, first and foremost, I must thank my fantastic editor, Laurie
Chittenden, for sending me down this rabbit hole, and for display-
ing the utmost patience as I flailed around, trying to tie together a
million threads. Her input and guidance surely saved me from the
loony bin.

Speaking of crackups, an enormous thank-you (and vodka and wine
and whatever else she wants) to my agent, Barbara Poelle, for her advice, talking me off a dozen ledges, and stepping in when "I can't
even . . ."

I'm so grateful for the brilliant folks at St. Martin's Press, all of whom work like fiends to turn my messes into legitimate (and gorgeous) books. I'm also lucky to have the best publicist in the business, Katie Bassel, and one hell of a marketing team. Thank you also to the sales force, who do so much to get my books onto shelves. And thank you to Lisa Padilla for the use of her daughters' names, Markie and Alex.

I must also thank my family—Dennis, Paige, and Georgia Bilski—for suffering through my writing anxieties and always being up for a research trip. You three make everything worthwhile.

I've dedicated this book to my father-in-law, Tony Bilski, who was himself a displaced person from Poland. Like Alicia, he spent several years at a camp in Germany before emigrating to the United States. Huge thanks to him for answering so many questions, and to my mother-in-law, Pat Bilski, who is always supportive and never objects to my intrusiveness.

If I listed all the friends (Hi, Karen! Hi, Lauren!), tennis partners (Erin! Anne!), and family members (Lisa! Brian! Amanda! Mom and Dad!) who suffered through my kvetching about this book, the acknowledgments would be thirty pages long. But, I remember every single one of you and am eternally grateful.

Have I mentioned? This book was a challenge to write. It was really, really, really hard. And I complained. A lot. But that's what happens when you write about a real-life woman who was born abroad, during World War II, and who changed her name, age, and backstory with alarming frequency. It's also what happens when this woman dated one of the most famous Americans to ever live, and when Katharine Hepburn and Gary Cooper are mere secondary characters.

People always ask: Where does the truth end and fiction begin? This book is absolutely a work a fiction. I've included some fairly scurrilous storylines and accusations but, as with my previous novels, my goal was to make the story *plausible*. The article that sparked the story asked, "Did JFK and Alicia Corning Clark have a secret love child?" I took known facts and filled in the gaps to make a case for what *could've* happened. In short, this book is my hypothesis. Alas, I write fiction and am not a detective or an investigative reporter. Sometimes I had to fudge a name or a date, and the research was often conflicting. Despite the large volume of facts and data, I made many leaps and assumptions.

In the course of writing this book, I read thousands of articles from magazines and newspapers, some of which had to be translated from Italian. All quotes and headlines included in the narrative were taken from actual publications.

I conducted interviews—with some people who did not wish to be thanked—and also relied heavily on the documents available at the John F. Kennedy Presidential Library and Museum in Boston.

And I read books. Gobs and gobs of books—nearly two hundred at last count. There are untold numbers of biographies about John F. Kennedy and his family, and I've probably read 90 percent of them. Below is a list of those I found the most useful and/or the most intriguing. As with any research, I tried to strike a balance between serious biographies, salacious tell-alls, and highly generous reflections written by family or friends.

I truly hope you enjoy this journey with Alicia and that the story has you googling for days.

Alford, Mimi. *Once Upon a Secret: My Affair with President John F. Kennedy and Its Aftermath*

Berg, A. Scott. *Kate Remembered*

Bly, Nellie. *The Kennedy Men: Three Generations of Sex, Scandal and Secrets*

Bogner, Nahum. *At the Mercy of Strangers: The Rescue of Jewish Children with Assumed Identities in Poland*

Bowers, Scotty. *Full Service: My Adventures in Hollywood and the Secret Sex Lives of the Stars*

Bukowczyk, John J. *A History of the Polish Americans*

Collier, Peter. *The Kennedys: An American Drama*

Considine-Meara, Eileen. *At Home with Kate: Growing Up in Katharine Hepburn's Household*

Dallek, Robert. *An Unfinished Life: John F. Kennedy, 1917–1963*

Damore, Leo. *The Cape Cod Years of John Fitzgerald Kennedy*

Doerr, Anthony. *Four Seasons in Rome: On Twins, Insomnia, and the Biggest Funeral in the History of the World*

Epstein, Alan. *As the Romans Do: An American Family's Italian Odyssey*

Farris, Scott. *Inga: Kennedy's Great Love, Hitler's Perfect Beauty, and J. Edgar Hoover's Prime Suspect*

Fay, Paul B. *The Pleasure of His Company*

Goodwin, Doris Kearns. *The Fitzgeralds and the Kennedys: An American Saga*

Graham, James W. *Victura: The Kennedys, a Sailboat, and the Sea*

Hamilton, Nigel. *JFK: Reckless Youth*

Hepburn, Katharine. *Me: Stories of My Life*

Hersh, Seymour M. *The Dark Side of Camelot*

Jaroszynska-Kirchmann, Anna D. *The Exile Mission: The Polish Political Diaspora and Polish Americans, 1939–1956*

Kessler, Ronald. *The Sins of the Father: Joseph P. Kennedy and the Dynasty He Founded*

Leamer, Laurence. *The Kennedy Men: 1901–1963*

Leamer, Laurence. *The Kennedy Women: The Saga of an American Family*

Lertzman, Richard A. *Dr. Feelgood: The Shocking Story of the Doctor Who May Have Changed History by Treating and Drugging JFK, Marilyn, Elvis, and Other Prominent Figures*

Levy, Shawn. *Dolce Vita Confidential: Fellini, Loren, Pucci, Paparazzi, and the Swinging High Life of 1950s Rome*

Lincoln, Evelyn. *My Twelve Years with John F. Kennedy*

O'Brien, Michael. *John F. Kennedy: A Biography*

O'Donnell, Kenneth P., David F. Powers, and Joe McCarthy. *Johnny, We Hardly Knew Ye: Memories of John Fitzgerald Kennedy*

Otash, Fred. *Investigation Hollywood*

Perret, Geoffrey. *Jack: A Life Like No Other*

Pitts, David. *Jack and Lem: John F. Kennedy and Lem Billings: The Untold Story of an Extraordinary Friendship*

Porter, Darwin. *Jacqueline Kennedy Onassis: A Life Beyond Her Wildest Dreams*

Preil, Joseph J. *Holocaust Testimonies: European Survivors and American Liberators in New Jersey*

Reeves, Thomas. *A Question of Character: A Life of John F. Kennedy*

Scott, Henry E. *Shocking True Story: The Rise and Fall of Confidential, "America's Most Scandalous Scandal Magazine"*

Smith, Jean Kennedy. *The Nine of Us: Growing Up Kennedy*

Smith, Sally Bedell. *Grace and Power: The Private World of the Kennedy White House*

Spada, James. *Peter Lawford: The Man Who Kept Secrets*

Summers, Anthony. *Goddess: The Secret Lives of Marilyn Monroe*

Summers, Anthony. *Official and Confidential: The Secret Life of J. Edgar Hoover*

Taraborrelli, J. Randy. *Jackie, Ethel, Joan: Women of Camelot*

von Post, Gunilla. *Love, Jack*

Michelle Gable is the *New York Times* bestselling author of four novels, including her latest, *The Summer I Met Jack*. Michelle graduated from the College of William & Mary and, after a twenty-year career in finance, now writes full-time. She lives in Cardiff-by-the-Sea, California, with her husband and two daughters, as well as one bunny, one cat, and a newly rescued dog.